A BITTER FIELD

By Jack Ludlow

The Roads to War series

The Burning Sky

A Broken Land

A Bitter Field

The Republic series

The Pillars of Rome

The Sword of Revenge

The Gods of War

The Conquest series

Mercenaries

Warriors

Conquest

Written as David Donachie

The John Pearce series

By the Mast Divided

A Shot Rolling Ship

An Awkward Commission

A Flag of Truce

The Admirals' Game

An Ill Wind

Blown Off Course

Enemies at Every Turn

A BITTER FIELD

JACK LUDLOW

First published in Great Britain in 2012 by
Allison & Busby Limited
13 Charlotte Mews
London W1T 4EJ
www.allisonandbusby.com

A CIP catalogue record for this book is available from
the British Library.

10 9 8 7 6 5 4 3 2 1

ISBN 978-0-7490-0842-0

Typeset in 11/18 pt Sabon by
Allison & Busby Ltd.

Paper used in this publication is from sustainably managed sources.
All of the wood used is procured from legal sources and is fully traceable.
The producing mill uses schemes such as ISO 14001
to monitor environmental impact.

Printed and bound by
CPI Group (UK) Ltd, Croydon, CR0 4YY

To
Richard Mantle,
who as Deputy MD
oversaw my dismissal from ENO.
If his help was inadvertent, he is
in some measure responsible
for my publishing
30 novels over 25 years.
Thanks Richard.

CHAPTER ONE

Callum Jardine was practised in the art of looking relaxed when he was not – much more so, he observed, than those keeping an eye on his movements. The two men who had tailed him from the Marconi Wireless office, almost caricature Frenchmen in their berets, striped jerseys and too-clean blue overalls, were now sitting a few tables away, making a poor fist of their supposedly disinterested surveillance.

Their attempt to look like working men was risible; worse, they were fidgeting, acting as though he was about to get up any second, dash to the edge of the quay, jump into a boat and vanish, when in fact he was quite content, given he had nothing to do for several hours, to keep them in this café while he read his newspaper and consumed his *petit déjeuner*.

When not idly scanning the news he could watch the last of the fishing boats enter the harbour of La Rochelle to unload their overnight catch, which made it pleasant to sit and while away time on a fine late August morning, already warm and getting warmer, and to idly speculate about the history of a part of France he had never previously visited.

In a country where governments came and went with tedious regularity, in which politics and politicians seemed to operate on a revolving door, the same faces reappearing in various ministerial disguises, and one much given to strikes by dissatisfied workers, La Rochelle had an air of tranquillity belonging to a port and city that had been rich for millennia, a sort of bastion of a more conservative France.

The harbour reflected this longevity, dominated as it was by three medieval towers; they formed as well as narrowed the entrance to the inner anchorage, which made it easy to imagine how the locals had come by their wealth, with, over a millennium, ancient galleys and sailing ships needing to pass through that gap and pay for the privilege, an entry point for goods from all over the world, including at one time, highly profitable African slaves.

Little of that passed through now; the inner port had long been replaced by a large exterior commercial dock. It was now home to the fishing fleet and leisure craft: the yachts and motor vessels of affluent Frenchmen, the less significant craft of the weekend sailors as well as the bobbing small boats of indeterminate ownership that featured in every anchorage. The quayside reflected that change from commerce to leisure, being lined now with cafés and restaurants instead of the warehouses and ships' chandlers of the past.

What had not changed was the noise created by the women who descended on to the quay of a morning to buy the fresh catch of silver-bodied fish, as well as to poke at the piles of still-live crustaceans –

crabs, langoustines and lobsters – that were sold from sturdy tables. Such a sight reminded Cal of what he had witnessed as a growing child in Marseilles; his formative years had been spent in France, which allowed him to act and feel as relaxed as a native.

If he stiffened at all – and he tried very hard not to – it was brought on by the surprise, bordering on actual shock, of seeing a one-time fellow army officer, and more recently something of a comrade in a clandestine venture, approaching along the cobbled quay. What the hell was Peter Lanchester doing in La Rochelle?

As was Peter's habit, he presented the picture of the perfect Englishman abroad, very erect in his cream linen suit and panama hat, with an MCC hatband and a matching red and yellow tie. The highly polished malacca cane he was carrying was an affectation, there for no other purpose than to beat out a tattoo on the pavement to complement that of his heels, or perhaps to swipe a less-than-respectful Johnny Foreigner.

Fearing he might approach and call out his name, Cal slowly raised his copy of *Le Temps* and pretended to read the front-page story about the continuing crisis in Czechoslovakia, though without being too obvious and hiding his whole face. He need not have worried; Peter might look and act the part of the typical 'milord' on his travels but he was anything but a foppish fool and that raised newspaper seemed enough to tell him to mind what he said.

He stopped a few feet away and leant on his stick, looking around the harbour with an air of obvious frustration, as though the whole place had been built and designed to in some way thwart his purpose, a pose he held until the waiter emerged with a tray bearing two tiny coffee cups and a pair of morning stiffeners, probably brandies. That the fellow was about his occupation and there were two people waiting for their order impinged on Peter not at all.

In a loud voice and with an execrable French accent he demanded to be told the whereabouts of the Place du Maréchal Joffre. The waiter was naturally offended both by his peremptory manner and the level of his demand, which caused Peter to add in an even louder voice and more intemperate manner, and one carrying the implication he was addressing a complete dolt, '*Je cherche l'Hôtel Henri Quatre.*'

Even though the waiter stopped to answer and give him directions, this did nothing to modify Peter's tone or ease the look of irritation on his face – he wore the expression of a man absolutely certain he was likely to be lied to and sent in the wrong direction – which had him reiterate the question to ensure he was being correctly advised.

Finally sure of his route and the veracity of the instructions, mouthing an abrupt and graceless *Merci beaucoup*, Peter imperiously rapped his cane on the flagstones and stomped off, followed by hard looks aimed at his very erect back. He had upset the waiter and most of the customers by his attitude, but he had also given Cal Jardine directions as to where they should meet.

The imperious act had also underlined the uselessness of the tail: Cal's pair of watchers, unlike everyone else in the pavement café, had studiously avoided reacting to the scene, neither frowning nor producing the expressive Gallic shrugs of their fellow observers at such a display of Anglo-Saxon arrogance. He would need to lose them, but in a city centred around a port that had changed little since the seventeenth century he anticipated no problem.

Ordering another coffee in perfect French, albeit with a hint of Marseilles in the accent, Cal went back to his newspaper, once more wondering what Peter Lanchester was doing here in La Rochelle and, more importantly, why he needed to make contact with him in so brash a manner, indicating a need for haste.

That hinted at either danger or something very important, more likely the former, which had him reprising in his mind the precautions he had taken. There was a cargo of Czech ZB26 light machine guns sitting on a barge by an isolated inland farmhouse on the canal that led to the huge interior marshlands of the Marais-Poitevin and he needed to get them aboard a ship that night.

In the end speculation was wasted; he would have to meet with Peter and see what was up, so he picked up the bill from under the ashtray, extracted from his pocket enough francs to cover his purchases, plus a few coins as a *pourboire*, then stood slowly and stretched, like a man newly arisen from his bed. Such an act would cause no comment; it was, after all, not yet eight o'clock.

Then he made a point of yawning as he looked around the active inner port, at the wooden fishing boats with their dirty beige sails now furled, at the weary-looking crews working on their nets, sniffing at the maritime and fresh-fish smell of the place, before patting his jacket pockets like a man checking for his keys, folding his paper and sauntering off.

The two watchers were not far behind, but too much so for a city full of narrow alleys enclosed by high buildings. These led to cobbled, crowded and constricted main streets designed for carts not motor vehicles, each with its charming shaded walkway, low colonnades supported by thick stone pillars, a feature of the city, which, at this time of day were thronged with locals heading to work in their shops and offices; losing a tail was child's play.

Peter would not be in the named hotel, but watching from a place where Cal could spot him, and he had chosen well – a small, quiet square, hard to enter without being seen, with him loitering in a far corner well away from the hotel entrance. The panama hat, so distinctive, was rolled in his hand, the striped tie was in his pocket, and standing as he was in deep shade, his cream suit was visible without screaming out his presence.

Sure he had been spotted, Peter headed away, cane silent, with Cal following in his footsteps, crossing several busy thoroughfares into side streets, and then on to a long road lined with shops. Peter then slipped into a baker's, allowing Cal to walk on by and stop to look into the window of a newly opened tool shop, thus accomplishing a standard check to flush out or make life awkward for anyone following.

Exiting, baguette under his arm, Peter passed him and finally, having slipped through another alleyway, stopped at the entrance to a seedy block of apartments. He waited till Cal was close before proceeding to enter and did not speak as he was followed up the narrow stone stairs, through a door and into a rather dingy and poorly furnished living room smelling of stale smoke.

In fact he said not a word until he had, having placed his baguette, hat and cane on a table, crossed the linoleum-covered floor to the shuttered windows and opened one to examine the street below, talking quietly over his shoulder.

'We lost them, old boy?'

'Lost who, Peter?'

'The chaps following you.'

Cal threw his paper on the table. 'You're sure I was being followed?'

Peter turned and even in the gloom of the half-shuttered room Cal could see his enigmatic smile. 'My dear fellow, if HMG suspects what you're up to, then you can be damn sure the Frogs do too.'

'What am I up to, Peter?'

'Don't jest with me, Cal.' Peter jerked a thumb in the general direction of the sea. 'Somewhere out yonder is a ship waiting for your cargo.'

'There are lots of ships out there, Peter, it's a bloody port.'

'British-registered, foreign-crewed, coastal type, with the kind of shallow draught that will let you land your weapons on a beach or in some sheltered Galician cove.'

A lazy hand was waved to a chair and Cal sat down, Peter following suit and crossing his long legs to expose one highly polished brown shoe, posing the question as he took out his cigarette case and extracted what he always referred to as a 'gasper'.

'How am I doing, old boy?'

'It always amazes me, Peter, that you seem to know more about what I am up to than I do myself. It's like Hamburg all over again, especially you turning up like the proverbial bad penny to warn me of impending trouble, and the question this time is the same: how much of what you're asking stems from knowledge and how much is deduction?'

'Did I not save your bacon in Hamburg, Cal? If I had not turned up when I did the Gestapo would have stripped off your skin with hot pincers.'

'I think I have already repaid that favour, but the question stands.'

'Bit of both, given La Rochelle, while a charming spot to visit, is not your sort of town – too provincial and very short on the louche entertainments to which you are partial. But it does happen to share the Bay of Biscay with the northern coast of Spain where the Civil War still rages, though only God knows how, given they should have utterly exhausted each other by now.'

Peter paused to tap the end of his cigarette several times on the table, but it remained unlit. 'There are guerrillas operating in the mountains of Cantabria and they need weapons and ammo to keep up the fight, while you, who make your way in the world by the supply of same, have, thanks to your previous exploits, good contacts with both the folk who will provide them and those with the money to pay for the purchase.'

'Anything else?'

The reply had to wait till his cigarette was alight and the first welcome drag was exhaled, to form a cloud of smoke around Peter's head.

'Yes, old chap, when you forge an End User Certificate saying the light machine guns you are buying from Czechoslovakia are for the Irish Republic it tickles the old hackles.'

'Your hackles?'

'Not only mine, but it does not make life any easier when it transpires they are in fact for Spain.'

'You're sure that's their destination?'

'If you are involved, yes.'

'I thought you would have been pleased given what we have done in the past, though I am curious at your earlier mention of His Majesty's Government.'

Peter was handsome in a sharp-faced way, with his black hair slicked back to leave a widow's peak, but it ceased to be as attractive when he frowned, as he was doing now, making him look like a peevish schoolmaster.

'I have to tell you, Cal, I am back with the old firm and the powers that be in the Government insist on Blighty being neutral. They want nothing to do with Spain and their national bloodletting.'

'A fact that has been made perfectly plain these last two years,' Cal snapped; the indifference of Britain to the plight of the Spanish republicans tended to get under his skin. 'As neutrality it's a farce, given the arms embargo is being, and has been since the outbreak, routinely broken by the Germans and Italians.'

'You forgot to mention the Russians.'

'Most of whose ships have been sunk by Italian submarines, whilst the Royal Navy just stands by and looks on. HMG should be blushing to the roots, not worrying about what I am up to.'

'I don't make policy, Cal.'

'It's not so long ago you seemed as committed as I am to fighting the likes of Franco, or was the buying and shipping of weapons to Ethiopia two years back just a lark? I seem to recall a lot of talk about stopping Mussolini, and while I am aware you are not much of one for ideology, I would be disappointed to find you have done a complete volte-face and signed up with the denizens of the Right Club.'

Peter, to avoid answering what was clearly a question, stood up and went to a rather faded curtain, which, when twitched back, revealed a tiny kitchen, into which he disappeared as he responded.

'Would you like some coffee, old boy? I can make some if I can work out this infernal pot the Frogs use.'

'So, you're back with MI6?'

'I am.'

'Comfortable?'

The reply came through the curtain with some venom. 'Salaried, old chap, which for some of us is a most compelling requirement.'

'And your previous . . .' Cal paused. 'I hate to say "employers"?'

Having been a victim of budgetary cutbacks at the start of the decade, Peter had been recruited by a group of moneyed or politically connected individuals who were worried about the inexorable rise of the European dictators, allied to the fact that His Majesty's Government were doing nothing to put the kibosh on them. To such people a trained and competent intelligence operative, British to the core, was just the ticket.

The assumption that he had done their bidding for a decent stipend Cal had taken as read. On the grounds of proper appreciation he never worked for nothing and he doubted Peter would either, but he did have a private income, which he knew Peter lacked, given it rarely went unmentioned when they met.

Recruited from Hamburg, where he had been involved in getting Jews out to safety with some hope of prosperity, he had been engaged to work for those same interests, tasked to buy guns and get them into Ethiopia, then being threatened with an Italian invasion.

A few surprising names apart, Cal had never been vouchsafed the identity of the well-placed members of this secret group and he was damn sure he was not about to be enlightened now. He did know they had money, political contacts or both, and the ability to employ them in places in which they could be of use.

'Still in touch, of course,' Peter replied, 'and helpful it is, given there is some hope the mood might just be beginning to swing their way on reining in the dictators. Not at the top, you understand – Chamberlain is still convinced his policy is the right one – but let us say since Anthony Eden resigned the ground is shifting very slightly under the feet of those committed to appeasement.'

'About time.'

He reappeared holding the enamel coffee pot. 'Damn thing works on steam, I gather.'

'Don't fret on my account, Peter, I've had several cups already while I was having a bit of fun with those fellows watching my movements.'

'I knew you were in some kind of trouble, as soon as you raised that damned paper I knew it. Took a bit of quick thinking, that did.'

'Which does nothing to explain your presence in La Rochelle. I hope you have not come all this way to tell me to desist.'

'Would it matter if I had?'

'No, and since we are not at home I don't see how you could.'

'There are ways, old boy. For instance, I could always tip off the chaps at the old *Deuxième Bureau*, tell 'em what I suspect, though judging by the way you are being tailed it looks as if they are aware already. Weapons for Ireland they won't give a damn about but they are hotter than we are on Spain.'

Peter shook the pot. 'Do you know how to work this damn thing, Cal? You are, after all, practically a native.'

'I've told you I don't want coffee.'

'Selfish to the last, as always. What about me?' Peter replied peevishly, the cigarette jerking between his lips as he looked around the poorly furnished room. 'Because of what you are up to I had to rent this dump. A hotel was out of the question.'

Even if it struck Cal as unusual, there was a certain logic in that; every French hotel registered their guests by their passports, names and home address, while the completed forms were collected by the local gendarmerie, leaving an undesirable record of who stayed where and when – even with false papers, for anyone involved in intelligence, it was probably better to stay out of the system if you could.

Cal stood up and took the battered blue pot, waved the smoke out of his face and went past Peter into the kitchen, to where there was an open tin of ground coffee. The filling of both the base and the metal filter he carried out while talking, also the lighting of the gas onto which the pot was placed, his mind working on a couple of nagging inconsistencies.

'Surely you have not come all this way to have me show you how to make coffee French-style?' he asked eventually.

'No. The powers that be I mentioned want your services and I have been sent to rope you in.'

'To do what?'

'The usual, old boy, to risk life and limb for little or no reward.'

The coffee pot had to begin to make a bubbling sound before Cal replied to that, which left a very long conversational gap. It was like Hamburg all over again, where Peter had turned up with information that Cal's activities had come to the attention of the authorities, bringing the threat of possible arrest by the Gestapo. That had led to a very hairy and hurried departure not only for them, but also for a Jewish family he was in the process of extracting. Escape had been a close-run thing in which he had only avoided being taken up by the amount of time and effort he had put into setting up more than one escape route for himself.

As he heard the water bubble he was thinking that was one thing he now lacked unless he abandoned that cargo. La Rochelle was not on the route to anywhere, it was one of those places you came to or went from, or left by sea, and if his position was threatened he had few alternatives on how to avoid anyone seeking to arrest him.

That he was in a risky business went without saying, and that was made doubly so by the nature of who those weapons were for and the fact that there was a French embargo on weapons to Spain as well. What was irritating him now was the resemblance to Hamburg; it was just too pat and the similarities were too great.

Yet he could not just dismiss what was on offer until he knew the threat it posed to that which he was already engaged in. The men fighting against Franco's forces in the Cantabrian Mountains needed those weapons, and job number one was to get them loaded aboard ship and on their way.

'How's that coffee coming along?' Peter called.

'Nearly there.'

'Fetch out the old *confiture*, Cal, there's a good chap, the old stomach is rumbling somewhat.'

CHAPTER TWO

'**M**ust have been a bit hairy in Czechoslovakia, Cal, buying and shipping out your cargo with the nation mobilised for a possible war with the Hun.'

Peter had emptied the coffee pot and chewed steadily on his bread and jam to the point of swallowing half the loaf, a time during which Cal Jardine had kept off the subject and stuck to conversational generalities to allow himself time to think; now he was being dragged back to the present and what might become a dilemma. For a moment he wondered whether to answer, but given what Peter already knew it seemed harmless to oblige.

'The order I made was placed and the paperwork sorted before the crisis blew up, but the Czechs honoured the deal, which was pretty straight of them considering they had Adolf breathing fire. Not that they were surprised; they knew Hitler was bound to come after them once he'd swallowed up Austria. How did you know about the false End User Certificate, by the way?'

'Our military attaché in Prague got wind of it and sent a standard report to London. That was where the Irish connection first raised questions, given how sensitive we are in Blighty about possible shipments to the IRA.'

Cal was thinking that such an explanation did not clarify why Peter was here.

'We had to be sure, Cal, they were going to where the certificate said. I also have to admit it was a damn clever ploy, given our chaps are busy licensing the same weaponry for use by the British army and, of course, the Irish would follow suit, piggybacking on our research and approval. I hope it was worth whatever you forked out to get the Czechs to fall for it.'

If it was clever, the real reason that he had been successful in his purchase was more to do with the Czech factory having no desire to question him too closely about his bona fides: his papers were in order as far as they could see and the people he claimed to represent appeared sound.

In reality they were not looking too closely; they badly wanted his money, or to be more precise, the Spanish republican gold with which he was prepared to pay, as did a government under threat from a powerful neighbour, keen to amass foreign exchange, so extracting a false certificate from the relevant Czech ministry had been something of a formality in which no one had even demanded an illegal payment.

It was a good deal; the weapons he had bought were perfect for guerrilla warfare, a new pattern of easily portable light machine guns deadly in that kind of close combat. It was a ground and vehicle weapon, and added to that, so low was the recoil, they could be fired from the hip while on the move, all of which Peter listened to with polite interest; if he knew Cal was stalling, which he was, he gave no indication of it.

'You can tell the staff wallahs from me they've bought a good infantry weapon.'

'Sorry to disappoint you, Cal, but I doubt your estimation would carry much weight with the military brass and even less if I passed it on from MI6, given the army think we are all overeducated dolts. Anyway, to cut to the chase, we're not interested in guns; what the firm is after is your opinion of the Czechs as a nation.'

'Do you mean the Czech Czechs, the Slovaks, the Ruthenians, the Poles, the Hungarians or the Sudetenland Germans?'

Peter sighed. 'Do you have to complicate things?'

Cal felt he needed to make the point even if the world was less ignorant now than it had been a few months before, because Czechoslovakia was very much in the news, with German newspapers ranting daily about the 'plight' of their racial brethren in the border regions called the Sudetenland.

Yet, even on the front pages of the world, few appreciated how much the nation was a construct nation of peoples hacked out of the dismembered Austro-Hungarian Empire, with a dozen languages and rivalries going back centuries. Like most of his fellow countrymen, and most unfortunately the people in power in London, Peter did not appreciate the problems that produced.

If the Sudeten German minority were the most vocal in the search for concessions to their racial background they were just one of half a dozen similar problems facing the Prague Government, given every ethnic group had, to varying degrees, jumped on the federalist bandwagon. Tempted to explain, Cal decided not to bother; the nub of the question was not about that.

'Despite the bleating of their minorities, the Czechs are an honest bunch who run a democratic government that others of a similar ilk should support. How does that sound?'

That got an idly raised eyebrow. 'Like a *Daily Herald* headline and easier said than done, old boy.'

'But not impossible,' Cal responded, his voice becoming more animated. 'They have a reasonable military, good equipment and a fortified mountainous border with Germany that would take a serious commitment of manpower to get through, one perfect to aid an assault from the west by a combined French and British army.'

'I'm not sure that's actually answering the question I asked.'

'I am, Peter, given it's the only one that matters. They would have made a perfect partner before Hitler marched into Vienna, but sadly the border with Austria is a flat plain and difficult to defend. By being supine over the *Anschluß*, we have fatally weakened and are going to lose a useful potential ally unless we do something to stop it.'

'That does assume Adolf wishes to go the whole hog, old boy, and swallow the country up.'

'Something tells me you have not got round to reading *Mein Kampf* yet. I seem to recall telling you to do that with some force two years ago.'

'Picked it up, of course, but it's terribly turgid stuff, a perfect cure for insomnia, in fact. I have never got very far when I try. Nod off every time.'

'Then let me precis it for you, once more. Adolf Hitler wants back all the bits of German-speaking Central Europe they and the Austrians were forced to give away at Versailles and if he can't get them by threats he will go to war to recover them. He's already remilitarised the Rhineland and swallowed Austria in a coup, two things he listed in his ever-so-turgid book, both of which should have been stopped. Not many politicians keep their written promises, but he is one who will.'

Peter sighed and lit another cigarette. 'While our lot seem to have promised there will never be another pan-European war.'

'They don't have the power of decision, Peter. Hitler does! Has anyone in London looked at a map and seen what possession of Czechoslovakia does to the defence of Poland?'

'He's after them too, I suppose?'

'He wants to wipe out the Polish Corridor and take back Danzig, and the Poles won't give them up without a fight.'

'So, tell me how you managed to get them out with all that flap going on.'

'The guns?'

'What else?'

'Would I not bore you?'

'Cal, old boy, you often make me wonder what drives you to get into so many scrapes, but bore me, never!'

'While I am wondering if you have just come to La Rochelle or were waiting for me to arrive.' Peter Lanchester grinned and flicked off a bit of ash. 'You were waiting for me, weren't you? Not that you have tried very hard to hide the fact that you have this apartment for one day and possibly more.'

'Was I?'

Cal pointed to the jar of French jam. 'That was not opened this morning, was it, and if you only just booked into this place it would need to be.'

Peter pulled a face, the one an errant child might employ when

24

caught in a fib, but Cal suspected he was only playing out a game. 'It might have been left by the previous occupant.'

'In a rented apartment it would have been pilfered by the owner, the agent or whoever cleans the place, a fact of which you too would have been aware. So that tells me you want me to know, because, Peter, if some of the people you are again working for are as thick as two short planks, you are not.'

'I will take that as a backhanded compliment.'

'So?'

'Being the servant of two masters, though not at the same time I hasten to add, has certain advantages, but it turned out that prior to my recall to the Secret Intelligence Service, certain elements in the firm became aware you were active and where.'

'How?'

'Various whispers, some of which I picked up.'

'You were listening?'

'On behalf of those for whom I worked, Cal. I have to admit a particular interest in what you are up to, given what you choose to call my "previous employers" thought we might be required to ask for your services again after Ethiopia.'

'I could have used more of their help in Spain.'

Peter had got him the use of a freighter to ship a load of weapons to Barcelona the previous year. Once on board he was soon disillusioned as to the depth of the favour, being presented with forged documents to sign that made him entirely responsible for what was in the holds, should the vessel be stopped and searched.

'The interests I worked for might be anti-fascist, Cal, but they are not pro-republican, while I am damn sure they have no time for anarchists. And that does not even begin to explain how little they are enamoured by the level of Russian involvement. They are, after all, people with a visceral dislike of Bolsheviks.'

'One of these days I look forward to you telling me who they are.'

'While I would be fascinated to hear the tale of how you managed to buy a shipload of German weapons for the Spanish republicans and get them out through Hamburg, when the Nazis are committed to supporting Franco.'

'That is a tale which will cost you a good dinner.'

'Don't you think it's time you treated me, Cal, given you're the one with the private income, while I am now what Karl Marx called a mere "wage slave"?'

'So, the trade was pegged in Czechoslovakia, but where did you pick up that I was involved and, more importantly, headed for La Rochelle?'

'SIS landed me with the job on my re-engagement, given I know you from our army days. The trade was flagged in Brno, from a contact in the arms factory paid to tell us when stuff was going out the door, regardless of to where.'

'I should have thought of that,' Cal said.

'At first, given he's pretty low level, he did not know who was buying, and naturally, given the reasons already stated, the firm was deeply curious and finally alarmed when they checked with our lot in Dublin and a false EUC emerged.'

'That does not finger me.'

'But then you contracted in a certain name for a ship to pick up an unspecified cargo here and that belonged to one of my previous contacts, who passed the info on to me, really to check the risk factor that it might be breaking the embargo. And lo and behold I find the vessel has been hired by a Mr Moncrief.'

Peter was looking pretty smug, but really what had caught Cal out was a chain of coincidence: British sensitivity about Irish terrorism in the six counties of Ulster, the contacts Peter had, plus the fact that he had supplied the false Moncrief identity to help him smuggle those weapons into Barcelona two years before. Then he had gone back to work for the Government and failed to keep that fact to himself.

'And naturally you had to let your new masters know that Moncrief was me and, very likely, the cargo was not destined for Dublin?'

'No need to take that tone, old chum, chap needs a feather or two in his cap from time to time and they were impressed. Having brought home a bit of early bacon, and knowing in part our relationship, I was given the task of looking for you.'

'Which involved?'

'Checking the trains that had left Brno, the goods they were carrying and their destinations, as well as who might be shifting them and to where. Dublin-based company, agricultural equipment, staggered journey with some odd stops and switches that took over a month – two and two, really.'

'So having made four?'

'I'm not here to interfere, Cal, but to enquire if you are planning any more little adventures.'

'I might be.'

'In Czechoslovakia?'

'It's possible.'

'In that case, as I have already mentioned, we want your services in what is now a very interesting part of the world.'

'You must have people there already.'

'Shall I just say there is an official policy and one that runs somewhat counter to that, which makes it an arena where we have to tread somewhat carefully.'

'To avoid alerting the Foreign Office and I presume some people in MI6 itself?'

Peter Lanchester thought for several seconds before nodding, initially unwilling to acknowledge that he worked in an organisation which, quite apart from the time-servers was staffed by some very rabid right-wingers indeed, agents whose loyalties might be split.

'And if the answer is no?'

'I go back to London with my tail between my legs and admit to those who sent me that I failed in my first field operation, which will not do much to raise my standing.'

Cal leant forward and looked Peter right in the eye. 'Assuming the answer is no, let me tell you what I would do if I were in your shoes.'

To avoid his eye, Peter deliberately looked at his toecap. 'Do we share a shoe size, old boy?'

'I would make the proposition and if I was turned down I would slip along to the *hôtel de ville* and seek out whoever it is who is in a position to alert the *Deuxième Bureau*, given there's bound to be someone in place for that purpose.'

Peter was now looking distinctly uncomfortable, a condition that was not eased by the bitter tone in which Cal continued.

'Then I would say to them that there is a cargo of light machine guns plus enough ammo for an extended campaign coming into town to be loaded on to a British cargo vessel, bound for Spain, and I would even provide names.'

'That would be awfully devious, Cal.'

'Yet I suspect I have just described your instructions from on high. I have been tracked halfway across Europe and if I am being tailed in

La Rochelle it is not by the French, it is by MI6, all for the purpose of blackmailing me into working for them. Those two following me were just to give you leverage, were they not?'

There was no reaction to that, the eyes stayed on the shoe.

'Just as they were also not the idiots I took them to be, they were supposed to be spotted so you could give that little performance on the quayside.'

'At least you must acknowledge it was convincing.'

'Who are they?'

The reply was not immediate but slow in coming; no one in the intelligence business likes to give anything away unless they have to. 'Couple of chaps from the Paris embassy, who were only too keen for a bit of cloak and dagger to relieve the boredom.'

It was not hard to anticipate the next question, given the way Cal was staring at him. 'Who, if they don't hear from me, will return there forthwith.'

'Do they know about my real name or my shipment?'

'Of course not!' Peter replied, eyebrows shooting up, leaving Cal to wonder if the shock was real or as feigned as his quayside rudeness. He was far from convinced he was being told the truth.

'The question is, Peter, will you carry out your instructions to the letter or will you, for old times' sake, if I decline your offer, manufacture a fudge that lets me get clear?'

Peter Lanchester looked Cal straight in the eye, tapping his fingers on the oilskin cloth covering the table. 'I hope you are not expecting me to be embarrassed. It is often the case that in the intelligence game one is put in an invidious position, Cal, you know that.'

'I accept that, but I don't know what you are going to do, given the position you are in – indulge an old companion, or obey your new bosses and hang me out to dry. When it comes to shipping weapons to Spain the French are worse than us and quite brutal in their methods of extracting information. I don't fancy ending up having to answer any questions they might pose about who helped me get this far.'

'Then give me an answer.'

'I will, on one condition.'

'Which is?'

'I'll say yes or no when my cargo is loaded and on the way to Spain.'

'You're not going with it?'

'No, my involvement ends once it's on board.'

That brought another long silence as Peter contemplated the offer, and it was clear from his expression that what occurred to him first were the manifest drawbacks.

'Such a course puts all the aces in your hands. What if you renege once it is loaded?'

'I give you my word I will not and my answer will be based on a realistic appreciation of what I can usefully do.'

'Not something my chiefs would accept.'

'They don't know me, you do. I am not giving them my word, Peter, this is personal between you and I.'

That led to another long silence and a stare between them that was locked and unfriendly, until Peter finally gave way. 'Oh all right, but you'd better bloody well keep it, for if you break it I will get the blame for that and I give you my word that those I represent will help me to ensure you will suffer more.'

'Meaning I'll have to shut up shop in the arms trade?'

'Meaning, old boy, you will never dare set foot on home soil again, for the moment you do you will be arrested and thrown into choky for a very long time.'

'I assume I would get a trial.'

'While I am certain you would earn a conviction. You're a British subject breaking an official arms embargo.'

Cal looked at his watch. 'It is about time for me to move, Peter. I have a schedule to keep.'

'Which involves?' Now it was Cal's turn to be guarded, to husband information best kept secret, which clearly annoyed Peter. 'I have to know and I have, after all, been fairly open with you.'

'I radioed the ship from the Marconi office this morning, which is, I assume, where your embassy chaps picked me up?'

'Another bit of brilliant Lanchester deduction. I guessed you'd have to radio the vessel to say the cargo was ready to load.'

'It will anchor in the outer roads late this afternoon and I have to get the goods into the commercial port and alongside before certain customs people go off duty.'

'Folk whom you've bribed?' Cal nodded, as Peter hauled himself to his feet. 'You'll have to wait till I get changed.'

'Why?'

'I doubt my present attire is proper wear for what is proposed.'

'You intend to come along?'

'Cal, if you think I am going to let you out of my sight, you have another think coming. I am going to stick to you, in that vulgar expression the squaddies we led used to employ, like shit to a blanket. Now do me a favour and start to clean the place up so there is no trace of either of us ever being here.'

'Is that necessary?'

'Compulsory, old boy, standing orders now that one is back in harness.'

'Did you not rent it?'

'Got one of the embassy chaps to do that and it is paid for till the end of the week.'

Surprised as he was, Cal complied and that took time, wiping every surface and handle, shutters included after they had been shut and locked. Then there was the coffee pot, the knife Peter had used, gas knob, kitchen surfaces as well as the tabletop and the backs of the chairs.

Peter Lanchester came out of the tiny bedroom backwards, using his handkerchief to do the doorknob and edge, nodding appreciatively when he saw that Cal had used a bag he had found to take with them the remaining food and any rubbish.

He was dressed in dark-grey flannels and a blazer, everything else in a valise he was carrying. Last of all, after the front door had been wiped, was the key, cleaned and flicked under the door. Once at the entrance to the apartments Peter allowed Cal twenty paces before following him to where he had parked his car, a small, two-door, green Simca, in a road off the quayside.

CHAPTER THREE

The route out of La Rochelle avoided the main road that led eventually, as all roads in France do, to Paris. They drove instead through the south-eastern suburbs, an obviously working-class quarter, across a bridge, then on to a narrow *pavé* road that ran alongside the south side of the Canal du Marais-Poitevin, just wide enough for two cars to pass, tree-lined on one side and with a shallow inland storm ditch to prevent flooding from the adjoining open fields.

It was also, bar the odd shallow bend, as straight as a ruler and far from busy, cutting through a flat, featureless agricultural landscape dotted with windmills and the odd *manoir*-type farmhouse, with the waterway and the occasional barge using it to the northern side.

There was no attempt at haste; Cal kept the speed down, not because he feared any kind of police presence, but for the simple reason that it was unwise to do anything that might draw attention.

Both side windows were open to let in a welcome breeze; with the sun now high in the sky, the day had become hot and a bit sticky, increasingly so as they left behind the cooling breeze from the sea. That also had the advantage of extracting Peter's almost-constant cigarette smoke.

What conversation they exchanged consisted of general chat about the increasingly feverish situation in Central Europe, thanks to the rantings of Hitler, plus a shared if constrained fuming at how Mussolini had not only got away with his criminal invasion of Ethiopia and the even more iniquitous use of poison gas, but had then had that conquest recognised by the democratic nations in the hope that it would deter him from forming an alliance with Germany, the conclusion being it was a flawed policy.

That moved on to the projected outcome for the republicans in Spain and it was far from sanguine. They were steadily losing ground to their fascist-backed opponents while simultaneously trying to get out from the grip of the international communists and commissars Stalin had sent to help in their campaigns – emissaries who had proved to be, as friends, just as dangerous as the troops of General Franco.

Railing at the stupidity of that, as well as Bolshevism in general, and getting little response, Peter eventually noticed that his companion was uncomfortable discussing the failings of the communists; in fact Cal abruptly turned the conversation to what was happening socially and politically in London, and when he enquired as to why he was a bit touchy, Peter was told to mind his own business.

He was thus left in the dark about a subject his companion found too painful to talk about: both the loss he had suffered at the hands of the communists in Spain and the revenge he had taken for what was, in truth, a bereavement. Not a cold-blooded killer by nature, events had forced him into that mode and it was not a memory that, in either cause or effect, was in any way joyful.

A lorry coming in the opposite direction, one of a width that forced them to pull hard to the side and stop between two trees to let it pass, curtailed a rather strained exchange. Sitting with the engine idling, Cal quietly asked, his eyes firmly fixed on the rear-view mirror, if there was any reason Peter could think of as to why they might be followed.

'None whatever, old chap, unless you have been careless.'

'I try not to be, as you know, but then if you found me . . .'

'The question is being posed because?'

'We picked up a car just as we left the centre of the city. You must have noticed that Hispano-Suiza roadster that was parked by the roadside?'

'Not terribly interested in cars, old boy.'

'Well it pulled out immediately we had passed. Nothing unusual in that, except that it is still with us and the hood is up, which is hardly fitting when it's so hot. Added to that, it has kept to the same speed as us ever since.'

'Why is that strange?'

'It's a J12, capable of well over a ton.'

'Not on this road, surely?' Peter said.

'Be great fun on this road,' Cal insisted.

The passing lorry cut out the sunlight, easing past with about an inch to spare. With the road clear again Cal moved off, his eyes rarely off what was happening behind, the lorry being forced onto the side embankment and skirting the ditch to get past the wider Hispano-Suiza.

'You think it's the law?' Peter asked.

'Not in that kind of car, it costs a bloody fortune. Bugger stopped when we did, as if he didn't want to get too close, and is now moving again, but not getting any nearer. If I was driving that kind of motor I would have been right up the arse of this little thing, flashing my bloody great headlights and leaning on the horn to get by.'

'You sound just like Toad of Toad Hall, old chap,' Peter responded calmly, before adding, 'I take it that it might be worth a few precautions.'

'Look under your seat, Peter; attached to the bottom there's an oilskin pouch with a Mauser inside.'

'I'm not sure that's very wise,' Peter replied. 'If I am fingered here I will be in the soup regardless, without firing off a weapon on foreign turf.'

'Just do as I ask, Peter, there's a good chap. You came along because you elected to do so, not because you were invited.'

'Fair enough,' came the reply, after a moment's consideration.

The gun was fetched out and one of the two detached full magazines inspected, before being rammed home and the weapon cocked, though with the safety on. Cal kept to the same pace as before, there being no point in increasing speed; this Simca could not outrun any kind of roadster, never mind one of the best on the market.

The careful speed was maintained until they passed, on their right, a ramshackle *manoir* so run-down it was shorn of windows, fronted by a clutter of delapidated farm buildings with a couple of canvas-topped lorries parked outside, which seemed to be a workshop for farm equipment, judging by the amount of rusting metal and tractor attachments scattered about.

Cal sounded a tattoo on his horn, before swinging on to a narrow bridge with a low stone parapet that led to the north side of the canal, followed by a glance upstream to check the barge containing his cargo was still moored where he had last seen it. Now hidden by the line of trees that enclosed the canal on both sides he increased his speed, jamming his foot to the floor; if it gave him a pleasing sensation of haste, it was, he knew, useless by comparison to that of the car behind.

The road ahead split again and he screeched round the right-hand bend, gunning through the gears to another junction and swinging left onto an equally narrow, long and straight road that led north away from the canal – not that he expected to fool anyone and get away.

He had only one aim: to see if it was indeed a tail, or if he was being overcautious; that was answered within minutes when those big twin headlights abreast the low-slung black body appeared once more in the rear-view mirror. Cal immediately killed his speed, noting that the tail slowed as well. They were definitely being followed, but by whom?

What he had said to Peter had to be true: it was unlikely to be official, and not just for the value of a car that cost as much as a Rolls-Royce. If it was the French equivalent of MI5, seeking to enforce their national embargo on weapons destined for Spain, they would have been much more professional and thus harder to spot.

Such people knew their job and they would not be daft enough to assign one very obvious tail – and to find out what? The only thing could be the location of the weapons with a view to seizing them, which meant they had to be as aware of his intentions as his passenger.

'Where is my cargo, Peter?'

'Not a clue, old chap.'

'Take a guess,' Cal responded with obvious impatience.

A sideways look showed Peter smiling. 'The last place I had it pegged for certain was at the railhead in Marans.'

'From which you deduced what?'

'Seemed an obvious place to transfer to the road, old boy, given it runs all the way to a major port on the Bay of Biscay and the trains running into said port are risky when it comes to being searched – which could be bad news if your manifest and papers don't pass muster. All it would take is the opening of one case to establish you are not shipping tractor parts.'

'Not a barge?'

'No,' Peter admitted ruefully when he realised what he was being told. 'You fooled me on that one.'

'La Rochelle was no more than presumption, then?'

'I flatter myself when I admit the answer to that is yes. With you involved and Spain the destination it had to be a Biscay port and Nantes and Bordeaux are too big, while Rochefort, the only other alternative, is an active naval base and too risky.'

'Will you stop being so damn smug and deduce what would happen if the French knew as much as you?'

'I have no indication that they did.'

'That's not what I asked, but if they had they would not need to chase us around the countryside, would they?'

The answer came with a languor that riled Cal. 'You refer, of course, to the Johnny who I assume is still following us.'

'You know, Peter, sometimes your sangfroid can be a pain in the arse. Now do me a favour and use your not-inconsiderable brain. I am reasoning that whoever is following can't be official. Discuss.'

'It is sometimes very pleasant, old boy, to get under your skin.'

'But?'

Peter's chin hit his chest as he ran over things in his mind.

'If the Frogs knew as much as I did, and with vastly superior resources, they would know exactly where your weapons are and could pick you up when they liked, whatever mode of transport you used. In fact, they might have done so already to ensure they did not miss you, unless of course, they are waiting to find out who is either helping you or who in the port has taken your filthy Spanish lucre.'

'In which case they would not allow themselves to be spotted?'

'You would have no idea they were even watching.'

'My thinking too, which leads me to the same conclusion as before. Whoever is on our tail cannot be either the local plod or the *Deuxième Bureau*.'

'Then who?'

'Ask me another,' Cal replied, before falling silent for a few seconds. 'We need to stop and see if we can flush them out. There's a small town ahead called Dompierre-sur-Mer.'

'Rather a shortage of the *mer*, old chap, wouldn't you say?' Peter responded, still in that laconic way, looking around the crop-filled fields to either side of what had once probably been ancient marshland reclaimed from the sea. 'But we lack an alternative, given there's nowhere to hide around here that I can spot.'

'In this case the best place to hide is in the open.' Cal nodded ahead to the first building at the edge of what was a far from substantial settlement, then looked at his watch. 'Time I bought you that meal you were so keen on.'

'I doubt this hamlet we are approaching has the kind of treat I had in mind.'

'Which was?'

'The Connaught or the Savoy,' Peter ventured, 'perhaps with the freedom of the wine list.'

'I fear you'll have to settle for peasant fare, old chum, and the *vin du pays*, so, find somewhere to conceal that gun and prepare to reprise your "Englishman abroad" act.'

Dompierre was typical of thousands of small French towns, a run-down and desolate sort of place that had not been on the coast for centuries, with no industry, living off the produce extracted from the surrounding fields, and a few buildings, none of any size and mainly looking in need of repair, the whole clustered round the local church. It had the air of so many places in rural France – somewhere time had passed by or never even discovered.

Yet it was a working hamlet, it still contained a few of the necessary small shops in a central square dominated by the ubiquitous war memorial to the dead of the *Guerre Mondiale*: a butcher, a baker, both just closing for the two hours of lunch, a still-open newsagent which was also a *tabac*, as well as a small brasserie with outside seating under a sun-bleached awning advising the benefits of Ricard pastis.

Cal parked the Simca near the brasserie but in the shade, attracting a few curious glances from those still about. The reaction to the two-seater Hispano-Suiza J12, as it glided in seconds after, low and sleek, the engine purring, actually made the locals stop and stare; it was a rich man's motor in a place were such things were rarely to be seen.

Parked well away from the Simca in full sunlight, hood still up, engine off, it just sat there for what seemed an age. By the time the passenger got out, Cal and Peter were sitting under the awning, awaiting the beers they had ordered.

He was tall, exuded even at a distance an air of arrogance, and looked to be in his early twenties, broad-shouldered with blond curls, in a double-breasted light-grey suit of a good cut, somewhat crumpled from having been sat in a hot car, that over an open-necked big-collared shirt.

He stood by the open door looking around like a tourist, at the church, the Calvary cross of the war memorial and the now-shuttered shops, though it was obvious that his sweeping looks were taking in the two men he had followed.

Then his lips moved and whatever he said brought out the driver, a shorter fellow, who looked even younger with his brown cowlick hair, dressed in a leather blouson over a dark-blue shirt; he also made a point of not looking in their direction as he fetched out a beret to cover his head.

'Cal, I have no idea who these two clowns are, but they are rank amateurs.'

Peter imparted that soft opinion as the owner of the brasserie placed the two draught beers on their table, looking up longingly just after he did so towards the Hispano-Suiza, which had Cal engaging him in a conversation of the kind people indulge in who love cars – the beauty of the lines, the size of the engine, which was a V12, and the potential speed such a vehicle could achieve, the conclusion that not only was the fellow driving it a lucky man, he was, along with his passenger, also a complete stranger.

Then he asked for some food and, with Peter's assent, agreed to a couple of omelettes and a side salad.

'I have never understood this obsession with motor vehicles,' Peter said, when the owner had gone; he had some French, but nothing like the fluency of Cal Jardine. 'But I take it we have fixed these fellows as not being local.'

Cal nodded and sipped his beer while keeping an eye on the two youngsters, the shorter of whom looked like a teenager, now conversing in a way that indicated they were trying to decide what to do. The conclusion had the tall one in the crumpled suit heading for the *bijouterie-tabac*, which had a sign outside to indicate it had a telephone, both men watching till he disappeared inside.

'I doubt he's gone for a paper,' Cal said.

'Calling for instructions, perhaps?' Peter essayed. 'You'd best fill me in on how close your cargo is.'

'Did I say it was close?'

Peter looked at his watch, trying and failing to hide his impatience, which actually pleased his companion; it was equally enjoyable to get under his skin.

'Lunchtime now, your barge has to be in the port, I suspect, during the hours of darkness, as will your freighter. But you have to allow time to get them alongside, more for loading so the vessel can sail at first light, and barges are slower than the lorries I thought you were using. How am I doing?'

'So far so good.'

'And can I add you are going to have to fully trust me anyway, much more now that we seem to have come across a slight impediment to that smooth transfer you earlier anticipated?'

'That set of buildings just by that bridge we crossed.'

'When you tooted the horn in that rather curious manner?' Cal nodded and did so again when Peter identified that as a warning to get ready to move.

'Who's waiting?'

'French sympathisers and a couple of Spaniards who will take the cargo on and land it.'

'Not communists, I hope.'

'Not a chance, they are Basques and they don't like Madrid, whoever is in charge.'

'Why the lorries?'

'I had them as backup, just in case anything went wrong getting down the canal.'

Peter allowed himself a grim smile. 'So it's not a careful plan designed to go like clockwork?'

'Take my word for it, Peter, should you ever indulge in the business of running guns, it never can be.'

'Advice I shall cherish. Is there an alternative to moving them now?'

'Not an easy one, given I've already sent a message to the freighter to enter port.'

'Here comes our chum,' Peter hissed.

Without being too obvious, they both observed the well-built suit returning to the car with his swaggering gait. If unable to hear what he said, it was a barked instruction that got both driver and passenger back in their seats, the engine firing with a bit of a roar through the twin exhausts, before it slipped out of the square heading inland.

Oil, vinegar and a basket of bread arriving allowed Cal to ask about the roads around the town and where they led, the conclusion, after much waving of hands, that there was any number of ways by which anyone could go anywhere, back to La Rochelle or inland to Niort on the *route nationale*. More importantly, he established that one of them would take the roadster back to that bridge without having to come back through the town.

'So what's the plan, Cal?' asked Peter when the owner had gone.

'Wait a mo,' he replied, standing up and walking towards the *tabac*.

In an exaggerated fashion, Peter stretched out his legs and lifted his beer to his lips, calling loudly after Cal, 'Do get a move on, old chap, this gun of yours is going to ruin the cut of my blazer. Oh, and fetch me some gaspers, will you, British if they have any.'

'You'll be lucky.'

Peter did sit up when his omelette came and he ordered two more beers before tucking into that and the bread. His plate was clean by the time Cal returned, his face set hard.

'Something tells me the news isn't good.'

'No.'

'Am I to assume whoever runs that shop overheard something?'

'No, I bribed her to ask the telephone operator what number our suit just called. Told her to say he had left his wallet.'

Peter clicked his fingers. 'As easy as that?'

'Look around you, Peter. When do you think was the last time anyone in Dompierre saw a hundred-dollar note?'

'I doubt anyone in this dump would recognise American currency of any denomination.'

'They do, this was a country awash with rich Yanks until the Wall Street Crash. Anyway, our madame of a shopkeeper did and that's all that matters.'

'Which, I assume, you flashed under her nose.'

'I just asked her if she knew anywhere close by where I could change one and waited for the reaction, which was pleasingly negative.'

It had been a pantomime of regrets, but Cal had seen avarice in the old woman's eyes at the sight of the high-denomination foreign note, one that became more valuable with each passing day in a country with a falling exchange rate; it was probably equivalent to half a year's profits in her *petit magasin*.

If his explanation of what he wanted had sounded false to the point of being risible in his ears, even in his perfect French, that *La Patrie* was in danger from foreign spies and he was offering a reward to thwart them, it had been enough to persuade her, once the note was in her hand, to call the operator with the required excuse. Having got the number, he then made a second call, pretending to be the fellow returned for his wallet, asking to be put through to allay any concerns.

What he heard from the other end set Cal Jardine's mind racing; if you live on the edge of danger or discovery all the time it is easy to become paranoid, but it is also necessary to exclude nothing from your thinking, especially the very worst possibility, like that on which he was reflecting now as he began to pick on his salad and munch on his barely warm omelette.

'So what did you find out?'

'Our blond-haired chum phoned the La Rochelle headquarters of the *Jeunesses Patriotes*.'

CHAPTER FOUR

A period of silence followed while both mulled over the significance of that discovery, not least in the fact of how they had come to the attention of what was in essence a private army. Cal knew the name well, Peter Lanchester only vaguely from the not-very-comprehensive reports in the British press, but he was well aware of the fact that France, in this fractious decade, was no different to his home country when it came to political disruption.

Oswald Mosley's Blackshirts were only the most visible of those who demanded radical change in Britain; there were outfits even more extreme while France was awash with organisations like the *Jeunesses Patriotes*, *Action Française* and *Solidarité Française* or *Les Camelots du Roi*.

These groups ran through the gamut of right-wing monarchists all the way to the outright fascist, but they did have certain things in common. They were all aggressively anti-Semitic, anti-socialist gangs of thugs, the main difference between them being in the level of violence they employed.

When it came to causing mayhem, the hot-blooded French left the British fascists looking placid; indeed they would stand comparison with the Nazis when it came to challenging socialists, communists and Jews on the streets and taking on the government. Street battles were endemic and collectively they had sought to storm and torch their own parliament in Paris two years previously, which led to them being outlawed.

All it meant, in truth, was they went underground until the smoke cleared. Then they could come to the surface again and operate more or less openly in a country where the state authorities, the police and internal security outfits were more likely to have some sympathy for their aims than any great desire to forcibly curtail them.

That would be particularly true in an isolated city like La Rochelle, which, judging by the obvious wealth of the conurbation, was probably a bastion of right-wing conservatism, where oversight by the law had to be minimal given the *Jeunesses Patriotes* felt safe to the point of openly answering the headquarters phone with their name.

Regardless of their chosen designation the French right had one other thing in common: all the groups were solidly anti the Spanish republicans, whom they saw as bedfellows of the greater enemy, the Bolsheviks of the Soviet Union, and would act as unpaid spies when it came to stopping any weapons getting into anti-Franco hands.

The *Jeunesses Patriotes* were an ultra-violent paramilitary group modelled on Mussolini's Fascist Youth or the Spanish Falangists. It was made up of university students and the sons and daughters of the rich and a higher bourgeoisie determined to protect their privileged existence and their money.

They espoused in particular a virulent hatred of communists, despised socialists, reviled Jews, and they were as an organisation known to be prepared to kill, their activities formed and funded by the champagne millionaire Pierre Taittinger and like-minded industrialists.

'Who did you tell where you were headed, Peter?' Cal asked finally, picking at his food.

'Only the people who needed to know.'

'From where did you tell them?'

'The Paris embassy.'

'In code?'

'Of course.'

'Which means you used the Cipher Room?' Peter nodded, making the connection immediately: the clerk who coded his message would have to know the contents prior to encryption. 'You're sure those two chaps you brought from the Paris embassy were ignorant about my cargo?'

'I can't be certain, Cal, but there was nothing in the message I sent to alert them to the truth, nor in their behaviour when in my company. You were not referred to by name and nor were any details of your shipment. I merely informed those I had to that I was pursuing my assignment to La Rochelle. How the hell that got passed on to a French fascist party I cannot tell.'

'I don't think these young sods are following me, Peter, I think they are following you and that information could only have come from London.'

'Unlikely,' Peter insisted, without hesitation.

'You seem very assured and I'm not confident you can be, given our previous conversation.'

'I have good reason to be, Cal, but why is not something I am yet prepared to discuss with you.'

'Indulge me. Air the thought.'

'There's no point. Besides, if someone in London blew the gaff, and I fail to see how they could, they would surely tell their French equivalents in the *Deuxième Bureau* and that would have meant either of the scenarios we discussed before this wonderful *repas*.'

'Meaning I would not have got this far?'

'Exactly, you'd be sitting in choky thinking about rubber truncheons. And I might add, given we are where we are, in the middle of bloody France and these chaps pose what seems to be an unquantifiable threat, is there any point right now in speculation about what got you pegged?'

'There is, Peter, plus a scenario that's even more troubling. Someone knows and has let slip to the wrong people that there is a cargo of very high-quality weapons on the way to Spain—'

Peter cut across him. 'Which the *Jeunesses Patriotes* will be determined to stop.'

'Maybe yes, maybe no. We've got two proper Charlies on our tail who don't seem to care about being spotted, but it's bloody obvious what they are after. When they make a phone call it's not to the gendarmes, it is to the headquarters of their organisation, which just happens to hate the present centre-left French Government and would love to bring it down – something they cannot do peacefully.'

'I'm not following you, old boy.'

'What if the *Jeunesses Patriotes* are not trying to stop the weapons from getting to Spain, but are trying to steal them for their own use here in France?'

'When did that notion occur to you?'

'Between making that call and coming back here.'

'Don't you think you are jumping a bit too far along the old conspiracy trail?'

'It's possible, Peter, but you think it through and come up with another answer that makes sense. We've got both the weapons and ammunition to equip a substantial force and what appears to be a couple of young thugs who are part of a group of mad bastards trying to get their mitts on them.'

'Hand them in,' Peter conjectured, 'feather in the old cap, sort of thing?'

'These kids and their backers don't want to impress the Government, Peter, they want to kick it out and very likely line the ministers up against a wall and shoot them.'

'It might be wise to recall that they are only kids, Cal.'

'They're old enough to kill and have shown more than once they are capable of doing so.'

'Street battles, heat-of-the-moment stuff.'

'Say I'm right and they do want to steal that cargo. What happens to the likes of you and me, what happens to the people waiting to help me if they do? If they are not planning to hand in the guns they are not planning to hand us over to the authorities either.'

'Say you're barmy?'

'Is it worth the risk?'

'No,' Peter replied, standing up, 'and I hope while you were doing all that thinking you came up with a way to put the mockers on the blighters.'

'Where are you going?'

'To buy those fags you forgot to get me, which will also, as I enter the shop with the telephone, make our chums wonder what we are up to, given I should think one of them is watching us.'

Cal nodded, but made no attempt to ascertain if there was any truth in what had been said.

'I expect, by the time I get back, that you will have formulated a way out of this mess that does not risk me getting shot at again. Why is it every time I get involved with you I seem to be at some risk of an early grave?'

'You don't have to be part of it.'

'If you are right, Cal, and I am still to be convinced that you are, then it's too late for that. How soon do you have to get that cargo moving if it is to go out tonight?'

'Quickly; it will take at least eight hours to get to the canal basin, then right through to the port and clear customs in a way that does not arouse suspicion.'

'Do you have to lead our Johnnies to them?'

'No, Peter, I have to lead them to a place where they can be dealt with and I also have to get a barge moving without anyone working out what it's carrying. So go and get your fags while I pay our host.'

Cal checked his watch as they pulled out of the square heading back to the bridge, waving away the excessively pungent smoke of the cigar-thick French cigarette Peter had just lit up.

'I am going to presume they don't know where the cargo is; for instance, like you, they have no idea it's on a barge. If they did, why tail us, given there is only one way out to sea?'

'And in order to tell their mates they have located them they need a telephone, which means they must come back here, since we doubt there's one closer that they know about.'

'Their chums can't move to intercept until they know where to go. So maybe we should lead them to that farmhouse and set a trap.'

'Which neither you nor I would walk into, Cal.'

'But then we would not have been spotted if we wanted to tail anyone, would we?'

'Are they stupid or just cocky?'

'Bit of both and certainly the latter, I'd say. I don't recall ever meeting a French *über*-patriot but they are of a type, no different to their German counterparts, full of themselves and sure that God, ideology and history are on their side.'

As if to prove what he had just said the Hispano-Suiza appeared once more in the rear-view mirror, a fact that Cal passed on. The situation was the same, driving without haste, except this time as they crossed to the southern side of the bridge he stopped and waited, seemingly indecisive, looking left and right, his tail pulling up likewise before his wheels hit the crossing.

'Seven minutes,' Cal added, looking at his watch again. 'Say ten minutes to get to that phone, make the call and drive back to the bridge. He's bound to drive like a bat out of hell.'

Peter reached into his pocket and pulled out a penknife, looking very smug indeed as he opened the blade. 'Except, when he gets there he will find the instrument does not work.'

'You cut the connection?'

'No point in just being a passenger, old boy, and I reckoned you had paid the old biddy who owns the shop more than enough to cover the repair.'

Cal nodded and moved off, driving straight into the jumble of barns to pull up beside the two lorries, slightly annoyed as they got out that two of the men who had agreed to aid him came out of the largest barn to greet them and thus made their presence known.

It would have been pointless to chastise them even if he had the power, so he just smiled and raised his hand in welcome, while telling them to get ready to move; he planned to be well away from here when the roadster came back.

The roar of that car's twin exhausts alerted them to the fact that any previous calculations, such as sending the lorries in different directions, were useless. The Hispano-Suiza swept over the bridge, turned right and, with the driver's foot right to the floor, shot off down the road to La Rochelle.

'One assumes,' Peter said, with his usual studied calm, 'that the chums are already on their way and our Johnnies have gone to meet them and chivvy them along. We have been humbugged, old boy.'

Cal's response was not calm, it was a loud and foul expletive followed by a stream of rapid French as he informed those he had brought with him – another quartet had emerged to make six in all – about the danger they were in, that followed by a set of rapid instructions.

The most important were to despatch the two Basques to tell the owner of the barge, who had stayed aboard to guard it, to get it moving towards the port and an insistence all three ignore anything else that happened around them.

He was still talking as he dashed to the nearest lorry to open the passenger door, reaching under the seats to pull out a roll of sacking, which, when rolled open on the ground, revealed the matt black metal and wooden stock of one of his Czech ZB26 light machine guns, complete with spare barrel and the front bipod, which he began to assemble and load, before dragging out and opening a canvas backpack to reveal several box magazines.

'Peter,' Cal said, removing and handing over his jacket, 'take my car back over the bridge. Get it out of sight, then cross back over and keep an eye on the road from La Rochelle. Oh, and you might need that spare clip for the Mauser.'

His old army comrade was looking at the machine gun and he was clearly worried. 'You can't start a war, Cal.'

'I'll try not to, Peter, but these sods have to be stopped and I don't think blowing kisses at them will do the trick. Now please do as I ask and quickly, we don't know how long we have and I need to think of a way to throw them off their game.'

With no idea of numbers or the level of the arms they might be carrying, Cal knew one very pertinent fact: with lorries likely to be against cars he could not outrun them, which would mean whatever he did, flight would only bring on a contest and in the open country, where he would be at an even greater disadvantage than he was at present.

So he had to think of a way to stop them getting into these farm buildings, a place he could easily be driven out of unless he was prepared to use the machine gun, and that might bring about, depending on how aggressive those heading this way were and regardless of his own disinclination, the need to kill.

Given no alternative that is what he would have to do, but quite apart from the bloodshed there was a second consideration in terms of the discreet smuggling out of a barge-load of weapons. It would hardly help to have the whole region, and probably the town and port as well, crawling with gendarmes after a gun battle and several fatalities.

He was also responsible for those Frenchmen, dock workers who had come along to help their fellow anti-fascists in Spain. They might be committed enough to run the risk of arrest but they were not armed, only along to provide the muscle he needed to load the weapons on to the ship, and now a quartet were looking at him waiting to be told what to do and right at that moment he was struggling for a solution.

It was the recollection of the lorry he had passed on the way here as well as how difficult the squeeze had been that gave him the idea, but just blocking the route would not be enough and he cast around for an added factor, looking at all the old bits of farm equipment until his eyes lit on a large drum surmounted by a lever pump.

The commands might have been rapid but the obedience was frustratingly slow from men who were willing helpers but not fighters. Cal was obliged to not only repeat his wishes but to cajole and push them into compliance before he could get the lorry started and back it up so the drum could be loaded on the back.

While they were doing that he went to find something easily combustible once soaked with petrol, alighting on a bale of straw, and then he had to get them to understand his aim, which took a quantity of arm waving until the nods looked convincing and he could get back behind the wheel and start the engine.

With the loaded light machine gun and spare mags on the seat beside him he eased the lorry out over the rough ground, which risked that drum being tipped off over the dropped wooden tailgate, obvious by the shouting telling him to slow down as it bucked and swayed over the deep dried-out ruts that criss-crossed the yard.

That ceased as they made the smooth surface of the *pavé* road, where he could also jam down on the accelerator, not that it produced much in the way of pace in a vehicle old and fatally underpowered.

It was just as well he had no need to go far; Cal wanted those thugs who were on their way to keep looking at what lay behind the lorry, to be able to easily see what he intended they should: the second one making a getaway.

On a long straight road and in his slightly elevated position he saw the first of a long convoy of some ten cars coming in good time, the J12 in front, not racing but at a steady pace that was somehow more threatening than all-out speed.

As the gap between them closed, he could plainly see that each vehicle looked to be full of young men in dark-blue belted raincoats and berets, an alarming choice of uniform on such a warm day; they had no fear of being seen for what they were.

Those with open tops, which now, at the front, included that Hispano-Suiza, were crowded with individuals who were making no attempt to hide their weapons either, and while it was hard to tell at a distance of what they consisted, Cal suspected they would be a combination of pistols, hunting rifles and shotguns, hopefully more of the latter given their poor range.

Sure he had come as far as he needed he eased on the brakes and turned the wheel first left, then right, so the lorry slewed across the road, coming to rest at an angle and completely blocking it, the front bumper resting against a canal-side tree, the tailgate hanging over the ditch, an act that halted the approaching convoy.

Then, grabbing the machine gun and backpack he jumped down and called to his Frenchmen to do likewise and run for it, with instructions to get aboard the second lorry and wait, he following at a walk, his nose twitching at the overpowering smell, holding the light machine gun by its carrying handle.

Peter had recrossed the bridge and was coming to join him, the Mauser in his hand, while to his right the sound of chugging told him his barge was moving towards the port, puffs of smoke coming from the stack, the man on the wheel looking straight ahead, smoking pipe in his mouth. Never speedy, he hoped to get it past the lorry before he had to act, just as he hoped those young thugs would see it as just another barge on a well-used commercial waterway and not guess what it was carrying.

'They should stop and have a gander,' he said, once Peter had joined him. 'Then, if they are still up for it, come forward on foot, thinking we are using the lorry as cover, by which time the barge should be well on its way.'

'Are they armed?'

'Heavily and openly.'

The answer made Peter glum. 'So they show no fear of the authorities, then?'

'Apparently not.'

It seemed pointless to add it was still lunchtime in rural France, so the chance of a passing gendarme was zero. Besides, if this crew were so open in their weapon-carrying, it had to be because they felt utterly safe from interference by the forces of the law, evidenced by their openness in identifying themselves on the phone, and it could be worse – Cal felt they had to work on the assumption of official collusion, not indifference.

'There's no cavalry coming over the hill, Peter, we are on our own, and before you ask me how far I am prepared to go, let me remind you they are likely to be killers.'

'I got that impression myself, Cal,' Peter replied, hauling on the Mauser to cock it with a loud click. 'But then, old chum, so are we if forced into it.'

CHAPTER FIVE

It was not a long wait, but agonising nevertheless, trying to work out what they would do, with the notion of them firing on the passing barge a worry. Before him the surface of the *pavé* road, reacting to the post-midday heat of the sun on the surface, gave the impression of being distorted, a mirage in fact, and he quickly realised it presented a problem: that wide and dark liquid streak on the road was fading too fast with evaporation.

The barge being invisible he had to duck through the screen of trees to locate its position, then relate that to the blocking lorry, relieved to see it seemed to be past the point of any danger, just chugging along undisturbed and unremarked upon, being such a common sight.

'Peter, a match.'

Peter passed over his box of red-tipped Swan Vesta, which Cal slid open to the maximum he could achieve without the whole contents tumbling out, taking out four and holding them together.

Lit simultaneously on the sandpaper to create a good flame, he then ignited the rest in the open box.

When that flared up he knelt and threw the whole thing into the long streak of stinking, rapidly evaporating petrol that had been pumped out as the lorry progressed from the farmyard to its blocking position, jumping back as the fuel flared up with a whoosh that, had he not moved quickly, would have cost him his eyebrows as well as the front of his hair.

The blue flame snaked towards the lorry tailgate at some speed until it reached the bale of hay that lay below the dropped tailgate and that, soaked with petrol by his French helpers before being thrown off, went up like a Roman candle firework, the fire licking around the drenched planked floor until that too was alight, rising to surround the large half-empty drum.

They watched as heat did the rest and in short order the drum went up with a thudding boom, sending streaks of burning fuel in all directions, especially into the ditch, and setting fire to the canvas covering of the body as well as the cab. Cal had taken up a position on the canal side of the road, close to the treeline, lying behind the ZB26 on its bipod and squinting through the sights, waiting for what he was sure must come.

With the road blocked the *Jeunesses Patriotes* could not use their cars and with that furiously burning lorry they could not use the canal side or the ditch either; they would have to take to the open fields to the south, in this case one of ripening wheat. The first sign of movement was, as Cal expected, tentative and cautious, maybe one or two at most moving in a wide arc.

As soon as he saw their warped shapes through the smoke, flames and air distortion he put a single shot as close over their heads as he dare, on the grounds that you don't have to kill a man to make him take cover, the crack of a passing bullet will do the trick just as well.

Peter had taken up a position behind one of the trees that lined the canal to block that route, and he would do the same to anyone who showed themselves – less of a possibility given the flaring fuel had already set light to the lower branches of the tree against which the lorry was resting and was beginning to blacken the whole trunk.

The flames were licking outwards on the slight breeze and a column of black smoke now rose into the sky, one that would be visible for miles and might attract the kind of attention that would force the opposition to abandon their aim. As if to underline that, there was a second huge boom as the fuel tank of the lorry went up.

The next act was to let the enemy know what they would face if they tried to break out into that open field. With deliberate aim he emptied the magazine in one burst covering the immediate area by which they would need to advance, which set into the air the heads of corn at the top of the stalks. The message was plain: that was not a safe way to go.

What followed was a surprise that had him rolling sideways at speed to get behind a tree, trailing his weapon behind him. The two flying grenades emerged from those flames and black pall of smoke to land on the road and bounce forward with a rattling sound, coming to a halt halfway between him and the conflagration before they exploded, sending bits of shrapnel thudding into the tree trunks and sending a blast of air past Cal Jardine's ear.

'Peter?' he yelled as the sound and blast dissipated.

'I'm good.'

Cal rolled back out onto the road and ramming down the bipod he jammed home and emptied another magazine. This time there was no chance to take careful aim, though as yet reluctant to kill he fired too high to hit anyone, still hoping the sound of passing shot would make them hesitate and take cover.

Peter Lanchester, falling back from tree to tree, was close to him now and able to say that, with the flames licking the canal bank, there was little chance of any attack from that quarter unless they were prepared to swim. Cal shouted back, asking him to keep going backwards, to get to the farmhouse and order that second lorry on its way.

The words were barely out of his mouth when bits of tree began to fly, chips blasted off by sustained and accurate rifle fire of an intensity that would make it dangerous for Peter to move into the open.

This was not suppression fire, it was meant to kill, so it was time to take off the gloves. The next burst of fire Cal put into the edge of the wheat field sliced low through the stalks, and as soon as he had emptied the mag he slotted another one home, calling to Peter to move when he fired.

'How's your ammo?' Peter yelled.

'One in the slot and two mags spare, one I need for my own move back.'

'Any more available?'

'There's a bargeful on the way to the docks.'

'Time I entered the fray, old boy.'

'Right,' Cal replied, smiling at the studied unflappability, which was Peter's trademark act and it was a performance; having seen him in action he knew him to be a very effective fighter.

Half emerging from behind his tree Peter held the Mauser forward in both hands, spreading his feet to fire, which he did rapidly, inching left as he did so, then scooting away at a crouch as soon as he heard the click of the empty chamber.

He threw himself to the ground and rolled off the road as fire was returned. Covered by the ditch he slotted home the spare mag before crawling back towards the buildings, this while Cal put single shots into the field.

He stopped because the return fire had ceased, which did not indicate to him that the *Jeunesses Patriotes* would be giving up the fight, more that they were trying to figure out some new manoeuvre to circumvent that burning lorry and the light machine gun fire. Thankfully those two grenades seemed to constitute their entire stock; there had been no repeat.

The sound from behind him of the lorry engine was welcome and he suspected they would hear it too – he had given instructions to gun it up to a screaming pitch for that very purpose. As he heard the note change and the first gear noisily engage, he opened up with single shots again, a spread of fire in an arc designed to curb any response.

In that he failed; the sight of that lorry, lumbering out from behind the nearest building, brought the heaviest volley yet from that wheat field, but nothing struck home till it was already halfway to the bridge, which hinted at frustration and pleased Cal – he hoped what they thought they were seeing was the cargo of weapons they so hankered after disappearing beyond their grasp.

The fire had steadied by the time it lurched onto the bridge, with a multitude of holes appearing in the canvas covering, other shots slamming into the side planking, but in truth the only person at risk was the driver – a separate instruction had been for the others to jog behind the cab or, at a crouch, the wheels, which would give them protection, that enhanced by the bridge parapet.

Within seconds it was out of sight but to the man lying on the roadway it seemed like an hour till the firing ceased. Cal's mouth was like leather and the acrid smoke that filled the air was affecting his throat. The blocking lorry was still blazing away merrily, the heat consuming the non-wooden parts of the vehicle, the tyres especially, which increased the choking smoke.

Yet it was obvious the height of the inferno was past as most of the fuel had been consumed. It would burn for a long time yet and the smoke might increase with the tyres smouldering, but it was diminishing as a blockage and might, in fact, provide cover for an advance.

It was time for him to depart as well, though that was the tricky bit; while he could use the trees as cover to get close to the bridge, he would have to come out into the open to get on to the crossing and for several seconds, even moving flat out, he would be exposed. Even an idiot would know where to concentrate their fire; every weapon that could be brought to bear would be aimed at that gap between the last tree and the low stone parapet.

A glance across the canal showed that swimming was not an option; the bank opposite was too steep to get out, and while he might be offered assistance from those who had already crossed, it was not aid he could count on. His instructions had been for the lorry to go on and for Peter to wait by the car, so it was too risky to hope anyone else might anticipate a need he had not thought to include.

Taking the last spare magazine from the backpack he stuffed it into his shirt, flinching slightly as the cold metal touched his hot sweating skin. Then, grabbing the handle of the ZB26, he tossed the backpack head-high and out into the open, moving as soon as the first shots began to rip it to shreds, thankful he was not facing any kind of automatic weapon; the worst he could suffer was a second bullet from a bolt-action rifle and it took a moment to work that, even for a professional soldier.

Also he hoped for an element of surprise, which is not conducive to good aiming, especially in the untrained. There was no time to go round the parapet and no thought of hurt as he dived over it, landing on his shoulder and immediately hauling himself up, ignoring the scrapes to skin and the painful jarring of bone. He rested the muzzle on the top of the stones and put half a dozen bullets into the wheat field as a warning for his opponents to stay still.

Crouched down he counted to ten, then raised himself again to fire off another short burst to create the impression he was going to hold this new position. In reality he was crawling away within a second, using his knees and elbows, not easy with the ZB26 as well, to get to a spot where the tree cover was thick enough for him to stand up and run.

Peter Lanchester was beside the idling Simca and the passenger door was open. Within seconds both men were inside and the car was moving, Cal holding the light machine gun upright between his knees and breathing as if he had just finished an Olympic marathon while simultaneously reloading.

'Left-hand fork, Peter,' he gasped.

'You sure? The lorry went right.'

'Yes.'

The car swung round the bend and took only seconds to cover the hundred yards or so Cal Jardine wanted, during which time he had wound down the car window and manoeuvred the muzzle out, forced to lean back so it was resting on the sill. With trees on both sides of the canal and the still-billowing smoke, what he was looking for was not fully visible until he was right abreast the main target at the front.

Slowly and deliberately he put several bullets into the front wheel of the Hispano-Suiza roadster, shredding the tyre in the process, before shifting to blast the cars lined up behind, this as Peter, unbidden, drove the car at low speed so all Cal had to do was work the trigger.

His last bullets he saved for the rear vehicle of the *Jeunesses*'s convoy, a low-slung cream and black Citroën. This he shredded from one end to the other, tyres included, and, as soon as the magazine emptied, Peter pressed the accelerator to the floor, with Cal dropping back into the seat exhausted.

It took a second or two to get his breathing back to something like normal, but soon he was pointing out to his companion that, narrow and empty as it was, he was driving dangerously by going too fast as well as being on the wrong side of the road – just as well, as, before ten minutes had passed, they were forced to pull very hard to the side to let past one rushing police car, soon followed by two more.

The fellow driving the lorry had been told to take himself and his companions home using back roads and to find a way to hide the vehicle. The Simca presented another problem; it was not a model of which there were many about, being a new design and fresh off the production line.

So it was too obvious, given its colour and the fact that it would likely be reported to the authorities, number plate included. They had taken the route that led north to the main highway, then followed that west to the outskirts of town where they stopped to both breathe and consider.

'I take it,' Peter asked, 'that I am sitting in what was your way out?'

'I was going to drive back to Paris once the cargo was loaded, sell it, and then head home by train.'

'And now?'

'Too risky, given we have no idea of the depth of what we are fighting. I'll have to get rid of it and think of something else. You?'

'I told you, Cal, I'm sticking like—'

'I got it the first time.'

'And you still intend to oversee the loading of the weapons?'

'That is what I am contracted to do.'

Peter nodded, he had expected no less; in a game fraught with danger, the possibility of dying in the act was a given – in fact, no different to being a serving soldier. Then there was the problem of reputation, quite apart from any sentiment to the republican cause; running guns was as much Callum Jardine's profession as intelligence gathering was that of Peter Lanchester. You just did not quit when the going got hard if you wanted to stay in the game.

Getting back into La Rochelle, Cal explained, presented little difficulty; they could walk into the suburbs and catch the bus. First the car had to be put behind some trees and then, while they were out of sight of the road, they had to clean themselves up using saliva, a handkerchief and the car's mirror, though they could do nothing about the foul after-combat taste in their mouths.

Personal clean-ups completed, Peter went to work on the car in the same way he had on that La Rochelle apartment, wiping the steering wheel, door handles and all of the instruments and switches, removing all traces of their fingerprints, Cal watching him silently and in doing so was gifted a sudden realisation, brought about by what was happening now, added to the feeling of curiosity he had experienced prior to abandoning Peter's apartment that morning.

Peter's blazer was marked from where he had rolled across the road into the ditch, but apart from that he was more or less all right and a bit of hand brushing removed most of the dried muck. Cal was more scratched and bruised and his shoulder ached, while his shirt, quite apart from the stains, was ripped both at the elbows and the front, which left his companion unhappily lending him one of his spares.

'Jermyn Street for you, old chum,' Peter insisted, 'the minute we get back to Blighty. I'll be having a few items in replacement on your Turnbull & Asser account.'

Cal was not listening; he was crouched down breaking up the ZB26, laying the parts on the shirt he had just removed. 'This will have to go in your case, Peter, I'm afraid.'

'What!' Peter demanded, looking over his shoulder from the tree against which he was pissing away the last of his two beers.

'You don't expect me to just leave it.'

'Might I point out to you, old chum, that it is somewhat oily, and that shirt of yours is not going to stop it damaging the rest of my kit, not least my cream linen suit.'

'Still got that knife of yours?'

'I have.'

Passed over, Cal used it to cut out the upholstery from the back seat of the car, wrapping his broken-up weapon in that before closing the case and handing it over.

'There you are, Peter, satisfied? Best I carry it, given what it contains. Now let's get back onto the road and get walking till we find a bus stop.'

'I'm curious as to how you are going to reconnect with your barge.'

'So am I.'

The walk was not far, though in still-flat open country at once fraught with the fear that some of their recent opponents might appear. Once in a built-up area it became easier, and having found a stop, they took a hot and crowded bus marked *Centre Ville* into town.

There was a definite frisson in the air when they got there, people talking and gesticulating, a lot of gendarmes around and the ringing of the traffic-clearing bells of police cars, which forced them into the backstreets and a welcome drink in the dark recesses of a small, dingy and far-from-clean workers' bar.

'And to think I always equated you with luxurious living.'

'We don't know what connections these sods have, Peter, or yet how they got onto us.'

'On to *you*, Cal,' he replied, pedantically.

'And I thought you wanted to be part of my gang.' Cal joked, even if, deep down, he felt Peter to have been the cause of the problem.

'Can't afford the laundry bill, old chap, or the seamstress to repair the kit, and that says nothing for the catering.'

'HMG doesn't pay you enough.'

'Understatement, Cal, they pay a pittance.'

At Cal's insistence, they took another bus to *Le Port* on the grounds that a taxi was potentially traceable, buying their own *billets* and sitting apart, with both keeping an eye out for anyone official seeking to board and examine papers.

Once in the port and seeing no sign of anything that posed a threat, they walked up the canal towpath, thankfully with the sun going down and the heat of the day dissipating. His fear of not finding the barge proved to be an unnecessary worry; the men crewing it had stopped outside the basin on the edge of the industrial zone where it joined the canal coming in from the south, before a branch that went through to the commercial port.

His two Basques and the French owner were sitting on the deck, quietly smoking and looking innocent. After a quick look to ensure no one was watching, they approached the barge, jumped aboard and immediately disappeared below into the cramped and stuffy cabin.

'And now what happens?' Peter enquired.

'We wait until the right people have come on shift.'

'Are you not a little light on muscle for what you have to do?'

'I am, but thankfully we have you along.'

'It's at times like these,' Peter sighed, pulling out his packet of French cigarettes, 'that I wish I'd paid more attention at school.'

With nothing much to do till the sun went down, and neither willing to indulge in much more useless speculation as to how the *Jeunesses Patriotes* had got on to Cal's cargo, they turned to talking about old times, which tended to sound rosy in retrospect and had been bloody awful in fact.

As subalterns, they had first met in the dying weeks of the Great War at a time when everyone thought the retreating Hun were beaten, but they were not; their retreat was orderly and designed to inflict maximum casualties when, as they often did, they made a stand. Jerry was always forced to fall back but no position or trench was surrendered without a hard and costly fight.

When those times were reprised there was no mention of any deep friendship between the two, more a degree of natural mutual respect, given that first quality had been absent. It was more than just an inability to connect, it being a bad idea to get close to anyone at such a time.

No two men who had lived through those days could discuss them without recalling, even if they avoided mention of it, the losses they had witnessed, both in fellow officers and the men they led; anyone being killed was bad, but a close friend dying could break those who survived, men who lived on the very edge of what could be tolerated by the human spirit.

Both had stayed in the army, Cal for personal reasons, Peter for the lack of a real alternative and, meeting again in the part of Mesopotamia destined to become Iraq, there had been no flowering of friendship at all – Captains Callum Jardine and Peter Lanchester had been on two sides of an argument about the tactics being employed to contain the Arab insurgency.

Peter, like most of his contemporaries, saw nothing untoward in bombing villages or pounding the insurgents and their families with artillery – the end justified the means. Cal disagreed so vehemently he had eventually resigned his commission, though, unable to settle, he had become, almost by accident, a gunrunner and advisor to various freedom movements on guerrilla warfare, much of the art of which he had learnt from his Arab opponents.

The Peter Lanchester he had known before Hamburg, as an acquaintance not a friend, seemed typical of a type that saw England as the centre of the universe, though they would nod to the useful contributions of the Celtic fringe in the making of Great Britain and the Empire. But they saw the unemployed as work-shy, Jews as devious Yids, Arabs were wogs and not to be trusted, while anyone

Latin, especially South Americans, could be dismissed as a slimy dago.

In that, Peter had seemed typical of his class and the company he kept, the denizens of ex-military officers' clubs and the golf course bores who saw anyone not Anglo-Saxon as somehow incomplete. Yet he had proved to have another side; he hated Fascism as much as did Cal and had the brains to also, like him, see leaving it to grow unchecked as a threat to everything he valued.

It was Hamburg and after that had got them closer, though both, if asked, would probably have plumped for being semi-chums rather than deep pals. Yet Cal, who knew he was the one who harboured the resentments, had come to respect Peter more.

The shared experience of acquiring and illegally shipping guns had created a sort of bond, which he would have struggled to define, given the disparity of many of their views; the only thing of which he was sure was that in a crisis, Peter was utterly reliable.

CHAPTER SIX

When the time came to start the donkey engine and move it was dark, the only light the faint glow coming from the city spill, until they were in the well-illuminated dock area. Peter was not allowed to see but only to hear the exchange between Cal and the *douaniers*, noting that it lacked for nothing in the sound of formality, down to the thud of stamps being banged on the false cargo manifests; if money changed hands, that was carried out in silence.

He was allowed out of the stuffy cabin only when the barge was out in the harbour, with Cal pointing to the set of lights – three horizontal white and one red – that identified his freighter, which they edged alongside, throwing up heavy cables so they could be lashed, metal to metal.

The ship had a derrick which did the actual lifting aboard and a crew to do the stowing; it was getting the boxes out of the barge hold that constituted the toil, which was carried out stripped to the waist, took all night and left the two Brits and their companions with sweat-soaked bodies and aching muscles.

When it was finally empty they and the Basques went aboard the ship, the latter disappearing to the crew quarters while Cal went to talk to the captain, returning to say that he had arranged that they should be taken into land down the coast by the ship's motor boat the following day. He could then allow the barge to cast off and return to the canal system and its home berth, not a problem now that it was empty.

As the engines of the freighter began to throb through the ship and the anchor chain rattled aboard, Peter had first dibs at getting properly washed and shaved, Cal doing likewise using kit he had borrowed. By the time they cleared the outer roads they were tucking into what Peter called a proper breakfast in the master's cabin: eggs, bacon and sausages and toast, with a mug of strong tea.

'None of that French muck,' he insisted. 'No wonder they get so fractious with each other when they start the day on nothing but bread and bloody jam. You can't think straight on a rumbling stomach, old boy.'

That consumed and it being the beginning of another hot day, it was two deck loungers on the shaded side of the main housing and some very welcome sleep.

They were still on deck and awake, sipping gin and tonics and with the sun now dipping into the western horizon, when they turned to the subject closest to Peter's heart: the recruitment of Cal to work in Czechoslovakia, a request to which he was sure he had more than qualified for an answer, while the man in question still had doubts about that, as well as other matters.

'It might be best to tell me what it is you want and it would also be helpful to know what it is you are trying to achieve.'

The response from someone normally so unruffled bordered on the impatient. 'I take it that is a yes, old boy?'

'No, Peter, it's a bloody question. Who is running this and why? Next question, what is wrong with using your own people?'

Peter stood up and went to the deck rail to look out over the sparkling waters of the Bay of Biscay, which reflected in the depth of their blue the colour of the sky, taking out another gasper and lighting up, drawing slowly several times and exhaling clouds of spent smoke. Cal wondered if he was really thinking or play-acting, increasing the tension in order to make more dramatic what he was going to say.

'If you repeat what I am about to say to you, I will probably be chucked out on my ear or slung into Brixton for a breach of the Official Secrets Act.'

Then he spun round to give Cal the kind of look that made sure he knew what he had just said was serious. 'The word from on high – not, I might add, on any piece of paper anyone has ever clapped eyes on – is that Britain will not even contemplate going to war over the Sudetenland, and if we don't budge the French won't either.'

'They have a treaty with the Czechs.'

'They won't honour it without the backing of Perfidious Albion and that's not likely to be on offer.'

'Not even if it could be proved to be a mistake.'

'Of course it's a bloody mistake and I don't need you to tell me that!'

'Sorry, but that does not answer either part of my question.'

'Needless to say there are folk in SIS who do not see my return in a wholly benign light, given what I got up to just prior to being called back in.'

He was not talking about Ethiopia but London. A couple of serving SIS operatives, either for money or conviction, one a pilot, the other a navigator, had helped to purchase a plane and had then flown a semi-exiled General Franco from the Azores to Morocco so he could take part in the senior officers' revolt.

It was a moot point if the rebellion would have been as successful without that intervention, given he was the man who could guarantee the participation of the hardbitten colonial troops he had at one time commanded in a country where the metropolitan army was useless.

Peter, on behalf of his previous employers, had been shadowing the pair prior to their departure in an attempt to discover their intentions in the hope of putting a block on what they intended, albeit he had no idea of the plan. In that he had utterly failed, but it said a great deal about the outfit of which he was once again part. It was obvious the pair could not have acted as they did without at least a nod from some of their more senior colleagues.

'How many of your colleagues are actually pro-Nazi?'

'Pro-Nazi might be calling it too high, but they are definitely anti the Soviets and anyone who travels with them, which includes any government called a "Popular Front" and loaded with socialists and trade unionists.'

Peter was alluding not just to Spain but to the coalition which had run France for two years, to introduce such wonders as the forty-hour working week and paid annual holidays, the underlying point being that, for all his protestations about his colleagues not being actual fascists, one or two must be flying pretty close.

'Whatever their views, the number is less significant than their mere presence, which makes it near impossible to meaningfully formulate a strategy on the dictator states so we can properly advise the Government.' Peter sighed and flicked his fag over the side. 'And before you ask, I am sure there are quite a few crypto-communists in the outfit as well, equally, if not more, discreet.'

'Surely you work in compartments?'

'We do and I must say this, there is no leak of military secrets to Jerry or anyone else we can trace, it's the political we're adrift on. Let's leave it at this – there are chaps in SIS who can see no further than the lead editorials in the *Daily Mail*, a fair few who would not even object to Oswald Mosley as prime minister.'

'Come on, Peter, the man's a bombastic farce.'

'I seem to recall some folk saying that about the fellow we used to jokingly refer to as "Herr Schicklgruber". Calling Hitler that in Germany now can get you a very swift bullet in the brain. Anyway, that's by the by; with the rivalries in the department, getting untainted advice to the top so they might make the right choices is proving difficult. The way things are we have no method of properly altering their stupid policy.'

'So you need outside sources?'

'More than one and people not at all connected with the establishment, yet they also have to be folk who have personal relations where they are needed.'

'How many people did you set out to tell you were coming to La Rochelle?'

Peter was slightly thrown by that question, even if he had known that eventually it must arise; Cal was never going to leave the uncertainty over betrayal dormant, but he did no more than hold up two fingers in reply. 'Just don't go asking me who.'

'I wouldn't expect an answer if I did, but I would like to know how important they are.'

'Top floor.'

'This is all a bit nebulous, Peter.'

'Goes with the job, I'm afraid.'

'I'm curious as to what's in it for me?'

That produced a wry smile. 'Fighting the good fight, which always tickles your fancy—'

'Hardly enough,' Cal interrupted.

'How about the freedom to operate unhindered in your chosen field?'

'Which I am doing now.'

'You won't be, Cal, take my word for it. Things leak out and certain folk are spitting blood at the rumour that you got those embargoed weapons to the Spanish republicans.'

'It's still just a rumour I take it?'

Peter understood the question, not that he enjoyed it being posed. 'If you are asking me if I let on about helping you, or any precise knowledge of what you did, the answer is no. I did nothing to expose you and I must add that I find the question itself offensive.'

'Sorry,' Cal responded, unabashed, 'I had to ask.'

'If we could get enough good info to put some backbone into HMG, maybe they will stand up to Hitler, or at least make some noises in that direction. That is what we need and we have no means of getting to such a position through an intelligence service that is not countered by those who think we should just let the Nazis do as they wish in Central Europe, many from a genuine desire to avoid another bloodbath like the last show. You have certain contacts in the Czech Government—'

'Do I?' Cal interrupted, suddenly guarded.

'Come along, old chap. You spent months setting up the purchase of those weapons and no doubt greased a few palms in the process, but to get away with what you did, that fake End User Certificate, there had to be at least one person in a high official position who went out of their way to assist you, and probably more than one.'

All he got for that statement was a bland look and a request that he sit down, given the sun was at his back, becoming low and blinding. That break was extended when the captain's steward, who looked to be Malay, appeared to give them a refill and advise them that dinner would be in half an hour, for if they were in a rather low-class freighter, the captain was ex-navy and a man who adhered to certain standards in both dress and comportment.

'Look,' Peter said, once the man had gone, leaning forward from the edge of his lounger. 'I can very well appreciate that you would want to keep to yourself the names of who you dealt with in Prague or Brno and I do not for one moment want you to disclose them. But to deny the existence of at least one high-placed contact is to insult my intelligence.'

He paused again, allowing Cal's silence to acknowledge that had to be the case. 'What we require is that you get back in touch with him or them and find out how far the Czech Government is prepared to go to defy Hitler—'

Cal's interruption was brutal. 'Which they cannot do alone.'

'. . . and what they need from HMG to make that possible.'

'Now you're insulting my intelligence, Peter. What they need is general mobilisation in the UK and France as soon as Hitler acts up and, much as it pains me to say so, the backing of the USSR.'

'We thought maybe Poland?'

'The Poles won't lift a finger to aid the Czechs. You have heard of a place called Teschen, I take it?'

'Vaguely,' Peter replied with a bored look that preceded a deep swallow.

'My regiment was posted there after the armistice in 1919 to stop the Poles and Czechs killing each other for possession of the coalfields, and bloody hard going it was, a full-scale armed conflict, just when we thought all that was over.'

'A few thousand on each side, Cal, and the odd armoured car! It wasn't much of a war.'

'It was enough of one for me. The Poles, who, I would remind you, have a military government, think they were hard done by in the plebiscite that followed and established the border, cheated in fact by the slimy Czechs. They have been smarting ever since.'

'They're a bit given to grievances, the Poles, old boy.'

'They're also a bit given to doing something about them. Half a sniff and they will take the Teschen region back and challenge anyone to oppose them. The only thing that's stopping them is the Czech army, and if they are fighting the Germans—'

'Enough, Cal, please. I don't need a lesson on the last twenty years of European history.'

'A point on which we fundamentally disagree!' Cal snapped. 'Our whole country needs a lecture on precisely that, especially the idiots in Downing Street.'

'Let's leave the Poles out of it, and the Russians for that matter. I can tell you, flat out, HMG wants nothing to do with Stalin.'

'If you want to put a spoke in Hitler's ambitions, Peter, unpalatable as it is, you will need the Russians, just as we did in 1914. Necessity makes for strange bedfellows.'

'Shall we get back to the subject at hand, Cal, which is the need to find out how far the Czechs are prepared to go to stand up for themselves?'

If he was expecting an answer to that question he did not get one, and what Cal did say threw Peter Lanchester completely.

'Are you sure you are working for HMG?'

'What!'

'Don't take this personally, but it is the nature of what I do to be suspicious . . .'

'Something that has not gone unobserved,' Peter growled.

'Much as you don't want to, I think you are going to have to be open with me about certain things, or this conversation is going nowhere.' The silence that followed was, to Cal Jardine, a clear indication that there were indeed 'things'. 'For instance, I would like to see the passport on which you travelled to France.'

'Whatever for?'

'Because it has to be your own and that is worrying.'

Peter took refuge in sipping his G and T, so Cal had to press.

'I can think of only one reason why you did not use a hotel in La Rochelle and why we had to go to so much trouble to clean up that apartment you were staying in, and the car for that matter. Your prints were all over both and you are not travelling on false papers.'

Peter shrugged and smiled, though it had a forced quality to the recipient. 'I told you, standard procedure and, I might add, it was done to protect you as much as me.'

'I shouldn't need it, given I do have a false passport.'

'You can't be too careful.'

'Which is only a viable reason if you suspect my real identity has been leaked to the French, a leak that could only have come from London, and if that is the source, then it is from the outfit you claim to work for. Now you are asking me to go into Czechoslovakia for those same people, a prospect that does not fill me with confidence that whatever identity I use will remain a secret.'

'Will you accept my reassurance that, in the present case, your own name is known to only three people?'

'What about the shipment of arms?'

'That was known to a whole raft of folk, coming in the way it did as a standard bit of intelligence. But all this is straying off the point, Cal, because the only real one is: are you in or not?'

'Sorry to be a spoilsport, old chum, but it's chapter and verse or no can do. I need to know where you stand with those for whom you work and what the risks of exposure are once an operation is in place.'

Peter drained his drink and stared out to sea for half a minute, obviously weighing up the odds of being open, and his voice was low and for once forcefully earnest as he finally spoke.

'I am going to tell you, because I trust you, Cal, but I do want you to know there is not another soul in the world to whom I would impart what I am about to say.'

'I'm flattered,' Cal said, his surprise evident. 'Given we have not always seen eye to eye and we have been, how shall I say, on opposite sides of most arguments.'

Peter now looked like a man who had been put on an embarrassing spot, not blushing exactly but close to it; if there was one area where he was utterly typical in the possession of a national characteristic, it was in anything to do with any revelation of personal regard for another man.

'I don't dislike you, if that is what you are driving at, which was not always a statement I could readily and honestly have made before our little escapade in Hamburg and what followed. You are, without doubt, one of the most awkward buggers it has ever been my misfortune to deal with, but I do not think you will betray a confidence.'

Having gone as far as he was prepared to nail their relationship and got a complicit nod he felt secure to carry on. 'When it comes to how bad things are in SIS I have not told you the half of it. In order to seal off the possibility of being wrong-footed, Quex has set up a separate bureau.' Seeing the eyebrows rise at the name, Peter added, 'Admiral Sir Hugh Sinclair, boss of MI6, or SIS if you prefer. "Quex" is his nickname.'

'I won't ask why.'

'I am part of that bureau, code-named Operation Z, which is housed in a separate set of offices to the main body—'

Cal cut across him. 'And in order not to alert those considered unreliable you cannot use the normal facilities of the main organisation, like the acquisition of false documentation on which to travel?'

'If I had asked for a false passport it would have set minds wondering about what I was up to.'

'Which should be none of their business.'

'My dear chap, when it comes to being nosy SIS would not give ground to the most assiduous suburban curtain twitcher – hardly surprising when you consider it, given the job we all do entails sniffing out secrets other people want to keep.'

'In the end, obviously, even taking those precautions did not work, Peter, and if what you have just told me is true, then where you had come from and where you were headed to was definitely leaked in London, and whoever did it either knew or guessed what you were on the trail of.'

'It saddens me to say that you are very probably correct, though I'm damned if I know how or whom.'

'You went to Brno and, I presume, talked to the SIS contact there?'

'I did.'

'Then some bugger did as you did and put two and two together. Christ knows there's not much more there to interest British intelligence in Brno other than an arms factory. Who, apart from you, is staffing this new lot?'

'A couple of chaps like me, dragged back in, and even they are being kept in the dark about what I'm up to, just as their operations are a mystery to me. The idea is to avoid those on station at the various embassies as well, and seek to get information from the people carrying out business in those places in which we are interested. Naturally, what most are doing is legit, but one who is not, such as your good self, could be a priceless asset.'

'Your idea?' Peter nodded. 'I take it this old lot are not too enamoured of what your boss is up to with his new incarnation.'

'They're bloody livid.'

'Enough to seek to queer the pitch and get you and I killed?'

'Not me, old boy, for in their wildest dreams they would not imagine that I would get so close to the actual movement of weapons.'

'Me, then.'

'In your case it would, to such people and should the information surface, be a pleasure to have done so. You may well see yourself as some kind of "holy warrior", but you might be surprised at the number of folk that observe you in quite a different light.'

'They don't seem to be too fond of you either, Peter, because whatever you say, you too could have been killed and no one seemed concerned enough to tell you so.'

'Sadly, no.'

'But the question remains, say I agreed to go back to Czechoslovakia, what am I looking to do?'

'Find the means to stop Jerry,' Peter replied, 'and for the love of God do not mention the Russians again.'

Now it was Cal's turn to stare into the middle distance for several seconds, while he weighed his words. 'Perhaps your best hope lies in Germany, not Czechoslovakia. Adolf is round the bend but I got a hint from a contact in Prague his generals are not. What they don't want is another war until they are good and ready, and that to them means another ten years at least.'

'SIS is more interested in what you think about the Czechs.'

'While I think you need to get back to London and find out who set the *Jeunesses Patriotes* on to your mission, because someone did and they did not give a damn how many people might be killed in the process.'

'And you?'

'Gentlemen,' called the dark-skinned steward, before Cal could respond, 'the captain wishes you to know that dinner is about to be served.'

'I need to know,' Peter insisted.

'And I need to eat, sleep on it and think.' Seeing his companion swell with the air needed to blast him, Cal added, with exaggerated politeness, 'And I do think it would be bad manners to keep our host waiting, don't you, old boy?'

CHAPTER SEVEN

Lying in an upper bunk inside a stifling cabin, with Peter Lanchester gently snoring below him, his nasal rasping accompanying the steady rhythmic thud and vibrations of the ship's engines, Callum Jardine was thinking, and not of the dangers he might face in doing what had been asked of him; one question that mattered kept recurring, without him being able to nail a definitive conclusion: could he be of any practical use?

He did have some contacts in Czechoslovakia and they were pretty good, the most important in this regard being the twin heads of both Czech Foreign and Domestic Intelligence whom he had met very briefly – he suspected they were determined to check him out, which was a necessary precaution for a country threatened by powerful neighbours.

The one who approximated to the head of MI5 had been a rather brusque character called Colonel Doležal, whose only concern was that the weapons should get off Czech soil as soon as possible, without wind of the shipment getting to any other body than those who were the end recipients, while he sought assurances that once delivered the secret would remain that.

The Foreign Intelligence chief he had found the more amenable, but that was, he suspected, because General František Moravec wanted something. In that murky world of international espionage and gunrunning, especially where money was involved, the notion of truth was not a given – people lied or acted for profit and sometimes did not care a damn what mess they left behind.

He had found the Czechs to be pretty straight as a rule – there had been no requirement for bribes – and in any case, people like Moravec did not provide aid in clandestine operations for payment.

Their price for cooperative silence was information, and, after years of running guns and dealing with those complicit in the game, Cal Jardine had amassed a depth of knowledge of the world in which he moved, both in the movement of weapons and other matters.

He knew what rumours might have a basis in truth and also had the ability to dismiss many that were fantasies, which was all grist to the mill for a man whose occupation depended on the ability to garner disparate facts from the countries surrounding his own and make connections denied to others.

Their conversation had then become general, almost friendly, and had inevitably turned to the present crisis with Germany and where that might lead, moving on to discussion, initiated by Cal, about the wisdom of training and deploying irregular forces as well as the various forms of sabotage that could be employed to penetrate enemy positions and destroy their rear communications.

It was an area where Callum Jardine had a lot of experience, gained in fighting in Iraq, the Chaco War in South America, and in training bands of Zionist settlers in Palestine to defend themselves against attacks by Arabs who resented their arrival from Europe to cultivate what both considered their ancient land.

He advised Moravec to think of guerrilla tactics in advance and not wait until an invasion happened, the trick being to train men and provide them with caches of the things they needed – handguns and rifles, grenades and explosives, as well as the means to detonate them – along with a list of pre-identified targets, choke points for any invaders, which could be reconnoitred and in some cases prepared in peacetime.

There had been a gentle enquiry as to Cal's availability to help in such training – it was, after all, a specialised field – politely declined, given he was not a free man until his consignment of machine guns was on the last leg of its Spanish journey, but he did not entirely rule out the possibility at some later stage; it was, after all, what he did.

It was Moravec, in the course of their conversation, who had alluded – and it had been no more than that – to the reluctance of Hitler's top generals to plan for an invasion of his country, fearing a simultaneous invasion by the French; had that aside indicated a truth based on sound verifiable fact or wishful thinking?

What could he find out in Czechoslovakia that the British Secret Service did not already know? Not very much, he surmised, but he was willing to try. More to the point, could that hint from Moravec provide a way to achieve what the people Peter Lanchester represented sought, given the level of doubt that any other course was possible, and where, if it could, did he fit in?

The more he thought on what Peter had said about the attitude of HMG, the more he saw it as a stance fully backed up by what he read in the newspapers – nothing definitive, but telling and disturbing trends about the status of British Government policy.

Neville Chamberlain had dropped so many hints in so-called off-the-record talks to journalists, both foreign and domestic, as to lay down a marker as to where he stood on the Sudetenland question and it was not on the side of intervention.

He had sent a mediator, it was true – a fellow Cal had never heard of called Lord Runciman – to broker a deal between the Czechs and the Sudeten minority. There was talk of a plebiscite in which the people could vote for what they wanted, but that mission of mediation, according to what he had read in the French newspapers, did not seem to be getting very far.

Then there were the editorials in London papers like *The Times* – day-late copies which he had picked up at various stops – which if they did not spout actual Government policy had a good idea of where it was headed, with leaders asking questions as to why the Czechs were being so intransigent about granting rights to their minorities, which made it sound as if the British and French Governments would go to any lengths to appease Hitler.

There was no doubt in Callum Jardine's mind that Hitler had to be stopped and the sooner the better. He had spent too much time in the country to harbour any illusions about the intentions of the so-called Führer of the German Reich, and had seen at first hand the effect of a totalitarian police state on the behaviour of the mass of its citizenry.

Even in a big sprawling city like Hamburg, home to millions, the presence of the state was all-pervasive, with formal political opposition neutered in every aspect of what had once constituted normal life. The communists had been rounded up or fled in the first year of Hitler's rule, the social democrats or anyone mildly left of centre cowed into silence by public beatings or selective incarceration in numerous concentration camps.

In the camps they were subjected to a brutal political re-education, a fate the Nazis were equally willing to hand out to any member of a former right-wing party as well if they did not put enough verve into their '*Heil Hitlers*' or dig deep enough into their meagre wages to support that fraud upon the public called *Winterhilfe*.

Such overbearing weight did not even begin to account for what had happened to Jews, Gypsies, the mentally retarded and those considered sexually deviant. Conformity was all, strikes were banned, unions suppressed and all other organisations, from workers to Boy Scouts, subsumed into things like the Nazi-created German Labour Front or the Hitler Youth.

When it came to the rights of the citizen they were quite simply whatever Adolf Hitler or one of his satraps decided they would allow. No one openly complained and even in private it was wise to be careful for there were those all around at work, and even in your own street or tenement, just looking for someone to denounce to prove their own loyalty to the party and the Führer.

Until the beginning of the year the structures of the German army had been intact, but even they were now subject to Hitler's will. He had removed Blomberg, the Minister of War, somehow got rid of the head of the army, von Fritsch, and appointed himself Supreme Commander. Those running the armed forces were his personal appointees, beholden to him, so now, even for the army to rise up and remove the Nazis would take a lot of nerve.

Every facet of German life was controlled, every organisation, military and civilian, including their own party organs, spied upon;

it was claimed half the office walls in the Berlin ministries contained hidden microphones and that officials, for their own safety, even if it was not proven, communicated in writing or whispers to avoid the attention of the *Geheime Staatspolizei*.

By decree, the Gestapo were not subject to any law; you could be arrested on a whim and just disappear, it being their decision, if they put a bullet in a victim's brain or tortured them to death, as to what the victim's family were told. Often nothing was said; at other times a wife, father or mother received an urn of ashes accompanied by the terrifying mantra that their loved ones had died while trying to escape.

Lost in this gloomy introspection Cal had to remind himself that he had managed to live for many months outside the attentions of the state and had, in that time, helped many Jewish families to escape to a safer place, not only with their lives but with the bulk of their portable possessions.

This had been achieved when most Jews wishing to depart Germany were forced to leave with no more than what they could carry in a single suitcase, and that after having paid hefty bribes or transferred valuable property, houses, businesses and works of art to the SS for a pittance.

If there was no underground movement, the German state still possessed an underbelly in the big cities: a black market in scarce goods particularly, the best customers now those with the means to pay, the higher-ranking Nazis and the industrialists and employers who had done so well out of the suppressed workers.

Criminals and those who lived the life of the quasi-legal had a natural survival strategy, particularly in the big commercial and industrial cities where once the Reds and socialists had ruled, places where people still had the guts to make jokes debunking Hitler and his satraps, the most obvious of those being Berlin – no wonder the Führer hated the place.

Cal's beat had been the Hamburg quarter of St Pauli, a place of hucksters, whorehouses, prostitutes in windows and highly suspect drinking dens dedicated to fleecing their itinerant customers – visiting sailors or provincials come to test out the fleshpots – a district where they also showed a cunning ability to circumvent the endless freedom-limiting decrees.

Was there enough of that commodity in an institution like the armed forces to curb Hitler and his plans for expansion? In many ways, especially in its codes of conduct, it was still the Kaiser's army – the officer corps hidebound in its traditions, fiercely clinging to its codes of honour and obedience, those hiding, in too many cases, the hypocrisy of professional ambition.

A lot of questions, few definitive answers, but the other nagging uncertainty was natural: should he get involved at all? Though he had been active in many places either fighting, training or supplying weapons, the last four years seemed to have been an ongoing fight against Fascism in its various incarnations, first in Hamburg, then Ethiopia and lastly Spain; this was no exception.

Yet if he lacked one thing it was an ideology; his politics did not go much beyond a hatred of any government dedicated to killing or imprisoning innocents to maintain power, and that included Communism. Peter was not the only person who openly wondered at what triggered his actions; Callum Jardine often asked himself the same question.

Was he a soldier of fortune, an international crusader or out of his mind, nothing more than a psychotic thrill-seeker, never happy unless he was in some place where the bullets were flying or there was order to be circumvented? He had never known the answer and it did not surface now as sleep took over.

What the captain of the freighter called his 'motor launch' was a bit less than that – one of his lifeboats fitted with an outboard motor – and since he did not want to re-enter French territorial waters, that meant in excess of a three-mile boat ride in a vessel that seemed designed to ship water over the bows in any kind of sea, and the one on which they were travelling was excessively choppy.

Their destination was the sandy beach on the southern shore of a low-lying peninsula called the Ile d'Oléron, a rocky sandbar jutting out into the Bay of Biscay, which became an island at very high tide. In a country with such a huge and fragmented coastline, the chances of being intercepted by authority were low, while the island was a place to which folk travelled for sea and sunshine, so that strangers excited no comment.

Peter's small suitcase had been replaced with a sailor's ditty bag and once on land it was a hot and dusty trek to find first the road which acted as a spine along the island, then wait for an infrequent bus to take them to the mainland and a town big enough to have a railway connection to the regional capital of Angoulême and the main route north.

The journey back to and across Paris to the Calais boat train provided ample time to talk, eat, doze, make a decision and plan; there was no thought of stopping en route, which would have required a hotel and the necessary registration. Bar that, it seemed all the difficulties lay on the opposite side of the Channel.

'If I'm going to do as you ask, I have to put in place my own plan,

94

because I tell you this, Peter, I will deal only with you and I would ask that you tell no one where I am, what I'm doing and to whom I'm talking.'

'You can't do this alone, you need money, papers and the means of keeping in contact as well. What if I seek to come out to help you?'

'Do you know Prague?'

'No.'

'Matters not, we have to work out a way to stay in contact.'

'Funds?'

'Demand a lump sum of money from SIS, a decent one, and bank it in your own name, payment to be sorted out when the operation is complete. Transferring money to Czechoslovakia is too risky, too open to being picked up, and besides, that will avoid currency controls.'

'Do you still have funds there?'

'That's a question I don't need to answer.'

Peter nodded; he thought he just had, but it was moot if they were his own or what was left over from his work for the Spanish Republic. If it was the latter, then the use of them for the purpose outlined lay on Cal's conscience, not his.

'Are you sure you can get good enough papers without my help?'

'One of these days I must introduce you to some of my more low-life contacts.'

'One of these days I might need them, which is certain to be true if this goes wrong.'

'There's no other safe way. If you can't trust the SIS people who provide false documents not to blab, neither can I, so I will set up a new identity and you and I will organise the method of communicating. But I stress it has to be secure, just you and me. No

SIS, no Quex, and if that person trusts you as much as I do, maybe we can do something useful.'

'He will ask for some assurance that you can be that.'

Cal grinned. 'With your charm, Peter, that should not be a problem.'

The remark failed to amuse. 'And the other matter will be left to me as well.'

That was a statement not a question and judging by the look that accompanied the words it was not something Peter was looking forward to, for the other thing which had been discussed on the way home, and it could hardly be otherwise, was the level of contact which existed between certain people in SIS and European right-wing organisations.

'I don't see how I can help in that regard,' Cal added.

The acknowledgement of that truth came with a sigh.

They parted company at the Gare du Nord, Peter going to Calais while Cal took another set of trains north through Brussels to the Hook of Holland, so landing at the port of Harwich instead of Dover, which was a precaution to avoid their arrival being connected. This, in terms of security was possibly excessive, but as Cal insisted, that was a commodity no one ever died of.

From there and by the boat train he went to his old London haunt, the Goring Hotel, a rather stuffy establishment behind Buckingham Palace, a place once frequented by the wife of a monarch and now used by a very respectable, rather conformist clientele, which suited him, since anyone not of the right type stuck out a mile.

That he arrived looking a touch grubby by comparison to his normal self did not raise an eyebrow, though there was bound to be curiosity in regard to someone who tended towards the well dressed; Mr Jardine was a good and loyal customer, inclined to tip well, and he would soon be back to normal – his luggage was stored in the hotel basement and every room had a well-stocked en suite bathroom.

It was while he was lying in the bath, enjoying a good soak in the company of a bottle of Sancerre and cogitating on how to keep going and maintain arm's-length contact with Peter Lanchester in a strange country, that he had what he considered a good idea. The best solution if a crisis blew up would be to have a trusted intermediary and he knew just where to find one.

'Hello, Vince.'

Backed on to the boxing ring ropes in his Old Kent Road gym, covered in perspiration and with his head in a protective helmet, arms up to ward off the rain of blows being aimed at him, it was not the most apposite time for Cal to introduce himself, especially since the distraction made his situation worse and he got a blow to his ear that looked hard enough, had he been wearing them, to have rattled his false teeth.

Vince Castellano was no mug as a pugilist; he had been more than handy in his younger years, good enough to box for and win many bouts for the regiment of which both he and his company commander, Callum Jardine, had been part. It was that ability which had gone some way to mitigating his punishments for the many offences Vince had committed against King's Rules and Regulations – the colonel did like a winner.

His problem now was the age of his sparring partner, who looked to be no more than twenty, tall, strong and muscular where it mattered, plus the fact that his blood was up and he was enjoying himself so much that the call to back off went nowhere.

Thankfully Vince had guile to compensate for the differences and when he took the blow he fell away far and fast enough to regain some control, to parry what came next and get past his opponent's guard. The short jab to the jaw stopped him dead and the shout to calm down finally registered.

'Thanks a lot, guv,' Vince gasped, hanging over the ropes. 'Just what I needed, a clout round the ear 'ole.'

'The boy looks good,' Cal replied, nodding to his equally puffing partner.

'He would be if he had any brains. Thick as a brick he is, ain't you, James?' The lad nodded as Vince pulled off his gloves, then his helmet, shaking his head and sending beads of sweat flying in all directions. 'Is this a social call?'

'Not really.'

'I hope you ain't come to get me into trouble.'

Cal knew to smile. 'Would I?'

'Let me get washed and changed.'

Vince was quick and within ten minutes they were sitting in a smoky pub, a fug to which Vince was quick to add with a lit cigarette, drinking pints of bitter, Cal not coming to the point right away but catching up with his old one-time sergeant, whom he had not seen since the fighting they had shared in Barcelona and the Catalan countryside. But curiosity was not long delayed and nor, it seemed, was Vince in any ignorance of what was happening in Czechoslovakia.

'If my paper is right they are in a bit of shit. What do you need from me?'

'I need my back covered and I might need a way of communicating that does not involve telephones or bits of paper.'

'With who?'

'Your favourite companion, Peter Lanchester.'

'Old snooty bollocks, eh,' Vince laughed. 'Not that I dislike the sod as much as I used to when he was an officer. We got on quite well on the last job. How long we talking about?'

'I doubt more than a month.' When Vince looked into his beer Cal quickly added, 'Look, I know the gym is important . . .'

'Runs itself now, guv, really, and as you just saw I am having a bit of trouble at the old sparring. Getting too old.'

Cal wondered if, in fact, Vince was bored. He had been a terrific if troublesome soldier, a good man in a scrap, bouncing from sergeant to private and back again at regular intervals, but whatever joy he took from his training of youngsters – as he often said, keeping them out of jail – seemed to have withered. He sensed something of the same in Vince as he had himself, an old soldier's recklessness that came from never being willing to just settle back into Civvy Street.

'Good money I hope?'

'Same as before, Vince, twenty quid a week and all found.'

'I don't get a raise?'

'Make it guineas.'

'Done,' Vince said, pulling out another cigarette. 'When do we leave?'

'I have a couple of things to sort out. I'll ring the gym, but sort out your passport and pack a bag.'

The reply was a nod to the empty pint glass. 'Another one?'

'Things to do,' Cal said, downing his beer and standing up, his hand waving. 'I would leave you here to choke on the smoke but I need you to have your photo taken.'

'What for?'

'Safety. We might be going into Germany as well.'

'That means danger money,' Vince replied, with a laugh, 'but I'll waive that if I get a chance to chin a few Nazis.'

'You can do that at Hyde Park Corner or the East End.'

And he had. Vince was not one to let folk like that do as they pleased. If Mosley's Blackshirts came out, so did people like Vince to do battle with them. That got a loud and dismissive snort.

'They're not real Nazis, they're fairies.'

Peter Lanchester had, as was required, made his report to Admiral Sir Hugh Sinclair, leaving out nothing about the dust-up outside La Rochelle and the suspicion that some kind of leak had come from London.

'Is that a line of enquiry you intend to pursue, Peter?'

'Only with your permission, sir.'

Quex nodded at what was the correct response, if not one he always got from his subordinates. It was in the nature of the game of which he was part that you needed to recruit mavericks and misfits – to Sir Hugh the man before him was of that stripe.

Some had mere harmless eccentricities, like his Berlin man's insistence on rattling around the German capital in a very obvious Rolls-Royce. Yet others were subject to a variety of types of paranoia, seeking and seeing, even inventing conspiracies where none existed, though they were less harm to the aims of the country and the service than those whose caprices tended to allow them to miss what should have been obvious.

More dangerous still were those with an agenda of their own, and what he had been told tended towards that being the case in La Rochelle, though the motives were mired in a great deal of conjecture.

Only three people had known the actual destination of those weapons, but there were enough folk under him who had strong views on events in Spain. Not that whoever had set that in train would necessarily have wanted to see anyone killed, but their personal ideology might have blinded them to the possible results of their actions.

'Best left with me for the time being, Peter,' Quex said, 'though I am getting some grief from Noel McKevitt on the Central European Desk regarding you wallowing about in his patch. I think it would be best if you mended the fence there by having a little chat with him.'

'I don't know him well, sir.'

'I'm sure you'll find him charming,' Quex responded, his tone wry enough to hint at the exact opposite. 'Now let us turn to Jardine – is he in?'

'I believe so.'

'Did you talk to him about Kendrick?'

'The subject never came up, sir.'

'Good. Might make him nervous to know that our man in Vienna has been arrested by the Gestapo.'

The older man was looking at his desk, this while Peter wondered if he would be enlightened any further on what was a very strange case indeed. Captain Thomas Kendrick, acting, as did most SIS station operatives, under the guise of being a passport control officer, had not only been arrested, but also interrogated in what was still a baffling case to SIS.

He had been on station for two years, so it was a fair bet that the previous Austrian Government had known precisely his role and that would have devolved to the Nazis when they marched into Vienna earlier in the year to effect their so-called *Anschluß*.

Why wait five months to act and then why, against all protocol, announce to the world in screaming headlines that you have arrested a British SIS officer for espionage when there was no evidence in London that Kendrick had done anything remarkable?

'The Hun are sending us a message in this Kendrick business, Peter, telling us they can arrest who they like and whenever they like and use it for their damned propaganda.'

'We could expel Kendrick's German equivalent in London, sir, who is, after all, engaged in exactly the same kind of game.'

'We should, Peter, but orders from on high tell me to stay my hand.' The look Peter Lanchester got then was a hard one that silently told him not to pursue that remark. 'But it may impact on Jardine. Perhaps he should be made aware that it is not just us who want him to take up the baton, which I suspect you could arrange.'

As a way of telling his man that he knew he still had his previous connections, Quex could not have chosen a better way without actually saying so. It was also by way of an order.

'I can leave that with you?'

'Yes, sir,' Peter replied.

'On second thoughts, don't drop in on McKevitt until I have had a sniff around. I still think you should do so, but perhaps when we are a little longer along the track.'

CHAPTER EIGHT

If the pub in which he had drunk with Vince was a smoky den, the Lamb & Flag in Covent Garden was equally bad, though the clientele tended to be better heeled. The walls and ceiling were dark and so nicotine stained they were near to the colour of the dark-brown wood of the bar, as well as the furniture that lined the outer walls.

Cal, being a non-smoker, was not much of a man for pubs because of that, but at least at the Lamb, in the summer, you could drink outside on the cobbled cul-de-sac and enjoy the warm weather. There was no piety in his being a non-smoker; he had, like every young man of his generation, been once addicted to the weed.

He had decided to give it up when he had seen a fellow officer on the Western Front take a fatal bullet in the side of his head a second after he lit up. Some people said cigarettes could kill; he knew they could, just as he knew that the desire for one was best avoided when you could not be certain of a decent supply.

Snuffly Bower smoked like a chimney; he was also a man so enamoured of his expensive camel-coloured Crombie overcoat that he would wear it on what was a warm day. The rest of his clothing was of equal quality, if a little loud in the dog-tooth check. Again, as usual, he had on his brown bowler hat and was at a full table surrounded by fellow drinkers, all of whom, in too-sharp suits and shifty appearance, had the air of those who existed on the edge of the law.

An illegal bookmaker by trade and undoubtedly a fence, Cal had often wondered what Snuffly's given name was, though he had no doubt how he had come by his moniker by which he was known. Snuffly's lips never moved without the accompaniment of a twitch of his substantial purple hooter and a loud sniff, followed by a touch of his knuckle as, like that of a gloved boxer, it swept across the tip.

His illegal beat was the nearby fruit and vegetable market and in this locale it was well established that he was king. Anyone who wandered into his patch from nearby Soho or from south of the Thames would be welcome as long as they were not on the fiddle, for if they were, he could be brutal. The hail-fellow-well-met, which was his natural front, was just that; Snuffly was a villain to his toecaps and a very handy man with the knife he always carried.

'Mr Jardine, as I live and breave!' he cried when he spotted Cal in the doorway, before turning to his companion. 'Move your fat arse, Freddy, old son, an' let a real gent park his.'

Freddy slid out quickly, with Snuffly still beaming. 'What can I get you?'

'I'm on my feet, Snuffly, it's my shout.'

'Did I not say he was a gent?' came the reply, aimed at those still sitting with him. 'Pint of Bass then, Mr Jardine, if you don't mind.' The nose twitched, the air was inhaled and the crooked thumb moved. 'You up west for a bit of fun?'

Cal just shook his head before moving to the bar to order a whisky and water as well as Snuffly's pint. By the time he had been served and turned to go back the man was on his own and soon they were sitting side by side talking in subdued voices. To begin with it was small talk: business was bad, the coppers were bent and there were folk – 'You would not believe it, guv' – who did not see the need to make sure that his life was peaceful.

As soon as it got to the real purpose of Cal's visit, Snuffly removed his brown bowler hat, put his elbow on the table and held it out so it covered their faces; he had, as Cal knew from past visits, a morbid fear of lip-readers.

'I need two passports and driving licences to go with them.'

As Cal said this he passed under the table the set of photographs he had just had done as well as a slip of paper with the necessary details, names and addresses taken from the telephone directory, to cover himself and Vince.

'One of these days you must tell me what it is you get up to.'

'One of these days, Snuffly, I will,' Cal replied, which was as good as saying, 'In your dreams.'

There was no temptation to ask where Snuffly got his passports, not that he would have got an answer any more than he was prepared to provide one himself, but it had to be the case that some of his contacts were 'dips' working the West End and beyond: the theatres, hotels and, further afield, the train stations.

Either that or they were housebreakers; it made no odds – the documents he had provided for Cal in the past were of top-notch quality and, since he also obviously had a forger on tap, quick as well.

'Need a few stamps on them too, Snuffly, to make them look used.'

'Will be done, Mr Jardine.'

Cal reached into his jacket to fetch out his wallet, only to feel an immediate hand on his arm, surprisingly firm in its grip from a man he never associated with physical strength. 'No need for a down payment, guv, is there?' Sniff. 'Not for you.' Sniff. 'You can pay when you collect.'

Cal smiled and nodded, pleased because he suspected it was a lot harder to get an account with Snuffly than it was to get one at Coutts Bank, just down the road on the Strand. He exited to streets full of the detritus of the nearby market: abandoned boxes, discarded paper blown on the wind and the odd drunk – hardly surprising in an area where the public houses, to cater for the thousands who worked and came here to trade, opened at six in the morning.

The taxi driver smoked too, so that by the time it dropped him in West Heath Road, and once he had paid off the driver, looking across to the heath under its canopy of trees in full leaf he was tempted to go for a stroll to clear his lungs. That had to be put aside till later; the man with whom he had an appointment was ever busy, and even if he considered him a friend, it was not a good idea to keep Sir Monty Redfern waiting.

The first surprise was to find a strange female answering the door when he had his hat raised and a winning smile on his face to greet someone else entirely. Expecting a young lovely, what he was presented with was a rather dumpy woman in shapeless clothing, with untidy hair on her head and a great deal more of that on her face, none of it made more attractive by the guttural voice with which she enquired as to his reason for calling.

'Where's Elsa?' he asked, once he had been shown into the large drawing room overlooking the garden that Monty used as an office.

If the furniture was as valuable as the substantial Hampstead house, which ran in total to some twenty-eight rooms, the man who owned it did not look the part of a Jewish millionaire. Careless about dress, Monty looked his usual scruffy self. For all his wealth he rarely polished his shoes or worried about the crumpled state of his clothing.

'Our little beauty is in Prague, Callum, doing good work with refugees.'

The name of the Czech capital gave him pause, but Cal decided not to mention it as his destination for the moment. 'How bad is it?'

'As bad as it gets with that bastard Hitler breathing down people's neck. Already they are moving away from the Sudetenland, and not just Jews, but those with eyes to see that the Nazis won't stop at that. The Commies they will shoot and the socialists can expect a holiday in their concentration camps for some gentle education. Thousands are trying to get out, and if the Germans do invade you and I might have to do a bit of business again.'

It was Monty who had financed Cal's work in Hamburg; the aforementioned Elsa had been part of the last family he had managed to extract – herself, her father, mother and her three brothers – and it had taken the assistance of a reluctant Peter Lanchester to actually get them to England.

Elsa Ephraim was indeed a beauty, so unlike her successor: young, lithe and inclined to have her employer cursing his age as well as what his wife would do to him if he so much as let one eye wander in her presence; Mrs Redfern would be more than happy with the replacement.

'If she safe there, at her age?'

'Hey, Callum, am I safe here when she is walking around with those legs of hers? And that figure and those eyes, my God!' He looked to the heavens before adding, in a less jocular voice, 'Elsa is eighteen now anyway and can get out when she wants. I spread a few shekels and got her a British passport. And if she does get into trouble I will blame you. If you had not been so busy with those damned Bolsheviks in Spain I might have asked you to go and do the job.'

'They were anarchists.'

'And that is supposed to make me feel better?'

'I can't imagine Papa Ephraim was happy about her going to Prague.'

'He was not and neither was I, 'cause she was good at her job. But that girl has balls, I tell you, and can she argue.' Monty raised his hands to the heavens and grinned, the wide mouth under that prominent nose spreading in mischief. 'Hey, maybe she told her Papa he would be my father-in-law to get him to agree.'

'Or your wife.'

'You want I should have a stroke?' Monty replied. 'I don't have to tell you who chose Marita.'

'The lady who answered the door?' Monty nodded, gravely.

The talk of her attractiveness and any hint of impropriety with Elsa was, of course, an act; Monty might like the fantasy but he was more of a father figure than an old lecher, a man who, while he had a huge and very profitable business to oversee, was too preoccupied anyway for such a game. He spent most of his time running his various charities, as well as harrying his fellow Jews, both in Britain and around the world, to provide money, sanctuary or both for those in peril from the Nazis.

'And the Government is being as stingy as ever with visas, I suppose?'

Jewish immigration was a hot political potato, not aided by a residual and far-from-disguised anti-Semitism in the upper reaches of British society, peopled by the kind of dolts who admired Mussolini and Hitler for bringing order to their countries, while blithely shutting their minds to the measures used to achieve it.

No Jew fleeing persecution could get residence without someone to sponsor and promise to support them; they would not be allowed in if they were going to be a burden to the taxpayer. So Monty spent as much time lobbying for those permits as he did seeking the funds to support emigration.

'It's like drawing teeth, the crooks,' Monty cried, 'and the Americans are no better, bigger crooks than us even, with the space they have.'

Time to drop the bombshell. 'It so happens that I am off to Prague, as well.'

Cal was thinking that Monty hid his surprise well, just as well as he managed to keep off of his face that his mind was working to see if there was some connection.

'You can look Elsa up, maybe?'

'Maybe not.'

'So it is not open-door, this visit to Prague?'

'No.'

'Does old Monty get an explanation, maybe?'

'I was going to ask you to lend me some money—'

'Boy, do you know how to spoil an old Jew's day,' Monty scoffed, cutting across him.

'—or at least make some available. Quite a lot, in fact.'

The reaction was typical, but Monty did not make the obvious comment, which was 'why?' He knew very well that Callum Jardine had his own private income, just as he knew where it came from, the profits of his father's successful trading in both France and Germany before the Great War, both countries in which the family had taken up residence.

With a blood connection to one of the great trading dynasties of the world, Jardine *père* had been in a position to make a great deal of money doing deals in a fluid market, buying and selling goods to ship between the Far East and Europe. His son could have done the same had he been so inclined and his cousins would have backed him; blood was blood to the Scots as much as it was to the Jews.

'I can carry a certain amount of money and I will do so, but to conceal big sums is impossible, apart from being too risky. I did some business in Czechoslovakia recently . . .'

'I won't ask in what.'

'The trouble I had in transfers, getting to Switzerland and back again, held everything up for weeks and that was before the Nazis marched into Austria. In what I am proposing to undertake, if I do need funds, and there is a chance I will not, I don't think

I will have the time to put the arrangements in place, and I am certainly disinclined to travel the way I did previously now that Hitler controls both the borders and the route.'

'Makes sense,' Monty replied.

'You do trade in Czechoslovakia, don't you?'

'A bit,' he shrugged, 'but maybe not much longer.'

'Even if you still do business in Germany?'

That got Cal a hard look. 'So, shame me. I have mouths to feed.'

Monty's business was chemicals; he had built up an international trading empire over several years and, being Jewish, he would seek opportunities and profits wherever they could be had. If that included Nazi Germany and Fascist Italy so be it, though he no doubt salved his conscience by the way he used the money he made to aid those he saw as being in ideological peril.

Cal was one of the few people to whom he had been open about that; he had been obliged to in order to fund Hamburg and he was not ashamed of it. He had started out as the child of immigrants selling bags of bicarbonate of soda door to door in the East End of London as a youth, for pennies. That was also something Monty never forgot: he knew where he came from and he was never going to risk going back.

What his international contacts gave him was an ability to shift large sums from country to country, even to the notoriously difficult Nazi Germany, without anyone taking too much notice, while it also allowed anyone purporting to act on his behalf to withdraw levels of cash in foreign banks that would not raise an eyebrow. At the same time, with a phone call, he could raise credit in another country in a way denied to mere mortals.

'I need access to an amount of money that is too open-ended to calculate, as well as a letter of credit and documentation saying I am representing Redfern Chemicals, and I will guarantee redress when I come back home.'

'Cal, I know you are not on your uppers, but that could be a lot of lolly. I would hate to see you needing my charity.'

'The loan is not to me, Monty, it's to the British Government.'

That narrowed the eyes. 'I am not skint but I think they have more lolly to spread around than me. And why should I give those crooks a loan, already?'

'Don't worry, I intend to give details.'

Which he did, leaving out nothing: the machine guns for Spain were explained, if not appreciated, as well as how he had been found and asked to help, every part of that except the firefight he had got into outside La Rochelle, but most importantly why he needed to avoid taking money directly from the Secret Service account. Monty listened without interruption, nodding occasionally, then frowning at one or two of the proposed actions or suppositions as to where matters might go.

'So you might need cash in Germany, as well?'

'I shouldn't, but you never know. I like to think if I end up there, people will act from principle, not for money.'

'Take it from Monty Redfern, Cal, if you think like that you will be sadly disappointed.'

'I know it's a lot to ask for.'

'It's too much to ask for, Cal.' Sensing the disappointment he was quick to explain. 'You I trust, and I mean that with my life, but these crooks in Whitehall would promise the moon to get what they want, then say it's cheese when the time comes to pay.

I deal with them already, my boy, and I know that what I say is true.'

'I could try and get some kind of guarantee,' Cal replied, wondering what kind of sum Peter Lanchester could get committed in the kind of arrangement they had discussed, or indeed, whether he could get any committed at all.

Cal said that without the faintest idea of how he might achieve such a thing. The only matter on which he was certain was this: that if he needed sudden large sums of money while abroad, and his experience told him he might, the Government machine moved too slowly to oblige, quite apart from the fact that there was no way of keeping such transactions secret from the kind of people who had already got him and Peter Lanchester into trouble; getting funds from HMG could be fatal.

It was with obvious caveats that he outlined what he hoped would happen with SIS and Monty softened somewhat; he was happy to match any sum already committed as long as he had assurances that Cal would be in a position to reimburse him. If he sensed the assurances he was given were speculative he had the good grace to keep that to himself and he did have one possible solution.

'Look, in Prague, you go see Elsa. She knows how to contact me, and if the need is a good one – and she will have to be convinced – then maybe we can do something.'

'I'd still like the documentation.'

Monty nodded. 'That's easy, I'll have Marita do the letters and, because it will make you safer, I will send cables to Germany and Czechoslovakia to say that a representative of mine might call to do some personal business.'

'I won't be travelling under my own name,' Cal said, pulling out the same details he had given to Snuffly Bower, 'and as well as your letters I need you to use your clout to get visas for Czechoslovakia and Germany.'

Monty shook his head and took the proffered list. 'God alone knows why you do these things, Cal, but if it is any help, I am glad you do.'

CHAPTER NINE

He returned to the Goring to find two messages, one from Peter Lanchester asking him to be at the Savile Club at seven that evening, with the added information that it was important. There was no explanation as to why but it was not a summons he thought he should ignore, which was not entirely the case with the second one.

That was from his wife, a slightly irritable missive to say she knew he was back in London and why had he not called – no doubt someone spotted him at the Goring. Among the many reasons that might make people like Monty Redfern wonder why he did what he did, Lizzie Jardine had to be numbered as a possible part.

She was a wife he could not live with, a woman who, because of her staunch Catholic upbringing, would not countenance divorce but who, nevertheless, did not see her religion as being a bar to either infidelity or making him miserable.

He could not look at any note from her without the recurrence of the very unpleasant memory which had blighted, probably, both their lives, certainly his own. On his surprise return from the Teschen region he had found his wife in bed with a lover. Still in uniform, still armed with his pistol, he had pulled it out and put a bullet in the man's left eye.

That had made the Jardines a true cause célèbre. Quite naturally he had been arraigned for murder, which led to a trial at the Old Bailey. What had surprised society more than the act was the fact that he had been acquitted, it being termed a crime of passion. To this day Cal knew wherever he went he attracted both comment and interest, not least from women, who saw him not only as a good-looking man, but also as a dangerous but enticing prospect.

'Lizzie.'

'Darling, you are being cruel again.'

That voice, that tone. 'I only got back yesterday.'

'Am I allowed to know from where?'

'Somewhere that you would find extremely boring.'

'If I was with you I might not be bored.'

'Lizzie, if you were with me you would be throwing the crockery at the walls after twenty-four hours. Bored no, furious yes.'

'That is mean.'

'No, my darling, it is true.'

Such events had happened too often; the usual pattern was a night out with Lizzie in which she would introduce him to all her louche, and to Cal's mind, tedious friends, the kind of people reported in the society columns of the daily newspapers as though what they did – basically the same thing night after night – was of interest. It always ended in tears, too often in the morning.

'Binkie Forrester is having an end-of-the-month bash tonight and I have no one to take me.'

'Have you already told the poor bugger who was down to escort you to find another partner, or are you waiting for me to weaken?'

'You sound as though you don't believe I can be without a man on my arm.'

'I've never known you struggle.'

'*Plllleeeease?*'

How many *P*'s and *L*'s had she managed to get into that request?

'I have an appointment tonight already.'

The voice was sharper. 'When?'

He should have lied; why was he too weak to lie? 'Seven.'

'I will be ready at nine, do not be a beast and leave me to go to Binkie's alone. It would be too shaming.'

'I'm damned if I will,' Cal said, to a phone which had already hit the cradle at the other end.

'Going on somewhere, old boy?'

It was hardly surprising Peter Lanchester asked this; Cal was in full evening wear, black tie, starched shirt with pearl studs, tuxedo and highly polished court shoes. If he noticed the glare he got in return he managed to ignore it. Earlier, with a whisky in his hand, Callum Jardine had been adamant that his wife would go to hell, a resolve that had weakened as the time came to dress, partly because a couple more drinks had been consumed.

He looked around the well-appointed lobby of the Savile Club where he had been met, all highly polished panelling, sparkling chandeliers, and on the stairs that led to the public rooms, deep red carpet. If anything, the sense of plenty seemed to deepen his irritation.

'This your club?'

'No,' Peter replied before turning to the porter. 'Please tell Sir Robert that I will take our guest straight out to the courtyard.'

'Don't I even get a drink?'

'There are drinks waiting for us.'

Peter turned and made his way past the bottom of the stairs to a door which led out on to a flagstoned courtyard, entirely enclosed by the upper storeys of the building, Cal following. Being the time of year, though it was not sunlit, there was sufficient residual illumination from the sky to see clearly and warmth from the day to make the atmosphere pleasantly cool.

In one corner sat a table with two chairs, topped with glasses and bottles, as well as a club servant standing by to pour and serve, and by the time Peter's mysterious knight joined them both men had drinks in their hands. Seeing him emerge, Cal observed a tall fellow in a navy-blue three-piece suit, soft-collared shirt and nondescript tie, with a strong handsome face.

'Sir Robert Vansittart,' Peter intoned, having introduced Cal.

Vansittart took a drink from the club servant before politely dismissing him and he then addressed Cal in a deep bass voice, his eyes taking in his attire. 'I hope asking you to meet with me has not inconvenienced your evening?'

There was a terrible temptation to bark that he could keep him here all night if he wanted until Cal realised he was in danger of being brusque to no purpose. Whoever this man was it was nothing to do with him that Lizzie Jardine was a minx and he was too weak to resist her wiles, so he answered in a soft negative.

'Peter has told me a great deal about you.'

'Then given he sees me as a violent thug I am surprised you have

118

not come wearing some kind of protective clothing.'

Vansittart threw back his head to laugh and by doing so created an immediate and relaxed atmosphere for both of them. He then surprised Cal by softly saying Peter's name in such a way that he moved away from them and went to stand far enough off for them to talk without being overheard, which led to an immediate enquiry from his guest as to why.

'A necessary precaution, Mr Jardine, to ensure security. Please do not think that I do not trust our mutual friend because I do, but what I am about to say to you I cannot risk being overheard by a third party who might at some future date be asked to repeat under oath what we will talk of. To do so would put the person in a very invidious position and do little for my own. Shall we sit down?'

They did so and there followed one of those pauses a man employs to gather his thoughts and ensure that he is going to produce them in the right order. 'First of all, I would like to say that if you and I were to discuss the personality of Chancellor Hitler we would find ourselves in full agreement.'

'I would like to put a bullet in his brain.'

'Then perhaps not in full agreement, but I have watched his rise to power with some trepidation and from what Peter has told me you would share my view that he is a man determined on disturbing the peace of Europe. You will understand that matters are very febrile at the moment, with the Nazi Party Rally about to commence and the very real fear that the Führer will up the tension in Central Europe.'

'Can I ask, Sir Robert, what is your position?'

Vansittart produced a slight self-deprecating smile. 'You're sure I have one?'

'Fairly certain.'

'I was until the beginning of this year the Permanent Undersecretary at the Foreign Office and as such I advised Lord Halifax and through him the Cabinet. I'm afraid that in that capacity I rather upset the PM, who promoted me to be his Chief Diplomatic Advisor.'

No slouch, then, Cal thought; this man had been the top civil servant at his department. That opinion received an immediate cold douche.

'As such, that leaves Mr Chamberlain free to ignore anything I say.'

'Did the Foreign Secretary share your concerns when you were advising him?'

Vansittart saw the merit in the question. 'Lord Halifax has the reputation of being soft on Nazi Germany, having been much lampooned in cartoons after what was supposed to be a private visit a year past, which somehow got turned into something more official by leaks to the press from the PM's office.'

There was a pause to let the import of that sink in; the idea of a prime minister undermining his own cabinet colleague was a startling one to Cal, but only, he realised, because he had never thought about it. In truth, knowing his fellow humans as he did, and politicians being that, he should not have been surprised.

'Let it suffice to say that Lord Halifax has a different view to that with which he is credited, and even if I am not in my previous place, he listens with great attention to my advice and not just because of the mauling he received in the press. It is common to describe politicians as fools but they are often far from that, Mr Jardine. He saw what needed to be seen upon his visit.'

Vansittart took a long sip of his gin and tonic, Cal suspected to again gather his thoughts. 'Peter tells me you have always wanted to know who it was who formed the group that facilitated and paid for your services in getting those weapons to Ethiopia.'

'He was always very reluctant to oblige.'

'It might save a great deal of time if I tell you I was one of the people who coordinated matters, many times, within these walls and in strict defiance of Government policy and my own responsibilities.' He produced a slow smile as he looked around the enclosed courtyard. 'If they could speak we would all end up in the Tower.'

Cal nodded; this man fitted the impression of what had been needed to smooth the progress of the buying and shipping of arms to the Horn of Africa, a combination of money and real political clout. He doubted he was one of the money men, but he could make things happen in other ways.

'You will know that the nation's policy towards Germany under our present government is, to people like us, a troubling one. The prime minister holds one view, while officials like myself hold one that is wholly contrary to that.'

'Not all officials, I would hazard.'

The slight shake acknowledged that. 'There are many who do not, but understand this: the policy of appeasement has one aim, and that is the maintenance of peace in Europe and the avoidance of another bloodbath. I must tell you that the aim of those who oppose the present policy is exactly the same.'

'Though the method would not be.'

'No, but I was present at the writing of the Treaty of Versailles, Mr Jardine, and I am of the opinion, as are many others, that Germany has grievances from that document that require to be addressed, as does Mr Chamberlain. Where we fundamentally disagree is that such changes should be considered while Hitler or anyone like him holds power and seeks redress by either bluster or force.'

'Then you have two problems, the first that Hitler does not bluster, he gambles, the second being that Chamberlain is prime minister.'

'Chamberlain gambles too.'

'Dangerous when there can be only one winner.'

Cal had said that rather sharply; he felt he was being treated in too condescending a manner regarding matters that any thinking person could arrive at without a lecture. Not that such truly angered him; he was dealing with a man who marshalled his thoughts and opinions as a matter of course and spoke in the careful language of diplomacy and bureaucracy, which had to be measured to ensure he was completely understood.

'The PM is a man not without a certain degree of vanity.'

'Is there such a man?'

That made him laugh again and shake his head. 'It is the level of that sinful quality which causes trouble.'

'Are you saying Mr Chamberlain has an excess of it?'

'He is convinced that his political genius can find a way out of what seems an intractable problem, and added to that he is as devious as a fox circling a hen coop, which, if you will forgive an extension of the metaphor, would serve to describe his Cabinet.'

'Who could stand up to him if they wished?'

Vansittart shook his head. 'Every person at the Cabinet table is there as a personal appointee of the PM and every one of them has striven all their political lives to get their feet under that table. Regardless of their private doubts the leaving of a cabinet position is too awful to contemplate for many, and for those seeking Chamberlain's chair akin to political suicide.'

'Anthony Eden too? He resigned.'

'Do not think he surrendered the Foreign Secretary's job with either good grace or easily. Anthony was always a thorn in the Chamberlain side, not least for his popularity with the public, quite apart from the fact that he was seen as a more fitting representative of the nation than the man above him.'

'Not just as the Glamour Boy?'

'He is lucky in his good looks, of course, but he has a fine mind. Given those qualities, his popularity with the public, the fact that he was appointed by Stanley Baldwin and does not agree with the PM's policy of appeasement, while representing himself as a potential successor, Neville took great pleasure in engineering his resignation.'

'Engineering?'

'That is what you do with a rival for your office . . .' He paused to smile. 'With a civil servant like myself you kick them upstairs.'

'I can't say I feel sorry for the man. After Spain, and what has been allowed to happen there, Eden does not stand too high in my estimation either. I doubt the non-intervention policy would have been half as effective with his efforts, which virtually handed the nationalists all the aces in the pack. If there was a time to stand up to Italy and Germany it was there.'

'It would be interesting to discuss the Iberian Peninsula with you, given Peter tells me you were active there, but not at this time, because matters in Central Europe are more pressing. So I will now tell you something that Peter could not. We have had emissaries from Germany, people of various standing, who have tried to pass on to the Government that there are many groups who are as worried as we are about the direction in which Hitler is heading.'

'With good cause.'

'Unfortunately the Government has paid no attention to them.'

'What about the people you . . .' Cal had to pause himself to find the right word, 'coordinated?'

'Naturally we took their views more seriously, but whatever we have in terms of ability to act does not include political power, nor is there the slightest prospect of that changing, given the PM commands a solid majority in the House of Commons.'

Tempted to mention what František Moravec had told him in Prague about Hitler's generals, Cal reasoned it would add nothing to be told that Britain was not the only place such tales were being spread; besides, Vansittart probably knew.

'Do you mean the Government or Chamberlain?'

'In some senses they are the same thing. Each time some emissary arrives the PM listens politely to what he is telling us, then refers the information to our Berlin embassy for a view, and unfortunately we have, in our ambassador there, a man, if you will forgive the vulgarity, so enamoured of Hitler it would not surprise me to find him kissing his bared posterior.'

Cal grinned. 'Maybe sometime we should discuss the meaning of the word "vulgarity".'

'Every time noises are made about opposition to Hitler, Sir Nevile Henderson insists we ignore them as having no basis and that to give them credence upsets the German Government. Given that is right in tune with the views of the prime minister, such dismissals are then used to persuade the Cabinet of their lack of value.'

'Peter intimated to me that the present policy is to go to any lengths to avoid another war.'

'Unwise of him to do so, perhaps, but tending towards accurate, I'm afraid, and in Chamberlain we have a man not averse to letting

Hitler know this through non-official channels, such as the American press.'

'Not the leaders in our own newspapers.'

'Those too!' Vansittart replied bitterly; clearly most of the British press did not find favour with him. 'So what we need, Mr Jardine, is some kind of irrefutable proof that there does indeed exist enough opposition to Hitler to be meaningful or, if it can be produced, something that clearly demonstrates his addiction to acting in bad faith.'

'Sir Robert, half the nation hates him and everything he stands for and I know that from my own time in Germany. But they are, like you and your friends, people without power, and I fear that even you do not understand the nature of the way that country is run.'

'On the contrary, I do, Mr Jardine, for I too have been there. Even in an official capacity it is easy to see that, left unchecked, the Nazi ideology will poison the whole of Europe.'

Vansittart suddenly became more animated, though such was his self-control it was nothing rabid.

'Hitler is using the threat of some great Bolshevik conspiracy to get his own way and he must be stopped. Not that I do not see Communism as an equal threat to our way of life and one that must one day be challenged and defeated.'

Taking a deep breath, Vansittart sought to regain his normal urbane manner.

'What I am saying, Mr Jardine, is this. In what you are about to do you have our blessing – that is, those who oppose Government policy – as well as any resources we have which you might need to employ in your task. Bring to the Cabinet table irrefutable proof that Hitler can be stopped by his own people and then perhaps that purblind dolt who heads our government can be made to see reason, or perhaps be forced to do so by his colleagues.'

Sir Robert stood up as Cal was thinking that the tasks Peter Lanchester had talked about had just been extended and he was not sure he welcomed the idea. Tempted to mention it, he was not really given the chance.

'Needless to say, this is a conversation that has never taken place and should it emerge that we have even spoken on such a subject I will deny it. You are going to take risks on our behalf and for that I thank you, but do not be in any doubt that people like myself are taking risks too, though not with our lives.'

'Has Peter been allotted the funds I might need?'

'Peter has access to anything you might need, but we have to be cautious. When you are dealing with a man who delights in conspiracy, as Neville Chamberlain does, you must not give him sight of one, for he will exploit that to his own ends.'

'I wonder you didn't resign – in fact you could do so now.'

'I would dearly love to have done so previously, Mr Jardine, but the PM moved me and when he did I was replaced with someone who agreed with anything he cared to say. Now I have at least a certain amount of access and to lose that by what would be an empty gesture would not aid matters. Good luck.'

Then he was gone, passing Peter Lanchester and indicating he wanted an equally quiet word. They conversed by the door of the lobby for a few moments, heads close, then Vansittart disappeared and Peter then came to join Cal.

'He's a decent man, Van, don't you think, old boy? Chamberlain's been very shabby in the way he has treated him.'

'Did you find out anything about La Rochelle?'

'Not yet,' Peter replied, slightly thrown by the abruptness of the enquiry.

'That's a priority. If what your Sir Robert is hinting at is true and the answer does not lie in Czechoslovakia, I am going to have to go back into Germany, and being betrayed there will be a damn sight more inconvenient than what happened in France.'

'I am working on it, but I have to be careful not to create the kind of suspicion that will alert certain people. That can only make matters worse.'

'Let's have another drink, shall we?'

Peter nodded towards his attire. 'Are you not due somewhere?'

'I am, but the person concerned has never been on time in her life.'

'A lady, what?' Peter cried, clearly curious. 'Far to go?'

'Connaught Square,' Cal replied with a trace of defiance. It was wasted; Peter knew that was the Jardine family home but he was not going to invite a rebuke by saying so.

CHAPTER TEN

'If I did not know you better, Callum Jardine, I would suspect you are already tipsy.'

He had drunk more than normal, probably for the purposes of Dutch courage, but whatever the reason it meant he was not prepared to reply in his usual sardonic manner.

'Lizzie, you don't know me at all.'

She was doing it again, standing where the light flattered her, just under a soft standard lamp. She had not been ready when he arrived, leaving him to pour another drink and wonder at the change of furniture – it seemed to take place between each of his visits. Last time it had been all white, now it was predominantly black lacquer, with the most alarming charcoal-grey and white zigzag carpet.

She too was dressed in black, in a garment that flickered with each tiny movement as the sequins that covered it caught the light. This was Lizzie's usual opening gambit, to look seductive and vulnerable, and it had always affected him in the past. Yet now he felt different, less engaged, an observer more than a participant in her game and he knew in his heart it had nothing to do with alcohol.

Lizzie Jardine was still beautiful, not as she had once been, the debutante catch of the year who had taken the eye and heart of a young and newly commissioned Scottish officer preparing to go off to war. Then she had been a gamine creature; almost bird-like in fact, going on to fill out with full womanhood, making her a true beauty in her prime years.

What was different now? The figure had not changed much, though he suspected there were things needed to keep it tight. Was it the fine crow's feet around the eyes, now too deep to be entirely hidden by make-up, or the small vertical lines rising from her upper lip?

He was not as entranced as he had been in the past and suddenly he knew why: Spain had cured him. There he had fallen deeply in love with a woman who was everything Lizzie was not and it had nearly cost him his life, that fight against a force as dark or perhaps darker than Fascism.

Whatever, if Communism had robbed him of the future he envisaged, the consequence of the affair was present now, for looking at Lizzie he felt none of the magnetic pull he had suffered from previously.

'Well?' she said, spinning slowly and sparkling as she did so.

'The taxi is waiting,' he replied, putting down his empty glass.

He helped her put on her short cloak, which exposed him to the smell of her perfume warmed by her flesh. Previously a cause of an immediate physical reaction, that was also absent and somehow she sensed it and the knowledge was in her eyes when they met his own, though as was her way it was selfishness that held sway.

'I do hope you are not going to be beastly, Cal, you know how rude you can be to my friends – and me, when I check you. I don't want my evening ruined.'

'I promise not to be rude,' he replied.

Moments later they exited the front door and descended the exterior steps to the pavement, where stood the throbbing taxicab. Opening the door he took her elbow to aid her to get inside but he did not follow, instead taking out his wallet and passing to the driver a five-pound note.

'The lady will tell you where she wants to go. There is more than enough to cover the fare and keep the change for yourself.' With that he went to the open door, his voice firm and his look steady as he shut it. 'Goodbye, Lizzie.'

The delighted cabbie took off immediately he heard the door click shut and all Cal was left with was the vision of her perplexed and pixie face staring out of the back window – that and a feeling of release that lasted all the way as he meandered across Hyde Park. It was maintained down the back wall of Buckingham Palace, as he made his way back to the Goring Hotel, there to sleep like a lamb.

It took several days to sort out what was needed, not least the false documents from Snuffly Bower, but when he did pick them up they were, as usual, perfect and they were delivered to Hampstead so Monty could get him visas. At Cal's request Peter provided a document signed by Sir Hugh Sinclair that would indemnify Monty Redfern for any expenses incurred in pursuance of the task he was undertaking.

He also had him withdraw various sums of money in different

currencies – dollars, korunas and German marks – in mixed denominations that could be concealed in a money belt, funds for which he was obliged to sign. The longest wait was for the necessary visas, but they finally arrived along with Monty's letters of introduction and – a nice touch – business cards for Redfern International Chemicals.

The other item, not actually asked for and sent to the Goring, was a briefing on the way the crisis had developed: newspaper cuttings in the main, plus comments from various Government officials, one of which was a note signed by Vansittart, in which he assessed the spokesman for the German Czech minority, Konrad Henlein.

The leader of the Sudeten German Party had visited London three years previously to present his case to the British people: in essence that he sought no union with Germany, just political rights for his people. Vansittart's view, and he had met Henlein in the company of Winston Churchill, was that he was a reasonable fellow and no demagogue.

In later notes he had added that he thought he, like everyone else, might have been duped by the fellow's unthreatening manner because of the overwhelming evidence that Henlein had moved further towards Hitler in the intervening years to become a spokesperson for the Nazi aims of conquest.

There was also a lengthy report from the Central European correspondent of the *Daily Telegraph*, who had done a sweep through the disputed areas of Bohemia and Moravia, and for once it was quite a balanced piece of reportage, which saw the Sudetenland question from both sides.

In his view the German minority had complaints but they were minor; the Czech nation was democratic, the Sudetenlanders had the right to vote and had several political outlets across the spectrum, from Nazis through social democrats to the Workers' Party, the first two of which had sent strong groups of elected representatives to the Prague parliament where they were free to plead their cause.

If there were grievances these were caused more by Czech insensitivity rather than anything approaching oppression, though discrimination in official jobs was rampant. He had noticed a certain haughtiness about the Czechs, who saw themselves as both more gifted and upright than others and that would rub particularly hard up against those with a German background.

Quite apart from employment, there was also the fact that the German children were taught in their own language, not Czech, while added to that there was bound to be a certain amount of friction caused by the local bureaucracy, which was naturally staffed by the national majority and tended to favour Czechs over Germans in disputes.

But that did not disbar the aggrieved from a right of appeal to a higher court in Prague, where their sensitivities were accorded equal rights with their opponents. Reading it, Cal Jardine thought they might have a moan, but, rabid Nazis apart, the Sudetenlanders would regret it if they ever got Hitler and his kind of government.

The briefing absorbed, there was shopping to be done to replace what he had left in La Rochelle, the kind of sturdy footwear and hard-wearing clothes that would stand constant and possibly outdoor use, as well as a couple of books. A visit to Stanfords in Long Acre provided maps of Czechoslovakia as well as a guide book, and he also bought two canvas holdalls, one green, the other beige, then went to work to scuff them up a bit so they looked well used.

If folk taking a mid-morning stroll wondered at an individual playing football with such items in St James's Park, before dropping them into the duck pond for a thorough soaking, they were too British to enquire.

The bags, once dried out, he had fitted with stiffener boards at the base in matching material, which, with a little glue, would serve as false bottoms. In these he and Vince could hide Snuffly Bower's passports and papers; they would go in under their personal passports but carrying nothing that was not necessary.

Whatever they used to travel had to be light; the only quick way into Prague, and one which, unlike the Paris-to-Prague express train, did not cross German territory, was by aeroplane from Le Bourget, just outside the French capital, and the airlines were damned fussy about luggage weight.

After several unreturned phone calls from Lizzie he decided it was time to write to her and bring some kind of closure to their relationship and that was hard to get right. He had no desire to make her homeless but she was occupying a prime town house, far too spacious for one person and an abode he would certainly never live in again.

That he intended to sell, and give her enough to buy the lease on a flat in Mayfair or Belgravia, she could choose. There was no question that he would provide for her financially but that had to be both reasonable and agreed, which he would rather do amicably than through solicitors and she had time to think about everything as he was off on his travels again.

The letter signed, he left the envelope at the desk to be posted. Then it was off to the Savoy Grill, one of the two books he had bought in hand, to tie up any loose ends and buy Peter a lunch he certainly felt he owed him from La Rochelle.

As usual, as he crossed the panelled dining room to join him, passing the mirrored pillars, several sets of eyes noted his arrival and followed him; if there was one thing that never seemed to fade it was the notoriety of his being a killer. Odd that for once, after composing his letter to Lizzie, it made him feel euphoric, not angry, and instead of glares being aimed at interested female glances they got winning smiles.

Peter waited for Cal to be seated before speaking, and was discreetly quiet when he did so. 'As far as I know your name is still not in the frame for what happened in La Rochelle.'

'Where you saved my bacon,' Cal replied with a beaming smile that actually surprised his companion. He took a menu and the wine list and surprised him even more. 'So perhaps we should push the old boat out. Call it a reward for all that labouring you did on that barge in the harbour.'

'I still feel a twinge in my lower back from that toil, Cal, and it has done nothing for my golf swing. I have concluded I was not born for honest toil.'

'Have you found out anything at all?' Cal asked, his head buried in the wine list.

Peter had rehearsed the answer, determined to ensure that Cal saw there was a high degree of uncertainty in what had emerged from the enquiries of his boss, with the added caveat of the need to protect a service of which he was now part.

What did emerge made absolute sense of the delay in talking to the man Quex had mentioned, which led Peter to think there must have been suspicions about the fellow prior to what had so recently occurred.

'It has been narrowed down to those who had access to the

intelligence from Brno, then run that against their known affiliations and interests etcetera. No proof, of course, there never can be, but our eye has alighted on the fellow who runs the Central European Desk.'

'Named?'

'Sorry, old chum, no can do for reasons of security, but I can tell you he's an Ulsterman and staunch Unionist, with all the neuroses that go with that patrimony.'

'I take it he is now being watched?'

'Monitored, but discreetly, and I am going to have a chat with him myself in a day or two.'

'Monsieur?' asked the sommelier.

'A half of the Chablis Fourchaume to start and a bottle of the 1920 Richebourg.'

'I say!' Peter responded, before seeking to curtail his response; he did, after all, want the sommelier to think he drank wine of that quality all the time. 'Must say you seem rather cheerful, old boy.'

'With good cause, Peter; I have just initiated a formal separation from my wife. Not a divorce, she won't agree to that, but I feel as if I have broken some evil spell which has been cast on me for many years.'

'She's still a fine-looking filly.'

'Feel free, Peter, I'll give you her number if you like.'

'Too dangerous, old boy, whatever you say. I don't want to end up as another notch on your bedpost.'

There was a bitter tone to the reply, in contrast to Cal's initial light mood. 'The notches there are not mine, Peter, they are all of them hers.'

No doubt because a change of subject was politic, Peter pulled an envelope from his inside pocket.

'These are the names of our operatives in both Prague and Berlin, plus a code to effect an introduction. I know you want to stay out of their orbit, but it might be necessary to invoke their aid and they do have the means to get to me quickly, or you out in a hurry, if that is required. Usual drill, old boy, memorise and destroy.'

'Am I allowed to share these with Vince?'

'So you are taking the estimable fellow with you?' Peter asked, with just a slight trace of pique that such a fact had been kept from him till now.

'I have to trust someone, Peter, and since I can't trust your lot—'

'All right, I get your point.'

Cal passed over the book, of which he had another copy, a collection of short stories by Chekhov, handy because in Russian literature there was the constant use of obscure letters in names and place designations that made it hard for anyone to get a handle on, quite apart from the fact that as a means of sending coded messages, without a copy of the book it was near-impossible to decipher. There was no requirement to explain; they needed to be able to communicate outside normal channels.

'Usual drill, Peter, story number first, page number in that story second, then the line and the letter reading right to left. I will let you know my location by telegram on arrival and only use it if absolutely necessary. Stories are worth a read too and short enough for you not to nod off. Now, shall we order?'

Lunch was Dover sole followed by a fine porterhouse steak, but the highlight was the choice of wine, the dusty bottle brought to the table to be examined, before being taken off for decanting. The cork, long and so deeply stained to be near black, was presented to show there was no rot, then the sommelier used his little silver cup to taste it before Cal was allowed some in his glass, that followed by much sniffing and swilling to aid the Burgundy to open out.

A nod saw both glasses filled, with Peter copying the tasting ritual. Rated as among the best wines in the world, a Domaine de Romanée-Conti was not something to be consumed in a rush, so the two lingered there for some time, reminiscing and planning.

Tempted as Cal was, there was no point in taking Vince Castellano for anything like a similar meal in Paris; he was not in favour of eating what he called 'foreign muck' and besides, there was no time, given they had airline reservations on a busy route that now provided the only convenient way into Czechoslovakia that did not involve a massive detour. It was a taxi from Gare du Nord to the airport, followed by a long wait to be processed through to a flight that only carried fourteen people.

Anxious French customs officers were behaving as if Cal and Vince were entering the country, not leaving, which perhaps only served to underline the nervous nature of everyone in Europe when it came to Czechoslovakia. Passports were scrutinised, luggage carefully examined, with both Cal and Vince staring at the man carrying out the latter task with the bland indifference of the seasoned traveller.

The country was of particular concern to France, who had had a strong hand in its creation, the same applying to Poland – building up allies on its eastern front to contain Germany, which was bound to be resurgent, had been its most serious political objective after reparations when negotiating the Treaty of Versailles.

She had also spent two decades and much treasure training the

Czech armed forces and building their defences; indeed there was still a military mission in Prague under a senior French general, that to give credence to a treaty of mutual protection that included Russia – a pledge to come to their aid if they were attacked by Germany and, of course, vice versa. Easy to sign, it was a damn sight more difficult to honour in the prevailing climate.

The daily newspapers they had read on the way over the Channel showed the rhetoric was being ramped up in Berlin as the delegate members headed to Nuremberg for their Tenth Party Congress, to be called, since they had taken over Austria in their manufactured coup, the 'Rally of Greater Germany'.

The whole of this was being faithfully reported as a wondrous event by the right-wing dailies, most notably Lord Rothermere's *Daily Mail*. In essence, if more measured, many of the others were not far behind, only the *News Chronicle* and the *Daily Herald* showing natural doubt, and the *Manchester Guardian* outright disgust.

All reported the rants from Hitler and Goebbels in the build-up to the Congress, about the supposed atrocities being committed by the Czechs against the poor beleaguered Sudetenlanders, whose only desire was, naturally, to be allowed to live their lives according to their own lights.

There was still no mention of any desire to be reunited with their brethren across the border, though Cal suspected from his briefing that was now the aim of Konrad Henlein and the *Sudetendeutsche Partei*, which he led, even if, as he did, he continued to deny it.

He had lived in Nazi Germany long enough to know the value to the state of the big lie: scream 'atrocity' loud enough and often enough on the radio and in the press and even the most sceptical observer begins to see reasons to believe it to be true, especially if there are no outlets to present an opposite point of view.

If that had been true in a country where the totalitarian reality stared one in the face, how much more effective was it in those supine democracies where the populace could barely comprehend the awful truth of National Socialism, people who would also, very likely, struggle to point out Czechoslovakia on a map.

Vince had an easy way of putting the whole thing into perspective; for him, all he saw in the *Daily Mail*, the paper which was most vocal in its support for Hitler, Mussolini and that 'turd' Oswald Mosley, was lies. This constituted a trio which, even with his Italian parentage, he hated with a passion. It was, in his pithy phrase, 'Pure bollocks, guv.'

Eventually they got aboard the twin-engined DC2 and it took off, lumbering into the air with a full passenger load and, flying from an airport to the north of Paris, it soon took them over some of the old battlefields of the World War. For anyone who had been there the scars in the landscape, though they were green and verdant instead of mud-brown now, were unmistakable.

From on high on a clear summer day the line of the trenches, gentle depressions now, stood out starkly in the fields of grazing land and wheat, running from north-west to south-east, as did the mass of craters that littered the otherwise fertile fields surrounding them, holes that regularly threw up body parts.

There were trees again where their predecessors had been reduced to matchwood, rebuilt farmhouses, and cows grazing contentedly in well-ordered pastures. When you thought of the millions who had perished on that restored landscape it was easy to see very good reasons to not want to go through the whole thing again.

Nor was it simple to equate the trouble of the country to which they were headed with the peaceful-looking parts of France over which they then flew, those that had been occupied but untouched by trench warfare, the very fields over which Cal and Peter Lanchester had advanced to battle.

That was until, just over the broad grey River Rhine, their passenger aircraft was buzzed by a couple of German single-engined fighters, seemingly, according to the steward, a common practice, a way of telling those on board that their passage in a Czech aircraft was only possible through German tolerance.

Just over an hour later the rolling hills of Bavaria gave way to the more broken country of Southern Bohemia, part of that chain of hills and deep forested valleys in which lay the formidable Czech defence line, copied from the French Maginot Line, which Cal had described to Peter Lanchester.

Not that anything could be seen of the artillery-filled cupolas and machine gun-bearing pillboxes, but to an experienced military eye it was very possible to understand how formidable it could be to advance into a terrain in which it would be easy to inflict casualties on and hurt even a well-equipped enemy.

The next cause for exhilaration was when the banking plane showed the numerous church spires of one of the jewels of the old Austro-Hungarian Empire: Prague, the city of a hundred churches, looked peaceful at this distance and that was maintained when they landed, to be greeted by folk who seemed grateful they had troubled to travel to their country, whatever their purpose.

Cal liked the Czechs despite their airs; they tended to speak German as a second language, which meant he could communicate, drove their cars on the left, were honest, if rather strict in their morality, and proud to be citizens of an independent nation, that proved by the calm way they had mobilised in May in the face of Hitler's bluster, getting to the colours some eight hundred thousand fighting men and forcing the Führer to back down.

Most had been stood down but it was obvious the country was still feeling threatened. There was a strong military presence at the airport and Cal had noticed both sides of the runway were lined with trucks, which could be driven on to the concrete strip to block it in the event of an emergency. The Czechs had an air force, but it was nothing compared to the Luftwaffe.

There were knots of soldiers on the route into the city and, even if the roadblocks had been moved to the side, evidence of a state of emergency was more obvious still the closer they got to the city centre. All the shop and office windows were still taped to counter the effects of blast and some of the larger buildings remained as Cal had last seen them, sandbagged at their entrances; this was a country on edge.

It seemed much more crowded than before and there were, too, beggars on the streets in a quantity Cal had not seen on his last visit, when he had passed through on his way to and from Brno. There would be refugees from the borderlands, and not just Jews or communists; anyone who dreaded the consequences of war would have tried to get out of the way of the feared invasion.

Much as he liked luxury, they needed to reside somewhere discreet, so the reservations Cal had made were at the Meran Hotel and in the names of the passports supplied by Snuffly Bower. He was now Thomas Barrowman and Vince, Frederick Nolan. They had discreetly switched their documents at the airport, once they had cleared Czech customs, their original travel papers going under the reglued false bottoms.

The Meran was an old family-run establishment, not in any way luxurious but central and not the sort of place in the lobby of which Cal was likely to run into the army of journalists now camping out in the Czech capital. On his previous visit he had stayed at one of the other top establishments, the Alcron, where he was known as Mr Moncrief, and that he would have to avoid.

The Czechs, not surprisingly given their staunch association with France, had adopted many of her customs; they operated on a similar system of hotel registration, in which the passport details were entered on cards to be picked up by the local bobbies before being sent on to the Ministry of the Interior where they were filed.

After a bit of juggling due to the influx of refugees, he and Vince managed to get separate rooms. They were lodged in a narrow building hemmed in on both sides by others of equal height. The hotel had a single front entrance, easy to watch, and at the rear the back doors led to a series of alleyways that would make it easy to disappear into a main thoroughfare without anyone in pursuit being sure of the direction taken.

Rule number one in a foreign country was to make sure you had a safe way out, and that could only be by a passage through Poland or Rumania and not by air or train, where papers would be bound to be rigorously checked, so a whole day was spent in doing what he and Vince had done in Bucharest two years previously.

They bought a reliable second-hand car for cash, in this case an early model of the Tatra 77, which if it looked odd to the Anglo-Saxon eye was at least, with its aerodynamic body, reasonably fast. Next came clothing, along with the necessary maps, non-perishable food and a supply of water as well as cans of petrol. Another absolute necessity was to have cut a couple of spare door keys.

It took time to do all that, even more in a strange city to find a safe place to park and leave the Tatra, Cal insisting it must be on both a bus and tram route that ran from the city centre. Once that was found, under the front passenger seat went their proper documents, passports and Cal's genuine driving licence; from now on they would operate on those provided by Snuffly Bower.

The last thing to do was to remove and hide the distributor cap in the boot of the car, thus immobilising the engine; the Czechs might be an honest lot, but with the number of refugees around, many of them people seeking to get out of the country right now – Prague alone had a population of Jews rated at forty thousand – there was a high risk of a long-parked car being stolen.

'Right,' Cal said, once they were back near Wenceslas Square. 'Food, a good night's sleep, and in the morning I will set about seeing what we can do.'

CHAPTER ELEVEN

The initial contact when buying those light machine guns, given to him by a Spanish republican envoy, had been a ministerial aide called Janek. He had a Catalan wife and worked at the offices of the Czech Finance Ministry as an aide to the minister.

To carry out the trade had involved Cal in several secret meetings with him, before he was passed on to others, but the notion of just calling at his home and saying hello was not one to contemplate. This was an operation in which there was no way of knowing where it would lead; he could not involve the man's family or jeopardise his livelihood.

Nor could he visit him at the ministry without raising questions about an association that was supposed to be for that one transaction only and had been kept within a strict circle of those who needed to be consulted and squared politically, both to process the payments and call in the necessary documentation to transport the guns out of the country. What had been done might have had the nod from above, but it was illegal and thus stood as a career risk to those who had participated.

Cal did, however, know the café at which the man took a cup of morning coffee before going to work and he was there before him, keeping his face hidden until Janek walked in, a clutch of morning papers under his arm. For someone not versed in the craft of the intelligence game, Milas Janek was good; there was no startled reaction, indeed no apparent reaction at all.

He made his greetings to the habitual morning crowd and indulged in the usual banter of well-worn jokes, probably about weather and wives, though being in Czech they were a mystery to Cal. He exchanged normal pleasantries with the staff and in every respect acted as if a man who could threaten his continued employment was nowhere to be seen.

It was instructive, though, to see him light up a cigarette, to notice the ever so slight tremor in the hand that held the match as it went to the tip, as well as the deep concentration he gave to his newspapers as he flicked through the pages. Having seen him in this place before, at another time and on other prearranged business, Cal was aware Janek was nervous.

There was nothing he could do to make him immediately less so, as he had no intention of speaking to him in public. The wait for him to finish was longer than normal; Janek was taking his time, no doubt wondering if Cal would go away, but eventually he had to make moves to leave. He would be due at his desk, just outside the office of the finance minister.

Cal was on his heels as he exited the café, heading out onto a bustling street made noisy by the volume of traffic and the passing of screeching tram wheels, in which getting to Janek's shoulder presented no problem other than the fact that he might be jostled by those hurrying in the opposite direction, and when he spoke, in German, his voice was low.

'I need to be put in touch with Moravec.'

Janek did not turn his head, staring straight ahead as he replied. 'Why?'

'For the good of Czechoslovakia.'

'Easy to say.'

'I'm not here to buy weapons this time.'

'Just as well, we need all the guns we have got for ourselves.'

'Moravec can answer certain questions I want to pose.'

Janek actually sounded surprised. 'You want to pose?'

'To which I need answers,' Cal hissed, deciding to take a flyer and make a claim that was way outside his brief. 'And so does the British Government.'

That broke his stride a little, but they walked on in silence for some twenty paces before Janek spoke again. 'That bench ahead, you see it?'

'Yes,' Cal replied, his eyes flicking to the named object some twenty yards along on the edge of the pavement, a double back-to-back seat shaded by a tree.

'I am going to sit facing the street.'

Cal immediately killed his pace – Janek had been walking quite fast – to open a gap between them and watched as his man did as he had said, dusting the seat with a flapping hand then easing himself down and opening one of his newspapers to cover his face. Cal sat with his back to him facing the shopfronts, crossing his legs and adopting the air of a curious bystander.

'Talk.'

There was no time for long explanations as Cal outlined what he was after and why. 'The only person who has the information is Moravec, but I doubt it is safe to just turn up at the Interior Ministry desk and ask for him.'

'You're right, the place is crawling with German agents, not all of them from the border areas.'

'The ministry, you mean?'

'The whole city!' Janek spat. 'Even I might be being followed.'

Cal glanced back to where Vince was standing, idly looking at shoes in a shop window. He was without a lit cigarette, a sign that he had spotted no one taking an excessive interest in either Cal or Janek.

'As far as I can tell you are not.' Cal spun and used the back of the bench to lever himself up, surreptitiously dropping a card into Janek's lap as he did so. 'Get Moravec to call me at this number and ask to be put through to room number 47.'

'What name?'

'He doesn't need that. Make it a personal visit and don't you speak to him on the phone. After that you are out of it.'

'A piece of advice.'

'What?' Cal replied, bending to retie his shoelace.

'Speak English on the streets even if you are not understood, it will be better for you. Your German sounds too good, too natural and nothing like the accent of a Sudetenlander or a German resident of Prague. Even they know it's considered unpatriotic to speak the language of our enemies right now and use Czech in public. My fellow countrymen are not too fond of real Germans at the moment.'

'Just get Moravec to call.'

Cal walked back the way he had come, passing Vince without saying a word. His minder waited for ten seconds, then began to follow, his eyes ranging over those between them looking for things he had noticed before: an item of clothing, particularly distinctive shoes, they being the one thing, unlike a coat or a hat, which could not be quickly changed.

The voice sounded different on the phone, soft and near to a whisper. He did not know the man that well anyway, having met him only briefly, but Moravec spoke in heavily accented English and got his tenses all wrong. That nailed him.

'St Vitus's Cathedral at the rear of the high altar, three o'clock.'

Cal put the phone down without responding; there was no need to, though he did wonder at such an obscure location, as well as the need to meet in such secrecy in what was his contact's own backyard. Still, Moravec was head of Czech counter-intelligence and perhaps being clandestine was a habit more than a necessity. Besides, he could do what he liked; it was Cal who needed him, not the other way round.

Gathering up Vince he took him to a restaurant in the old town, and when he ordered some food and a couple of beers, he took Janek's advice and spoke loudly in English, like a tourist, though there were precious few of those around these days, which guaranteed them a great deal of attention.

As usual, there were locals who overheard him and were eager to talk, either to practise their own language skills or to find out what his country might do to assist their own, not a conversation in which he could give them much of a positive nature without telling outright lies.

As they left, a card was pressed into Cal's hand with a guttural smiling invitation from the proprietor to return soon. Then it was a slow walk for Cal, Baedeker guide in hand, like a sightseer, through the old town and across the Charles Bridge, admiring the statues that lined it at intervals, flicking through the book to get the names of the various saints, with Vince his usual several dozen paces behind.

As Vince pointed out with a chuckle as they reunited in the cathedral entrance, if anyone was trying to tail Cal they must be going mad with the stopping and starting he had been doing. The upriver breeze had been welcome on what was a hot Central European day but the effect had faded by the time they had progressed uphill to Hradčany castle and the massive cathedral that lay within its walls.

Like all great churches St Vitus's imposed a degree of silence on all those who entered; no one spoke above a whisper as they examined the plaques in the walls as well as the statuary, most of which were in the high arched nave.

As Cal made his way to the rear of the high altar Vince had already dropped back, seeking to look inconspicuous, but both suspected that Moravec, if he was going to all this trouble, would have some of his people watching and that in itself provided what security was required to cover the meeting. Cal stopped when the voice spoke from behind a stone pillar.

'Mr Moncrief.'

Addressed by the name he had been using previously to buy those Spanish weapons, Cal responded in the affirmative.

'Or should I say Mr Jardine?'

'Either will do, General,' Cal replied.

But he did not add the name he was using on the passport he had acquired from Snuffly Bower, just as he had not vouchsafed it to Janek, on the very good grounds that he had no idea what this meeting would produce.

He had taken to Moravec on that first meeting earlier in the year but the man was the head of Czech Foreign Intelligence and he had fish to fry that Cal knew nothing about. Just as Moravec would not vouchsafe to him things he did not need to know, neither would Cal be entirely open in return.

'I never expect you to meet again.'

Moravec had chosen to speak in English, when they would have both been more comfortable in German; Cal felt he had no choice but to do likewise.

'Nor I.'

'Our contact me tells, you are this time not in Prague on behalf of Spanish Republicans.'

'No.'

'If as he me tells, you are British Government representing, why not through the embassy work?'

'I only said that to get to you. I am not representing the British Government and have nothing to do with the embassy. I doubt the need to explain that to someone in your position, and besides, I am here for a quite different purpose to anything they might be acting on.'

'Only thing they acting on is seeking number of Jews to process, many out of the country trying to get. You would think they would London advise best way to deal with exodus is to tell to keep within own borders the Germans.'

'On pain of another war.'

'Exact!' Moravec responded, so loudly it produced a slight echo, showing a natural frustration at the lack of open support from the democracies. 'Instead in the London newspapers we read is we who in not give Hitler what he wants are unreasonable being.'

Justified as it was, Cal did not want to listen to condemnation of his own government or the stories Downing Street was feeding to the press to soften up opinion. 'The last time we spoke, you made mention of doubts in certain German minds regarding Hitler's intentions.'

'I did.'

'I wondered if you had any more intelligence on that.'

'Is that why you here?'

'The only way certain parties can see to aid Czechoslovakia is to bring to the attention of the British Government just how strong that opposition is, perhaps with enough power to alter the course of German ambitions.'

'Depose Hitler the only way that to do.'

'If it could be established that by standing up to him such an outcome could be achieved it might alter the nature of those press reports you have just mentioned. It might stiffen the resolve of those in power to oppose him.'

'Who you represent real, Mr Moncrief?' Again Cal found the use of that name slightly jarring, but he was left with no time to consider it. 'You have made plain it not truly the British Government by your own words.'

'Are there people in Prague, General Moravec, who think it would be best to let Hitler have the Sudetenland for the sake of peace?'

'Few only, but yes.'

'Then accept there are those in London who disagree with the way things are being carried out by our government and want to do something to stop it.'

'Names.'

'Some you will know, General, for they have the capacity to be open, and those you don't I will not divulge because they do not.'

Moravec did not reply and Cal supposed he needed time to think on what had just been said. He was leaning against one of the long stone pillars that supported the high arched roof, and even if he was not a churchgoer, he had often wondered at the effort and artistry that had gone into such constructions as these great cathedrals, many of which he had stood in with something approaching awe: Notre Dame, Canterbury, Chartres, Bourges.

Masons had chipped away at stone for decades to produce these smooth blocks that lay on each other and seemed to be bereft of mortar, had carved the gargoyles and decor, exactly reproducing the same design again and again, and then had come along men with lead, glass and vision to create the great stained glass window which now dimly lit the place where he stood.

It was not too fanciful to see that shattered, to see the great pillars break and tumble. In Spain, Cal had seen the effect of aerial bombardment. If the Luftwaffe was let loose over this jewel of a city then they would do to Prague what the Condor Legion had done to Guernica and tried to do to Madrid – destroy it – and that thought was in the mind of everyone who lived in the city.

'You suggesting,' Moravec said, eventually, 'we can something get with my help?'

Amazing though this wonderful building was, Cal had to again ask himself: why here? Why all the subterfuge? And then he recalled what Janek had said that morning. 'Why are we meeting in such secrecy, General?'

The sigh was audible and seemed to fit the surroundings in which they had met. 'Even in my own city, safe from the eyes of my enemies I am not.'

'German agents?'

'Those, yes, and traitors, like those you ask about.'

That induced an unpleasant thought: if there were forty thousand Jews in Prague there had to be, in what until twenty years ago had been part of a German-speaking empire, at least that number of Germans who had made their homes here during the rule of Vienna.

There might well be Czech traitors, but it also meant that spies, particularly those of an Austrian background, bilingual in Czech from having lived in the city all their lives, and prepared to back the Nazis, could operate in the city almost with impunity.

'Few, you said.'

'Too many if who are they we not know. Most nationals German do not Hitler want, not even all in the borderlands. They from their contacts over border know what he brings, but some are seeing for themselves a good chance to rise.'

'Do you have agents inside Germany?' Moravec just laughed softly; the answer was too obvious to require a reply. 'And perhaps contacts with those who oppose Hitler?'

'You want I should you tell, I think.'

'Yes.'

That brought a laugh that was loud enough to create another slight echo. 'Not safe for them, not safe for me.'

There was a definite truth in that; if the head of counter-intelligence felt he had to be cautious in his own bailiwick, how much more must he show that quality in dealing with his contacts inside the Reich, where the slightest suspicion of disloyalty was paid out with a bullet to the skull – and that was if you were lucky. To this man he was an unknown quantity in what he was up to at present and hardly worth immediate trust.

The problem for Cal was, without the help of someone like Moravec he was pissing into the wind. The more he had thought about it, the more he had seen the answer lying outside Czechoslovakia but he could not just go stumbling about Germany looking for contacts. If he did it was he who would get the bullet, but to just allow himself to be fobbed off having gone to the trouble to get this far was not an option either.

'Look, General, this is not about whether the people of whom we speak will act, it is about the notion that my government thinks they will do so if they are given encouragement. You are right that I do not represent either Downing Street or the Foreign Office but I do act on behalf of some very powerful people indeed.'

He paused to let that sink in, wondering what else he could offer.

'I also have access to funds, if needed, to both help and encourage those who might rise up, and something tells me, with the beginning of the Nuremberg Rally and what might emerge from that, we do not have long to make a case for the democracies of the West to act.'

'The first day of October, a month from now, Mr Moncrief, the day the Germans will invade.'

'You know this?'

'Told I have been, by those who have the orders read.'

Clever, Cal thought, though he was not surprised. He had rated, even on a very short meeting, that Moravec was as sharp as a tack and now he had just shown it. Without the use of a name or a title, he had just told him how high were his contacts in Germany. Orders like that had to be of the highest secrecy level, shown only to very few people, and they had to be trusted to keep their mouths shut. But someone had not.

'Have you told your allies?' He meant the French and the Soviets.

'Of course, and we also Major Gibson told, your SIS man at British embassy.'

Who would have surely passed that back to London and it would have been given to those at the very top of the Government, which made Cal wonder why he was here. That did not last long; it was like those envoys Vansittart had talked of – it had either been discounted or not even rated as true.

'Force levels?'

'Foolish to attack without men enough.'

Was Moravec being cagey or did he have those facts too? Alone, that should have been enough to show the likes of Chamberlain that Hitler was talking rubbish when he claimed he wanted a peaceful solution. Yet Vansittart had described the PM as vain and convinced of his own political genius and leading a cabinet that would not challenge him. He needed more.

'I have lived in Germany, General Moravec, and I know, as do you, that to overturn the Nazi state will not be easy – too many ruthless people have a stake in its continuance. Likewise, those who might act will not do so unless they know it will have an effect. The ordinary Germans do not want war any more than the ordinary Czech or Briton, they suffered too much in the last show.'

Cal waited for a response, but none came.

'You do not have the ability to get them to act, otherwise you would be doing so. I mean no insult when I say that to those people your country is of no consequence. Only the threat of an attack in the West will give Hitler pause . . .'

Moravec finally responded with another laugh. 'You understand not, Mr Moncrief. An attack in West Hitler expects.'

'He doesn't have the manpower.'

'But,' Moravec replied, finally changing to German. 'Hitler is a madman. He believes all he needs is the will and success is guaranteed. Is that not how he rose to power in the first place? Go back to the hotel and wait. I need to think.'

CHAPTER TWELVE

Peter Lanchester had been somewhat disingenuous with Cal Jardine about the fellow he suspected might have dished them in La Rochelle, because, despite what Quex had told him, he had been doing a spot of gentle digging around to add some meat to what were, from his boss, suppositions.

It was absolutely certain, given the desk he ran, that the information about the shipment of light machine guns from Brno, as it should, had come to Noel McKevitt first; whom he had shared that knowledge with, apart from his own department, Quex and the top floor, was an unknown.

But it transpired he had been poking about asking questions since shortly after Peter had gone to Czechoslovakia, enquiries that had continued all the time he had been absent and had not abated on his return, no doubt prompted by the fact that he had not himself been asked to pursue a matter that fell under his area of responsibility.

'Do you know this Lanchester fellow?' 'Any idea about his areas of speciality?' 'Bit weak on the dictators I hear.' There had even been a blatant one. 'Anyone got a notion of where he is? I want him to do a job for me.'

Such enquiries might appear innocent to those he was asking, but the answers – fragments in fact from a culture of in-house and after-hours barroom gossip – put together, could form a picture that would make for uncomfortable reading for both parties. It was a fair guess he had found out about the Brno mission in the process; now, with Quex's clearance, Peter was finally making that visit to talk to him.

Physically, Peter thought, the man looked like the perfect undercover operator and he had once been that, having held the intelligence job at two important embassies, Paris and then Berlin, just before Hitler became chancellor. McKevitt's face was pinkish and bland, the forehead unlined, his receding hair fair and wispy, while his green eyes seemed, regardless of what was being discussed, devoid of expression.

It was said by some Peter had asked that he was a man you could insult with impunity, he would never show any reaction, only for those same people to find out in time that he was a fellow who never forgot an affront, being the type to lock it away and wait for an opportunity to pay back the slur in spades, quite often at the point where a rival needed to be removed or diminished.

Working for the Secret Intelligence Service abroad was not a task that could be glorified with the designation of 'spy', despite what the Gestapo claimed for Captain Kendrick; MI6 officers in foreign embassies usually held the lowly post of passport control officer, a job that could safely be left to minions while he got on with the real task of sniffing out bits of information the forces of the country they were stationed in would rather keep to themselves.

In a world where you could never trust anyone's stated opinion – the truth might be the polar opposite of what they said in public – McKevitt was one fellow who made no effort to avoid being pigeonholed. He was open in his admiration for firm government and never hid his hatred of trade unions under a bushel, particularly 'bloody miners and their Bolshevik chums'.

He was wont to tell anyone who wanted to listen or not, always in a particularly grating Northern Irish accent, that the best way to deal with recalcitrant workers was to shoot them. That he always followed such a view with a braying laugh did little to diminish the chilling effect.

The man was efficient, of that there was no doubt; he had run his embassy operations faultlessly and brought in good intelligence about the intentions of the political masters of the countries in which he operated, all of which was filtered and passed to the Foreign Office so that the diplomats could formulate Government policy.

In time, he had been brought into MI6 HQ in Broadway to command a regional desk for Central Europe – at the time of appointment not the hot potato it had become since the crisis had blown up in Czechoslovakia. Yet it was still not one of the senior positions in the firm, not the German or French Desk, and it was well known that was what he craved – the other obvious thing about McKevitt was his ambition.

'Quex heard you have been asking about me,' Peter lied, given his boss had said nothing of the sort, reverting quickly to the truth. 'He thought I should come in and let you know what happened in the operation I was tasked with, not that it is at all clear. Better you hear it from the horse's mouth, what?'

'He sent you to Brno, did he not?'

'He did, which I think he has the right to do, but I'm curious how you know about it since it was supposed to be top-floor only.'

Any hope of embarrassing him was futile. 'If I choose to make contact with the man we have there, that is my affair. What concerns me more, Lanchester, and you know it, is the job should have properly been left to me to initiate.'

The use of the surname was irritating; it was normal to get on to first-name terms with your SIS colleagues quite quickly, even if, as in this case, they were not well known to each other. McKevitt was being condescending and he was equally determined to show his pique at being sidelined.

'It was no doubt felt that, with what is going on already in Czechoslovakia, you had quite a lot on your plate.'

There was no reaction to what both men knew to be a lie and it was at that point Peter Lanchester realised how very rarely the other man even blinked.

'Not that there is much I can tell you,' Peter added, 'that you don't already know.'

'Not really my concern now,' McKevitt replied, and given his control of his features, there was no indication if that was the truth either.

In the life of an intelligence operative, working in several different countries, the name of the game was contacts. Few people go in for outright betrayal of their national cause – the odd one yes, for principle or money and they are gold dust, but mostly an SIS man will work on collective small indiscretions, the little things let slip by numerous folk he talks to that add up to something worthwhile in the whole.

Given McKevitt's way of openly stating his political leanings, it was a fair guess that many of those contacts he had made abroad would subscribe to his views; that was how you got talking to someone with inside knowledge, you shared in decrying the things that upset them, you created a fellow feeling that allowed for things that should be left unsaid to slip out.

Peter Lanchester knew that, just as he knew that if the man he was talking to had made connections with the right-wing zealots in France, like the *Jeunesses Patriotes*, the last thing he would do was be open about such an association.

'Just the same, Quex felt it best you are made aware of what I did and when.'

'Of things like that little dust-up in La Rochelle.'

It was hard not to tense at that; Peter had not expected any mention of it. 'You know about that?'

'One of the fellows you took there from the Paris embassy is an old friend of mine.'

You have been putting it about in asking questions, Peter thought, but why do so in Paris unless . . .? And when was the question posed, because there had been some delay in lining up that pair and the actual departure?

'I take it,' McKevitt continued, 'given you went to Brno to check out the illegal purchase of guns, there's some connection in the fact that you ended up there?'

Now he was being sarcastic, but there was no point in denying it, nor was his knowledge indicative of anything. The gun battle would have come to the attention of the French press, or perhaps that friend in Paris had put two and two together – indeed they might have still been there and not, as he had instructed them, heading back to Paris.

'I am assuming you were trailing the consignment, you being there I mean?'

Peter made the response as laconic as he could. 'All I know is there was a hell of a flap a few miles outside the port at the time I was expecting the guns to show up.'

It would have been quite unnerving to be the object of McKevitt's stare if one was not experienced; fortunately Peter was enough that to sit back in his chair and look relaxed.

'According to what I could glean from the local gossip there was a confrontation in which a light machine gun was employed and a couple of young blades wounded. Given the employment of such a weapon, as well as the mention of foreigners being involved, it's a fair bet that was part of the consignment I was looking for.'

'And how, Lanchester, did you find all this out?'

'By poking around a bit when I heard about it, the place was awash with rumour and gossip. Hospital first, then I found a local bobby who liked his beer too much and had been out at the scene.'

'And he told you what?'

'Apparently there was a burnt-out lorry blocking the road but no sign that it had any kind of load on board, so if it was those machine guns they must have been spirited away somehow.'

It was equally unnerving, this lack of any sign of a reaction; Peter Lanchester rated himself as no slouch in the game of which they were both a part and he had to believe that McKevitt was well aware of his true reason for calling.

It was nothing to do with concocting a tale to inform him of what happened, more a coded warning to stop poking around asking questions, the reasons being straightforward: to tell McKevitt to have a care how he behaved in future, if indeed – and there was no proof – he had behaved improperly in the recent past.

'Sure, you must be a fast worker to unearth all that.'

'Keen to impress, shall we say, being fresh back in the fold. Anyway, I lost all trace of the cargo and we have no idea where it went, if indeed the dust-up outside La Rochelle was to do with that. It was not something I was able to establish.'

'You did enquire at the local gendarmerie?'

'Good God no! Quite apart from the struggle I would have had to find a reason, I would have risked my cover.'

'Well I made some enquiries through Paris and I can tell you it was a damn sight more than a dust-up.' McKevitt pushed his chair back and folded his arms. 'Did you know there was a British cargo ship sitting in the harbour?'

'I assume there were several.'

'But not one in particular, say one chartered in Dublin by a character called Moncrief?'

'No.'

'Not that our Dublin lads think that's his real name. It sailed that very night.'

'But,' Peter said, leaning forward and looking like a man who had succeeded in something, 'was it loaded?'

'I have no idea and neither, it seems, do you. It's quite possible it was and the weapons got to their intended destination, which, I am going to speculate, you don't have a clue about either?'

'My assumption is that whatever was planned would have had to be aborted.'

'But you don't know for certain?' That brought forth a slow shake of the head, which in turn engendered a sharp response. 'Which means, Lanchester, it appears to me as if you made a right Horlicks of your first mission back, because you should know.'

'Perhaps,' Peter replied, forcing himself to look and sound the same, even if, inwardly, he was seething. 'But we will keep our eyes and ears open in case it resurfaces. How goes things in your bailiwick?'

'Now, why would I tell you? Everything that comes across my desk goes upstairs, Lanchester. Maybe, since you are one of Quex's new blue-eyed boys, you should ask him to let you see what I send him.'

It was interesting: most people being deliberately rude could not avoid accompanying it with a matching irate expression – McKevitt could.

'Look, old chap,' Peter said, glad to see that form of address produced a flicker in the McKevitt eye – it was an expression he obviously disliked. 'We know you are not waving flags at what Quex had decided to set up.'

'No, I'm not, and neither are the others who have put in years of uninterrupted service. Morale is at rock bottom.'

'But we are all on the same side,' Peter said, standing up, 'all trying to get to the right result, are we not? If I find out anything of use to you, I will happily pass it on and I hope – indeed, I am certain – you will do the same in reverse.'

'If you will forgive me, Lanchester,' McKevitt said, dropping his eyes to his desk, 'I have a rate of work to get through.'

'My old school head was less brusque than that bastard and that, sir, is saying something.'

Admiral Sir Hugh Sinclair, the aforementioned Quex, allowed himself a very slight twitch of the lips, not a smile but an acknowledgement that what was being said was true. 'He's an acquired taste all right, but it takes all sorts to do our kind of work, does it not?'

'And he's been asking far too many questions about me, sir.'

'Happens when one's nose is put out of joint, and his was very much so when he found out he was being bypassed.'

'How did he find out?'

'You turning up in Brno would not have gone unnoticed, Peter.'

That seemed to be too sanguine a response; better to seek to dig the man out. 'For my money he has pursued it beyond what is natural. I have it in mind, sir, to slip McKevitt some false information, to see if I can get him to break cover and expose himself.'

'Whatever you think of him, he is on our side.'

'I think he knows precisely what happened in La Rochelle and who was involved and he is not one just to sit on his hands. He's talked to both the Paris and Dublin embassies and, for all we know, asked them to dig further. It might be best to put him off any scent he picks up regarding Callum Jardine and those like him.'

'And how would he do that, Peter?'

You do not say outright to the head of an intelligence agency that his organisation is riddled with factions, that it is a hotbed of rumour and suspicion made worse by your recent actions, even if you know he is aware of the fact and spends much of his working life using that tension to good effect; Peter Lanchester had to be tactful but he also had to say his piece, for if McKevitt was devious, so was the man he was talking to.

'Just as a precaution, given my sole concern is to protect our man in place, who is, after all, not officially a member of MI6 and is therefore very vulnerable, even to the machinations of his fellow countrymen. Contact with Prague goes through McKevitt, which allows him to issue instructions that we would know nothing about, while withholding information he feels he has no need, or reason, to pass on.'

'You are implying that if he found out about Jardine being in Prague, he might not bother to let me know?'

Quex paused, having stated the obvious, albeit with a palpable air of disbelief.

'As long as you keep me properly informed, we will be able to deal with any problems that arise and, I might add, McKevitt's a clever bugger, who will reckon that anything coming from you is tainted and that will only excite his interest. Best leave him alone, Peter.'

Given the nervous state of František Moravec, the leaving of the cathedral was a damn sight more cautious than the arrival. Vince was well behind Cal as he reprised his sightseeing act on the Charles Bridge. When he stopped in front of the statue of St Elizabeth and managed to look both up and back Vince was very obviously smoking and made a point of shoving out his cigarette to flick off the ash; they had a tail.

That did not say who it was, it could be that Moravec had put somebody to keep an eye on them, but to accept that as the case was a bad idea; it was safer to think the worst, to suspect that by meeting with the head of counter-intelligence he had laid himself open to scrutiny by someone whose aims were not benign.

It also appeared that Moravec might be right: he was not able to operate unobserved in his own capital city. Cal made no attempt to identify who was doing the following – Vince had spotted him and would give him a description later – but it did mean that he would need to act upon it. Had anyone overheard the exchange in the church? Unlikely, they had spoken in near-whispers.

Sauntering on, still playing the tourist, Cal peered at buildings and statues. He had no intention of leading their man back to where he and Vince were staying, but made instead for the Ambassador Hotel, even if such a place carried with it the risk of him being recognised, being, he knew, the chosen watering hole of all the foreign correspondents.. A five-star establishment, it had a precious asset: more than one entrance and exit, which made losing a man on his own easy.

The lobby was abuzz with conversation being carried out in several different languages and, like every luxury hotel he had ever entered, there seemed to be an overabundance of well-dressed women, some, no doubt, of dubious purpose. But it was busier by far than the Savoy in London; diplomats too used the Ambassador, and right now every country in Europe felt they needed to have folk in place outside their embassy staff to tell them what was going on.

Cal moved through to the desk, engaged one of the receptionists to ask an innocent question, then went to one of the bank of lifts and allowed himself to be taken up to the fourth floor. He immediately dropped one floor and took another lift, a different one with a different operator, back down to the lobby and without looking around made for a more discreet exit, which took him through a residents' lounge.

'Jesus Christ Almighty, if it isn't my old pal, Doc Savage.'

The cracked American voice, reminiscent of someone with a bad throat, might have been behind him but he knew it to be female, just as he knew who it was, though such knowledge brought him no more pleasure than the nickname she had once regularly used to insult him – the moniker of some inane American cartoon character he had never heard of or read.

Walking on and ignoring it was not an option; he had to turn round and be smiling broadly as he did so. The last time he had seen Corrie Littleton she had been in some distress, in the latter stages of a recovery from a wound caused by an Italian bomb, pale-faced and all skin and bone, not that she had ever been fulsome; he had once decided she was rangy rather than skinny.

Now she was very obviously recovered and was no longer clad in slacks and a masculine sort of shirt-blouse he remembered as standard dress, but in a smart grey suit, jacket and pencil skirt, with an expensive handbag and shoes to match. Her hair, slightly reddish on the side of auburn, which she had worn loose, was now carefully arranged under a pert hat.

'Corrie,' he responded.

'Cal . . .'

He moved forward with speed, immediately taking her arm to push her towards a clutter of settees where they could sit down.

'Hey, buster.'

Cal's response came out of the side of his mouth as a desperate whisper. 'Do shut up for once, there's a good girl.'

'Hell, your manners ain't altered.'

'Let's sit and talk.' She tried to resist being put on her backside but he was too strong, and he made sure their backs were to the door he had just come through. 'And don't use my bloody name.'

'Oh.'

'That's right.' There was no need to say he was here on the same kind of business he had been doing when they first met and Cal did not bother to try and explain. Corrie Littleton might be a pain in the posterior but she was not dumb. 'What in the name of creation are you doing in Prague?'

She responded to his low tone of voice in a similar vein. 'Working, which I kinda guess is what you are doing too.'

'What kind of work can you be doing here?'

'That, from you, is typical, like a woman can't do any work. I am here reporting for *Collier's Weekly*.'

'You're a journalist?'

The reply had all the sarcasm he recalled so well. 'I always knew you were smart.'

'How did you end up doing this?'

'Thank Tyler Alverson. I thought if he could do it, so could I, and I must say he was sweet when we got back stateside. He put me on to people who could help, though that had to wait till I had fully recovered.'

Alverson had been with them both in Ethiopia and Cal had come across him in Madrid as well, when the city was under siege. A long-in-the-tooth self-confessed hack of a foreign correspondent, he was a man Cal liked and admired; he was also a fellow who was to be found where there was anything approaching action.

'Don't tell me, he's here too.'

'As far as I know he's in Berlin, though he might turn up in Prague to slam your guy Runciman when he's finished pussyfooting around.' Her raised crooked two fingers, on both hands, implied parentheses; the look in her eye was implicitly one of scepticism. 'He's supposed to be assessing the situation, as if we don't know what it really means. Damn bastard's been here for weeks and all he's done is play footsie with the Germans.'

'He might not have done, the situation's complex.'

Cal replied in that positive manner, even though he did not believe his own words. He had really only said them to give himself time to think, because Corrie Littleton's presence might present a complication. A reporter, she would be bound to want to know what he was up to, as would Tyler Alverson if he showed up.

'You staying here?' She nodded. 'Room number?'

'One of the best, 48.' Seeing that the praise did not register, she added. 'Overlooks Wenceslas Square.'

'OK. I am going to leave, but I will call you.'

'How about you give me your contact number and I'll call you.'

'No.'

'I could yell out your name, let the whole world know you are here.'

'You could, but if you want to guarantee I clam up, that would be the best way to do it. I will call – and tell Tyler if he shows up that I will talk to him too, but not to shout out if he sees me, and that goes for Vince Castellano.'

'He's here too?' Her eyes narrowed in a face that was attractive, if not conventionally beautiful. 'Sounds as if you and Vince are involved in something juicy.'

'Or maybe nothing at all, Corrie.'

'The Doc Savage I recall was not that kind of guy.'

For once, that nickname did not annoy him; it would allow him to communicate without the use of his name. 'I'll be in touch.'

'Give Vince my regards.'

His cockney friend was pleased with the message – he and Corrie had always got on – though Cal was less enamoured with what Vince had to tell him about what the fellow tailing them had done, in fact he was mystified.

'Sod went straight to the phone after you went up in the lift and I sidled over to see if I could cop the number he dialled. Missed that, but the bugger was loud enough to overhear his voice, not what he was saying, though. The thing is, guv, whoever the sod was talking to, he was doin' it in English.'

CHAPTER THIRTEEN

The telegram Cal Jardine composed and sent off to London was gobbledegook to anyone but Peter Lanchester; sent to his home address to avoid complications it was delivered before six in the evening. It told him he had made contact with those who could help and asked if anyone from the embassy might be tailing the head of Czech Intelligence and how many operatives were in place.

Unbeknown to both, such was the nervousness of the British state regarding events in Czechoslovakia that the sister service to the SIS had people in place to monitor that kind of traffic between the two capital cities. If MI5 did not know the contents of Cal's message or whom it was from, they knew to whom it was addressed.

Part of their job was to compile a list that kept the SIS Central European Desk informed. The register of the day's traffic was thus passed on to Broadway where the recipient's name set off the bells with the man who ran it; normally he was above that sort of thing unless it was deemed important.

Following on from Peter's previous trip to Brno and the subsequent trail that led to La Rochelle it smacked of conspiracy and produced in Noel McKevitt the kind of expletive-filled apoplexy he reserved for times when he was alone and unobserved, the kind that turned the air blue and had those outside his office exchanging looks and shrugs.

They were messing about in his patch again without telling him and there could only be one reason for such behaviour – they were acting to achieve something he could not support and the only thing he could think of was some kind of attempt to embroil the country in Central Europe that went against Government policy.

It also, after a period of thinking, occurred to him that unravelling that might give him some leverage to demand answers to any number of questions, and that had him send off a message to the station chief in Prague, basically asking him to check on new arrivals of British nationality in the capital or Brno, journalists and diplomats excluded, as a Code One priority – there should not be too many with the continuing crisis.

Then he turned to flicking through his address book for the number of an old colleague, asking for an outside line; this was not a call to risk being overheard by the switchboard.

'Barney, it's Noel,' he said into the telephone, having forced himself to calm down. 'Sure, I was thinking it's a long time since we shared a jar and a chat an' it being Friday and all . . .'

The recipient of the call, Barney Foxton, had been in his job long enough to know what that meant: I want to ask you questions I dare not pose over the telephone; and that led him to speculate what it might be about – not for long – given he knew the post McKevitt held.

'Both been snowed under, Noel,' he replied.

That was followed by a short pause that allowed time for speculation. The Ulsterman must want something and Foxton was speculating about his own needs in these troubled times; what could MI6 have that might be of use to him, something for which he could trade?

'I was thinking,' McKevitt continued, 'that we might have a pint. How about that nice little snug bar at the Salisbury in St Martin's Lane?'

Good choice, Foxton thought: a busy pub and homosexual haunt on the corner of an alley that joined two main thoroughfares, a tiny bar with two doors, one to the street and another to the main saloon, a load of mirrors so you could keep an eye on everyone who came and went without actually looking at them and a clientele that would be too busy with their own concerns to care about anyone else's.

'Why not?'

'This lunchtime, say one o'clock?'

He's keen, Foxton thought, having failed to drag up anything he could ask for; still, a favour in the bank usually paid off in time so, provided what McKevitt was after did not pose too many problems, he would help if he could.

'See you there, Noel.'

Peter Lanchester had looked at his deciphered message and wondered what he could do about the major part of it. He had no idea why the Prague station might be following the head of Czech Intelligence to find out who it was he was meeting, while added to that was the certain knowledge that probably the only man in London who had any clue about the answer was Noel McKevitt.

Asking would get him nowhere, in fact it would only alert the Irish bugger to the fact that he was messing about in his pond again, so it was with some surprise that he got a mid-morning telephone invitation to come over to Broadway for a chat, that accompanied by an explanation that left him unconvinced.

'You know, Peter, I think I let my annoyance get to me the other day. It will not come as a surprise to you that people like me are a bit unsure what Quex is up to with your new set-up.'

Now I am suddenly 'Peter'. 'Perfectly natural, Noel, but I can tell you without a shred of doubt any worries you might have are misplaced.'

'An assumption that it would be best to operate on, would you not say? So why don't you pop over and we can talk about what you picked up in Brno and beyond.'

'I'm not sure I picked up any more than you will already know and what we have already discussed.'

'Only one way to nail that, given I don't know to the last T what you found any more than you are aware what I am familiar with . . .' The rest was left up in the air.

'Is this about running guns, Noel?'

Peter heard a single sound that he supposed was laughter, though it equated more to a cough. 'Not my concern; as you know, my patch is Czech land and environs but you have been there and I have not, at least for years, so . . .'

It was too much of a coincidence; I get a telegram from Prague, then a call from McKevitt, but if that was the connection, turning down the invite would make him even more suspicious than he clearly was already.

'Can't do this morning, how about after lunch?'

'Best make it three-thirty, then, I have a meet arranged that might take me till then.'

He was still pondering on that when the door opened and a messenger entered with a slip of paper, which was handed over, an answer to his request to Quex to be told how many people were on station for the SIS in Prague.

Usually it would be two at best for such a troubled location, more likely one in normal times, it being a bit of an intelligence backwater, while the likes of a major capital might run to a trio or even four if there was trouble brewing. Prague at present had six, four having been hauled in from the neighbouring stations at the request of McKevitt after the May mobilisation of the Czech army.

It was quite indicative of the surprise Quex had felt that he had followed the number six with three exclamation marks; that meant the Ulsterman had increased the Prague staffing without clearing it with his boss, which was stretching his level of accountability somewhat. Would Quex have him in for a haul over the coals or would he do what normally happened, quietly seethe and say nothing, putting it in the memory bank for a later date?

There was never a good time to run an external intelligence service but now was particularly bad, given the way appeasement was pulling things in two directions. By its very nature MI6 required as staff people who, though they might rank as misfits, could think for themselves and often act without instructions, while keeping your cards close to your chest, even with colleagues, was essential. The idea in theory was that everything came together at the top; in practice it was often the very opposite.

Yet Peter's main concern was to get an answer to Cal. He had said it was important, so the first stop when he left the office at lunchtime was the post office, where he sent a telegram with the single significant letter.

Moravec came on the phone for a second time, again not identifying himself, to arrange another meeting at the same location and time, surprised when Cal insisted on knowing which entrance he would use. It was only catching him on the hop that got an answer, as well as the hint no meeting was possible without the information.

The question came about through what had been talked about the previous evening, once they had established that Cal had not been followed back to the Meran Hotel; what to do about Corrie Littleton was less pressing than nailing what was happening with Moravec.

Vince was adamant there had been no sign of a tail on the way to the cathedral, only afterwards, which implied Cal had been picked up because of the meeting and possibly tailed speculatively rather than because of any direct suspicion, though why that should be someone who was English was too much of a mystery to even go near.

Yet could they assume that the man who had followed Cal had been alone? Had someone stayed with Moravec, which implied the kind of resources that had prompted the telegram sent to London? With or without an answer something had to be done about it. Cal had been lucky to get clear once, it would be tempting providence to expect to do so twice.

'The only solution, guv, is to get there ahead of your man and see what he brings with him.'

Cal nodded slowly. 'If it's two we leave without making contact.'

'And if it's only one?'

All that got was a slow grin as Cal picked up the phone and asked to be connected to the Ambassador Hotel. The card from the restaurant where he and Vince had eaten was on the table, and once he got through he arranged to meet Corrie there that evening, though when she asked the name he was obliged to spell out both that and the address; Czech was a language that imposed that on visitors.

Wanting to get to St Vitus's Cathedral early he and Vince took a cab to the main railway station, then after a walk through the concourse they exited to take another up to Hradčany, paying the cab off away from the castle and entering to take up a position which gave them a good view of the huge open square before the Golden Gate entrance to the church.

Too extensive a space to be crowded on a weekday, they spotted Moravec easily as he walked into the square – from what they could see, without minders of his own. It was Vince who pointed out the man following him some twenty paces back, the same 'geezer' he had spotted on Cal's tail the day before. It still did not make sense to either of them but that was by the by; the man had to be got rid of to avoid a repeat.

Moravec went straight in through the high and imposing doors, followed by his tail and in turn by Cal and Vince, who split up once they were inside, making their way up separate sides of the nave. The

Czech Intelligence chief was by the same pillar as before and as he opened his mouth to speak Cal cut him off.

'Why would anyone from British Intelligence be tailing you?'

'I not understand.'

If the explanation was swift, Moravec's smile was slow, though he did nod with understanding as Cal related how the man had been overheard on the phone. As they were speaking Vince was approaching the very same person outside one of the numerous small chapels, a smile of enquiry on his face and a cigarette in his left hand, which he waved before his lips and pointed in the universal signal that he wanted a light.

If his man were a staunch Catholic he would object that to smoke in a cathedral was sacrilege, disrespectful in the extreme. He wasn't, because he nodded, patted one of his pockets, then reached into it, his eyes on those of the still silent Vince and so unaware of the clenched fist that was just about to crack him right on the point of his jaw.

In the seconds that this silent exchange had taken place Moravec had gone from a smile to a low chuckle. 'English? The language none in my office speak. German yes, French too, Czech obviously . . .'

If smoking in a cathedral was uncouth, shouting at the top of your voice had to come a close second. Vince was looking over a lit match, the cigarette in his lips, fist poised and his feet in place for the very necessary stand and balance that you require to deliver a blow that would knock out a man.

It got to be no more than an extended twitch, because he heard his name and the following 'No!' echoing around the huge church, in a voice so loud and reverberating that it must have stopped every other visitor in their tracks and made those saying their prayers wonder if God had decided to speak to them.

That had Vince looking around and shrugging in embarrassment, before holding up the cigarette and spinning away. He had taken only a few steps when he saw Cal walking hurriedly towards him looking concerned, an attitude that evaporated as he observed that Vince's proposed victim was still standing. Yet concentration was not allowed to slip – they did not address each other, Cal doing a forgotten-something mime before retracing his steps, Vince on his heels.

'He's Moravec's minder,' Cal hissed as soon as they were out of view. 'He only followed me to see if I went back to the embassy.'

'He came close to being a crock of shit.'

'Swearing in a church?'

'I like that,' Vince replied, irritated. 'I can't swear but I'm allowed to knock a bloke spark out. So what's happening?'

'Don't know yet. I best go back and find out.'

He did, but Moravec was gone.

Like most pub conversations between two middle-aged fellows, that in the snug of the Salisbury began with old times and old campaigns, their connection going back to the days when as younger men they had sought to thwart the intentions of the Irish Republican Army in the Six Counties of Ulster, just work for Foxton but a cause close to his heart, blood and religion for Noel McKevitt.

That lasted through the consumption of one of their two pints of bitter; the second took them on to the situation and the prospects of war in Europe, which was where McKevitt wanted to be. 'It'll come, Barney – and, by Jesus, I hope we are ready for it – but not over anything I deal with in my area of responsibility and not for several years yet, if I have anything to do with things.'

'Can't be sure, though, can we?'

'Let me tell you, it's damn near official policy, man. Chamberlain knows what's right, and I have that from the lips of a cabinet minister friend of mine.'

That was accepted; Barney Foxton did not ask who or how McKevitt came by such a high-level source, one he could refer to as a friend.

'But that's not to say there are not people trying to queer that pitch, I can tell you, and that's where I need your help.'

Too long in the tooth to react, Foxton nodded, said nothing, sank his pint and accepted the offer of another, content to wait till McKevitt sat down again and got to the real reason for this meeting.

'One of the telegrams that came in from Prague last night went to one of our own MI6 boys. I have to tell you I think the sod is up to something out there and he's not telling me about it.'

'Naughty.'

Foxton replied as required but was not surprised; he worked in an organisation that was similar in its fractures. The only thing troubling him was the flush on McKevitt's cheeks, given he had always been an opaque fellow, famous for his cool head. Now he was positively animated.

'It's worse than that, Barney, it's bloody dangerous! You've read the papers. It's all very well for those lefty bastards to say we should stand up to the likes of Hitler. With what, I ask you, and if he wants to duff up his Yids and take bits of the middle of the Continent back, who are we to interfere, eh?'

'I don't like the bugger, Noel.'

'D'ye think I do! He's a loon, and I say that having seen the shite close up. Honest, he has eyes that would melt metal and is daft enough to start a fight in an empty room. So the last thing we would want to be doing is givin' the bastard an excuse, which is what might just happen if some folk are not stopped from poking about where they are not wanted.'

Tempted to calm him down, Foxton instead posed the obvious question. 'What is it you're after, Noel?'

'If the certain party I mention to you gets another telegram from Prague, I want to know what it says.' Seeing Foxton swell up for a refusal, McKevitt was quick to keep talking. 'It's domestic, so I can't ask for it, but you can.'

'If your boss asks my boss—'

The interruption was swift. 'That won't happen.'

'It needs a warrant.'

'What if I were to tell you, Barney, that my boss might be part of the problem, might be working against our own government, what would you say to that, I ask you?'

'Are you having me on?'

'God, I wish I was, but the sod has set something up that makes me wonder and I can smell it has something to do with the Czechs who would be quite happy to see us bleed so they can hang on to their miserable little country.'

Just like the Orange Order, Foxton thought, but he kept that to himself. Not that he got much chance to air any thought – McKevitt, a man normally the picture of calm, was close to bursting with rage, no doubt brought on by the drink.

'We wandered into the last lot, did we not, Barney, and do you think if we had known the cost we would have done so? Well we damn well know the cost now and it's likely to be worse, what with bombers in the hundreds an' all. There's a crisis brewing and it could go either way if we're not careful . . .'

'You're asking for a hell of a lot, Noel.'

'And don't I know it. I can kiss goodbye to my job and pension if this gets out, but I tell you what, to avoid seeing those Flanders fields soaked in blood again, I would do it.'

'I'll have to give it a bit of thought.'

'Do that, Barney, do that, and rest assured, if you want anything from me in return, in the rules or out of them, sure you only have to ask.'

The first thing Barney Foxton did when he got back to his office, following on from a quick and very necessary visit to the Gents, was to tell the switchboard that if Noel McKevitt rang they were to say he was out. Not normally a man to talk to himself he did so when he put the phone back down.

'You can blow your pension if you want, you Irish nutcase, but I'm not blowing mine.'

Sir Hugh Sinclair looked at the copy of Callum Jardine's telegram from Prague as well as the reply and he compared them with that which had been given to him by Peter Lanchester. He had no need to decipher the original as long as the cryptic characters compared properly and they did.

Getting the information from MI5 had been relatively easy and had nothing to do with an exchange of favours. Sinclair had spent many years seeking to combine the two services but had been rebuffed time and again. For all that, his opposite number, Vernon

Kell, the head of the domestic intelligence service, knew that he had not given up hope, just as he knew that such affairs and infighting tied everyone up in such a Gordian knot of bureaucratic nonsense as to be a nightmare.

So any request that seemed reasonable from Sinclair was met, and if Kell wondered at the secrecy surrounding the application for telegram transcripts, and the demand that it stay strictly between the two of them, that too was easy to accede to.

His secretary entered to advise him his car was waiting, with a frown that was intended to impart that keeping waiting a high-powered delegation from Paris, including the French PM and Foreign Minister, was very bad manners indeed, but he was less concerned than she.

They were with their political equivalents and that always went on too long; such people were too fond of the sound of their own voice to adhere to a timetable, quite apart from the fact that they seemed to derive some pleasure from keeping in suspense those people they referred to in private, or certainly thought of, as their minions.

Part of the visiting party included his counterpart in French Intelligence and he would share with that man the fact that he had an independent and covert operation going on in Czechoslovakia, one in which he was happy to communicate the results, albeit the French were well placed there themselves.

Naturally he would be expected to ask for something in return and he would, out of a curiosity prompted by what Peter Lanchester had told him on his return, request a record of the calls from abroad made to certain proto-fascist organisations in France; that such records existed he had no doubts.

The telegrams were locked in his desk drawer; his briefcase was waiting for him to take out, within it the latest digest of intelligence from the Central European Desk. Emerging to cross a sunlit pavement, Sir Hugh reflected that it was probably sunny all the way across the continent of Europe. Odd that what he was carrying hinted at dark and threatening clouds.

CHAPTER FOURTEEN

'I think the thing that set me up most was the sea journey back to the States.'

Corrie Littleton was talking about her convalescence in what had, so far, been a very pleasant dinner, during which she had, surprisingly, asked for wine; Cal remembered her as a strident teetotaller, but as a result of her serious wounds, she had turned to alcohol to ease down from a possible morphine addiction.

'And not just the sea air. On the transatlantic there was the dishiest doc you have ever seen in your life. Boy, do those sailor's whites make a guy look good, especially the shorts.'

'You should see me in a kilt.'

'Do you mind, Cal, I'm eating,' she replied, forking some goulash into her mouth, only speaking again when that had been consumed. 'So when are you going to tell what game you are playing here in Prague?'

'Who says I'm going to tell you?'

She threw back her head and laughed. 'You better had, bud, 'cause I am a hot reporter these days.'

She had been something of a thorn in Cal's side in Ethiopia, forcing diversions on his objectives in a search for her archaeologist mother, that not aided by a tongue that seemed, in his case, to be made of acid. Yet she could handle a gun, complained little of the discomfort of travelling and proved she was a woman by making moon eyes at an aristocratic, arrogant French flyer.

It was also true she had been stalwart when called upon, helping, without any experience at all, to run a field hospital in which it had been necessary to quickly overcome any natural squeamishness and deal with the horrendous wounds caused by modern weapons. In short, Corrie Littleton was quite tough.

'So you'd best just open up.'

Recalling the way he had lost contact with Moravec, Cal was thinking right now there was nothing to say. Then Vince nudged him and he saw coming through the tables the bloke his boxing friend had nearly floored. The young man said nothing, just dropped a card onto the table by Cal's side and carried on. Corrie Littleton tried to snatch it but failed; after a quick look it went into a pocket.

'Whose side are you on?' Cal asked as a way of diverting her. 'The Germans or the Czechs?'

'I'm supposed to be neutral.'

'Hard to be that,' Vince said.

'I agree, and when it's the little guy against Goliath there's really only one side to be on.'

'Is that the policy of your rag?'

'It's not a rag, Cal, it's a magazine and they don't have a view either way and nor do they want headlines. What they need is a set of features that sells copies. How the place is, under the threat of invasion – are the locals coping, what do they think of the democracies, not just here in Prague but in the Sudetenland as well? And to do that I need to go there and be free to operate openly.'

Cal did a good job of looking sorry for her; Vince did it better – he meant it.

'With what's happening in Nuremberg the Czechs have got kinda jumpy about journalists travelling around the border areas and they're insisting they need police escorts. I'd need accreditation papers to do my job.'

'You can go as a private citizen, I think.'

'What would be the point of that? My request to go there is with the Interior Ministry but they seem to be taking their damn sweet time to process it.'

'It must be crowded in those parts right now,' Vince said.

'Not so, Vince, the head honchos up there are not talking, so all the journos are stuck with the political shenanigans here in Prague, all writing the same copy. Quite a few will be lighting out for Nuremberg, where at least something's happening.'

'Mass hysteria is happening.'

'Which I don't want to cover anyway, because my stuff is supposed to be human interest. I don't suppose you have any pull in this neck of the woods, do you?'

'If I had, why would I use them on your behalf?' Cal replied, avoiding the implications of that query, not that he could oblige.

That got him sight of a paprika-stained tongue. 'If they take much longer I might just be obliged to shimmy over to the Nazi Party Rally. I've got accreditation for the Reich and it will be exciting on the last day when Hitler speaks, though that will be crowded.'

'Take my word for it, the place will be heaving with lunatics.'

'I was talking about journalists.'

'What makes you think I wasn't? What are the chaps in the bar saying about what's happening here in Prague?'

'To a man they're saying it stinks. That Lord Runciman guy Chamberlain sent over is a patsy, going through the motions, judging by the speech he made today at his latest press conference. And where has he gone off for the weekend to find out how the Czechs feel? To spend time in the castle of some well-heeled German aristocrat up north near Carlsbad called Prince Hohenlohe, that's where. The word in the bar of the Ambassador is it's all a set-up to sell the victims down the river.'

'Typical reporters' talk.'

'Don't knock it, some of those guys have seen it all and are too long in the tooth to fall for any old line.' Another mouthful of goulash later, Corrie added, with narrowed eyes and what Cal thought was her best effort at a winning smile, 'But if I can't do the Sudetenland my readers would sure like a tale of derring-do and gunrunning. I can do it off the record, no names or places.'

'Pity I can't oblige, I always wanted to see my name in print.'

'You will one day, buster, but it will be on a charge sheet.'

They continued to spar throughout the main course, into the dessert and coffee, she probing, he fielding, watched by a mainly silent and amused Vince Castellano, who knew there was something between the pair other than the apparent mutual antagonism that peppered their conversation, until finally Cal indicated he and Vince had to go.

'Anything to do with that card you pocketed?'

An index finger was used to tap the side of his nose before Cal asked, 'You OK to get a cab on your own?'

'I'm a big girl now, Cal,' Corrie replied with a girlie lilt.

Having seen her into the aforesaid taxi he and Vince walked up the street till they saw their man emerge from a doorway several yards ahead – a gap he maintained, turning left then right into a backstreet so ill lit it had Vince on edge, eyes darting and fists clenched in case of trouble. The car Cal had been alerted to on that card was waiting, engine purring, and the two men got in, the lead fellow now in the front passenger seat.

'Does he speak English?'

Cal could only mean the driver, who had engaged the gears and moved off without a word being spoken. 'No.'

'You do?'

'Yes.'

'How well?'

'Three years at the London School of Economics.' There was a mid-European accent, but not much of one. 'Most of my fellow students went to the Sorbonne and are French-speaking.'

'Why did you follow me?'

'On the general's orders, to see where you stayed.'

'He must have known I was at the Meran as soon as he made the phone call I asked for.'

'A clever man might book into more than one hotel to make sure he was not exposed.'

'And the Meran is where you picked us up tonight?'

'Yes.'

'Inside or out?' Cal saw the young man's shoulders shrug as if it made no difference; it did to him and he asked again.

'I was outside in Wenceslas Square.'

'So you did not enquire about me at the Meran reception desk? Ask who was staying in room 47?'

The silence was the answer and that was not good; the last thing Cal wanted was people seeking information on him at a hotel reception desk, especially since this youngster would have had no name with which to enquire, which was bound to raise curiosity about him as a guest. Anonymity was a precious commodity to be preserved if possible, which was why he had not told Moravec the name he was travelling under at the cathedral.

Irritated as he was, there was no point in crying over spilt milk. 'Where are we going?'

'To the old Jewish cemetery.'

'Why there?'

'It's safe.'

There was a temptation to probe about that, to ask if it was as bad as Moravec had made out, or was it just the paranoia of a man who spent his life in the spying business? But there was little point, so he just sat back and relaxed as the car weaved through the light night-time traffic, crossing the river, until they stopped by the long wall of the old cemetery, alighting to walk to the gate.

There was a moment outside while checks were made on both sides of the gate but finally they went through into the gloomy interior. Moravec was waiting for them inside and, without speaking, they set off on a walk through the now defunct graveyard, packed with tilted headstones, with the other two well back to avoid them being overheard. The intelligence chief was not even about to trust the young man he had sent to fetch them.

Cal could hear Vince questioning the young fellow, not in any pressured way, just curious about his time in London, what he had studied, what he thought of the place and had he come across any fascists at the LSE, but inside those replies there would be nuggets of information that might provide clues for future use, given neither had any idea exactly where this was heading.

On a clear night with a near-full moon and a sky full of stars, even in a part of the city low on the spill from street lighting there was no need for any extra illumination, though it did give a ghostly air to both their surroundings and the Moravec-Jardine conversation as they walked down the gravel paths that criss-crossed the burial ground.

Cal was wondering what Moravec wanted with him but was equally determined not to initiate anything; he would wait to hear what the intelligence chief had to say and that became frustrating, as Moravec seemed to want to talk about anything and nothing, thankfully mostly in German.

He was treated to a potted history of the Czechs, without doubt and unsurprisingly in the Moravec exposition the cleverest and most industrious of the former inhabitants of the old Austro-Hungarian Empire. Quite naturally that included a comprehensive list of the manifest failings of the rest of the groups with whom they competed for imperial attention in what had, until its dismemberment in 1919, been a somewhat rickety edifice.

To the Czech way of thinking it was made up of lazy Slovaks, mercurial Hungarians, puffed-up Poles, insular Ruthenians and double-dealing Rumanians, all beholden to soft overfed Austrians, with the rest, a good dozen races, not, it seemed, to be considered as human at all and a polity riven with the kind of deep-seated anti-Semitism that made men like Hitler.

'And you can see how we Czechs did not just tolerate the Jews, but lived alongside them in harmony and mutual industry. There were no pogroms in Prague and as of this moment we are walking through a thousand years of Jewish history.'

Then he was on to the German minority, grudgingly admitted to be hard-working and industrious, though politically they had nothing to complain about, with the whole separatist campaign being orchestrated, if not forced, from Berlin.

Konrad Henlein, the leader of the SdP, was far from the most rabid of their number and, while he was strong in demands for regionalism, had never been a National Socialist. It was only pressure from others, rabid Nazis, and their success in the polls that had forced him to even consider incorporating the Sudetenland in the Reich.

According to Moravec, Henlein had been quite amenable to the Sudetenland regions remaining part of the Czechoslovak Republic, albeit with concessions, a position he maintained until he was outmanoeuvred by the National Socialists, who were being heavily backed financially from Berlin.

With less money to spend on elections Henlein had lost an internal struggle for votes against a faction led by an outright Nazi who was now his deputy, a thug called Karl Hermann Frank. He had then moved to the extreme right only to maintain his own position as leader of the ethnic Germans.

While what Moravec was telling him was of some interest it did not answer the central question of what this clandestine meeting was for. On and on he rambled until finally he came to the point, which was that the invasion was scheduled and the question as to how that knowledge would be received in London if it could be proved beyond doubt that it was not just some outline plan – the reason it had been dismissed before – but a real one ready to be executed.

'It would have to harden their attitude to Germany.'

'Enough to stop Hitler?'

'It's possible,' Cal replied, thinking of his conversation in the courtyard of the Savile Club. 'I can say no more than that.'

'We cannot give up control of the Sudetenland without losing the means to defend the rest of the country. I suspect you know this.'

'Of course.'

'You asked about the Germans who fear Hitler will ruin their country?'

Cal did not speak; this was what he had come to Prague for.

'That attacking us was bound to cause another war. Three we know of tried to change his mind, wrote strong memoranda saying it was madness, von Neurath, the Foreign Minister, Generals Blomberg and Fritsch; all were got rid of. Now General Beck, the Chief of the General Staff, has resigned, but it has not been made public.'

'If a man of that stature took such a course there must be others willing to follow him?'

'None as yet, they are behaving like sheep. Everyone who knows what is planned has been told it is Hitler's unalterable will.'

That sounded like the Austrian Corporal all right: 'unalterable will' was one of his favourite sayings and a mantra adopted by those who worshipped him and his creed, as though the mere application of willpower could achieve whatever was desired, regardless of obstacles. It was an uncomfortable truth that, up till now, against all the odds, the little moustachioed bastard had been right.

'Most of his senior generals are terrified of what he proposes and fear that he will use his leader's speech at Nuremberg to declare his intention to invade.'

That was only a few days away. 'Will they act if he does?'

'If your country was at risk like mine, would you rely on a group of German generals to save you?'

'No. Is there any prospect of help from elsewhere?'

'The Polish jackals will not give us aid, they will not even let the Soviets cross their land to help us because they are itching to take back the Teschen coalfields, this while the Hungarians are circling like vultures too, waiting to feed on our carcass. Without help from the West we are doomed.'

'You're still negotiating.'

That produced a snort, which was supposed to pass for a laugh. 'Let me tell you, my friend, a few days ago our president called in the two deputies Henlein has appointed to deal with us. He gave them a blank sheet of paper and a pen and asked them to write for themselves the conditions by which we could avoid a conflict, guaranteeing to accept whatever they wrote in advance.'

'That sounds like surrender.'

'It was not quite, but I think they were shocked. Oh, these men, they wrote such a list and Beneš accepted it in a bid to avoid our country being smashed. Then we had a riot up north in Moravia, engineered by the German deputies, in which they claim a policeman struck a deputy with his whip. You will not yet have seen your English papers reporting this, but suddenly we are again, in Germany, killing innocents even if no one died. And what happened to those terms that our president agreed to?'

'Don't tell me, no longer acceptable.'

Then, surprisingly, he reverted to his grammarless English and the previous point. 'If we you give proof absolute of what Hitler planning, what with it would you do?'

'What kind of proof?'

'The details of attack.'

That required a long pause; was he being offered such proof? 'Get it back to London, put it in the hands of those who could make use of it.'

'The newspapers also?'

'Perhaps. That would not be for me to decide.'

Even in the gloom Cal saw the smile. 'Politicians the newspapers fear when they do not them control.'

'Why do you speak in English when your German is fluent?'

'Not fluent my English, is it, like Vaclav?' Finally the young man had a name. 'I am wound, but practise I must, my friend, if I need flee. If Germans come, a bullet only I can expect.' The switch back to German was seamless as was the change of subject. 'There are only four places where this truth you seek exists.'

I seek, Cal thought. *So this is where he's going?*

'Naturally, the entire plan is at the headquarters of the German army in Berlin, along with those for defending at the same time the Rhineland from a French invasion.'

'I hope you're not going to suggest I go burgling in the Bendlerstraße.'

The idea of Cal picking the locks on those Berlin offices tickled him and caused him to chuckle, before going on to say where other plans were kept, equally impossible to get at: Hitler's Bavarian retreat, the Berghof, high in a large fenced-off and SS-guarded compound in the Obersalzberg, another set with the designated field commander who was, at this moment, engaged in training his troops for the invasion under the guise of autumn manoeuvres.

'You seem to know a lot about something supposed to be a secret.'

Moravec was too wise to fall for that bit of fishing. He obviously had good sources right at the top of the German state but they were not going to be discussed. 'Case Green . . .'

'Which is?'

'The name of the plan for the invasion of Czechoslovakia; the one for the defence of the West is Case Red. The Sudeten German Party does not have the plan but it holds documents given to Henlein by Hitler only five days ago relating to the invasion plan for Bohemia and Moravia, so that they know what to do when it comes.'

'Such as?'

'What assets to seize or destroy, where the *Wehrmacht* columns will seek to penetrate our defences so that they can cause mayhem in the rear areas, as well as their own targets to attack, like roads to block, certain bunkers and the Czech police stations.'

'Is it not lunacy to give the details to such amateurs? From what I know they are not soldiers but street fighters at best.'

'That is what has happened and it also proves that Henlein is in Hitler's pocket. The man is no more than a puppet.'

Cal was trying to imagine that on the table of Chamberlain's cabinet room and the effect it would have; it would blow the appeasement policy out of the water and expose the Sudeten German leader as a fraud.

'And you know where this is kept?'

'It is in the possession of Henlein.'

'Then why don't you just break in and steal them?' Cal asked, though he suspected he knew the answer.

'That riot I told you of, the man who was supposed to have used his whip, was dismissed. So was the police chief and six more of his men.'

That was followed by a deep sigh and a long and windy explanation of the constraints Moravec was under. He had strict orders himself from the president's office to do nothing that would make a bad situation worse while the British envoy, Lord Runciman, was in the country; in short, nothing that would antagonise the Germans or give the democracies an excuse to walk away from supporting Czechoslovakia.

To launch an assault on the building in which those documents were located was out of the question when the slightest act like an arrest, even for the proper imposition of order as it had been in Moravia, was blown up by the German press into an atrocity, another excuse for Hitler to rant on about the 'plight' of his racial brethren. That impacted in the West, weakening the hand of those trying to press for a policy of standing up to him.

The police in the Sudetenland had even stricter orders now to avoid provocation. Following the riot and the dismissal of Czech officials, they had been required to stoically bear it when the more rabid Nazis took to the streets to taunt them.

They had been backed up by the Sudeten German *Freikorps*, a group based on Hitler's SA, who had hurriedly rushed to their side, with their uniforms, flags and arms, to parade through the streets where the riot had taken place singing *'Deutschland über Alles'* and the *'Horst-Wessel-Lied'*.

Konrad Henlein would not take part in the negotiations with the Czech Government or any other body – Moravec suspected that was again on Hitler's orders – and nor would any of the other top men in the SdP like Frank. It was becoming increasingly clear there were no concessions which would satisfy the Sudeten German Party: every time their terms were met they upped their demands – this, he was sure, on instructions from Berlin, so the Führer would have his 'excuse' to invade.

Not that standing off made any difference; Goebbels, or at least the German newspapers and radio stations he controlled, just made things up. They screamed daily about fabricated Czech atrocities: the beating of innocent civilians, children included, women being molested and in many cases raped, brutal police raids in which houses were reduced to rubble and furniture thrown out into the streets to be smashed, assassinations of activists and all the usual claptrap of Nazi propaganda.

'My hands are tied, I cannot move, for if I even attempt to do so against the express orders of the Government, someone in my department will leak my intentions before I make a move, perhaps even to the Germans, and next day it will be banner headlines in the *Völkischer Beobachter*.'

So your outfit is split, just like MI6, Cal thought, though he did not say so. His other thought was to thank God he was a free agent, and it was that which underlined what Moravec was driving at: if he could not act he needed someone to do it for him, hence this little walk and talk.

The Czech was angling for him to be that someone. He had a lot of sympathy for his plight, but natural caution kept him from speaking even if he had a shrewd idea what was coming, not something to contemplate without serious consideration. If Moravec was frustrated by his silence, and he probably was, he hid it well.

'I now know for certain you are not connected to the British embassy.'

And I won't ask how you know, Cal thought; Moravec would have people in every embassy that employed Czechs as drivers, cooks and interpreters, which was just about everyone except the Germans and Soviets, the latter too paranoid to ever employ locals in their legations.

'How do you know this document is where you say it is?'

'Trust me to do my job.'

'A spy in place, perhaps?'

'You would not answer that, neither will I.'

It was time to nail him. 'If you want help, and it sounds to me very much like you do, you're going to have to answer that and a lot more besides.'

'Go back to your hotel. There you will find a package waiting for you. Examine it tonight and I will call tomorrow and arrange another meeting.'

The package was bulky and when it was laid out it covered not only the bed but the floor as well, information relating to a small town called Cheb in Czech, Eger in German, which Henlein and Frank were using as their personal headquarters and from which they were running their political affairs.

No doubt they had chosen Cheb for the very good reason that it lay only a few miles from the German border; Henlein's house was even closer in a hamlet called Asch, practically right on the boundary line. The SdP leader was taking no chances on a crackdown; any hint of trouble and he and his family would be in Germany and safe from arrest.

Frank had his HQ at the local Nazi Party HQ, which appeared to be a substantial edifice, while Henlein's was over two floors of the Victoria Hotel, which was a three-storey classical-styled building in the centre of the town opposite the Cheb-Eger railway station, through which ran the Paris-to-Prague Express.

The detail of both locations was comprehensive: the package contained maps of both town and hamlet, as well as the surrounding country, photographs of the streets around both Henlein's house and Frank's HQ, and building plans of the hotel itself, where anything really vital would probably be kept.

There were armed members of the local *Freikorps* guarding the Victoria, day and night, their strength and a rota included, as well as the number of people employed there during the day, all checked as being of the right stripe, because it was still a working building so there was also included an estimate of the rate of occupancy by guests.

The only speculation was the location of the safe that contained the details of Hitler's invasion plan – they would have to be kept under lock and key – which was assumed to be in Konrad Henlein's own suite on the first floor.

Everything being, of course, in German, Cal spent as much time translating for Vince as he did examining the documents himself. The Londoner was swift to one conclusion.

'They must have a bloke on the inside, guv, and he's got to be close to the boss man, not just one of the hotel staff. If you've read it right this practically tells you what this Henlein bloke had for breakfast.'

'They must have the place under permanent surveillance too, Vince. You don't compile all this without you can watch them day and night, which makes me curious. How come the Heinies haven't spotted they are being clocked?'

'Heinies?'

'That's what Henlien's men are called, and every other Sudeten German now, I shouldn't wonder, even if they are dead against him.'

'Maybe his lot are thick.'

'They'd have to be blind, deaf and dumb not to suspect they are being watched by Czech security, and there's another thing. Moravec says that he cannot trust everyone in his own department.'

'So how many folk know about a file like this lot?'

'That's right, and if they do, would they go so far as to betray the secret? That means it's possible the likes of Henlein will be aware that this file we are looking at exists.'

'He must be well on guard for somebody trying to break in to his bit of the hotel.'

'I think that's what Moravec is going to ask us to do.'

'An' I'm thinking we shouldn't touch it with a bargepole.'

Cal had a map open now and was fingering the route to Cheb from Prague, as well as the distance to the German border, which even at a generous estimate could not be more than half an hour.

'There is another alternative. Old Henlein must be nervous, ready to run if he thinks he's going to be arrested. He's not going to leave something like that behind, is he, and it's not going to be in his house.'

'You think he could be spooked into doing that?'

If Cal was smiling at the thought when he looked up, such a feeling was not replicated in Vince's expression and it was not necessary to say why. They were two strangers in the country and on the face of it they had no means of bringing about what was being discussed.

'I don't know yet, but having seen all this, I can't think that Moravec does not have something like that in mind.'

'One that keeps him clean and might get us in deep shit.'

'You're not suggesting we don't give him a hearing, Vince?'

'I might,' Vince sighed; he knew his old company officer too well, knew when an idea had taken hold that excited him. 'But I'd be wasting my breath.'

'And this might be too good an opportunity to turn down. Cast-iron evidence of what Hitler is up to is just what we need, and those plans do just that.'

Once everything was tidied away and Vince had gone back to his own room, Cal sat down with the laborious task of composing another telegram to Peter Lanchester, this time outlining what he thought was on offer.

CHAPTER FIFTEEN

Peter Lanchester's 'chat' with Noel McKevitt had not started well and ended badly, though he had noticed on entering the Ulsterman's office that there was a strong smell of drink on his breath. His eyes also had that slight glaze which comes from a too-liquid lunch and perhaps it was that which led to a surprising loss of control from a man so well known for the lack of passion in his demeanour.

There had been a seemingly interminable discussion of Brno and what he had observed there, tedious because Peter had nothing to say which he suspected McKevitt did not already know, but eventually it led to where it was clear he wanted to go, even if he said he was no longer concerned: had Peter found out the identity of the fellow who had illegally bought those weapons?

'You didn't question anyone at the arms factory?' McKevitt asked, for the first time slightly querulous when the answer was negative.

'That was not my brief, Noel, and besides, given we surmise that the End User Certificate was known to be false by the managers, I doubt asking questions would have got me very far. They would have just clammed up, while I was not inclined to seek out and interrogate your source.'

'Not your brief,' was the response, accompanied by a slight frown. 'You were given this job by Quex himself—?'

A sharp interruption was necessary. 'I do think that is a question you should put directly to him, Noel.'

'Would it be breaching any confidentiality to tell me what the parameters were? For instance, was your mission to stop the shipment or just to track it?'

'As you know,' Peter responded, prevaricating, 'it had already left Brno when we were alerted to the transaction.'

'Which makes me wonder, Peter, if the man we pay a stipend to there is either as quick or as loyal as we would hope. We should have known about this deal before it was concluded.'

The idea that the fellow's loyalty might be to the country of his birth was not one to raise; it may well be he had done the minimum instead of the maximum.

'I'm curious, Noel, where this is leading. I am happy to talk to you about Brno, even if there's not much to say, but I am less so to discuss an operation with anyone not directly connected with it. It would, in fact, be a breach of both confidence and protocol.'

'Do you not see, Peter?' McKevitt replied, rather pedantic in the way he used that expression. 'We have been made to look like fools.'

'We cannot be certain of that; there's no evidence those weapons ever got out of France.'

Maybe it was the drink, maybe the way he was being stalled, but the man lost some of his habitual detachment.

'Christ, we would be a poor Secret Intelligence Service if we relied on evidence. You have admitted you were in La Rochelle on the trail of those bloody machine guns. One phone call to the French would have put the kibosh on any attempt to get them through France, never mind out of the country. Why was that call never made?'

The temptation to ask if he had made any calls around the same time was so hard to resist.

'Now if you did not do that,' McKevitt continued, 'there had to be a motive for it, and I am curious as to what that could be. I am also curious, Peter Lanchester, why a few days after your return from this particular cock-up you are in receipt of a telegram from Prague?'

'That is none of your business.'

'Anything to do with Czechoslovakia is my business and the list of such telegrams and the recipients lands on my desk as a matter of course. What I want is the contents.'

Peter stood up. 'Have you never heard of Chinese walls?'

The tone of the response was icy. 'I'll give you Chinese walls, or maybe they'll be prison walls. I am not a man to mess with, Lanchester, as you may find out, and don't be sure that there is anyone, however high and mighty, who can protect you. There's something going on that I should know about and I intend to find out what it is. Maybe you would like the weekend to think that over.'

'We are all here on sufferance, Noel, including you, but I will pass on to Quex your concerns as to how he runs SIS.'

There was pure devilment in what Peter said next and he had no knowledge of what Quex had been up to.

'And while you are busy monitoring the telegram traffic from Prague don't be surprised to find there are certain communications between London and France that are also under surveillance, by the *Deuxième Bureau* if not by us. I'm wondering if a request to them for certain information would go unacknowledged.'

'You've lost me,' McKevitt replied, his face expressionless.

'I wonder,' Peter barked over his shoulder as he went out of the door.

After a day of endless talking at Downing Street, during which many a bellicose statement had come from the French delegation about standing up to Hitler, meeting more measured assertions from their British counterparts, it was fairly plain to Sir Hugh Sinclair that matters had not moved on one centimetre, never mind an inch; it was all talk and no go.

There had been no time to beard his French counterpart, Colonel Gauché, during the day, both men being too busy advising their own superiors, but as usual there was a formal dinner in the evening and they were seated next to each other, where, conversationally, they competed to see who could most mangle the other's native language.

For all the difficulties that entailed, communication was achieved as they discussed what might come out of the forthcoming gathering of the Nazi bigwigs in Nuremberg. Gauché had a very good intelligence operation in Czechoslovakia – hardly surprising given they were formal allies, with a proper signed treaty and France had bankrolled a lot of the Czech armaments through loans and subsidies – but when it came to Germany the British had the upper hand.

A free flow of shared information was never possible with two intelligence agencies – not even internally did they always cooperate – but within the bounds of mutual jealousies and natural Anglo-Gallic mistrust they did help each other and the Frenchman saw nothing to trouble his conscience in having one of his men examine the records of foreign calls made to such outfits as the *Jeunesses Patriotes*.

'The call,' Sinclair said, '*C'est* from *Angleterre, dans le* middle *de Août.*' Then he flicked a finger over his shoulder. '*Votre* glass *c'est* empty, Colonel.'

The Frenchman replied, but not in words Sinclair was sure he understood; the man was nodding and that would suffice.

While Vince was reading his day-old *News Chronicle* Cal had his nose buried in the freshly delivered German newspapers that had come in on the overnight trains which still ran over the disputed border as though there was no problem. It was one of the features of Prague that you could buy almost any newspaper published in the world if you didn't mind old news.

The Czechs prided themselves on being internationalists, as people with a world view, not a narrowly parochial one, and in the cafés and bars in normal times you could get into a well-informed discussion about what was happening in the four corners of the globe; not now – even the foreign press was full of what was taking place in Bavaria.

If there was a deep fascination, allied to a visceral fear of what the Nazi Party was up to in Nuremberg, it certainly, in Cal's mind, would never extend to the speeches, which were the usual Aryan claptrap mixed with justifications for no freedom, low wages for workers and the need for vigilance against foes, who would be manufactured if they did not exist, all wrapped up in nice language about the beauty of their ideology.

Any discussion about what they might be asked to do had been put to bed; Vince had been reassured that Cal would do nothing without having a good look at any problems first, but he had persuaded his boxing friend that what was on offer might fulfil the requirement of what he had been sent here to do, without the need to cross into Germany. Quite apart from that, if it could be done it was too good to pass up.

When Moravec phoned, Cal was translating some of the more florid and ridiculous bits from the newspapers to Vince in a cod German accent that had them both laughing. The call put an end to that; he advised Cal to take a tram to a station called Geologica for noon, probably chosen, Vince ventured when he looked at the tram routes on his town map, because it was the only one a foreigner could pronounce.

For Cal, having sent off his telegram to London and with a bit of spare time before the rendezvous, it presented a good opportunity to look over their own means of emergency extraction, that ugly Tatra car parked in a side street gathering dust. Having ensured it was untouched, it was back on the busy tram system to the aforementioned station, in his hand his canvas bag containing the information that had arrived the night before.

When they alighted Vaclav was waiting, as if an aspiring tram passenger, but once they had moved away and he had checked no one was following, he spun on his heel and walked quickly to get past them. With all the usual precautions he led them to where Moravec was waiting in a very different vehicle, a limousine; this time Vaclav was the driver.

Naturally the talk turned to what he had sent them and Cal's impression of the information, to which there was only one reply – that it was comprehensive enough to qualify for praise as to the amount of detail, but it did not answer the pertinent question, this while he was vaguely aware, by the position of the sun and the time of day, that having originally travelled south-east they were now heading north in a wide arc around the city.

'I am taking you to meet someone who might answer any questions you have.'

'He is?'

'The man who compiled much of what you were given, as well as the person who is still in charge of the surveillance on Henlein and the SdP.'

They drove on for about an hour out through the suburbs and into a pleasant countryside, leaving the main road for narrower tree-lined avenues, finally turning up a wooded drive and stopping at a farmhouse with a barn big enough to accommodate the car, the doors being closed once it was driven in so it was out of sight of the road.

Vaclav headed off down the drive to keep an eye on the road, Vince opting to follow him and help, knowing that, being unable to understand German, he was likely to be no more than a spectator at any discussion.

Cal and Moravec approached the door of the house, which was opened by an invisible hand, and they entered the darkened interior, progressing through to a sunlit and rustic dining area, full of the tempting smell of cooking, without a word being spoken.

The man they had come to meet could have sat for a poster of the perfect Aryan as seen by those lunatics who prated on about ethnic purity in Germany. He was tall, having several inches on Cal, broad-shouldered, with neat blond hair, piercing blue eyes and chiselled features that extended to a square jaw, as well as being deeply tanned in that bronzed way so loved by the old *Wandervogel* movement.

'Captain Karol Veseli.'

As he said this Moravec took off his hat and threw it on the table, where sat a bottle of plum brandy and several glasses. Compared to this gleaming specimen, the intelligence chief, stocky, his suit crumpled, with his mop of greying hair, weary broad face and tired eyes with heavy bags beneath, looked like he was from another species.

Cal, who without vanity knew he was attractive to the opposite sex, felt he would hate to compete with this bloke for female attention and that was made worse when the sod beamed at him with teeth so white they seemed to flash, before a hand came out to be shaken in a very firm grip.

'A drink, first,' Veseli said, uncorking the bottle and pouring three glasses of clear liquid. 'Then we can talk and finally we will eat.'

Whatever was bubbling on the stove smelt delicious, so that was something to look forward to. With the drink there was, of course, a clink of glasses and a toast to Czechoslovakia, made standing, before the contents were downed in one go. They then arranged themselves around the table, Cal emptying the bag to spread out the files and photos, posing an important question as he did so.

'Where is Henlein?'

'In Cheb during the day and Asch at night.'

'He hasn't gone to Bavaria?'

'No,' Moravec insisted. 'He dare not be seen in Nuremberg. To do so would blow open the fiction that he is acting independently.'

'Before we begin,' Cal asked, now that everything was laid out, 'I need to know if, as I suspect from all this, you suppose what you seek is in Henlein's offices at the Victoria Hotel and not at Frank's headquarters?'

'Yes.'

'To be sure of that you must have someone on the inside?'

The two Czechs exchanged looks but it was Moravec's call and he nodded. 'But we will not reveal the name.'

'Naturally. But is this person in a position to aid any attempt to get to the written details of the invasion and Hitler's instructions?'

It was Veseli who answered. 'To do so would expose the agent, who is able to tell us everything the leadership of the SdP are doing and thinking.'

'So I assume that I would not be given contact with this person?'

'No!' Moravec replied, emphatically.

Cal nodded; he had expected nothing less, because whoever that asset was he looked to be too precious to put at risk even for such a prize. 'Can I ask if you have planned an operation to get hold of these documents?'

'If we were certain that an invasion is imminent,' Veseli said, 'we would use the full power of the state so our police and army can counter the attempts of the Sudetenlanders to carry out the kind of tasks they have been set.'

'Always assuming,' Moravec added in a mordant tone, 'that we have allies in the West to help us fight the German army.'

'So,' Cal asked pedantically, 'is there a fully worked-out plan in place that does not depend on an imminent invasion?'

Moravec paused for several seconds before he replied, Cal thought more for effect than anything else; he wanted it to look as if the answer was being dragged out of him. 'There is.'

'But you cannot carry it out?'

'For the reasons I gave you as we walked around the Jewish cemetery.'

'Is it one that I could execute given the right circumstances?'

'I believe so,' Moravec replied. 'Otherwise I would not have brought you to this place.'

'And if Henlein takes flight, which he is bound to do under the circumstances of German invasion, what then? He would not want to fall into your hands, would he?'

That got two nods.

'So you must have more than just a pre-planned assault on the hotel; there must be one to take him between there and his house, which he might go to on the way, or a place where you could ambush him before he gets to the German border?'

That got Cal a full flashing smile, in truth no more than an acknowledgement that he had discerned the obvious; these people had plans in place for any eventuality.

'Naturally,' Moravec said, 'should the invasion come, our police would storm Henlein's hotel and Frank's Nazi HQ to find evidence of their activities, things that could be shown to the neutral press to increase pressure for their aid. They would not, we think, be able to remove or burn all the files in time and if they did so prematurely that would alert us to the aggressive movements of the German army.'

'You know, you should do it now and tell your president to go to hell.'

'To which he would say, the consequences would bring on that which we most fear. Imagine Hitler's closing speech at Nuremberg on Monday if we do that, and besides, both locations are well defended, Henlein's house less so, but there are plenty of locals in Asch who would come to his aid to fight us, so taking even that would not be easy.'

'Even if you took him by surprise?'

'A difficult thing for a Czech to do when they cannot even get into his hotel if they are local, and no stranger would be allowed entry unless they could prove they were ethnic Germans.'

'Go in numbers?'

'How many? Remember, in Cheb too he is surrounded by his own kind who would be keen to protect him.'

Veseli took over. 'And how can we surprise him when we would need the army to take the place?'

'Understand,' Moravec interjected, 'that apart from manning the defensive emplacements in the borderlands, most of our troops have been withdrawn from the disputed provinces to locations where they pose no threat to the German minority. Left in place it would be too easy for Goebbels to claim the soldiers were committing atrocities.'

'Even the police in Cheb are kept in their station unless an incident occurs they must deal with, and they have strict instructions to stay well away from the Victoria Hotel.'

'I need copies of those ambush plans and I need to go and take a look to see if there is any way that I can implement what you dare not.'

'You need more than that, my friend,' the older Czech replied. 'You need a reason to be there.'

'Understand, sir,' Veseli said, the honorific making Cal wonder to whom he was talking until he realised that in introducing his agent Moravec had not given him any name. 'Cheb is not a large town and it is ninety-ten per cent ethnically German, Asch almost wholly so.'

He paused to make sure Cal understood.

'They are doubly suspicious of strangers at the moment, regardless of their nationality, unless they know why it is they have come there, and given the number of members of the SdP in both places, any outsider would be treated a suspicious person as a matter of course and watched.'

'Presumably, then, you do not go under the name of Karol in Cheb?'

The two other men only exchanged a half a flicker of a look, but it was enough to tell Cal that Karol Veseli was not his real name, but certainly his given one in a Czech-spelt version and, he suspected, if asked to spell it, though it would sound the same, it would read very differently. Given his looks, added to what he had just said about Cheb, it was clear he could not move around there without arousing suspicion unless he was a long-term resident himself.

Cal knew something about small towns, having spent four years before the World War in a Scottish one and found himself an outsider to people who knew each other from their very first day at school right through to their places of work. Without those connections it was hard to discover who was cousin to whom and to understand all the local matters that constituted old enmities and long-standing grudges.

In such places you watched the generations come and depart, caught sight of the same faces in their main streets, shops and events, as well as seeing your fellow citizens procreate and age. Captain Karol Veseli, or whatever he was called, to do what he did in such a community, had to be either wholly or partly an ethnic German and he certainly looked like one.

So it was a fair bet he was a 'traitor' to his own kind, or a Czech patriot, depending on which side of the divide you occupied. Whatever, he was playing a very dangerous game in which there was only one price for exposure and it would not be just a bullet;

discovered, he would be ripped limb from limb.

'I doubt we would be sitting here if you did not have some notion of how we can visit there and move around freely.'

'Last night you were observed dining with an American female journalist,' Moravec ventured, his tone cautious. 'A Miss Corrine Littleton.'

There was no point in Cal asking how he knew her and her occupation; it was his job to know and Moravec already knew he and Vince had been followed to the restaurant. Question: did her job have a bearing on that card being dropped on the table? Had that been part of a jigsaw Moravec was toying with?

Cal knew also enough about intelligence work to realise that a lot of what went on was manipulation and he wondered if that was what he was being subjected to now. He had come to Prague looking for facts about dissent in Germany and now he was being edged in another direction entirely, not that it made much difference if the end result was the same.

'How well are you acquainted with the lady?' While Cal was considering how to reply to that, Moravec added, 'You seemed to be friendly from what was observed—'

That's all you know, Cal thought.

'—much more so than the men with whom she drinks in the hotel bar.' That got the older Czech a look of deep curiosity, to which he responded, 'The barman, who has good English, observes that they treat her with little respect, that if they are kind, they talk down to her.'

'Because she's a woman?'

'No, because she drinks little, but more because she lacks experience.' That was followed by a sardonic smile. 'You will know that such men have been in many places and seen many wars and perhaps they drink so much to forget what it is they have seen. To them our troubles are just another crisis. They are, I suspect, full of cynicism.'

Cal had met many a war correspondent in his travels, more recently in Madrid, and that was a description which entirely suited them; they drank like fish, would roger anything female that moved and looked willing, while they took not a word they were told at face value for the very good reason they had heard it all before.

'But your Miss Littleton is not that, which might make her perfect for what we have in mind.'

'For some time now,' Veseli cut in, before Cal could nail that statement, 'it has been suggested to Konrad Henlein that he should cease to avoid the international press, that he should stop hiding away in his hotel suite and grant an interview to a selected journalist from the democracies to insist he wants peace. What better time could there be than now, when the trumpets are blaring in Nuremberg?'

The person who would be pressing for that could be the agent they had in place, whoever he was.

'He will not countenance, naturally, a French or British publication, but an American one he is less troubled by, given there is a large German population in the USA to whom he would like to be able to speak and who could be counted on to put pressure on the US Government to give consideration to his aims.'

'Or,' Moravec said bitterly, 'his lies.'

'I take it he has agreed.'

'I think such an opportunity would please a young lady American journalist, don't you?' Moravec replied softly. 'And I can say a request would be received favourably from such a person.'

Cal recalled what Corrie had said about the borderlands being hard to get into without a police escort and the frustration that was causing her.

'I think any one of them would trip over themselves to get an interview with Henlein, especially if it was not the whole pack.' For some reason the thought of the way her peers were treating Corrie annoyed him. 'And for Miss Littleton it would be one in the eye to all those fellows you say are patronising her.'

'"Exclusive",' Moravec said in English, 'they call it, I think.'

'But she has been told she cannot go there without being escorted by the police. I can't see Henlein agreeing to having a Czech policeman present while he's interviewed.'

'Naturally,' Veseli added with a grave expression, 'for a woman journalist to travel to a dangerous part of our country alone would not be wise, and you are right that Henlein would not accept that anyone from the Republic should escort her . . .'

'But two British nationals?'

'No, we had in mind one only,' Veseli said. 'To drive her, look after her welfare and, of course, interpret.'

Moravec took up the baton. 'You can, after all, easily do such a thing for her.'

He was not about to respond to that right away, so it took several seconds, while he was under close scrutiny, before he nodded at the logic; she would have to have an interpreter and some kind of bodyguard would be wise, but how could that be squared with the local police?

'That, I think, can be arranged,' Moravec said, 'by my talking to

Colonel Doležal, while to Henlein, to lift such a requirement at his request would only look like the kind of Czech collaboration he now takes for granted.'

'You think we would be free to move around?'

'It would be part of the arrangements,' Veseli said, with such assurance Cal wondered if he was the inside man. 'Anything written about the area must include an impression of what it is like for the ordinary people, though not Czechs, and it would be unwise to approach the many social democrats who live there. That would cause Henlein unease.'

'And he would know, because?'

'You will be followed wherever you go.'

'I would need a car and a good one to befit my supposed occupation.' He was thinking of that Tatra he had bought, which was not the kind of vehicle to turn up in. 'And it can't be anything belonging to the Czech state.'

'A suitable one can be hired.'

'There's only one problem that I can see, quite apart from being unhappy without my own man or anyone else to back me up. Corrie Littleton would have to know what I am trying to do.'

Moravec waved a finger in dismissal. 'You tell your lady friend that through your contacts you have been able to arrange her a meeting with Henlein. She will, I think, be too excited about that to press home questions you do not want to answer about how it was arranged.'

'One thing I should tell you, Colonel Moravec – you are talking of a lady who knows what I do for a living and is already curious about what I am up to in Prague.'

'Ah! She is not, as you would say, a paramour?' Cal actually laughed, which brought forth two frowns to tell him how inappropriate that reaction was in such a serious situation. 'It was said to me she might be, given the lady is not married.'

Vaclav must have watched them for a while and observed their animated conversation, while Moravec had done his digging about Corrie Littleton, and they had come to a conclusion that was at total odds with the facts.

Right now he was not committed to anything, nor would he ever have been without he had surveyed the ground. What was on offer was a way to accomplish what he had come to Prague for, but regardless of what Moravec said – and surely he must know it even if he did not want to admit it – Corrie would have to be in on the deal to some extent.

'The only question that lacks an answer is what you are doing in Czechoslovakia.'

'I have certain documents, papers from a good friend, to cover that, both here and in Germany. In them it will tell anyone who asks that I am on the lookout for trade opportunities in chemicals.'

Moravec was impressed, but troubled. 'I had in mind a disguise for you as a German national.'

'I can't see the necessity, but there is one other thing: I am not armed and I don't like the idea of being in bandit country without the means to defend myself.'

It was Veseli – or whatever his name was – who replied. 'You cannot travel with weapons, it is too risky given our police might search your car, but maybe they can be discreetly provided when you get to Cheb.'

'Fine.'

'You must get Miss Littleton to send a telegram to Henlein's press office at the Victoria Hotel asking for an interview and stating her credentials, while also insisting that she wants to give him and the cause he leads a fair hearing.'

'She will ask to come to Cheb with her own interpreter,' Veseli continued, 'and give your name and the nature of your business.'

'They will refuse unless she comes unescorted, and once that is granted by us, they will next seek to get her to come alone, but if she declines they will back down.'

There was no point in asking how Veseli knew all this, but Cal suspected he was running whatever agent they had in place, if he was not himself that person.

'Miss Littleton has not had her accreditation from the Interior Ministry.'

'That will be seen to.'

'Then it only remains for me to talk to her.'

'Time to eat,' Moravec said, showing a relish wholly at odds with his normal demeanour; clearly he was either a man who liked his grub or Cal's agreement had relieved him of the worry of a refusal.

As they ate – a very tasty lamb stew Veseli had prepared – they talked. Cal was only partly engaged in the general conversation, mostly background to where he was going and the people who mattered there, while he also had to consider the likelihood of anyone in the Czech borderlands knowing him – unlikely given he had operated in Hamburg.

Still, it would be a good idea to subtly alter his appearance, which could be done in small ways – the wearing of glasses, a different type of hat and even a haircut, though there was no time to grow a moustache.

Eventually, when the light of the day was fading, it was necessary to say farewell to Veseli and return to Prague. A lot of his thinking, in the back of the car, was how long it was going to take him to compose another telegram to Peter Lanchester outlining what he was about to do.

Also, if he was going to involve Corrie Littleton he would have to talk to her, and the sooner the better.

CHAPTER SIXTEEN

N oel McKevitt and Sir Thomas Inskip were not, in the strict sense, friends; the social milieus in which they moved were too far apart but they did share a certain philosophy, which made their conversation of more import than mere gossip. First of all they were united in their staunch Protestant faith – the vicar of their local church had introduced them – and secondly Sir Thomas had at one time been part of the intelligence community, which to McKevitt meant he was reliable.

Such an occupation had long been left behind by the older man; Inskip, a high-flying lawyer by profession, was a member of the Government, having been given by Stanley Baldwin, the previous incumbent of Number 10, the office of Minister of Defence Procurement, this despite the generally held opinion that he possessed a staggering degree of military ignorance.

Churchill, who had lobbied for the creation of what was, in effect, a minister for rearmament, had expected the job would be given to him. Baldwin thought differently; he had no desire to have someone so bellicose in his government, quite apart from the signal such an appointment would send to the dictator states he was determined to mollify.

Once deprived and Inskip appointed, a furious Churchill, with his usual facility for the killer phrase, had called it 'The most cynical appointment since Caligula made his horse a consul.'

Inskip's other trait was a blind loyalty to the serving prime minister, which manifested itself as strong support in the Cabinet for the policy of appeasement. Having lost ministerial office once in the National Government landslide at the start of the decade, Sir Thomas was not about to act in a way that would find himself out in the cold again, and it had to be said his aims were honourable.

Though he had never been a front-line soldier, he harboured, along with many of his contemporaries in age and experience, a horror of a repeat of the blind slaughter of 1914–18, the evidence of which, in maimed ex-soldiers, widows and unmarried women, was still very obvious even after all these years, a subject he had laboured long the night before at the Downing Street dinner for the French delegation.

In some sense Sir Thomas had helped to form McKevitt's thinking on Czechoslovakia, a country he had insisted was impossible for Britain and France to defend, an opinion he was willing to share with anyone who would listen, and who should be more inclined to do so than the man appointed by the head of MI6 to oversee matters in that country?

'Mark my words, Noel,' Inskip had pronounced after church one day. 'If we seek to aid that country we will end up with stalemate and a repeat of the Western Front, with all the death such a futile exercise

224

produced. I would not sacrifice a single soldier for such a policy and thankfully neither will the PM.'

McKevitt did not question Sir Thomas's assertion, he took it as fact, assuming, which was quite natural, that a man who spent much of his time with soldiers, seamen and airmen discussing their needs, with a quite brilliant legal brain, had been given a bona fide opinion by those who would have to execute such a course of action.

Yet it was also the case that McKevitt saw war as predictable; you could not hold the Berlin Desk and watch the rise to power of the Nazis without accepting that conclusion. In Hitler's *magnum opus* he demanded *Lebensraum* for the German people. If one nation needed to expand it could only be at the expense of another.

In addition, and this had been his primary intelligence target, within the higher reaches of the German General Staff it was a common gossip that another war was inevitable, with the date of 1945 almost pencilled in as the time at which they reasoned Germany would be ready both economically and militarily to confront their old foes.

If it was to come, then McKevitt was of the opinion it should be when Britain was ready for it, perhaps with the Americans as allies. In the meantime Hitler needed to be diverted to the east and as far as the Ulsterman was concerned he could go as far as he wanted in that direction.

Yet it was axiomatic that the department for which he worked would have to expand dramatically over the next few years to confront a range of emerging dangers and McKevitt had enough personal arrogance to see himself as ideally suited to head the more powerful entity.

Sir Hugh Sinclair had been good in his time but he was now sixty-five and must be nearing retirement, so when he was worried about being sidelined in a way that obviously diminished his standing, it was quite natural to call at Inskip's office and express his concerns.

'Sir Hugh is up to something in my backyard, Sir Thomas.'

'I judge by your tone you have no idea what that is?'

'While I see my superior as deserving of my respect, sir, I am also a servant of the government of the day, and what concerns me is that he is stepping outside his brief of support for the declared policy and at a very dangerous time.'

That had no need to be mentioned; even the proponents of the 'policy' were becoming uncomfortable with the word 'appeasement', which had originally been coined as a description of the need to satisfy the legitimate concerns of the dictator states. In a couple of years it had morphed into a means, in too many minds, to let them do whatever they wished to avoid conflict.

'Deliberately so?'

'We occupy a murky arena, Sir Thomas, so I would not wish to be so specific. But if my concern is genuine I have no means of finding out the truth. Right now I believe he might be colluding with the Government of Czechoslovakia to produce some rabbit that will force our country into an anomalous position.'

That too required no spelling out; the press, with the exception of the *Daily Mail* and *The Observer*, was split on appeasement, with even *The Times* occasionally posing awkward editorial questions, while the public mood was febrile and uncertain. In the social circles in which Sir Thomas moved – his club, his legal chambers and the drawing rooms of people of property – it had unqualified support.

But out in the country, certainly in the industrial north, the mood was not, by the accounts he was receiving, the same. His position involved him in visiting the factories and workshops where armaments were being designed and produced, an unpleasant task to a man as fastidious as he but one that could not be avoided. Even some of the military officers he was obliged to deal with were beginning to voice doubts.

'If he is engaged in such a venture, Noel, then he is exceeding his brief. Are you sure he is not just seeking information in the normal manner?'

'If he was doing that in Central Europe, Sir Thomas, he would go through me.'

Inskip nodded slowly; oversight of the intelligence service was outside his responsibilities but he knew who to talk to. 'I shall have a word with the Home Secretary.'

'I wonder,' McKevitt advanced gently, 'if it might also be wise to alert the prime minister?'

Quick to see a way to underline his loyalty, while not willing to appear to be guided by the man to whom he was talking, Inskip, the highly paid and quick-witted barrister, produced a ready answer. 'An idea I had already considered, Noel. If what you say is true, Neville will be incandescent.'

'Would you wish me to act as a conduit, sir?'

That involved a look into the Ulsterman's eye, which was steady, as it should be for a man seeking in no way to hide his own hopes and ambitions, this while Sir Thomas Inskip was wondering if such an association and the information it could produce would help him to where he wanted to go, to one of the great offices of state in the gift of the prime minister: the Exchequer, the FO or the position of Home Secretary.

'It can do no harm,' he nodded. 'I will instruct my civil servants that, should you call me on the telephone, you are to be put through to me on my private line. Now, if you will forgive me, Noel, I must dash – I'm invited to lunch at Cliveden by Lady Astor.'

McKevitt thought that a perfect way to tell him they were very different people; Sir Thomas Inskip thought so too.

'Hey, Doc, I ran into a friend of yours down the Jewish Emigration Centre yesterday, nice kid called Elsa. Went kind of weak at the knees when I mentioned you, like she had a crush on you or something.'

That strident greeting, said in a loud and carrying voice, turned every head in the lobby of the Ambassador Hotel, busy with all sorts of folk; for a man who liked to be discreet it was anathema.

'Do you ever talk softly, Corrie?'

'Only when I carry a big stick.'

The arm was taken with the same force as previously and Corrie Littleton found herself propelled to a quieter corner of the hotel, an act that did nothing to diminish the interest of the other folk present.

'Is that how you got pretty little Elsa out of the cradle?'

'We're just good friends.'

'Well we're not, so ease off with the third degree.'

'Sit down and shut up, Corrie, and listen to what I have to say to you.'

'That adds up to three things I don't want to do, buster!'

He had to drop his voice. 'But you would like a trip to the Sudetenland, wouldn't you?'

About to produce a scathing response, she must have seen in his look that he was serious; she sat down quickly and he joined her. 'You on the level?'

'Better than that, Corrie, I think I can get you an interview with Konrad Henlein.'

'Early morning and you're drunk already! That guy hasn't given an interview to a non-German newspaper for two years and the last one, from what I hear, was one of your Brits called Ward Price who the guys tell me is a Nazi himself and a prize shit.'

'He works for a bigger one called Rothermere.'

'What the hell, we've got Charles Lindbergh.'

Cal knew she was stalling. 'Henlein is holed up in the Victoria Hotel in Cheb and if you put in a request for an interview it will be positively received. Do you want that I should go find another journalist to offer this to?'

That shut her up; there was nothing like professional rivalry to achieve her silence.

'I am talking about just you and him, an exclusive, as well as a look around the town and Henlein's home base in Asch, with maybe the chance to talk to the locals, and me along to interpret and make sure you don't get yourself shot by some ardent Nazi thug.'

'No cops?'

'No.'

'Why?'

'Don't you mean why you?'

'No, Doc, I mean "why?" You might come across as all charm, Cal Jardine, but you are one devious son of a bitch.'

'I've always admired your command of the English language.'

'One of these days I'll give you my personal dictionary, but right now I would like to know what is in this for you.'

'Typical, you try to do someone a favour—'

229

'Cal, I don't give a goddam what you are up to, I just want to know what it is that you get out of this offer.'

He had known he was never going to get away without an explanation, but he had enjoyed guying her a little. 'Care to go for a walk?'

'What's wrong with right here?'

Thinking of Snuffly Bower and his paranoia, Cal replied, 'Lip-readers.'

As they exited the hotel, to a salute from the liveried doorman and a look that asked if they wanted a cab, Corrie spotted Vince Castellano and her body movement presaged a greeting.

'Don't say hello,' Cal whispered, 'Vince will follow us.'

'To?'

'To make sure nobody else does, or gets too close to hear what I am going to say.'

'Part of me is saying I should get my arm out from yours and walk away.'

'But the other part is screaming "story", yes?'

They walked several paces before she answered. 'So, shoot.'

'I need to go up there to do a bit of a recce. Don't ask why or what because I won't tell you, on the very good grounds that it is best you don't know.'

Expecting an objection Cal was surprised she remained silent; maybe learning to be a journalist had cured her of shooting from the lip.

'You will have your accreditation by tomorrow and I will drive us both to Cheb, where you will be taken to meet Konrad Henlein for a full interview at his headquarters.'

'What's the angle?' Cal explained about Henlein's aim of appealing to the likes of the American German Bund. 'They're Nazis, Cal, and on his side already.'

'He also wants to get his message across to the other Germans in the USA. It's a big community and it might get him a better hearing in Washington.'

'Depends what I write.' That was both true and significant; Corrie had gone from doubtful to committed. 'How the hell did you arrange this and who the hell did you set it up with?'

That he ignored. 'He won't speak to the press from the other democracies and I doubt he would be happy with any of the big American names who are over here and have already made their positions plain.'

'Whereas?'

'You are an unknown quantity.'

'You're avoiding the question.'

'Let's just say I know the right people, have a job to do and I will be travelling as your chosen escort and interpreter under a false identity.'

'Jesus.'

'Look, I am a guy you have never met before until you arrived in Prague, but we got along.' He outlined what she had to do to get a response, which he assured her would be positive even if she insisted on her own German-speaker being present. 'And it might be a good idea when we get there to let them think we are lovers.'

'I think this is where I bale out,' she snapped, in the manner of the girl he knew so well.

'This is your chance to do so,' he replied, determined she should know he was serious. 'Once we're committed you will have to live with whatever lie suits.'

'You mean I might be interrogated.'

'Meaning you are going to be in amongst people who are suspicious as hell and they will probe you, your motives and your connection to me. And as for pretence, you are going to have to act like you have some sympathy for what Hitler is trying to do. It's the only way you'll get the story you want.'

'I get to write what I think?'

'You get to come back to Prague and file, which, once it appears in your magazine, should make all those guys you drink with in the bar, who think you are a novice, want to cut your throat.'

'You been watching me?'

'Not me.'

'People you know?' He nodded. 'One question, why are you doing what you're doing?'

'The idea is to keep whole the country we're in and stop a German invasion. If I can do what I want, it may be possible to get Britain and France to stand up to Hitler.'

That made her ponder, but in reality it could only be one of two things: he was either acting for those he had worked for in Ethiopia or the Czechs themselves. She knew what he thought about Fascism, given she had heard him talk about it too many times to be in doubt about his feelings.

'Look, there is danger in this, I won't lie to you, but it is more to me than to you. In a sticky spot you can always claim you were deceived about me, wave your press credentials and scream for the American ambassador.'

'How do we get to this Cheb?'

'I told you, by car, which I will drive.'

'Long journey?'

'Depends on checkpoints and things I don't know about. Could be four hours, could be ten.'

'When do we leave?'

'As soon as we get the go-ahead. You happy with what you've been told?'

'Like hell I am, but if I'm going to be sitting in a car with you for all that time I guess it will give me a chance to grill you properly.'

'My real name and what I am up to is off-limits and I need your word on that.'

That made her stop walking and look up at him and there was a note in her distinctive cracked voice, deeper that usual. 'You telling me, Doc, that you would accept my word?'

How do you say to someone, *I know what you are made of; I have seen you embrace danger and a cause when you could have walked away; struggle through tents full of the dead and dying doing a job for which you had no training and do it superbly; that, in fact, for all the sparring we indulge in, you are admirable?*

'Corrie,' Cal replied, 'you might be a pain in the backside but you're an honest pain in the backside, so if you give me your word I know you will keep it.'

'Boy, are you a master of the compliment.'

'Do we have a deal?'

They had walked ten paces before the answer came, which pleased Cal; he did want her to think it through.

'We do. Do I wait to hear from Henlein?'

'Yes, but I will know the response before you do.' That got raised eyebrows. 'Pack a small bag and be ready to go at a moment's notice, but don't call down for a porter or say anything to the hotel desk. I will call you on the internal phone and you can carry it down

233

yourself. And try to stay out of sight of any of your colleagues, who are bound to ask where you are going if they see luggage.'

She giggled. 'Mata Hari lives.'

'Corrie, this is not funny. If anyone does spot you and asks, say you're going to check up and try to get a story on the plight of those Jews seeking to get out over the Rumanian border.'

CHAPTER SEVENTEEN

The summons for Sir Hugh Sinclair to attend a private meeting at 10 Downing Street with the prime minister was uncommon indeed – he normally briefed the Home Secretary – so much so that it engendered in him a desire to know what was going on before he obeyed the summons.

So he telephoned next the First Lord of the Admiralty, Duff Cooper, who was a member of Chamberlain's Cabinet, albeit one who was vocally unhappy with the present policy, though only in private conversation. That required Cooper to make some enquiries before ringing back.

'Neville thinks you are up to something, Quex.'

'It's my job to be up to something, Freddy.'

'I can't be certain, but I think Inskip has been whispering in Neville's ear that you are acting against Government policy.'

'Indeed. No details I suppose?'

'Sorry, old chap, can't oblige.'

'Thanks anyway, Freddy.'

'Be just like being had up before the beak, I shouldn't wonder.' That was followed by a laugh from a man who did that a lot. 'And what a beak.'

When Sir Hugh arrived in Downing Street it was to see fishing rods being loaded into the back of the PM's Humber, along with a basket for his catch, making the head of SIS wonder how anyone could call standing flicking his rod by a riverbank at this time of trouble correct behaviour. When he was shown into the Cabinet room it was to find the PM dressed in tweeds and plus fours, obviously ready for departure.

Normally in a wing collar and black coat, such country apparel did not improve Neville Chamberlain's appearance; he was still the pigeon-chested fellow of caricature, tall with his slight stoop and that vulture-like face dominated by dark heavy eyebrows over the nose about which Duff Cooper had made his jest.

The only person present was his newly appointed cabinet secretary, Edward Bridges, so fresh to the job that he took no part in the conversation; surprisingly he took no minutes either as Chamberlain began to speak in that rather high voice of his, not, Quex noted, while looking him in the eye.

'Sir Hugh, I would like your latest appreciation of the state of affairs over the Sudetenland.'

'I briefed the Home Secretary only two days ago, sir.'

'I'm well aware of that; has anything altered in the meantime to change your opinion of events?'

'No, sir, I fear that Lord Runciman's mission is mired in intractability, that whatever President Beneš offers will be rejected and that the whole of Henlein's campaign is being orchestrated from Berlin.'

'You have taken no unusual steps in Czechoslovakia that would fall across the line of Government policy?'

'No, Prime Minister, and neither would I contemplate such a course.'

'Matters are coming to a head, Sir Hugh, perhaps as soon as Herr Hitler's leader's speech at Nuremberg. I want nothing between now and that occasion to in any way give the German Chancellor or the leadership of the Sudeten German Party cause for concern. It could be, in short, turned into a flashpoint from which things would either be said or done from which even the best intentions could never recover.'

'Do you have any specific instructions, sir?'

'Only that your task is to support the elected government.'

'As always.'

Only then did Chamberlain look directly at him and there was nothing benign in his eye.

'Your car is waiting, sir,' Bridges said, failing to disguise that he had been instructed to remind his boss, in short, to curtail the exchange as soon as the PM had issued what amounted to a warning.

'Ah yes. Do you fish, Sir Hugh?'

'Sad to say, only in troubled waters, Prime Minister.'

'They can be smoothed by application, but not by anyone acting in excess of their instructions.'

What had been said to him and by whom? There was no point in asking with the beak nose bobbing in dismissal. As he exited the heavy door Quex was tempted to look at the watch he wore in his waistcoat, to let Chamberlain know that he had dragged him up from Victoria for an interview that had lasted all of two to three minutes and that in consequence he was annoyed to be treated worse than a servant; he did not do it from a lifetime's habit of concealing his emotions.

Making his way down Whitehall and then across Parliament Square and along Millbank, with the tip of his unnecessary brolly beating out an increasingly angered tattoo on the pavement, it did not take long to nail the potential culprit who had engineered this event but the question remained as to what to do about it.

If it was McKevitt, then he was entitled to his concerns about policy; Quex did not run a dictatorship but an organisation that had ample room for the free airing of views, even of dissent.

But the protocol was that such a thing was internal, it was not to be taken outside the walls and if the Ulsterman had done so it was not merely because he disagreed but that he had another motive, and given his ambition was close to an open secret, that did not take long to arrive at either.

Still ruminating on that, he returned to his office to find the latest telegram transcript from Peter Lanchester, which told him what was being planned in Czechoslovakia, which in order to approve meant all he had to do was nothing. Was it the right policy to pursue?

In a very acute sense it went right against what he had just been told by the PM – it was active when Chamberlain wanted passivity and if the truth emerged it would not be a warning he would be given but the door.

Two problems combined in one solution: he needed to check the machinations of McKevitt, keep the operation that Lanchester had alerted him to in progress while ensuring if it all went tits up the blame lay squarely at another door. The finger was soon on the intercom buzzer to his secretary.

'Ask Noel McKevitt to come and see me, would you, as soon as he has a moment free?'

Translated that meant 'immediately' and was taken as such by the recipient. McKevitt knew that Inskip had passed on his concerns, just as he knew their knowledge of each other and shared interests were well known.

That meant Quex was going to be hauled in and told to mind his p's and q's on Czecho and he had enough respect for the man to think it would not take his boss long to unearth the connection; the call from the top floor told him he already had.

He was thus well prepared to face Sir Hugh Sinclair's wrath with the certain knowledge that he was fireproof – there was no way he could be sanctioned for merely doing his job and if he was it would go all the way back up to Downing Street; the man under threat was the man he was going to see.

'Noel, nice of you to respond so quickly. Do take a pew.' As his backside hit the chair, Quex followed up that jolly greeting. 'I've just had an interesting chat with the PM.'

'Really,' McKevitt replied, putting as much marvel into the tone as he could and also wondering why the old man's secretary had stayed in the office, taking a chair well away from the discussion.

'Aye, he's worried about Czecho – and who can blame him, what?'

Beware of the cat that smiles, McKevitt was thinking, for if the old man was not actually grinning his tone was too jocular for what he had just gone through.

'Wants nothing to upset the apple cart,' Quex continued, 'and as I pointed out to him, that will not be easy, what with the Hun stirring things up. Look what they did to Kendrick in Vienna.'

And what, McKevitt thought, *has that got to do with the price of coal?*

'He fears an incident that will somehow compromise his sterling efforts to sustain the peace. What chance do you think there is of something cropping up in, say, Prague, that the Germans could exploit?'

The temptation to say 'You would know better than I' was one that had to be suppressed.

But he was not going to give this old sod the answer he wanted, which was that such a scenario was unlikely, so that, at some future date and backed by the testimony of his secretary, he could openly claim to have asked for a reassurance only to find it not forthcoming. Best seek to be non-committal, not definite, opaque.

'Sure, if they tried anything, it might be there all right.'

'Exactly my point to the PM, they may attempt a repeat of what happened to Captain Kendrick.'

'Prague is not Vienna, sir.' Presented with a chance to be sarcastic he was not about to pass it up. 'The Gestapo has, as far as I'm aware, no power of arrest there.'

'True, but any accusation that excessive numbers of our chaps *in situ*, and you know the numbers better than I, are involved in using their skills to aid the Czechs might appear in the German papers at any time.'

'I felt that more muscle was needed there, sir; it is after all the present hot spot in my area of responsibility and it could impact on its neighbours.'

'And very apposite that was to move more men in, but how will the Hun see it? What if they publicise the number of our Prague agents in the same way they splashed on Kendrick, with the added information that the establishment has increased threefold. Shipping in more bodies might come back to haunt us, and even if it's untrue what they claim, the mud, the PM fears, might stick and, I have to tell you, he was even more alarmed to hear we had reinforced the station recently, thus increasing such a risk.'

'I considered it worth an extra effort to keep the Government informed.'

'And, my dear chap,' Quex cried, 'it was a brilliant ploy at the time, which I told the PM.'

'But not now?'

'No, it now involves a risk Mr Chamberlain does not want to take! With his agreement I've decided to pull out all our chaps in Prague, including those you have shipped in from other stations. They, of course, can go back to their previous posts.'

The thought could not be avoided: *he's heard about my request to search for new arrivals and he wants to put the mockers on it to give his man, and now I am convinced there is one in place, a free run.*

'Only it has to be done with maximum discretion, Noel, and we cannot risk even a coded cipher. So I want you to go to Prague yourself and close down the operations there. It must not, I repeat not, be revealed to either the press or the Germans that we have done so.'

'To ensure discretion will take time. Embassy folk have wagging tongues.'

'Yes, it will, though shipping the extras back should be straightforward.'

'When do you want me to go?'

'I would have thought soonest done soonest mended, wouldn't

you? You can go in on a diplomatic passport, so I would like you to drop everything else and travel as soon as you can.'

McKevitt made a good fist of looking thoughtful, but he had come to one conclusion while Quex was still talking. 'It might be best to get everyone out as soon as possible, over a day or two, including the regulars, and stay around to clear up anything outstanding myself.'

'Good thinking, I'm sure with you there any risks will be sealed down tight.'

Making his way back to his own office, McKevitt was nearly laughing. The old man had just handed him the keys to unlock his suspicions and, while he was there, he would find out what was going on and put a stop to it, but not before he had laid at the door of those who needed to know the truth that Sir Hugh Sinclair was not only losing his touch, he was actively thwarting the policy of those who employed him.

Odd that Quex was happy too, for Jardine, by the time McKevitt got there, would be long gone from Prague and the Ulsterman had no way of connecting anything to him, doubly so given he was travelling under an assumed name.

The man might seek to stir things up but that would only play into Quex's hands, and if it all went up in the air and an incident did occur, how could he carry the can for anything, when the head of the relevant section was on site and in control?

For all Veseli's certainties it was an anxious two days and a testing exchange of telegrams before on the Saturday morning the invitation came from Henlein's press office to say the visit was on and that two rooms were waiting for Corrie in the Victoria Hotel.

Moravec phoned Cal to confirm, again without using either his name or hers, that Corrie would be given full access to the SdP leader on the Sunday. Cal then called the Ambassador Hotel and alerted Corrie that he was on his way and for her to be ready to move.

Throwing economy to the winds – it was Moravec's money after all – Cal had hired a really luxurious and very powerful German-made car, a dark-green Maybach Zeppelin with a soft top, a V12 engine and a top speed that exceeded a hundred miles an hour if you had the courage to push it hard.

It was also a very weighty car which, apart from a tank, would smash to bits anything it hit – if he had to run he wanted to do so in something hard to catch and impossible to knock off course. He had also bought a good camera, a long lens and several rolls of film, as well as a hunting knife which he would just leave in the car to be found if anyone wanted to search; hiding it would only make it seem suspicious.

'I like the bins,' Vince said, when Cal tried on the pair of rimless spectacles he'd bought. 'You'll look a bit like Himmler now you've got your barnet cut short.'

Cal ran a hand across his now-short red-gold hair, then nodded to the telegram he had compiled for Peter Lanchester, lying by the open book of short stories.

'I don't know why I bother with coding messages. I could get you to telephone Peter and talk to him in cockney.'

'Only one problem, guv, he wouldn't understand a bleeding word I was saying to him.'

'True, I struggle enough.'

Cal had begun splitting the notes in his money belt; half he would leave with Vince and the rest he would take. His friend had a simple way of keeping the currencies separate: they went into different pockets.

'You say you're going to get tooled up when you get to this place.'

'That's the deal, I've asked for a Mauser.'

'A bloke doing the job you're supposed to be at would not carry a shooter.'

'He's about to become a reformed character.'

'One who's out on a very long limb, guv, and as for involving Corrie, well . . .' The undertone of what Vince was saying came down to the fact that he was unhappy about being left behind. 'She's a game bird, but this might be pushing it a bit.'

'She will have instructions to dump me if I'm exposed, say that I used her.'

'Corrie won't do that, guv.'

'Why not?'

'Because,' Vince replied with slow deliberation, 'she fancies you.'

'Rubbish. I've got to send that telegram to London,' Cal responded, ducking the implications of that statement. 'I'll get dressed, then let's get my own bag packed and into the car.'

'You taking all the documents?'

Vince was referring to those hidden in the Tatra.

'No point, and if they were found they would only get the noses sniffing for more. You sure of what to do if the balloon goes up?'

'How many times do you want me to tell you?'

Vince had instructions, if the emergency was so dire as to be irresolvable, to think only of himself, to go to the Jewish Emigration Centre and find Elsa Ephraim, using Cal's name and that of Monty Redfern – she would know how to get him out to safety if he could not use either of his own passports, and given the money he was holding there was always bribery.

'Just as long as you remember not to try and come and get me.'

Leaving his backup man in Prague was essential to maintaining that vital link with London, and the temptation to move him closer to the place where Cal would be operating had to be put to one side. There was still a deep nervousness about leaks or even active disruption from the offices of MI6 and nothing Peter Lanchester had sent so far indicated such a threat had been either positively identified or neutralised.

There would have been more alarm had it been known that a man from the Prague station, one of those brought in from Bucharest, was trawling the hotels with a Czech interpreter for a list of guests from the United Kingdom, with an emphasis on those newly arrived; an attempt to save time by checking the flight manifests of the Czech airline, the quickest way in, had been rudely rebuffed.

Having been at it for two days and starting with the luxury places, it was Saturday before he got to the Meran, and he and his man entered just as Cal and Vince exited carrying the canvas bag.

The Czech made for the desk, the MI6 man standing back, where he went through the routine of being jolly with the man at reception, agreeing that times were bad for everybody except those with rooms to let, before asking if there were any people staying who might need his services as an English interpreter.

That was not an absurd thing to ask; Czech was a Slavic language that only the locals spoke and even then it broke down into several dialects and that was before you got to Slovak, Ruthenian and Hungarian.

It had no international presence, so that any visitor from any country, especially Britain and those with Latin-derived tongues, struggled to get the bus or tram, never mind do business; even fellow Slavs from neighbouring countries would have to strive hard to be understood.

The reply he got, that of the only two British guests staying, one, a Mr Barrowman, certainly spoke fluent German, was responded to with initial disappointment, though he did ask about the other, only to be told the receptionist had never exchanged a word with him, but he could if he had to – thankfully he spoke a bit of English and French.

'Been here long, have they, 'cause they might have picked up a bit of Czech?'

'A week . . . or was it Tuesday they checked in? Not sure.'

'Been here before?'

'No, they made the reservation from London, though by telegram, so they must know Prague well.'

'Still, friend,' the interpreter said, pacing out his questions so that it did not seem like an interrogation. 'Even German might not be enough if they are here to do business, eh? Are they businessmen? Would you give them my card if I left one?'

The receptionist shrugged and accepted the proffered card; there was no harm in it and his interpreter visitor bade him a hearty farewell, then walked out onto the street followed by his MI6 employer, who listened to what the Czech had been told.

He reckoned this pair fitted the bill more than any of the other names he had turned up, not that he knew, apart from finding British passport holders with no known reasons for being here, precisely what the bill was. Still, it was not his job to decide that – such a task fell to the station chief – and he had many more places to check.

'OK, Miklos, on with the motley, what!'

Miklos had studied hard and reckoned himself a good English speaker, but as he watched his employer head off he wondered what the hell he had just said.

There was one thing Cal had forgotten to cover and that was because he was not in the same profession as Corrie Littleton. A good journalist never goes anywhere, and especially to somewhere dangerous, without telling the person who employs them, in her case her editor in New York, and nor would she go off without leaving a forwarding address.

That was a telegram she composed on her account at the hotel because the first thing a journalist learns is never to spend their own money and never be entirely truthful about your expense account either, because spare cash is not only handy, it can be essential for both work and pleasure; you cannot, for instance, submit a chit for sexual gratification in some foreign whorehouse.

Some of those males she drank with sparingly in the bar of the Ambassador were given to visiting such places and were not deterred by a female presence from mentioning it. They were also, to a man, experienced reporters, who knew that a good way to keep ahead of your competition was to know what they were up to.

Thus, on arrival at their hotel in the location of a story, and even before they made friends with the bar staff, they would approach the concierge and slip him a decent sum to keep them informed and their competitors in the dark about what they themselves were up to.

Where Corrie, in her lack of practical experience, fell down was in not doing first that; then what she should have done when she gave him the telegram was to slip him something to stay quiet because of the name and destination that would leap out even if he struggled with English.

It was doubly unfortunate that a very experienced English correspondent called Vernon Bartlett spotted her on the way out of the hotel after Cal had called for her to come down.

'Where are you off to, young lady, and by the side entrance?' he asked, coming in from a late-morning constitutional walk.

'Nothing doing in Prague, is there, Vernon, so I thought I'd go down to the border and see how many Jews the Rumanians are letting in.'

'As many as have the means to bribe the border guards, I should think.'

'Still . . .'

'Well, good hunting,' Vernon replied, moving to go in for a cup of coffee and one of those big cream cakes so loved by the Czechs. 'We shall miss your gracious company in the bar.'

'"Gracious" is not the word I would use, Vernon, "debauched" is more appropriate. Did you stay on last night?'

Nearly everyone was leaving to go to Nuremberg for Hitler's big speech, an event enough to give an excuse for a leaving bash.

'No, I could see it was turning into a real session so I baled out not long after you.'

'There'll have been some fine heads this morning.'

'I'll say, there was not a soul at breakfast, bar me.'

'I took mine in my room.'

'To avoid the groans of those who stayed up, I suppose. We should run a sweepstake on who misses the Munich train, someone's bound to.'

'Well,' Corrie said, with as much veracity as she could muster. 'Must be off, 'cause I've got a train to catch.'

As she made for the door, Bartlett did not go into the dining room; instead, not entirely convinced by what he had been told, he waited a few seconds then followed her, ready to duck out of sight if she looked back. The revolving doors to the side entrance were panelled in glass and he saw the rather severe-looking man who took her small case and put it in the boot of the big dark-green Maybach, the sight making him curious.

Vernon Bartlett had covered the Spanish Civil War in the early days and been in Madrid during the first nationalist siege of the capital in '36, staying in the same haunt as many of his peers, some of the same hard-drinking lot that were now ensconced in the Ambassador.

He was sure he had seen the same fellow now helping Corrie into the car in the saloon of the Florida Hotel drinking with two stalwart boozers, Ernie Hemingway and Tyler Alverson, and had been at one time introduced, which, with his press instincts, he remembered clearly.

He had no real knowledge of what Callum Jardine did, only that he had taken an active part in fighting the nationalists on behalf of the republicans, added to the fact that he was a man of some mystery who had not, the last time he had seen him, been wearing glasses or sporting a rather Germanic haircut.

What the hell was Little Miss Just-Started-in-the-Game doing with a character like that, and was she really going to catch a train? Next stop was the desk of the hotel concierge, and though it was just on the off chance, he had in his hand a twenty-koruna note which produced the information as to where Corrie Littleton was off to and what she was about to get.

'Well damn me,' Bartlett swore, when it was relayed to him, a precis of the contents of the telegram that a hotel boy had taken to be sent on Thursday morning, as soon as the telegraph office opened its doors. 'Cheb of all places – talk about the cunning little vixen!'

Of course, it was necessary to pay out more money to ensure that he was the only one privy to this information and as he did so he reflected on two things: that the life of a luxury hotel concierge was certainly an enviable one given the amount of cash they garnered for their favours, the other being that he was blessed as a fellow who could decline to get sloshed at the drop of a hat.

When he got to the dining room he observed that many of his peers had emerged from their rooms to drink copious amounts of coffee – Americans, French and British, nursing hangovers from the previous night's debauch in the hotel bar, all of them receiving a hearty greeting in a loud voice, accompanied by a backslap, that was certain to cause their heads to ache.

Over his coffee and cream cake Vernon Bartlett mused on what to do about that which he had uncovered; he was off to Nuremberg to cover the leader's speech at the Nazi Party Rally on Monday himself, and even if it was likely to be an occasion of thundering and repetitive boredom he was reluctant to change his plans – his editor would not be pleased if he did, especially this year, when Czechoslovakia was bound to be one of Hitler's topics.

Thankfully, he had been sent out a young tyro to help cover what was the biggest story on the Continent and do the kind of legwork a man of Bartlett's experience found too tedious: the daily briefings from the various Czech spokesmen and what that dry stick of a so-called mediator, Runciman, was up to, or what, more likely, he was avoiding, like coming up with any solution to the crisis.

Jimmy's travel accreditation had come through from the Interior Ministry days ago, but he wondered, as he played with the sugar in the bowl, what could the young fellow do? Certainly he could shadow Corrie Littleton and find out the exact nature of her assignment, which might be more than she had said.

If Henlein was agreeing to an interview, and he already knew the Sudeten leader to be a master manipulator in his relations with the press, it might mean matters were coming to a head in the disputed regions and for his paper not to be there would be seen as a failure, quite possibly on his part, because regardless of right and wrong, it was never the editor who was the latter, always the man on the spot.

'Ah! James,' he cried, as his assistant came into the room, looking as ever like the keen young chap he was, more student than adult. 'Just the fellow I'm looking for.'

Expecting to be invited to sit down, Jimmy Garvin was surprised when his normally urbane boss leapt up, grabbed his arm and aimed him straight out through the dining room door, Bartlett's voice a whisper as he explained to him what he wanted him to do.

'I shall be holed up at the Bayerischer Hof in Bamberg and you can keep me posted by telegram, and if it's really hot stuff, use the phone.'

CHAPTER EIGHTEEN

'Jesus Christ, Cal, you look like an executioner with those damn specs and that haircut.'

His hair now stood up from his head in a spiky sort of way, not the first time he had worn it like that; when you are fighting in the trenches short hair is a must to help you keep the lice under control. It is the same for doing battle in hot climates or travelling through South American jungles.

'Do I look suitably German?'

'You sure do, but I preferred it when you looked human.'

They had just pulled out into Wenceslas Square and into a stream of traffic and trams that made Corrie edgy; she was, after all, sitting in what, in her own country, would have been the driving seat and she was used to being in control of the car.

'Why the hell do these folk drive on the wrong side of the road, are they crazy?'

'Time to tell you who I am supposed to be and we have to concoct a story as to how I got involved in this as well.'

She reached down to her feet and pulled up her copious handbag to extract a pad and pencil.

'I'm not sure it's a good idea to write anything down.'

'It makes it easy for me to remember, and what do you think the chances are of finding anyone who understands shorthand English in this neck of the woods?'

Cal smiled. 'In my game you don't take risks.'

'In my game you must take notes, so shoot.'

He started talking and her pencil flew, which he let go. It had the advantage of keeping her from looking out of the windscreen and ducking in terror every time a car came too near or he swung out to pass another.

Mostly it was background: the name Barrowman, his background in chemicals, not as an expert but as a buyer and seller, the need to keep that vague since it was not the kind of thing two people meeting in a strange country would go into too deeply.

'We met in the bar of the Ambassador and I introduced myself.' He took one of the Monty Redfern-supplied business cards from his top pocket and handed it to her so she could spell his name. 'Hang on to that and keep it in your purse.'

'What was the approach?'

'You're a woman, single and we formed a mutual attraction.'

'Let's hope nobody looks me in the eye when I spin that one.'

'I invited you to dine with me, you did and we had a great evening, which ended in the bar. Use the name of the restaurant where we did eat in case anyone asks what you ordered.'

'Hell, I can't pronounce it, or half of what I ate.'

'Even better, because the trick is to tell as few lies as possible – for instance, that you have not yet filed a story back to the States because you are looking for an angle that no one else has thought of.'

'And that stuff about us being lovers?'

'For emergencies only.'

'Buster, the roof will have to fall in big time before that gets an airing.'

They were out in the suburbs now, which looked to be peaceful, but that did not last long because they came to their first checkpoint, Corrie making an unfunny pun about it being Czech.

The examination of papers was done with great courtesy; these young soldiers in their grey-green uniforms were conscripts, polite and, once they had perused her passport and seen the eagle, somewhat excited to meet a real American, which held them up longer than it should.

'Those kids were sweet. I ain't never been pointed at and called a film star before.'

'They didn't mean it, they'd say that to anyone from the USA.'

'Thanks.'

'Play on being American when we get to Cheb. Most people there will never have met anyone from outside their own area, often their own village, and everyone is enthralled by anything American. Being exotic—'

'That's a nice word.'

'In your case, inappropriate.'

At the main railway station Jimmy Garvin was buying his ticket, rather excited to be going on a chase for a story without Vernon Bartlett breathing down his neck, imagining a big splash in the *News*

Chronicle with a byline saying 'from our special correspondent in the Sudetenland'; it might not use his name, but he would make sure no one was in doubt who wrote it.

But he had to remind himself to have a care, so he took up a position on the concourse from which he could watch the comings and goings; neither he or his mentor had any idea if Corrie Littleton was on the train, she might have been lying about that too, and given they had shared the same hotel she knew his face too well for him to be spotted.

While he was there the Paris-Prague Express arrived and disgorged its passengers. As they filed through the exit gate – their travel documents would have been examined on the train – he wondered at the purpose of those coming to Prague: businessmen, diplomats and maybe even the odd news hound too. Even his young imagination did not stretch to a desk chief from SIS.

Noel McKevitt had felt liberated ever since he left London; stuck in Broadway for five years now, he had forgotten the excitement of being out in the field. In London crowds you paid no attention to anyone unless they were striking; from the point where he had stepped aboard the train at Calais he had felt his old instincts begin to sharpen. By the time he made the Czech capital they were back and fully engaged.

It was not those who stood out in the mass you needed to spot when active, it was the exact opposite: those who blended in with the background had to be looked out for, the face that appeared too often and never looked at you directly, identified by the smallest of features, the tilt of a head, the cut of a chin, a certain gait when they moved.

In five years of sedentary work he had filled out from the slim field man he had been in Berlin, but Prague had to be awash with German agents and some of those might be the people he had sparred with previously in the German capital, and someone would have been given the task of watching the incoming express – and that was before you put devious old Quex into the mix.

Suitcase in hand, he joined the queue for taxis and shuffled forward until nearly at the front. Four places from his turn he suddenly picked up his bag and left the queue, his concentration on those lined up behind, cutting back into the station, stopping and retracing his steps, then making for the front of the station and the car he expected to be waiting for him. If it was probably unnecessary it was fun to employ the old tricks.

His lift was there: Dawson, one of the men he had sent to this station from Warsaw, standing by the rear passenger door so that it could be opened and closed quickly, his suitcase thrown on the floor. It was moving before he managed to shift to a comfortable position, weaving out into the traffic.

'Have you got anything to cheer me up?'

'In what way, sir?'

'A name would be a start.'

'We've got more than a hundred and we're still trawling. It would help if we had some idea of what we're looking for.'

Noel McKevitt was not good with subordinates, being too abrupt, too demanding; he knew he was not the type to inspire loyalty out of love of his personality, so he had never tried, but he reckoned he was respected for his ability and that allowed him to be brusque.

'The best-manned station in Europe by a country mile and you can't give me an answer.'

The reply came back as swift and hard as his dismissal of their efforts. 'Before you have an answer, sir, it is usual to have a question.'

'Just get me to the embassy.'

Time was not on his side; he could stall Quex on the grounds of the need for discretion but not for too long. The old bugger would be monitoring what he did, so he had to come up with a way of nailing his man in a way that breached the usual protocols of dealing with British subjects abroad. Having had a long and silent train journey he thought he had the answer.

'Do we have the Czech equivalent of a police warrant card?'

'Not as far as I'm aware, sir.'

'Then we need to get one.'

The checkpoint soldiers outside Prague had been jolly, young and friendly but that seemed to diminish the further Cal and Corrie travelled from the capital, just as the queues to get through them got longer. That left them ample time to talk – it was a warm sunny day, the hood of the Zeppelin was down and Cal saw no need to race – in some part to reminisce, while Cal was aware of the little probing darts she threw to get information.

It took some time to realise that this was the first time they had been alone in each other's company; in Africa there had always been people around, on the old camel route into Ethiopia upwards of a hundred warriors, in the country numerous folk and at the very least Vince Castellano and Tyler Alverson.

Without an audience to witness and laugh at her jibes, Corrie became less sharp, and since she did not rile him, Cal did not respond, while added to that they had shared experience. He was also aware and wondering why he had not noticed before that she was much more feminine than she had been either on first acquaintance or on their subsequent travels – hardly surprising; it's not what you look for in the midst of a conflict.

It was not just the way she now dressed but also in her manner; she had always struck him a bit juvenile and added to that there was her endemic bumptiousness and strident views which she was not shy in expressing. He asked about her mother, an archaeologist he had met in Africa whom he thought crazed, and her father whom he knew she was fond of, but he was never going to get away without the classic query about his own state of matrimony.

'I once asked Vince if you were married.'

'And what did he say?'

'You'd think I'd asked for the number of your safe deposit box.'

'We boys stick together.'

'Look, Cal, if we are going into what you say we are that is the kind of question to which I need an answer. We are supposed to have only just met but hit it off, and if I don't know too much about that kind of deal I do know your marital condition is the kind of information people who are attracted to each other share. I need some background.'

'Get your passport ready, we're next.'

The man who leant through the window was no boy, he was a grizzled fully grown man with stubble and not much given to smiling as he demanded their papers in a gruff unfriendly way. There was the usual charade of looking several times at the passport photographs and then glaring at the faces, as if that could not be done in one go.

'This one's full of charm,' Corrie said.

Was it the nationalities that had him grunt that they should pull over or Corrie's plainly displeased attitude to the delay? Flippancy requires no translation. Cal suspected a bit of both, aware that the best way to make a passport checker's day – and this had nothing to do with the country in which they operated – was to give him an excuse to hold you up and make you sweat. It was even better if you lost your temper.

Cal swung the car out of the line to pull up beside a hut that had about it the temporary look of the many they had seen and eased past without trouble. Their checker had followed them and with another grunt he made a sign that they should get out of the car, to which there was no option but to comply. Being an American, Corrie thought differently.

'What the hell . . .?'

'Quiet,' Cal snapped, albeit he kept his voice low. 'Just get out and whatever you do smile sweetly.'

'What d'ya mean?'

'How does step out of character sound?' Seeing her swell up for a response he was quick to cut her off. 'Look, these fellows hold all the cards and they can keep us here as long as they want. Now let us do as he says.'

Forcing a smile Cal got out and went round to help Corrie do the same. Their soldier-checker gave them an unfriendly look, then walked off with an abrupt order to follow and they were led into the hut, where at a desk sat a man who was clearly, by his shoulder boards, an officer.

Their passports and Corrie's accreditation papers were handed over to him and Grim-face left. As he did so his superior fired off an incomprehensible question.

'*Nejesme české,*' Cal replied, using an expression that had become familiar in the last few days. '*Mluvite anglicky?*'

The officer shook his head and even Cal was thinking he was just playing a stupid game. With the passports he had in his hand he must have reckoned it would be unlikely they would understand him – so few foreigners did.

'Would a couple of dollar bills help out here?' Corrie asked; at least her voice was serious.

Cal was quick to squash that. 'If you really want to upset a Czech try to bribe him. They think it's what other people do, not them.' Then he turned to the man still ostentatiously examining the booklets, flicking through the pages as if enlightenment would fly out from the leaves. '*Sprechen Sie Deutsch?*'

He did not want to say yes – it was a matter of pride – but there was no alternative as Cal, seeing the answer in his eyes, explained who they were and why they were going north: for this fine American journalist to have a look and tell the world the problems the Czechs were having with the German minority.

Even if she did not understand, Corrie guessed he was laying on the charm with a trowel; it was in his face and it was with a slight feeling of shock that she realised she was thinking Callum Jardine was a handsome bastard, more so when he was being nice rather than being sarcastic.

Whatever he had said, the Czech officer answered with a stream of less amiable complaints that went on for some time before handing the passports back and calling for Grim-face, who was outside the door, giving instructions, she supposed, to let them through the barrier.

'So what was all that about?'

'Just a general warning not to trust the Germans to tell you the truth.'

'He took a long time saying it.'

'There was more, and none of it flattering.' Cal waved to the men lifting the barrier and gunned the Maybach through to admiring glances from those who dreamt of owning such a car, pointing up ahead as he did so to the gathering dark clouds. 'Looks like we are heading for some bad weather.'

'Yep.'

Noel McKevitt was perusing the list his men had got from the Prague hotels in the days before his arrival, marking those he thought most likely. Instinct, even if he acknowledged that he could be wrong, told him the man he was looking for would not be in any of the luxury hotels; if he were operating as he thought his target would, he would find somewhere more discreet.

He had sent for an interpreter called Miklos, who his station chief thought would fit the bill for what he wanted, being tall, well built and with a lived-in face. He was still staring at his ticks when the man arrived.

'Sit down, Miklos.'

That was responded to nervously; whatever the Czech had been told, and it should have been little, he had no doubt been informed that this was the big chief from London he had been brought to see.

'I need you to do a bit of play-acting, Miklos. Do you think you could pass for a policeman?' Sensing the hesitation, Noel McKevitt was quick to add the ultimate bribe and it was not money. 'I have made it plain in London that we cannot leave behind anyone who has worked for us if the Germans come. If they found out, that person would not live long, I suspect.'

'No,' Miklos replied, his seat shifting in the chair as he struggled with what he was being offered.

'Naturally we control the passport office here and, sure, I can tell you, SIS look after their own.'

'What is it you want me to do?'

The supposed warrant card, a forgery, would have been unlikely to fool anyone who spoke Czech and demanded to examine it closely, but the way it was flashed under anyone's nose meant even the locals could be counted on to accept it as genuine, because the question they were asked was so innocuous.

Two men, one of whom did not speak, merely wanted to know the room number of the various British guests in various hotels and when that was supplied, once it was certain the person was in his room, the two men would call on them to check their passports, a natural thing to do at a time of national emergency.

That the fellow asking had talked to some of them before, in the pretence of being an interpreter, the desk clerks who recognised him took as a fitting subterfuge, particularly as the fellow was excessively polite - as befitted a policeman in a democracy and wanted nothing more from them than information the authorities were entitled to.

Miklos was relishing the task, not least because of what it was going to gain him if he could satisfy this big London chief. There was not a person in the country who did not harbour fears for what might be coming – not one, Miklos suspected, who had not at some time thought how good it would be to get out of Czechoslovakia to somewhere safe.

Mr Barrowman and his fellow guest Mr Nolan were not first on the list that McKevitt had ticked, so by the time Miklos and his companion got to Vince Castellano the act was well honed. The knock at the room door was gentle and when it opened there was

Miklos smiling, with another bland-faced individual standing a couple of paces away with a clipboard and a pen.

'Forgive me, Mr Nolan,' he said, speaking slowly so as to be unthreatening, flashing his forged warrant card so quickly it was a blur. 'I am from the Czech police. Please do not be alarmed, as we are doing a routine check.'

Vince knew how to soften the Old Bill: be nice to them. 'Do you want to come in?'

'That will not be necessary, but I wonder if I could have a look at your passport?' Seeing Vince's eyebrows go up a fraction – everyone else had the same reaction – he was quick to add, 'I am sure you are aware of the number of refugees trying to flee the country, many of them employing false papers.'

'Are they?'

'Yes, and to ensure that they do not use those of guests visiting our country we wish to have a list of the numbers, which we can hold to compare against forgeries.'

Vince, again as had others, stood for a moment in consideration of whether to comply, but the man before him was smiling and his eyes looked pleading rather than threatening, so he turned and went to fetch the required document from his coat pocket.

This was taken, examined, then passed to the silent oppo who dutifully wrote down the number against the name, and then it was passed back. 'I believe your companion, Mr Barrowman, is not in the hotel and left with a bag.'

There was no option but to reply honestly, otherwise they might attract unwelcome attention. 'He's gone out of town on business.'

'Do you have any idea when he will return?'

'A couple of days, I think. It depends on how successful he is.'

'Really, it is good to find you and your countrymen still doing trade with us. Might I ask what business you are in?'

'Chemicals,' Vince replied, noticing the other fellow with the clipboard was looking impatient.

'You too are in chemicals?'

'No, sports equipment, boxing rings.'

'Then I hope you have success. Enjoy your stay in Prague, Mr Nolan, and please, I see you carry your passport with you – look after it well for it would not be helpful to anyone if it was stolen.'

CHAPTER NINETEEN

Jimmy Garvin got to Cheb long before the car carrying Callum Jardine and Corrie Littleton, though he was unaware of the fact. All he knew was that by jumping off the train as soon as it entered the station and running for the ticket barrier he had a chance to get into a position to see if she followed, unsure what to do when he saw there was no sign of her.

He knew, having looked at his watch as the train drew in, that it was bang on time, which led him to reflect on that often-quoted saw mouthed by those idiots who admired Benito Mussolini, that 'he had made the trains run on time'. Why was such an accolade never applied to an efficient democracy like Czechoslovakia?

Bartlett had told him about the car she had got into, so he assumed she must be coming by road, so his first task was to find himself somewhere to stay that was not the Victoria Hotel. Being a bit of a spa town, a sort of minor Carlsbad, there were quite a number of places dedicated to those taking the waters and he elected to walk to find one.

The difference outside the station – managed and run by Czechs – was palpable, the buildings flying flags showing more of the black-red-black ensign of the Sudetenland than the far fewer Czech tricolours. Added to that there was a grimness about those people he passed, their looks not aided by the wet weather, albeit, given the puddles in the road, the worst of the downpour had passed and was now just a light drizzle.

The choice of one flying the national flag was deliberate; Jimmy knew the object of Corrie Littleton's visit and he guessed she would park herself as close to Konrad Henlein as she could.

In a place with few visitors now – no one was coming for the waters in a potential war zone – he soon realised that in the hotel he chose he was the only guest; no wonder he had been greeted and fussed over like a saviour.

In the Maybach the hood was now firmly closed, the heavy rain beating a tattoo on the windscreen with which the small wipers were struggling to cope, creating a cocoon which closed them in and seemed to make more intimate their conversation, with Corrie now talking about her upbringing.

Cal knew she came from Boston but was now treated to the fact that she had gone to Bryn Mawr, which was apparently a prestigious and famous woman-only college in Pennsylvania, right up there with Harvard and Yale.

'But no boys?'

Corrie laughed. 'We were told we did not need them.'

'End of the human race.'

'To prosper, not procreate, but we could do that too if we went looking.'

'Did you?'

'Once or twice.'

The tone of that response was not a joyful one, which made Cal wonder if she had been let down in her past. He couldn't ask; he was not well enough acquainted for that and it did not fall in the need-to-know category regarding what they might face in Cheb.

'Is that a petrol pump by the roadside?' Cal said, peering through the rain, which was as good a way as any of avoiding that subject.

'What, again?'

They had stopped and filled the car in each sizeable town through which they passed – an eight-litre V12 engine used a lot of fuel – but that was not the reason; Cal liked as full a tank as possible on the very good grounds that you never knew when you were going to need it.

Corrie had broken him down earlier by refusing to be diverted, and in truth he could see that she needed the background she claimed, and he had to admit being married and the circumstances of his attachment. Oddly, like his last days in London, he found his wife a subject he could now discuss without the onset of gloom.

'I was young and going off to war, Lizzie was beautiful and . . .' Cal paused. 'You have to be facing that kind of thing to know what drives men and women to rush into matrimony.'

'You mean apart from stupidity.'

'Was it Doctor Johnson who said "the prospect of hanging concentrates the mind wonderfully"? The Western Front was a bit like that. No one told you but the average survival time of a subaltern when there was a big battle on was about two weeks. I was lucky – I survived.'

'But you were in love, right?'

'Very much so, but the time we had was too tight to allow for much investigation of what made us tick. My wife craves excitement.'

'And you don't?' Corrie said with disbelief.

'Maybe that was the mutual attraction, but my adventures tend to be outdoors.'

That confused her until the message struck home, which produced, 'Sorry I asked.'

'Don't be.'

'It's a bitch she won't give you a divorce. I suppose you've been a good boy yourself?'

He was not going there; one, he had not been and two, if you're a gentleman you don't boast about your conquests. Besides there was an affair he wanted to avoid mentioning because that would still be painful.

'I hope you are not preparing a profile for your magazine.'

'Make a good one, especially if you have had lots of love affairs. International adventurer with the soft heart of a romantic poet.'

Cal was suddenly very serious. 'Don't ever go thinking I have a soft heart, Corrie, because I haven't. If you run my name through your records I suspect it will come up even in the USA.'

'Why not save me the time?'

'It doesn't make for contentment.'

'Sounds like you did something real bad.'

'It was,' Cal replied, not seeking to keep the bitterness out of his voice. 'Another checkpoint ahead, so go to work on your smile.'

'Physician heal thyself.'

'You're right,' Cal replied; memory of the blood-spattered wall of his marital bedroom had made him glare.

'Right,' McKevitt snapped, looking at the first replies that had come back from Miklos. 'Get those numbers off by telegram to the passport office in London. I want the names on them checked for anything that isn't right and I want a rocket up their arse so they don't just bury it.'

'You still have not told us what it is you are after, Noel.'

McKevitt looked up at Major 'Gibby' Gibson, the Prague station chief, and gave him the coldest stare he could, which was coming it a bit high with a man of his age and experience, some twenty years in the service and an unblemished record.

'There are things you don't need to know, Gibby, but when you do you will be informed.'

Gibson wanted to reply that this was his patch, even if the fellow he was talking to was the man who ran the London Desk and, though junior in years, his superior. Though a hierarchy like any other government body, the SIS ran on slightly different lines and it was simply not done to override a station chief, and even worse to do so in such a public manner as to undermine his local authority. McKevitt in briefing everyone had done just that.

With the extra staff he had been given, plus his own skills and contacts, Gibson had done a good job of keeping London up to speed on everything happening in both the capital city and beyond, yet he had been obliged to drag men off what he saw as valuable work to meet the needs of Noel McKevitt, which might just have been acceptable with an explanation.

If it had displeased him to issue the orders, they had been received just as badly by those tasked to execute them, all professionals who felt they were being sidelined from proper intelligence work to do the kind of thing usually allotted at home to lowly beat coppers, and such a feeling had permeated most of the building.

Down in the basement Cipher Room he handed over McKevitt's list to the clerk who ran it and gave him orders to route it through Broadway. Coming from just down the road would ensure a faster response than anything from hundreds of miles away.

'And Tommy,' Gibson said. 'I'm in need of a little favour.'

'Whatever you need, Major,' the clerk replied, giving, as he always did, Gibby's old military rank; he was a man who was unfailingly polite to everyone, who knew the names of, and never failed to ask after, wives, children and girlfriends – in short, the major was popular.

Gibson went to a desk to compose, with the codebooks, a despatch of his own to Broadway, pre-dating it to the day the original instruction had come from the Central European Desk to check the British nationals.

In it he did not criticise McKevitt's demand – that would be counterproductive – but he did feel the need to point out how that would impact on the amount of hard information coming out of the Prague station in the coming days with his men so occupied.

When he handed it over to the clerk, Tommy read it, fingered the date and smiled.

'I owe you one, Tommy.'

'You don't owe me a thing, sir, happy to be of service.'

Tommy was typing before Gibson left the Cipher Room; that would land on Noel McKevitt's desk and he would only read it on his return to London, the delay being explained away easily as just one of those standard cock-ups that happen daily.

But it would cover Gibson's back if what was happening was questioned on the top floor, a standard precaution in any establishment where there was competition for the plum postings, added to a culture of passing the buck if things went amiss.

With the weather clearing a bit, and approaching what the ethnic Germans would call the border, it was just possible to see the troop concentrations by the roadside, tented encampments and lorry parks stretching into the misty distance under canopies of trees to protect against air attack.

At the next checkpoint there were tankettes, Tančik vz. 33s, that if they looked impressive to Corrie, Cal knew would be mincemeat to the latest armoured vehicles the Germans could put in the field, but what it told him, without the need to look at road signs or maps, was that they were now in the disputed areas.

The flags came next and increased the further north-west they drove, rising into the high hills, the not-quite-mountainous region of the Bohemian borderlands; to the ethnic Germans this might be the province of Carlsbad, but to the Czechs it was Karlovy Vary.

By the time they got to Cheb the red and black horizontally striped banners were ubiquitous, nowhere more so than on the Victoria Hotel itself, which was festooned with them, and just in case you did not know what it was, there were men outside in the dun-brown-coloured uniform of their *Sturmabteilung* counterparts across the frontier and, like them, wearing side arms in big leather holsters.

The incongruity of a uniformed porter rushing to their car as soon as they stopped nearly had Cal laughing, it was so out of keeping with everything else he could see, and that was replicated in the hotel reception, which if the lobby was dark and rather Teutonic in its decor, conformed to what was needed: a desk at which to register, couches on which to sit, pastoral scenes on the walls and vases full of flowers to give a peaceful ambiance, and two staircases leading off from the lobby.

'Miss Corrine Littleton, of *Collier's Weekly*.' She threw out a hand to indicate Cal, standing back because this was her show now. 'And my interpreter. I believe you are expecting us.'

The man behind the desk wore a pince-nez and had that superior air of hotel receptionists of not-quite-top-flight establishments everywhere, who always behave as if they are doing you a favour by letting you soil their pristine accommodation. This one had the added non-attraction of having in his lapel a Nazi Party swastika badge.

Out came a heavy ledger, and the receptionist ran a finger down what Cal suspected was an imaginary list – this was not the most desirable destination hostelry in the world right at this moment – then shook his head as if someone might have got something wrong by even thinking of letting a room, finally replying in rapid German to acknowledge the booking of two rooms.

'Did he say yes or no, Doc?' Corrie asked.

Cal took over, annoyed that already she was not calling him by the name on the passport, and went through, with some surprise, the usual registration process with their passports, which did not take long, and soon they were being escorted up one of the sets of stairs, followed by both porter and their bags, to rooms on the fourth floor.

'No elevator?'

'They're hardy mountain folk round here – and it's a lift.'

'What do we do next?'

'Wait to be contacted. That snotty sod downstairs will now, no doubt, tell whoever we need to meet that we are here.'

'I could sure use a drink.'

'Lobby, ten minutes,' Cal replied, 'so could I.'

Corrie was still complaining about her 'lousy Martini', Cal reading a local newspaper, when the woman Cal decided on first sight to call the 'Ice Maiden' appeared and came towards them, dressed in dirndl-type clothing as if the rest of her appearance was not enough to mark her out as German.

Her blonde hair was braided tightly from the front of her head to the back and she was stunning-looking, with clear skin and large bright-blue eyes, if a trifle severe of expression and, tellingly, with no sign on her hands of a matrimonial band. Being a gentleman, Cal stood up, but it was the still sitting Corrie she addressed.

'Fräulein Littleton?'

'I prefer Miss.'

That response was ignored. 'And Herr Barrowman, your interpreter, *Ja*?'

'You speak good English, Fräulein . . .'

'Metzer,' she replied. 'I help run our leader's press office. English is very necessary to counter the fabrications of the foreign journals.'

'Or,' Corrie snapped, 'to understand the complexities.'

She might as well have said 'lies'. Cal, seeing the eyes narrow, was quick to intervene, his voice genial, at the same time seeking to throw Corrie a warning glance; she needed, *he* needed these people to think they were sympathetic.

'Which Miss Littleton has come a long way to unearth. I must say I too will find it fascinating to explore the way you have united the people of Bohemia and Moravia into such a powerful political body. It's quite an achievement and one we discussed on the way from Prague.'

It was almost comical – indeed it would have been in peaceful times – the way her face changed at the mention of the Czech capital. It was as if someone had just farted and walked away from a bad smell.

'You must be tired after your journey, Herr Barrowman, and I have to tell you it is too late in the day to meet with Herr Henlein, there would not be enough time before he goes home to dine with his family.'

'How admirable that a man with so much to do, a man indeed of destiny, has time to keep his family obligations.'

'That is something he does every evening, Herr Barrowman, unless there is a crisis. The hotel houses his offices but he rarely sleeps here.'

'Well that suits me, Fräulein, I need to work up some notes.'

Cal noted the tone of Corrie's voice, which was not friendly, but it perfectly matched the utterly insincere smile with which the Ice Maiden responded; it was cold enough to freeze a volcano.

There was something in the air and Cal knew what it was: the Ice Maiden was smiling at him but not at her, which reminded him of the atmosphere Lizzie created when she saw a rival, something she was inclined to spot often and at a hundred paces. His wife could not bear it that anyone around her should be able to compete for male attention.

The Ice Maiden, even if he did not know her, was doing the same, but why was Corrie Littleton reacting in the way she did?

'I am sure you know already, Fräulein Littleton, what it is you want to ask our leader. A typewriter and paper will be sent to your room, Fräulein Littleton, along with ample paper so you may write up your article.'

'I was just going to make notes and do the composition when I get back to Prague.'

'But our leader would be very interested to see what you write.'

'And no doubt make some suggestions for alterations.'

'He must be careful not to be misrepresented.'

'I am used to my own machine.'

'If you struggle with what we send you, I am sure we can find someone to type for you.'

'Your kindness overwhelms me,' Corrie said, with very sweetly delivered irony.

'Might I suggest,' Fräulein Metzer said to Cal, her face going from frosty to smiling, 'that you dine in the hotel and we will set a time for tomorrow.'

'Sunday?'

'With the amount of things happening in our poor land everyone must work, even on a supposed Holy Day.'

'Time to freshen up,' Corrie said, finishing her drink and glaring at the German woman. 'I'm feeling a little soiled.'

'I take it a promenade after dinner would not be forbidden?' Cal asked, his tone pleasant to cover for Corrie's acidity.

The Ice Maiden's big blue eyes got bigger. 'What a strange expression, Herr Barrowman; how can such a thing as going for a walk be forbidden in a free country?'

Jimmy Garvin was sitting at the café attached to the station, wondering if he could avoid buying another beer and wishing he had the kind of expenses that went to the Vernon Bartletts of this world; the money they all spent in the bar of the Ambassador was staggering.

Not that he had been shocked by their excess, given it was exactly the same in and around Bouverie Street where the paper had its offices, a culture of drinking that often saw stories filed from the floor of a pub rather than a reporter's desk.

He did not know how lucky he was; the station café was Czech-owned and thus silent, while inside the hotel, those he was waiting for were sitting, trying not to look bored at the interminable speech being delivered from Nuremberg by Joseph Goebbels.

His voice was rather nasal and even if Corrie could not understand what he was saying she could recognise the tone of mockery in it, his jokes, which Cal knew to be heavy and unfunny, roared at by his audience as well as laughed at by many sharing the dining room.

No one talked; it was either considered impolite when the Minister of Propaganda was making a speech, or their fellow diners were afraid to look as though they did not believe every lie he was telling. The exception to the sarcasm was any mention of the Führer, which came with great '*Heils!*', and then he went into that standard Nazi trick of the ever rising crescendo of threats, which would be shattered against the iron wall of National Socialism.

The worldwide Jewish conspiracy would not halt the forward march of the German *Volk*; beware Bolshevism and the Slavic hordes, for the righteous anger of the Aryan master race was moving forward to face and defeat their machinations. During all this Cal had to struggle not to shout at the big radio relaying this, his only compensation the best part of a bottle of very good wine; Corrie only had one glass.

'Make out you're not feeling well,' Cal insisted as he drained the last of that and leant toward her looking concerned.

'What?' Corrie whispered.

'Mop the brow, clutch the stomach, unless you want to listen to all this drivel. He will go on for at least another hour.'

She gave a sterling performance of a woman in some distress, doing as he bid, clutching his hand and, with her auburn near-red hair and pale skin, able to look ill without really trying. Cal stood and helped her to her feet and with a backward glance of deep apology to the fascists still listening to Goebbels they left the room.

The sight of Corrie Littleton and her companion, under the canopy of light outside the hotel, emerging into the cool evening, had him draining the dregs he had been hanging on to, only to realise that when the time came to move, what he had consumed, several steins, needed to be got rid of. The hesitation, whether to use the toilet or not, allowed him to see that as soon as the pair walked on, a couple of Brownshirts appeared from the shadows to fall in behind them.

'That was not the finest meal I have ever consumed,' Cal said, 'but the wine was OK.'

'Take it for what it was, free.'

That brought a happy smile. 'It's nice to eat on someone else's expenses.'

'I hope my boss in New York knows about fine Moselles.'

'If you like I'll write him some recommendations, the Germans make some very superior wines.'

'He drinks beer.'

'Then he should have come instead of you, Bohemia is the home of beer.'

Cal, as he said that, made to cross the road, which naturally allowed him to look behind him. The two fellows in uniform and jackboots made no attempt to avoid his eye, indeed the way they were looking at him and Corrie, it was as if they were lining them up for the firing squad.

'We are being followed.'

'Big deal, we're not going anywhere.' Corrie looked back and waved, which made the pair look even more grim than before. 'Nice guys, cheerful.'

'The trouble with Fascism is that it allows the real shits to have a bit of power. Give an idiot a uniform and he will do anything you want him to do to keep it.'

For all his flippancy, it was worrying that they were being tailed, even if it was obvious. At some point Cal had to make contact with Veseli and there were no arrangements in place, which left it all to the other man.

'They're gonna demand to see what I write before we leave, aren't they?'

'Probably more than that, Corrie; once they've approved it don't be surprised if they want to cable it to New York for you.'

'Damn,' she spat, taking his arm.

'So I have to get you back to Prague in time to correct what they receive. Best make two sets of notes, let them see one, the flattering stuff, and keep the real copy on you at all times.'

That had Cal's arm squeezed tightly, which he enjoyed. 'Are you training me to be a spy, Cal?'

'Much more devious that that, my dear Corrie,' he grinned, 'I'm helping you to be a journalist.'

'"My dear?"' she said softly, and questioningly.

Their promenade had brought them to the crowded central

square, clearly the old central marketplace, where loudspeakers were playing Goebbels' speech to a large mixed assembly, many of them in uniform, some holding flaring torches, all listening intently one minute, then crying out in passion the next, and that made them stop.

'He's still going strong.'

'Public radio,' Corrie said. 'On the streets, just like Times Square.'

'You should visit Germany, they have this in every main street, square and in the railway stations – loudspeakers on the buildings and lamp posts to tell the population what to think.'

Cal had got it wrong about the length of Goebbels' speech, for the little mountebank was coming to the end of his peroration, his voice hoarse, his demands for the nation to be faithful to the Führer and his iron will like some gospel preacher, the crowd now screaming at his every word so that it melded into one indistinguishable howl, with the same from the far end of the square.

Now the radio started billowing out martial music as, no doubt, Goebbels was played off the podium to march down an avenue of thousands of cheering supporters, hundreds of banners, and illuminated with swaying searchlights. Both Cal and Corrie had seen the newsreels and whatever you thought about the Nazis it had to be admitted they knew how to stage such an event.

Not to be outdone the local Nazis in their brown uniforms were forming up, the civilians moving out to form an avenue down which they could pass; clearly they had decided to march through the town with their flaring torches and their own massive swastika banners.

Having assembled at the bottom of the square in ranks, a shouted order filled the air and they were moving. Cal and Corrie stood to one side as they came closer, the boots cracking on the cobblestones loudly enough to be heard even over the sound of their raucous singing.

The men were dressed like their escorts, who were now standing with their arms outstretched in their fascist salute: dun-brown uniform shirts buttoned to the neck, gleaming jackboots and riding breeches, a Sam Brown-style belt and shoulder strap and a swastika armband.

'That, if you don't know the tune, is the "Horst Wessel Song", Corrie. He was one of those idiots I told you about who was stupid enough to get himself killed in a street brawl with the Communists. Now he's a Nazi martyr.'

It was the soft, kepi-type forage cap that had stopped Cal from really looking at the man leading the parade, two flag-carrying acolytes a pace behind, goose-stepping with his arm up, a tall very Aryan figure, and it was only when he got really close and he could see the face that he realised that he was looking at the man he had been introduced to as Captain Karol Veseli.

The head did not turn, not even the eyes flicked sideways as he stamped by, so Cal, unsure if he had been spotted, raised his hat so that his face was in full view, an act which shocked Corrie.

'Jesus, what are you doing?'

'Making friends locally, Corrie, which, if you want your story, you better get doing too.'

Jimmy Garvin, well back, had been able to keep tabs on Corrie Littleton by just watching those following her, without having the faintest idea of where it would lead; he certainly did not want to be seen or to talk to her, it was more in the nature of something to do.

'Christ Almighty!'

He actually swore out loud when he saw that hat come off the head of the man he had been told was Callum Jardine and the sight did not fit with what Vernon Bartlett had told him, which, while not a fully formed picture, had been underlined by one very salient fact: Jardine was a rabid anti-fascist.

What was a man with his background, albeit that it was mysterious, doing raising his hat to a bunch of Brownshirt thugs? Jimmy Garvin might be young but he was not stupid and even if he did not know it yet he was already imbued with something that could only be called a nose for a story.

Right now he was thinking this was all wrong and there were only two conclusions to draw from that. One that Vernon Bartlett was wrong about this Jardine, or that this man with a funny background was up to something here in the Sudetenland, and he was inclined to plump for the latter. The question was, should he contact Bartlett and ask for instructions?

That he decided against that was hardly a surprise; handed a possible scoop no journalist, however much he's a tyro, is going to give it away to anyone else. The really hard question was, how was he going to pursue it?

At that same moment Cal was wondering about Veseli, even more certain that was not his real name in this neck of the woods. But he was less worried about how he was going to make contact; in that outfit he could walk right into the Victoria Hotel and just say hello.

CHAPTER TWENTY

Back in his room Cal checked to see if it had been searched while he was out, discovering that if the person who had done the looking had not been good enough, the job had been carried out very professionally indeed.

Not a sock or a shirt was out of place and his canvas bag was exactly where he had left it, as were the things he had used to wash and shave before dinner. The letters from Redfern International Chemicals, which he had left on the dressing table, would have been examined too.

Naturally, the bed had been turned down and the heavy coverlet folded back by the room maid, a standard act in any hotel, which had made it impossible to employ the normal precautions on the door. This would also cover for any small movements that occurred with his visible possessions should the searcher make a mistake.

The small slip of folded paper he had inserted into the base of one of the drawers was just where he had left it, but missing was the single strand of his now very short red-gold hair that had been folded inside, one so small it would not have been visible unless the person doing the scrutiny was looking for it and impossible to spot under artificial light on a polished wood floor.

There was no shock attached to the discovery; he was an unknown quantity in a place where suspicion had to be rife for the sake of what they were trying to achieve. He assumed that Corrie's room had likewise been done over while they were having their dinner and their promenade – at least one lucky person had avoided having to listen to Goebbels.

He was still not quite over the shock of seeing his supposed contact leading that parade but he had to assume that right now he was safe, just as he had to trust Veseli to make whatever moves he had in mind and they had to have been pre-planned. It was all very well being active, but sometimes passivity was the right strategy, as expounded by the creator of Sherlock Holmes.

A few things were necessary for a good night's sleep: a heavy oak chair should be shoved under the door handle, which, if it would not stop anyone entering who really wanted to, would create enough noise and delay for him to react. His fountain pen, a Montblanc *Meisterstück*, he put on the bedside table; you could get a good grip of the body, and the nib made a dangerous weapon. Next he rolled really tight a local newspaper he had brought up from the lobby, which jabbed end on into someone's face would stop them dead and used in the right place could even kill.

Having been given a room overlooking the front of the hotel, but to one side, so he had a good view under the front canopy, Cal, busy doing his morning exercises to the sound of church bells, was drawn to the window by the sound of mild cheering and several vehicles entering the square below.

Really it was the small truck behind the big Mercedes that was making the noise on the cobblestones, open at the back and containing two files of rigid SA men in greatcoats, a dozen in number, all with rifles between their legs, while there was another car in front with what also looked like bodyguards.

The Mercedes in the middle stopped before the front door and another escort leapt out from the front to open the rear door. All Cal saw of the man who got out, to a raised arm salute, was the top of a soft trilby hat and a besuited arm responding with a lazy salute.

It had to be Konrad Henlein but the question uppermost in Cal's mind was the size of the escort and its armament – if that was standard he would need half a company of trained infantry to ambush him, and Moravec and Veseli must know that.

Responding to the telephone he picked it up to find it was Corrie asking him if he was ready to go down to breakfast. 'Why, do you need an escort?'

'I just want somebody to talk to and no one speaks English.'

'Maybe Fräulein Metzer will join you.'

'That will not be a good start to the day, the stuck-up bitch.'

'Maybe she's shy,' Cal replied, just to tease her.

'Are you kidding me? She makes Garbo look like Mae West.'

'Must be the hair.'

'You know the question Mae asks? Well the gun's in Metzer's pocket.'

'I'm just finishing my morning routine.'

'No details please.'

'And I think our man has just arrived. Ten minutes and I'll knock at your door.'

Over breakfast Cal was given a written list of questions that Corrie thought he should ask, with Cal pulling out his fountain pen to make some alterations that changed the tone.

'You got to sucker him, remember, be soft.'

'After what we saw in that square last night that's going to be difficult.'

'It was never going to be easy.'

Next stop was a meeting with the Ice Maiden, who informed them that the leader had much on his plate – constant communications were coming in from Prague, other Sudeten towns and around the world – and he could only spare one hour at a time, but would do one in the morning and another in the afternoon.

'It may take longer than that.'

'Then more time will be found tomorrow.'

'How's your French?' asked Quex as Peter Lanchester entered his office.

'Not brilliant, sir.'

'I have received this morning a communication from my opposite number in Paris, Colonel Gauché, the transcript of a conversation that was overheard between an external telephone and the chateau of a certain chap called Pierre Taittinger, dated August twenty-ninth, and it's not about champagne.'

The paper was passed over and Peter looked at it, thinking it was much harder to read a foreign language than speak it, this as Sir Hugh continued.

'Now it would be very easy for me to have this translated, as you know, but I think that might set running hares that would go in all directions, so as of now, I want this to be strictly between you and I.'

Having got well past the *bonjours* and *bien sûrs,* as well as a long screed, which he suspected was general conversation about the state of the world, one word hit him very hard.

'La Rochelle,' Peter said, 'hardly requires translation, sir.'

'No,' Quex said in a dry tone.

Peter was looking at other obvious words, such as *je pense par camion*, but the one that was most striking was his own name and what he assumed was a description, as well as the fact that he, *avec deux autres hommes anglais*, would *arrivent par train le trente août.* Given those two facts, a watch on the railway station – La Rochelle did not have a mass of long-distance trains coming in – was all that was required to identify him.

'The trouble is,' Quex continued, 'that though this tells us the communication came from outside of France, it does not say from where and it definitely does not identify the caller, who did not at any time use his name, and nor did Monsieur Taittinger.'

Peter went right to the top of the page, reading out the opening words, '*Bonjour, Pierre, c'est moi.* Which means the voice was known to him, well known.'

'Precisely, and does it not also imply that it is one which is quite distinctive, given the interference on such lines?'

'What do you think would happen if we shoved this under McKevitt's nose?'

'He would deny all knowledge of it, quite apart from the fact that as of this moment he's in Prague.' Seeing the surprise, Quex added, 'To shut the station down.'

'That puts him awfully close to Jardine.'

'Who has, according to your latest communication, gone up to Eger to meet with Henlein.'

'It's called Cheb now, sir.'

'Don't be a pedant, Peter.'

Sir Hugh went into a deep study, with a face that implied it would be unwise to interrupt his thoughts, and judging by his expression they were not happy ones.

'You sure this could not have come from something Jardine did, some mistake he made?'

'I cannot see it, sir. When I met him he was very confident he had kept things tight; he is very experienced in that game and I can tell you he is a hard character to follow and impossible to tail over weeks without him spotting something.'

'Say you are correct, what could be McKevitt's motive?'

'Guns for republicans in Spain, sir, he is visceral about that.'

'Peter, he does not know they were for Spain, nor does he know that Jardine was involved, because if he did, I would know about it, for the very simple reason he would have been letting things slip to his political friends.'

'I did not know he had any.'

'I did, and if I'd had any doubt, I certainly found out only the other day.'

Peter Lanchester had a look of curiosity on his face, to which Sir Hugh was not going to respond; the fewer people who knew he had been given a wigging by the PM the better.

'Let us speculate that where we had a suspicion we now have confirmation that your problems in La Rochelle stemmed from our own organisation, but that does not, even if it points us towards one person, nail it down and it has to be that before I can even think of acting upon it.'

'How in the name of all that's holy did he find out I was going to La Rochelle when the communication I sent was to you and for your eyes only?' It was necessary to add quickly the only other person who should have seen it. 'It's certainly not your secretary.'

'No, if Miss Beard was to be leaking secrets the whole nation would collapse. It has to be coded and decoded, does it not? It might be an idea to find out how long the cipher clerk in Paris has been in his job. For instance, was he there a decade ago when McKevitt was station chief?'

'It could be this end, sir, he does tend to put himself about, I've found.'

'Which means one of six people could have tipped McKevitt off.'

'Only two are on duty at any one time.'

'So we need the duty roster and a copy of your signal.'

'Which as soon as we request it will alert whoever is the culprit, if indeed anyone is.'

'I fear you are in for a tedious time, Peter, for to avoid that we must look through many days of transcripts to avert suspicion.'

'I'll need your written permission, sir. A lot of what I will be reading is bound to be outside my clearance level.'

'As a way to seek to pass the buck, Peter, that was very neat, but not neat enough. I am far too old and far too busy to undertake such a task. Be so good as to fetch in my secretary and I will happily upgrade you.'

To get to the leader it was necessary to pass through the lobby, coming down the staircase that led to their rooms and taking the other up to the suite of offices where the leader worked, his the room overlooking the other side of the canopy.

Konrad Henlein was not as either Corrie Littleton or Callum Jardine expected, a strutting bully and obvious fascist. Every time Cal had seen a photograph of him he had been dressed in some kind of uniform and at some quasi-military occasion or a party rally. In his office he was dressed in a tweed jacket, twill trousers and was wearing a cravat in an open-necked shirt; he looked more like an English country gent than the leader of a rabid bunch of thugs.

That extended to his personality, which was mild-mannered and pleasant, his voice soft, with more than a tinge of Austrian in the accent. He smiled easily, and with his spectacles on, a rather bland face exuded a sort of schoolmasterly air. Thinking back to the report he had read, penned by Sir Robert Vansittart, it became clear why he had seemed to represent no threat.

Corrie, on being introduced, got an old-fashioned kiss on the back of the hand, Cal a manly handshake before they were invited to sit down in comfortable chairs in front of a set of large windows that looked out over the square.

What followed was a general set of enquiries as to the comfort or otherwise of travel by sea, air and car, as well as questions about America, Corrie's replies translated by the Ice Maiden, which lasted until coffee was served.

The snapping banners and scudding clouds outside took a lot of Cal's attention – there was quite a strong wind blowing – and he tried very hard not to look at the large safe which dominated the corner of the room, inside which he assumed was what Henlein had brought back from his talk with Hitler.

The place was simply furnished: dark wooden desk, the safe,

another table with a big wireless sitting on it, several upright chairs, maps on the wall and lots of photographs of Henlein with various famous people, a lot of them politicians.

'Sir,' Cal said in German, 'I think it would be best if you speak in short sentences that I can translate for Miss Littleton, given the way the two languages differ.'

'As you wish, Herr Barrowman. We do want to get things correct.'

Cal was wondering if Hitler was like this in private, for there was a very good chance this man had modelled himself on the Führer. Having only ever seen the Austrian Corporal ranting on newsreels it was hard to imagine, but it might just be the case. It made little difference; he still wanted to put a bullet in his forehead.

That had to be put aside and Cal, using Corrie's notes, asked the first question, which was about the problems that existed for ethnic Germans in a state run by another nationality, the big blue eyes of the Ice Maiden fixed on him when Henlein began to reply, her lips pursed as she made sure he translated correctly, interrupting once or twice on some minor point. When she was not looking at him, her eyes were fixed then on Corrie's flying pencil, as if it was spouting Czech propaganda.

In truth what they were getting was the same line that had been trotted out for a decade, albeit without any of the venom normally used by the kind of speakers who were all taking their turn at Nuremberg. The ethnic Germans were pure of heart and purpose, good citizens but denied what was their due by spiteful Czechs who were repaying them for hundreds of years of Austrian domination.

All they asked was to live in peace in their own lands and control their own destiny and any notion of wishing to be united with the German Reich in another *Anchluß* was a Czech lie to which, unfortunately, many misguided people in the democracies subscribed.

How he wished they would come and see for themselves. It was difficult to keep a straight face sometimes, though Henlein and the Ice Maiden had no such problem, because what they were being told lay at total odds with what both had witnessed the previous night.

When Corrie alluded to that, in a gentle way that irritated the Ice Maiden but drew Cal's admiration, Henlein was all sorrow; these things came about through the intransigence of the Prague government. By failing to give the Sudetenlanders their rights they allowed hotheads to gain ground. Everything they had seen was the fault of the Czechs.

'He's a smooth bastard,' Corrie whispered as they were shown out after the first session.

'If you use the same words over and over again, year after year, they come out pat and who knows, maybe you come to believe they are true.'

'We eating here?' she asked, gloomily, as they looked into a dining room full of the same kind of people they had sat with the night before.

'No, let's get some air. There have to be other places in town.'

'Christ, that was quick,' Noel McKevitt said as Gibby Gibson handed him the response from London, which lifted his mood.

He had a frustrating morning meeting with the military attaché about that false End User Certificate, in which he had learnt nothing he did not already know and was in a bit of a mood because of it. It seemed the dolt had not even bearded the relevant Czech ministry and demanded an explanation.

From being cheered by the speed of response, that evaporated when he saw that it had come from Broadway. 'You sent this through the office?'

'Yes, it was bound to be quicker.'

Noel McKevitt was wondering how many people would have been apprised of that and how high it would go. 'I would have been happier if you'd told me, Gibby.'

'And I, Noel, would be happier to be getting on with my proper job.'

'Your job is to do what I tell you.'

'But you're not telling me, are you?'

Not having mentioned that the station was going to be closed down yet, that waspish reply allowed McKevitt the pleasure of doing so now and he told Gibby Gibson with no attempt to soften the blow to a man who was bound to wonder what this meant for his future career.

'So once this job, my job, is complete, old cock, it's pack your bags and back home for you and your 2IC, Bucharest and Warsaw for the others.'

'That's mad.'

'Tell Quex, Gibby, not me,' McKevitt replied with a cold stare, 'the orders come from him.'

Turning to the list, the name of Nolan stuck out as the only one where there was a query, given the owner had applied for a replacement, claiming his original had been lost, and the name on the document should be a Mr Laycock of 156 Fulham Palace Road, London, address and distinguishing mark supplied. All the other numbers were genuine. He toyed with the notion of sending for a copy of the photograph but that would take too long.

'Where's the Meran Hotel?'

'Wenceslas Square.'

'Get me a car and some backup, I'm going there.'

'I don't know if you've noticed, Noel, but the folk you want to back you up are all out doing what you wanted already.'

'Then it will have to be you and me.'

'What about an interpreter?'

'We don't need one, the bloke we're going to call on is English.'

Gibson grabbed a copy of the hotels his other men were calling on that day. 'The people you might want to question don't speak English, so let's find Miklos first.'

Cal extended the walk around Cheb in search of a meal as much as he could, passing several possibilities, trying to memorise the layout of the place and relate to the pictures he had seen. One of his stops was outside the Nazi Party HQ, much more formidable in fact than shown in the photographs.

It had steel doors with firing slits and shutters of the same kind for the windows; they at least were not going to take any chances if the Czechs came for them. They would not succumb to mere rifle fire – they would need artillery.

A wide loop in what was not a large town centre finally brought them back to the hotel square and Cal then chose the station café right across from the Victoria for a bite to eat, which had Jimmy Garvin, who was sitting indoors, scuttling away to try to remain unseen, ducking out of the door and scooting towards the station entrance. Sadly, nothing catches the idle eye quicker than movement and Corrie spotted him.

'So there's another reporter here?' Cal said.

'Sure, but why is he avoiding me?'

'Probably best I don't answer that.' That got him a thump on the arm, which only deepened his grin. 'Anyway, let's see if they do a sandwich.'

'You're not planning on an outside table?'

'Why not?'

'It's blowing a gale.'

'We'll be OK.'

'You might, I'll freeze.'

'Don't they have wind in Boston?'

'They do, and people of sense avoid it.'

He had to accede even if he did not want to; there was no way he was going to tell Corrie of his intention to study the exterior of the Victoria Hotel, the numbers going in and out and how the guards behaved – he also hoped to be there when they changed.

Frustratingly there were no tables by the window, but as soon as one was vacated he picked up his food, moved, and since his concentration was taken by the front of the hotel, he sat in silence.

'Penny for your thoughts,' Corrie finally said.

'I was just thinking about what Henlein said this morning and how he lied so easily, and with that nice-old-man smile on his face. Then when you look over there at those two Herberts standing outside the front door with their feet spread and a glower for anyone passing you wonder what makes them tick.'

'Power.'

'Yep, even a tiny bit is enough.'

In truth he was thinking that even the hotel would be hard to attack; it was in a terrace, which meant a frontal assault on the door was the only option and that was after you had crossed a wide open space large enough to give those inside, forewarned, a very good chance to get out the back doors where there was very likely an alleyway.

The next thought was how he was going to get round the back to check it out without causing suspicion; it was not, after all, what a man like him would do, wander into some narrow passage going nowhere. It was one of those situations where the presence of Vince would have been handy.

'Guards changing,' Corrie pointed out.

A party of Brownshirts approached and with much rigid arm raising, shouting and stamping they performed a farrago of a military drill, which would have been comical to Cal if he did not know the nature of the berks doing it. He had seen men like them taunt and beat up Jews in full view of their fellow citizens, who even if they wanted to, dared not interfere.

Often they would assault anyone who showed insufficient enthusiasm in their salutes to the name of the Führer, or even some poor soul who looked at them the wrong way, sure that whatever treatment they meted out would not bring down on them any sanction – they were above the law.

'You done?' he asked, looking at Corrie's unfinished food, and when she nodded he added, 'Best have a wash and freshen up before we see the leader again.'

'He sure has nice manners,' Corrie said, rubbing the back of the hand he had kissed. 'Not like some people I could mention.'

With that Cal extended his arm, which was taken by Corrie with a smile. The wind tugged at their clothes as they made their way back to the Victoria, and they separated to go to their respective rooms to prepare for the afternoon session.

There was not much difference between that and the morning, exactly the same cosy atmosphere, with slight variations on the trotted-out mantras, but at least Corrie had got into her stride when it came to sounding sympathetic because she had seen that was the only way to draw Henlein out.

And he was enjoying himself; it was almost as if being denied the kind of international publicity he clearly craved he was bathing in the sound of his own glory, repetitious when it came to his patience in dealing with the separatist problem, calling as concessions things he had done to make life awkward for the Czechs.

It was the same as what was happening across the border, the same as that speech of Goebbels: the well-honed lie that sounded reasonable as long as you stuck to it and allowed for no one to question it.

'I feel you need more, Fräulein Littleton,' Henlein said when the time came to end the session, impatiently signalled by the Ice Maiden, each sentence translated by Cal. 'There are documents I would wish you to see, things Herr Barrowman could interpret for you to demonstrate how far backwards I have bent to avoid a problem turning into a crisis. Alas there is no time today, but I will ensure these things are made available to you tomorrow and then, in the afternoon, perhaps we can talk again.'

'That would be most generous, Herr Henlein.'

'And perhaps,' he added, with a scholarly smile, 'you will have outlined in some detail the article you intend to submit and we can discuss it.'

There was no choice but to accede to that and they were ushered out.

* * *

296

The clattering of Corrie's typewriter was audible through her door when Cal came to fetch her for dinner, another indifferent meal, this time accompanied by the drone of the Deputy Führer, Rudolf Hess. He was no man to rally the troops, in fact looking around he looked like the kind of speaker who would be able to send his audience to sleep – even Corrie knew that and she could not understand a word he said.

'A walk?' Cal asked when Hess had finished – they could not pull the same sickness stunt twice.

'No, I'm bushed, Cal, being lied to all day and having to smile takes its toll.'

'We'll go for a little spin tomorrow morning, have a look around.'

That got him a look of deep suspicion; he was not the type for a 'spin', but she said nothing, just smiled and nodded and they made their way to their rooms. Cal, when he entered his, noticed his canvas bag had been moved.

He also noticed when he lifted it that it was a damn sight heavier than when he had left it at the foot of the chair, not surprising really when he saw that it had inside a Mauser pistol in a leather holster and two full ammo clips. He had to hide it quickly when there was a knock at the door, which when opened revealed standing there, in full SA kit, Karol Veseli.

'*Heil* Hitler, Herr Barrowman,' he said, in a voice too loud given they were only a few feet apart, just enough for him to add a salute.

'Good day . . .?' Cal could not use a name.

It was instructive that as soon as Veseli's hand dropped it went to his lips to command silence, then a finger waved to indicate the room was bugged.

'*Standartenführer* Karl Wessely.' The same sound, but Cal assumed the surname would be a different, more Germanic spelling. 'I have come, on the instructions of our leader, to ensure that everything is in order with your visit.'

'It is, thank you.'

Responding to a crooked finger, Cal immediately stepped out into the corridor and shut his door, hissing, 'My room was searched last night.'

Veseli replied softly in German, 'I know, I ordered it. Leave the keys to your car at reception when you go to breakfast tomorrow. Tell them to bring it to you in an hour.'

'Why?'

'Matters are coming to a head, you will see.'

'I was going to do a recce in the morning between here and Asch.'

'The time for that is past. We need to act quickly.'

Reaching past Cal he pushed the door open, speaking normally. 'My *Freikorps* troop are having a rally tomorrow night in the central square, we would be most pleased if you and Miss Littleton would come and attend as my guest. There will be food and beer and we can listen to the speech of the Führer from the Congress Hall on the radio.'

'Delighted,' Cal replied, managing to make it sound as though he meant it.

'And perhaps we can talk together and I can introduce to you and your lady reporter some of my men, and they will relate to you the lies that are told daily about how we ordinary Sudetenlanders behave.'

'I'm sure Miss Littleton would be very grateful for that.'

'I will call for you at eighteen-thirty hours tomorrow. The Führer's speech begins at seven.'

Wessely/Veseli gave him another stiff salute and was gone, leaving Cal to wonder at what the plan was, because there had to be one and whatever was going to take place had to happen tomorrow night and he was not sure he was happy with that.

CHAPTER TWENTY-ONE

In a strange city, especially one where the language was difficult to understand and few spoke English, Vince Castellano was glad of the Automat cafés; there he could eat and drink by merely looking at what was on offer in the various compartments and putting coins in the slot so that the glass-fronted door opened.

He also thought it a good idea, since he had time on his hands, to locate the Jewish Emigration Centre well before there was any need to go there in a panic, but when he got there, having got lost a couple of times, he wished he had not.

The sight depressed him too much; he had seen this sort of thing in the cinema on the Paramount and Pathé newsreels but in the flesh it was much worse, the displaced flotsam of those dislodged by war or the threat of it.

There was no queue outside the building, more a mob of people desperate to get out of the country by any means possible, all ages from ancient beings in black round hats with long ringlets to wailing babes in arms, tired-looking men and women, all Jewish, surrounded by suitcases or wrapped bundles of possessions.

The whole seemed to move in a swaying motion, much like a tide, as rumours were spread from one to another, this while volunteers moved through the crowd with buckets of water and ladles to quench the thirst of those hoping for those magic papers that would allow them to cross a border.

If it was like this before the Germans invaded, what would it be like afterwards? And then Vince realised it would be quieter – there would be a lot less Jewish emigration if they were in charge instead of the Czechs. The temptation to go inside was killed off by the people besieging the entrance so he turned round to retrace his steps, map in hand, constantly required to stop and peer at the street names which were incomprehensible.

It would have been nice to travel by bus or tram but he feared getting even more lost by taking the wrong one and occasionally, in frustration, he cursed Cal Jardine for leaving him alone in such a strange city.

Yet many of the locals, seeing his confusion, took pity on him as he sought to compare street and map names, eager to help, and everyone, even without English, knew the name and whereabouts of Wenceslas Square, so if it took time to get back to the Meran, he got there in the end.

Having been surrounded, when he overheard any conversations, by an unintelligible babble, the sound of a loud English voice, even a slightly irate and Irish one, as well as people dressed in the kind of clothes he knew from home, was welcome, and he made to approach the two men who were in heavy discussion by a double-parked car, one of whom had a very military moustache and bearing.

'For the love of Christ, Gibby, tell Miklos to send the bugger on his way.'

He did not in the end get close, but wiping the half smile of greeting off his face, Vince spun on his heel and went to look at a poster stuck on the nearest lamp post advertising something, he knew not what.

There was a third person at the front of the car explaining something to an unsmiling policeman and he was the big benevolent-looking fellow who had come to his door and asked to see his passport the day before.

'Copper's only doing his job.'

'And I am trying to get on with mine, or hadn't you noticed?'

'There's no rush, Noel, he's bound to come back here.'

'You can't be sure of that.'

'Where else is he going to go? The clerk says his luggage is in his room.'

'We should get Miklos to work him over.'

'Miklos is not a real policeman, and anyway they don't do that sort of thing in Czecho.'

'Then they're too soft and deserve to be invaded by the Hun.'

'Has it occurred to you that your man, Nolan, might be genuine?'

'On a lost passport?'

Vince had pulled his hat down while he listened to the argument and then that was added to by an accented voice. 'The policeman says he doesn't care if we have diplomatic plates, we can't park here and must move.'

If there was a reply Vince did not hear it; he was already walking away, forcing himself not to rush, wondering what time he had, only registering after several paces the way that foreign bloke had said 'we'. Diplomatic plates? He ducked down the first alley then doubled back to the rear of the Meran and through the door.

The lift was opposite the reception desk so it was a run up the stairs, and when he got to his room door a full kick splintered what was not a very strong lock. Inside, Vince shut the door and waited, counting to sixty; the noise of splintering wood might bring out someone from the shared hallway to see what had caused it but they would have to be standing right outside the door to see the damage.

In that minute the whole gamut of possibilities ran through his mind but the one thing that was certain was that he could not stay here and he could no longer use that false passport, which had to be the reason that bloke was calling again. Diplomatic plates meant an embassy as well, but then he had heard the military-looking one say that the bloke was not a real policeman.

Was it the law after him or someone else? Assume the worst, it's safest. What would they do when they discovered he had flown the Meran? He had a choice, the Jewish Emigration Centre or another hotel and he did not fancy the former, yet if he went to another hotel and it *was* the law they would come round looking for an Englishman who had checked in that day.

That was when Vince nearly laughed; first off he set a chair against the inside door handle to keep it closed and went to the canvas bag Cal had provided, then he packed his things quickly and untidily, including the book of short stories, pocketed the key to the Tatra and was out of that door in three minutes, bounding back down the stairs.

Outside in Wenceslas Square, thanks to an insistent policeman, it had been necessary to let Gibby Gibson move the car and so Noel McKevitt had taken station in the lobby, this after he had sent Miklos to the receptionist to flash that false warrant card again and order him to alert the man with the wispy fair hair sitting over there if Mr Nolan came back and asked for his key.

But a quick recce had revealed the back entrance and Miklos, duty done, was sent to cover that, arriving seconds before Vince reached the ground floor and made for the back door. Well oiled, it opened noiselessly and there before Vince was the back of a big bloke looking up and down the street, his hands in his pockets.

Stick or twist? There was really no option and no time to consider if this man blocking his way was a proper copper. If he was here, and whatever he was, the front had to be covered too. Dropping his bag, Vince stepped forward. Miklos heard the soft plop of it hitting the ground and turned to see coming toward him, smiling, the man he had spoken to previously.

Small and wiry, Miklos reckoned the little fellow to be no match for him, a thought he was still holding when he woke up about ten minutes later, having not seen the jab that hit him in the midriff, nor the fist that clouted the side of his head. All he could do was groggily stagger through to the lobby and tell McKevitt, now joined by Gibby Gibson, that their bird had flown.

An hour later Signor Vincenzo Castellano, who knew that to stay on the streets was too dangerous, was just down the road at another big hotel called the Paris demanding a room in fluent Italian. '*Posso avere una camera?*' That was the language with which he had grown up, as the child of immigrant parents, and his name on the passport he had fetched from the Tatra was the Italian spelling.

Making a bit of fuss and waving his arms in a very Latin way, he had to hope that his British passport, albeit the details were recorded, would not cause anyone to be too curious. Just because he had got away from the Meran did not mean he felt completely safe; he was still a stranger in Prague without the ability to easily communicate and with no knowledge of the depth of the threat he was facing.

Was it time to get out through Elsa Ephraim? But could he do that without first getting in touch with Cal, because if his passport was blown, then so would be the other one Cal was using, and his real documents, without which he would be left stranded, were still in the Tatra. Vince had not been a soldier for many years, but he knew the self-imposed regulation by which you always tried to abide: never leave a comrade in peril.

Could he telephone or send a telegram to Cheb? But that would mean using the Barrowman name and there was no way of knowing what risk was attached to that, yet that had to be weighed against the risk of doing nothing.

In the end, given the language problems he might face at the other end, he opted for telegram and once that was done it was getting late in the day. Not wanting to drive in the dark, he decided to eat, then sleep, ask for an early call and head off at dawn.

'Do you have any idea how many hotels there are in Prague, Noel?'

They were back in the embassy, Miklos was being checked out and patched up by a first-aider and Gibby Gibson was wondering if he should slip a sedative to his increasingly unstable Northern Irish boss, who might have a reputation for being a cool customer, but was showing no signs of it now.

'I don't care, I want them all checked out.'

They had a description, taken from the reception desk at the Meran and handsomely paid for, but in terms of resources what McKevitt was asking for was out of the question.

'You might be better looking for the other chap, Barrowman.'

'How? The bastard could be anywhere.'

'If, as we suspect, he's travelling on false papers like his mate then he's committing a crime.'

'And?'

'If he's staying in any kind of hotel, his details will be registered as a matter of course.'

'Like in France and Germany, you mean?' McKevitt demanded.

'The embassy can inform the Czech authorities that they have reasonable grounds to suspect that a British subject is in their country under an assumed name for purposes of which we have no idea. I have to tell you, Noel, if they are given information like that, right now they will smell German spy.'

'Who do we tell?' McKevitt demanded. 'I hope you are not going to say to me "the police". If they are anything like the lot we have at home it will take them a week to get off their arse.'

'The man we want is Colonel Doležal, who runs the Czech equivalent of MI5.'

'They're not much better,' the Irishman spat, thinking of Barney Foxton. 'How well do you know him?'

Gibson knew the meaning of the question: could Doležal be trusted? 'Well enough.'

'Then let's get hold of the bugger and tell him the fella we're after is dangerous.'

'Is he, Noel?'

'More than you know, Gibby,' McKevitt replied.

'If I can tell Doležal why that is, it might speed up his search.'

But you would not see it as I see it, McKevitt thought, not see that a man who might drag our whole nation into a war was the most lethal kind of problem we could have – and how can you tell some Czech sod who would want us involved that I am trying to put the mockers on our staying out of their stupid little predicament?

'Hint he's a spy, Gibby, that will have to do, and Christ, with what's going on it should be enough.'

Having done as requested, Gibby Gibson waited till McKevitt was out of the way and made another visit to the Cipher Room, this time to send a cable to Quex himself. He wanted to ask if the outfit had any information on two men named Barrowman and Nolan, whom his station chief seemed intent on pursuing without saying why, though he checked first with Tommy that McKevitt had not sent anything similar.

'Hasn't been in touch with London at all, Major, since he arrived.'

'Not at all?'

That was peculiar; it was standard practice when chasing suspects to keep Broadway informed of progress – doubly so when they had only really got the names – not necessarily the top floor but certainly his own desk, to keep abreast of things whoever McKevitt had left in charge. What was the bugger playing at?

'If he does, Tommy, tip me the wink will you?'

Colonel Capec Doležal had a lot on his plate in a country prepared for war and in a city swarming with potential spies, so the request from Major Gibson only got attention because he was a good and trusted friend to his country and he sounded alarmed, as if this Barrowman might pose a substantial risk.

The name was added to what was a daily bulletin distributed throughout the country, a combination of police notices, intelligence dilemmas and threats to guard against that went out every morning.

In a nation on high alert there were a lot of warnings being issued to the various branches of government and the only way to distribute such alarms as needed to be disseminated and ensure they might be acted on was in writing.

With the name in question, police station commanders in Prague would have their men check the hotel registration files for the past ten days. Cables were sent off to offices in other Czech cities – they would print and send out what they received locally; the one place excepted from the full effect of this was in the disputed border territories where the staff in the telegraphic office were a mix of German and Czech.

So for places like Cheb it was added to a series sent off with the despatch riders who distributed the bulletin to the various checkpoints and army headquarters that covered the country, and even when the bulletin was received, care had to be taken about what to act on and what to ignore, given the potential for any act to stir up trouble.

Cal was doing his exercises again when the telegram from Vince was delivered to his door and when he read it, even if it was not in code, he reckoned that it was secure, given the chances of anyone being able to read a mixture of rhyming slang, cockney and seriously colloquial English in this part of the world was zero; it took him some time to decipher the series of short sentences himself.

Hubble bubble was trouble; *flown the coop* simple; could be *Old Bill* needed no explanation and nor did *done a runner*; *Nolan brief gone west, yours too probably, old one best* took some working out; *think about being on your toes* did not. *Trying for a meet – twelve dart finish. Will bell.* Vince.

The hushed curse made no difference at all and it was exactly the reverse of what he had expected; Cal thought if anyone got into trouble it would be him and he could think of no rational explanation as to how it could be otherwise. Vince had got into some difficulty and had been forced to leave the Meran, his false passport the cause, and that put both false identities at risk. Added to that, despite being told not to, he was on his way and fast.

What to do? He could not just bale out without an explanation and Corrie had her last interview with Henlein that afternoon. Added to that, something was going to go off that night, he was certain, which almost guaranteed, though not for sure, he would be out of here within twenty-four hours anyway.

Then it struck him: only he, Vince and Peter Lanchester had known the identities they were operating under; had Peter been obliged to tell anyone at Broadway and had their names been leaked to the Czech authorities from there? Looked at from every other angle it was the only thing that made sense, but not a lot. The only other people who knew the names were Snuffly Bower and the man he used to doctor the documents and they had no idea where he was.

'Breakfast time,' came the breezy call as he picked up his phone.

'Be along soon.'

'Bring that pen of yours, I've got a typed draft I'd like you to look over.'

'I've been promoted from interpreter to editor?'

'Guess so.'

He was not going to rush, so he went back to his press-ups and squats, thinking, and that told him if Vince was moving he had to stay still, quite apart from the fact that he could not risk travelling on the documents he possessed. Once he had his own passport then he could make some kind of plan, until then it was best to just carry on.

Both before he went to sleep and this morning he had been thinking about what his late-night visitor had said. Either something had occurred that meant Veseli had to make a premature move, or, more worryingly for Cal, they had got him here on a false prospectus – getting him to undertake some action immediately had always been the aim!

The way to turn that down flat was easy – keep his car keys in his trouser pocket. But Cal possessed a curiosity to a greater degree than any cat. Before he left the room he put the canvas bag with the Mauser, folded tight, in the cupboard – it was not a thing to be carrying around discreetly – and downstairs he did as Veseli had asked and left the keys at reception with the requested instructions.

There was little use for his pen on Corrie's article, it was so flattering it nearly made him choke on his fruit juice; in fact, he thought it might be too much so and it would be an interesting test of how seriously these people took themselves if they fell for it – no rational mind would, only a warped one could.

'We still going for that spin?'

'Of course, meet you out front in twenty.'

Standing at the desk, it suddenly occurred to him that it was here he had filled in the registration card as Barrowman. Did they give them to the Czech police? He tried to imagine one walking in to collect them and passing two Brownshirt thugs at the door. Tempted to ask he decided against it, for he could think of no way of phrasing the question that would not sound suspicious.

The first place the name Barrowman rang a bell was at a checkpoint halfway to Cheb, crossed by two foreigners that the officer in command could recall very easily – how uncommon was it to find an

American female journalist in Czechoslovakia at all, or perhaps just as unusual, a foreigner, an Englishman, travelling in his homeland, who could speak German like a native, though not with an accent he could place?

With the gift of a field telephone, though frustrated by the way the traffic had to be routed on a busy network, he was through to the Ministry of the Interior within half an hour. So occupied was he that he instructed his men to be lenient about letting the stream of cars and lorries going in both directions through the barriers.

Vince, who had set off from Prague at dawn, was one of the beneficiaries and in passing he made sure they would think him Italian as he shouted, '*Mille grazie!*'

CHAPTER TWENTY-TWO

'**G**ot him,' Gibby Gibson cried when he came off the phone to Colonel Doležal, before he wondered what he was getting so excited about. 'Your friend Barrowman crossed a checkpoint going towards Karlovy Vary two days ago in the company of an American female and I have even got the make of motor he was driving.'

'Not short of a bob or two,' McKevitt remarked when he saw what that was. 'A bloody Maybach Zeppelin, for Christ's sake. Any idea who the lass was?'

'Journalist apparently, she had accreditation papers but the name has not come through.'

'Saturday – we must have missed him by a whisker.'

'Rotten luck that,' Gibson replied insincerely.

'She had to come from Prague, Gibby.'

'You'd think so. Most of the journos stay at the Ambassador.'

Picking up the telephone Gibson added, 'And there can't be too many who are female.'

Annoyingly, McKevitt was drumming his fingers on Gibson's desk as he made the call but it did not take long to establish who the lady was and the fact that she was not presently in residence, but given Gibson was talking to reception, and not the concierge desk, that was all he got.

'She must have left some form of contact address,' Gibson insisted, his eyes going to the ceiling, given the time he was obliged to wait until the reply came through; they did not stay there when he was told.

McKevitt was equally surprised and he had read the latest briefing before he left London. 'Cheb! That's where Henlein had his headquarters, isn't it, and that other bugger Frank?'

Gibson nodded and waited for the obvious follow-up – like what was their man doing going there? – but it did not come. Instead he picked up the phone again. 'Should I tell Doležal we've found him?'

'No!'

'Noel, he will have men searching hotel registration cards all over the place to no purpose. You can't just leave him in the dark.'

'We've let him think our man's a spy. If we tell him, who will pick him up? Not us.' Still drumming his fingers, McKevitt went into deep thought, the conclusion surprising the station chief. 'I need a car, Gibby, and some cash.'

'You're going after Barrowman yourself?'

'I am, but I doubt that's the bastard's real name. Tell me, what's the situation with weapons?'

'You mean—'

'Look, this man is dangerous, Gibby, and he has to be stopped.'

'From doing what, Noel?'

'I can't tell you.'

'Is that because you don't know?'

'Have you told your team about closing down the station?'

'Don't change the subject.'

'Who in the name of Christ do you think you're talking to?' The question was on Gibson's lips: why have you not been in touch with base? But it died there, not least because McKevitt was not finished.

'You should be packing your bags, Gibby. And don't think it will go unnoticed that I had to come here to sort out a problem that you should have seen to.'

'I have no idea what you're talking about.'

'No,' McKevitt sneered, a very necessary adjunct to his bluff, 'you don't, which makes me think it might be time you retired. Now get me the use of an embassy car and a pistol with some ammo.'

'Sorry, Noel, that is something you will have to do yourself.'

The sun was shining, the hood was down in the Maybach, though being autumn the air had a chill in these high elevations that required Corrie to wear a headscarf and Cal his hat. But it was pleasant driving at a relaxed pace, quite often through thick forests, even if right behind them came a car, a tiny Hanomag, with two Brownshirts crammed into it, tasked to watch where they went.

The temptation to look in the boot when the car was brought to the front of the hotel had to be resisted and there was nothing in the passenger compartment that was in anyway untoward. He would just have to wait for an opportunity and to do that the first task was to lose the tail.

'Have you got used to being on the wrong side of the car yet?'

'Let's just say I don't think I'm going to die.'

'Good.'

Cal hit the floor with the pedal and the V12 engine responded immediately, Corrie crying 'Jesus!' as she was thrust back in her seat. There were no straight roads in these parts and they were not generous in width, which made the sensation of speed all that much greater, exaggerated as the tyres screeched round the bends.

As soon as the tail was out of sight, Cal was looking for a junction or at least where the road split, and that came at a fork, he taking the uphill line because it affected him not at all, but that near-toy car with two big blokes in it would struggle to keep up any speed at all. For all they were moving up a steep hill, the trees still hemmed them in.

At the top of the hill there were two bored-looking sentries in grey-green Czech uniforms standing before an entry into the woods shut off by a wire gate, but the approach of the car brought them to life and their slung weapons came off the shoulder just as the trees thinned to one side to show an extensive panorama.

Inside those trees there had to be some of the Czech defences, and on this kind of elevation and with the open ground below the hilltop, Cal assumed heavy artillery, which would be in a well-defended concrete cupola surrounded by pillboxes.

He slowed right down and went by at a crawl; these conscripts, which is what they looked to be, were likely to be trigger-happy and he had known men killed by not paying enough attention to another soldier's nerves. The speed also allowed him time to assess the field of fire he imagined the weapons could strike; that panoramic view looked as though it extended right into the Third Reich.

Past that and descending he really gave the car full throttle and soon they were racing through another dense tree belt so narrow occasional branches hissed along the side of the car and one or two hit it with a crack; if it had a serious purpose, driving like this was exhilarating.

Corrie showed no sign of fear; in fact, when a bit of straight road allowed him to look at her it seemed as if her eyes, staring straight ahead, were alight, her mouth was slightly open and her breathing seemed faster than normal – she was excited and enjoying the thrill as much as he was.

Sighting another ungated path into the trees he pulled hard over and shot up the lane, which had her sliding across the front leather seat to his side, coming to a halt with her body jammed against his. He could sense her, and the way her breath was still heaving was too obvious to miss, so spinning sideways he threw an arm over her shoulder and pulled her close.

She made no attempt to avoid being kissed, there was no stiffness or resistance and, as his tongue slipped between her teeth, he also knew that whatever else Corrie Littleton had done in her life, this was not the first time such an embrace had happened to her; she had been kissed before, because her tongue was also pushing forward to meet his own.

'Is this why we came for a spin?' she asked when they broke contact.

'Would you be angry if it was?' She shook her head. 'Neither would I.'

'That's a helluva thing.'

'I have work to do.'

'You betcha,' she said, her hand grabbing the back of his head, knocking off his hat and pulling him in till their lips were locked together again, and this time there was a trace of a moan, and whatever it is that signals from one human to another that they are willing was in Cal's nostrils now.

'You an outdoor girl?' he asked.

She knew what that meant. 'Heart and soul, Doc.'

'There are a couple of rugs on the back seat.'

'Is that planning?'

'It's a luxury car.'

'Maybe they are in the wrong place.'

'A walk?'

As she nodded he switched off the engine and Corrie took his hand to be pulled out of the driver's door, which she held tight till Cal got the rugs out, there for rear seat passengers to cover their knees to keep out the cold.

'You all right with this?' he asked, his own voice now slightly hoarse. 'There might be soldiers about.'

By way of a reply she led him away from the car and into the trees, holding his hand tightly – a pressure Corrie kept up until they came to a small clearing covered in fallen leaves. She looked at him and he nodded, then detached himself to spread out the rugs one on top of the other. Cal lay down and pulled her with him and immediately they were locked in an embrace.

He knew by what followed that Corrie Littleton was no first-timer; she knew the body parts that mattered on him as well as he knew those that excited her and was uninhibited at seeking them out. The usual awkward gremlins getting out of clothing were met with the kind of intimate laughter that comes with slightly embarrassed struggles.

In these trees there was minimal sunlight and it was not really a warm day, but racing blood made up for any chill, that and activity that started slowly and rose in pace as both parties to this lovemaking extracted maximum pleasure from the act. When it was over, her bird-scattering screams had subsided and the breathing had settled a touch, she spoke into his shoulder in a small voice.

'I hope you'll still respect me, Doc.'

'Don't see why I should, I didn't before.'

Her laugh filled the air and seemed to echo off the trees. 'Callum Jardine, you are a piece of work.'

'Which reminds me why I came,' he whispered in her ear.

That set her off again, pealing laughter, which had Cal thinking this was a wholly different person to the one he thought he knew and he preferred it that way.

'Can we just stay here for a few minutes?'

'What makes you think I have the guts to say no?'

They lay for some fifteen minutes, not talking a lot but sharing whispered intimacies, until eventually Cal rose up and hauled her willingly to her feet. Hand in hand, once they had sorted out their clothing, they walked back to the car, each with a rug, and once they were seated in the front Cal asked her to get the maps and camera out of the glovebox.

'It suddenly occurs to me we could have wandered into a minefield.'

'Bang,' she replied, as he handed her the camera.

'What are you like as a photographer?'

'As good as you are as a lover, Doc.'

Now it was his turn to startle the birds with his laughing.

It took a while and some map reading to get back on to the road to the town the Czechs called Aš, with many stops on the way: after tight bends, places where the road narrowed or where it was heavily enclosed by trees which, felled by blast, would block it completely – all possible points at which to spring an ambush.

At each one Cal took photographs, with Corrie insisting that he stand back to be snapped as well, and at no time did she enquire what he was up to; it was as though by making love their entire relationship had altered massively. She was happy and made no secret of it.

Asch was a pretty place nestling in rolling hills and surrounded by good rolling pasture. The houses, where they were not just grey stone, were painted in rose-pink and yellow and the style was similar to Cheb, with the tall steep-roofed buildings joining one another in long terraces.

The attempts to talk to what locals they came across were not a success: approaching anyone, even when Cal spoke to them in German, showed that they were an insular bunch not too keen to answer Corrie's questions, some so nervous it was as though the mere act of talking to strangers would endanger them.

'He might not have invaded,' Cal ventured, 'but it feels like Hitler's here already.'

They found Henlein's house by endless asking, as if they were tourists, Corrie's notebook put away, and the first obvious fact was that, like the Victoria Hotel, it was guarded, in this case by two armed dolts who refused to believe Cal's explanation and refused to allow him to use his camera. If they wanted photographs of the house they must get that from the owner.

'Time to go back and meet the big cheese.'

As she slid into the passenger seat, he finally went to unlock and look in the boot. There was a small wooden box there, one big enough to hold a couple of pairs of shoes, covered in a cloth, with a faint smell he recognised – the almond odour of slightly sweating nitroglycerine in the Nobel 808. The cloth once moved showed a pair of impermeable gloves over a packet of the green flexible explosive, a couple of detonators, a coil of wire, and underneath that a battery-operated plunger.

'You OK?'

'Yes,' he shouted back cheerfully, but he was not, he was concerned at what he was going to be asked to do. As he locked the boot lid he added, 'You want to drive?'

'Do you want to live?'

Unintentionally that was a very apposite question.

The delay in reacting to Gibson's despatch was caused by Sir Hugh Sinclair giving his weekly briefing to the Home Secretary, which took up half of his morning and meant he did not read it till he arrived back, and when he did so it was buried under a collection of other cables from stations around the globe. Miss Beard, his faithful and long-serving secretary, had not heard him curse often, but she heard it now.

'Get hold of Peter Lanchester at once and tell him to come immediately, then come back to take a message to be sent to Prague.'

Miss Beard was writing when Peter arrived, with Quex dictating that no action was to be taken in respect of either man, though all he knew of Nolan was that he was backup for Barrowman/Jardine, and they were to stay well clear.

'Get that off as a flash message as soon as it is coded,' Quex growled, turning to Peter Lanchester when she exited and throwing the cable across the desk. 'I don't know what McKevitt is up to but he has somehow dug out Jardine.'

'The man's a bloody menace.'

'Never mind that, get down to Documents and have them issue you a diplomatic passport, we've no time for visas and the like, I want you over there babysitting Jardine and making sure McKevitt goes nowhere near him.'

'He wouldn't block him, surely, if he found out what Jardine's after?'

Sinclair was thinking of his wigging from the PM again; as well as scarcely concealed desperation to avoid a war, he was now, it seemed, talking of going to Germany to meet Hitler face to face; it did not bode well.

'I would not put it past him, and besides, he must not find out. You can travel by train tomorrow, I hope, from Paris and that will take you directly to Eger.'

'Of course. But, sir, there must be more to this than meets the eye. McKevitt seems to be out of control.'

'The problem is he's not under my control at present, but out of that entirely he is not.'

Peter waited for him to expand on that, but he waited in vain.

Both he and his boss would have been even more alarmed had either been aware that, as they were talking, McKevitt was on the embassy secure line to Sir Thomas Inskip confirming that there was an operation taking place in Czechoslovakia the nature of which he was unaware and, *ipso facto*, so was the Government.

'What do you suspect?' asked a surprised Minister of the Crown, who hardly expected a call from such a location.

'I am still in the dark about that, sir, but there is no question that it is dangerous and possibly downright illegal.'

'And you have gone to Czechoslovakia to pursue this?'

'I have,' McKevitt lied – he was not going to admit he had been sent. 'Worse, Sir Hugh Sinclair has decided to shut down the station, an idea he says he discussed with the PM to avoid anything happening to exacerbate tensions.'

'That, if I may say so, McKevitt, does not square with what you have just been telling me.'

'No, he's playing some deep game all right. What I need to kill it off is the authority to override Sir Hugh, and only Mr Chamberlain can grant that.'

Accustomed to giving advice to clients as a top-flight lawyer, Inskip knew that would never be forthcoming because it had no validity unless it was in writing, and he doubted Chamberlain was fool enough to even contemplate such an instruction.

He also knew that anything he said on this telephone was strictly between him and the caller, while it seemed to him important that McKevitt should proceed; why should he not take the reins and act on his own initiative?

'I can try to get that for you, but it would take time. Do we have time?'

'I would say it would be tempting providence to think we have.'

Code, Inskip thought, *for you have no idea of that either.* 'It may be you have to act on your own until I can get the PM's ear and he's away on a fishing holiday.'

'That exposes me, sir, and I may have to act in a manner that could be seen as prejudicial.'

'If you deem it necessary then you must do so, and you know I will back you, McKevitt, if there's an enquiry.'

'Do I have permission to keep you informed?'

'A splendid idea, and I will liaise with the PM about the matter. In fact I will send him a message this very hour.'

'Thank you, sir.'

Phone down, Sir Thomas sat and pondered, reverting to his original conclusion that no such written instruction would come from Neville Chamberlain even if he knew what McKevitt was up to and approved. This was a situation in which he could act as a conduit, and if it proved to have merit he would gain credit; if it was pie in the sky, and it very well could be that, then he could discount all knowledge of it.

As to sending a message to the PM, the poor man was on a well-earned holiday, peacefully fishing; it would not be the done thing to impinge on that. Besides, he had plenty on his desk as the Minister for Defence Procurement, not least the latest costings for the new fighter just introduced to RAF service.

The price of building these planes was going up to over twelve thousand pounds per item, and though the people who flew the Spitfire claimed it was a wonder-plane, there was no evidence that it would match whatever other nations were producing, not least the Germans. It could, in aerial combat, turn out to be a dud.

'As long as you don't blame me if it's not,' he said to himself.

When the pair came back to the hotel from their spin the Ice Maiden was waiting for them, and judging by the look she gave Corrie, it was all her fault that they had lost their followers.

'That was very wrong of you to run away from those we have given the task of protecting you, Frau Littleton.'

'We don't need protection, surely,' Cal replied, 'and we did want to see some of the country.'

'The Czech army is out there and has been known to shoot anyone who they think is spying on their defence works.'

The temptation to say "That must include half the Sudetenland population" had to be suppressed. Then, as she had done so many times before, she smiled at Cal and turned her body just enough to exclude the other woman.

'But you are back, Herr Barrowman, and safe and that is all that matters.'

That changed when Cal got a peck on the cheek from Corrie; the smile was gone in an instant, before she added with sweet cruelty, 'And we had such a lovely drive, Fräulein.'

CHAPTER TWENTY-THREE

M ajor Gibby Gibson was well aware he was dithering; should he send another signal to London or not? Effectively he had been relieved of his job by Noel McKevitt, so in essence he had no authority to do anything at all and in between the worries he had there was the requirement to make arrangements to disperse the men under his command.

With the chaps from neighbouring stations it was easy, they had travelled light – pack your kit and take a train to Warsaw and Bucharest. With him and his assistant they would be giving up rented apartments, paying off people like cleaners, saying goodbye to long-standing friends, settling bills for mundane things like gas and electricity, and in his much younger 2IC's case disentangling himself from a rather torrid love affair.

'I think you should see this, sir,' said Tommy the cipher clerk, bursting into Gibson's office. 'It's a flash from London.'

Gibson was out of his chair before he had finished reading it, calling out for the Royal Marines he had stationed in Prague as legation guards to find Noel McKevitt and if necessary restrain him, only to receive the news that the man had taken a Humber Snipe from the pool and had left half an hour before.

'Did he indent for a weapon?' he asked the senior marine, a sergeant who was in charge of such things.

The reply was crisply military and given as if such a thing was an everyday occurrence.

'Webley revolver, sir, and twenty-four rounds of ammo. Nice to see the gentleman was familiar with the weapon, sir, handled it like an old pro, he did.'

London had to be informed and he needed to know what to do – a message which took time to encode and send. It was only by sheer luck it caught Peter Lanchester, who was leaving the building to hail a cab to Victoria for the boat train. He was hauled back smartish to face a seething Sir Hugh Sinclair.

'Change of orders, Peter,' he said, thrusting Gibson's signal in his hand. 'McKevitt is to be stopped by whatever means are necessary. Right now Miss Beard is typing a letter relieving him of all duties forthwith pending an enquiry into his conduct.'

'Can't we get the Czechs to stop him?'

'He's armed and travelling on a UK diplomatic passport – what would you say if you were a local and asked to intercept an armed British official roaring around in a legation car with dip plates?'

'I would wonder what is going on.'

'And you would ask for clearance to act?'

Peter nodded; he knew what that meant with someone carrying a gun: permission to shoot, which would entail at the very least the

Czech Foreign Ministry asking the ambassador, who in turn might well cable London for clarification.

'Exactly, and this would all be taking place in a country where, by official diktat, we are supposed to be playing it soft. Get to Eger, Peter, and tell Jardine to abort whatever he's involved in and get out of the country.'

'Regardless of what stage he is at?'

'Regardless,' Sir Hugh replied, very forcibly, as the required letter was placed in front of him for signature; rather suddenly his eyes misted over and this took on the appearance of a letter of resignation. 'Termination, Peter, nothing else will do.'

Peter just had time to send a telegram to the Meran Hotel for Vince to get out and he employed the same tactics of colloquial English, there being no time to code it. It read: *Gaff Blown, Scarper.*

Upstairs Sir Hugh Sinclair was composing another signal telling Major Gibson to stand down and do nothing; the last thing he needed was a bunch of SIS men running around Czecho trying to apprehend one of their own. Keeping that quiet might prove impossible.

Driving out of Prague, Noel McKevitt was excited; given the mundane nature of what he had been doing for many years – the life of an SIS man on station was not one of much adventure and being desk bound was even worse – he was shedding nearly two decades, going back to the days when he and men like Barney Foxton, young then and ruthless, had fought the IRA to keep Ireland under the aegis of the British Crown.

That was the last time he had carried a gun in anger, the same as that which lay beside him on the car bench seat. There was too, at the back of his mind, the knowledge that, while he could rise further in the service, to a man of his background – grammar school and front-line service in a common or garden regiment – positions like that held by Sir Hugh Sinclair were outside his natural reach; he did not come from the right part of the establishment.

Long-held instincts now crystallised into a powerful spur to what he was doing, for it thus followed, and always would even if he had been reluctant to acknowledge it in the past, that elevation to the kind of position he craved would only come from some bold stroke which would elevate his prospects.

Luck played a major part in advancement, that and birth, for, from what he had observed, ability was not a prerequisite if you went to the right schools and saw service in the Royal Navy or the Brigade of Guards. How many senior positions had he seen filled by eejits who had nothing but one of those as their only qualification?

At the first checkpoint he was waved through without trouble; the boys manning it had been educated to recognise the plates of diplomatic vehicles, with which they were neither allowed to interfere or search, and it would be the same at the ones he had yet to face. McKevitt could look forward to being in Cheb in under four hours, the kind of time that had only been possible before Czech mobilisation.

He had reckoned without the car, which on the open road and being pushed a bit hard – normally it was used in town and on short journeys – revealed a radiator prone to overheating, evidenced by the pall of steam that began to issue from the bonnet at the second checkpoint, forcing him to pull over.

Once the steam had dispersed, one of the soldiers keen to assist him identified the problem as a split hose and a very junior conscript was sent off to find a garage where a replacement might be located. So frustrated was McKevitt that he wanted to retrieve the Webley from under the seat where he had hidden it and shoot someone.

Up ahead Vince Castellano was having a miserable time; every checkpoint was taking over an hour to get through, the traffic backed up for at least a mile and everyone's papers being checked. Being foreign, he was pulled over for a more serious questioning every time which further delayed his progress and the nearer he got to his destination the jumpier seemed the soldiers.

It was well into the afternoon that he was obliged to pull over to the side to let past a stream of army lorries, some pulling artillery, and he wondered if the balloon had gone up, the only thing that reassured him the lack of a stream of refugees coming the other way. Then, on what this map told him was the border with the province called Karlovy Vary, he was halted altogether, the only consolation being that everyone else was too.

Peter Lanchester was back on the train at Calais wondering whether his stomach would ever settle down after a most appalling crossing in which he had been tossed around like a cork; would he be able to eat the food he had ordered?

The waves in the English Channel were notorious, made more disturbing by the narrowness of the sea and the way the gap between each rise and fall was so small. The whole thing had been accompanied by the sound of breaking glass and crashing crockery as the things normally used to feed and water people – no one was eating or drinking – were chucked off the shelves supposed to contain them by the peculiar corkscrew motion of the ferry.

Worse, the crossing had taken longer than normal, not aided by the difficulty of getting into Calais harbour, and he was in some danger of missing his connection to the Paris-to-Prague Express. The steward in the first-class dining room had assured him that the driver would seek to make up time, so he would just have to hope – and it seemed a forlorn one – that he could get to Cheb before McKevitt.

'And so, Fräulein Littleton, I hope you have everything you have come for,' said Henlein, once more taking her hand to kiss it while Cal translated. 'You will, of course, let me see what you intend to submit.'

'Before you leave,' added the Ice Maiden.

'Plenty of time,' Cal responded, his remark no longer met with warmth.

'Wessely told me he had invited you to our local rally tonight,' Henlein said. 'I too will be attending. It is good that we come together to hear the German Führer speak, for I am certain he will refer to us and our difficulties and what aid he intends to give us.'

That was said with such confidence that Cal wondered if Henlein knew what Hitler was going to say – not the words, for he was very much an instinctive orator, but the gist. It was not a thought he held long, for the time had come for him and Corrie to depart, and as soon as they were out of the door she could not resist a jibe.

'How does it feel to be frozen in ice like a woolly mammoth?'

'I don't know what you mean,' he replied, but he did.

'How long have we got before we are taken to the bullring?'

'A couple of hours.'

'We could . . .' she said kittenishly, taking his arm.

'Haven't you got typing to do?'

If it sounded like resistance it was only a formality.

Her nails dug into his arm. 'I've got nimble fingers.'

'My place or yours?'

Jimmy Garvin was bored stiff; he had actually called the Bayerischer Hof to inform Bartlett there was nothing happening, only to be told there was bugger all happening anywhere, certainly not in Prague, and what about him, surrounded by fanatical Nazis who kept trying to knock his eye out with their damn salute? It seemed churlish for Jimmy to point out that he was in much the same boat.

'She must have interviewed Henlein, Jimmy, if she is staying in the same bloody hotel. What about breaking into her room and seeing if there's anything worth pinching?'

'You're not serious, Vernon?'

'No, joking really, but you never know what a young and ambitious fellow will do to get on, what?'

'Meaning if I'd said I would do it you would not have restrained me?'

'Laddie, I'm a hundred or more miles away, how could I? Best thing to do is to make yourself known to Corrie—'

'I've met her, remember.'

'Don't be obtuse, Jimmy, there's a good chap. Let her know you're in Cheb, chat her up and use that devastating charm of yours to wheedle something out of her.'

Jimmy was about to say 'What devastating charm?' when he realised Bartlett was being sarcastic. 'She'll probably tell me to bugger off.'

'Not a word our American chums employ, dear boy, but nothing ventured. Now, I've got to dash, the car is waiting to take me and dump me amongst several thousand sweaty oiks in that damned Congress Hall so that I can listen to Hitler tell the world what a genius he is for the umpteenth time.'

'Are you not worried about being overheard?'

'Jimmy, I hope the Gestapo are listening in. The truth, for once, will do them a power of good.'

Lying soaking an hour later, Cal was not thinking about the second bout of lovemaking he had just been enjoying with Corrie Littleton, pleasant as that was, but about what might be asked of him when he met Veseli in an hour's time – and he knew it was not just going to be beer, food and listening to Hitler; that box in the back of his car was there for a purpose and it did not take a genius to work it out.

He was going to be asked to blow Henlein's safe, which was pushing things a bit; while he knew about explosives, there was a skill to being aware of the right quantity needed to blast open a lock of a hardened steel door without killing yourself in the process and this was no trial-and-error situation.

Also, it must have been planned from the outset; Moravec, he suspected, had suckered him into this, playing up his need for subterfuge in his own capital city, ramping up the nerves, dangling before him the enticing prospect of material that would answer his purpose without the risk of going into Germany.

How convenient it must have been, his turning up, a man with the skills needed, an expert in covert warfare, guns and explosives, abilities they had talked about months before. How long after he got Janek to initiate contact had Moravec seen that he might be the solution to a problem he was wrestling with?

Cal had to assume it had been from the outset and he had been manoeuvred, pulled and pushed like some puppet, with Corrie Littleton the icing on the Moravec cake, which, if nothing else, showed that the intelligence chief was not only very quick to see a possibility but capable of acting on it with equal speed.

The other fact, which was inescapable, lay in the certain knowledge that someone else had been set to undertake what he was going to be asked to do and stood down when he arrived as a better alternative.

The reason? He was a foreigner, the original person tasked to blow Henlein's safe and steal those documents had to be Czech, so was that sanction from the president to do nothing real or just another bit of flummery to suck him in?

Odds-on it was Veseli, but by using Cal, Moravec might get what he wanted, avoid censure if there was to be any and leave his best agent in place, which might not have been possible if Veseli did the deed.

How, if it was Veseli doing the job, had the Czech agent planned to get away? That, as Cal examined it, did not make sense. Once his cover was blown he was stuck miles from safety with everyone who had once trusted him baying for his blood, and he was not an easy man to disguise; even amongst Aryans he stood head and shoulders above them.

Imagining some of his Brownshirt thugs catching up with him and thinking of the treatment they would mete out should not have induced feelings of gratification, but it did; it was only a flight of the imagination and if Moravec had finagled him into this, Veseli must have known and been complicit.

The church clock striking six had him rise from the water; it was time to get ready.

* * *

'Jimmy,' Corrie said, as she opened the door to find the young reporter looking abashed, in fact hopping from foot to foot; she was, after all, wrapped in a huge bath towel.

'Sorry to catch you in . . . er . . . your . . . er . . .' he mumbled away at the towel. 'Thought it was time to come and say hello.'

'I'll say, but I would be more interested to know why you ran away yesterday.'

'I'm not supposed to be here,' he replied, in a flash of what seemed like inspiration until he realised he would have to run with the lie and he had no idea where to go.

'I guess you're trying to find a story that will get you out from under Vernon,' Corrie replied, unwittingly throwing him a lifeline. 'As you can see, Jimmy, I was just getting dressed.'

'Sorry.'

'Look, I am meeting someone in the bar in fifteen minutes.'

'Callum Jardine,' Jimmy replied, immediately realising that was a mistake.

The hand that grabbed him and pulled him inside the door was not gentle, nor was the way it was slammed behind him.

'How the hell do you know his name?'

Tempted to lie, there was not one he could think of and that left only the truth. 'Vernon knows him from Madrid and he saw you get into his car.'

'You little schmuck, you've been sent to tail me.'

'Instructed, Corrie,' Jimmy pleaded. 'I am only doing what Vernon told me to do.'

'Sit in that chair and say not another word.' Corrie went to the phone and asked for Cal's room number, hissing when he picked up his end, 'Doc, my room now! No, it's not that, it's serious. Quick as you can.'

She turned to see Jimmy standing over the typewriter and what she had written was lying beside it. 'Get away from that and sit down.'

'How the hell did you know we were coming to Cheb?' she demanded when he complied.

'Vernon knew.'

Pacing back and forth, she began to curse, because it could only have come from the hotel. 'That low-life snake! To think he acts like he's an English gent, when he is full of shit.'

'I say,' Jimmy protested; he was no stranger to foul language, only not in the mouths of the fairer sex.

'Don't you "I say" me.'

The gentle knock at the door heralded Cal and he was inside quickly, to be given a gabbling explanation of who Jimmy was and what he knew. When the 'how?' came it was Corrie's turn for contrition.

'It's standard behaviour, Cal, you gotta tell your editor when you go somewhere.'

'The telephone would have been better.'

'What, a transatlantic call for that? He would have had my ass.'

Turning to face Jimmy, Callum Jardine wondered why the youngster shrank away. Then he realised he was wearing his rimless specs, and with his *en brosse* hairdo, allied to the expression on his face, he must have looked to him like he was Gestapo.

'Relax.'

'Easier said than done.'

'I'm not going to hurt you, am I?'

'I don't know, are you?'

Cal had to shut this lad up, but how? One thing was for sure: threats would be counterproductive unless he was not prepared to let him out of his sight, indeed out of this room.

'Jimmy – it is Jimmy, yes?' That produced a still-fearful nod, even though Cal had smiled. 'I am going to need your help and so is the British Government.'

'You're working for the Government?'

'I am.'

'Doing what?'

'I can't answer that, and I am afraid, Jimmy, even if you were told you would not be able to write about it. If you submitted it to your paper . . . by the way, who do you write for?'

'*News Chronicle.*'

'Good newspaper,' Cal said, 'got the right ideas about Hitler. The story would be subject to a D-notice, in fact, I suspect it will be buried in the files of SIS for a hundred years or more, it's so sensitive.'

'So you might as well tell me what it is.'

'Corrie, get dressed, we are meeting Veseli in the lounge shortly.'

'Sure, I'll use the bathroom, but don't let that little bastard near my notes.'

When she had gone, Cal addressed a young man pained by the way she had described him. 'You must know about the Official Secrets Act, Jimmy.'

'I do, but I don't see what difference that makes if the story is not going to come out anyway.'

'It means I can't tell you anything, because if I do, I will suffer the consequences.'

'I don't believe you.'

'What don't you believe?'

'All of it, the Government, you working for them, D-notices.'

The sigh was audible. Cal had a choice: stepping closer, he could take this little bugger by his carotid artery and either kill him or render him unconscious and do so in utter silence. What then? He would either have a body to deal with or he would have to truss him up and for how long? And he could still scream blue murder as soon as he was released.

Suddenly he was back in that moonlit Jewish cemetery in Prague, with General Moravec, and it was something he had said which provided a possible solution to shutting this lad up at least as long as they were in Cheb.

'OK, Jimmy, how would you like a twenty-four-carat gold-plated scoop?'

'Politicians the newspapers fear,' Moravec had insisted.

CHAPTER TWENTY-FOUR

The *Standartenführer* was waiting for them in the lounge and as soon as Corrie saw him she hissed, 'What a hunk!'

'You trying to make me jealous?'

'Would it succeed?'

'I'm not the type,' Cal replied as Veseli gave a crisp Nazi salute.

'Nothing to fear, Doc,' she whispered.

Introductions followed with Cal comparing the stiff behaviour he was watching now to the more relaxed man he had met in that farmhouse with Moravec; in terms of German broom-up-your-arse carry-on it was faultless.

'But we must be on our way, it would not do to miss the arrival of the Führer.'

'God forbid,' Corrie replied, which got a flicker of disapproval from Veseli, leaving Cal to wonder at the man's self-control.

Living a lie must be intense, acting almost constantly against your natural instincts, never able to relax, probably even in private in case you inadvertently gave something away by allowing the mask to slip, and there had to be, at his age and with his looks, women in his life, people with whom he was intimate, and how hard was that?

As they exited the hotel, Veseli gave his men a salute, which was returned, with Corrie commenting that this was a nation – she meant the Germans – who would benefit from a mass amputation. Then he was off, striding down the road, saluting right and left as those who thought him one of their own, and seeing his uniform, were determined to acknowledge his rank.

'You're in for a fun night.'

That got him that arm squeeze again. 'I sure hope so.'

'Remember, I'm only human.'

'Not at all, Doc,' she said with feeling, 'you are a love machine.'

'Where did you learn to talk like that?'

'First of all at Daddy's knee, 'cause he was never one to avoid a cuss when I was around, and then at college. We Bryn Mawr girls are famous for telling it like it is.'

'Feminists?'

'You make it sound like a dirty word.'

'The dirtier the better.'

They reached the crowded old market square, which killed off their conversation. Down the side it was set with tables and in between them there were stalls cooking all kind of wurst, the smoke and the smell of the frying meat filling the air. Others were laden with bread and hams, added to which the tavern had set up a beer service on the pavement, with girls in dirndl clothing delivering steins to thirsty customers.

Within a minute both visitors found themselves holding steaming glasses of *glühwein* and being encouraged to drink up. It could have been a carnival except that now many of the surrounding buildings were festooned with a mixture of Nazi banners and the red-black-red flags of the SdP. They tended to turn the mood, for non-believers, into a sombre one.

'Fräulein Littleton, our leader wishes you to join him. He is about to have his photograph taken and he would like one which includes you.'

'Delighted,' Corrie replied in the correct and required tone; Cal knew she did not mean it because, distributed, it would give the wrong impression.

Veseli/Wessely took her gently by the arm to guide her through the crowd, which left Cal to look about him. He saw Jimmy Garvin with a big jug of beer in one hand, a sausage in the other, standing back and not engaging in conversation, no doubt composing a feature about mass hysteria for some future date.

Then Veseli was beside him, leaning over to talk quietly in his ear while he handed him a bratwurst, wrapped in a linen napkin. There was something hard inside, which Cal's fingers identified as a key. With the babble of conversation there was no chance of either being overheard and it looked as if they were having a friendly chat.

'Tonight, as Hitler is speaking, the Czech army will enter the so-called Sudetenland and stop all this nonsense.'

'I thought—'

'Never mind that. The key to his suite of offices is in your hand and a layout of the hotel is drawn on the napkin, showing the emergency exit from Henlein's suite. The papers are in his safe and you have been given the means to get access to what you came for.'

'I came under false pretences.'

'You must forgive the general and I for deceiving you – that was essential.'

'What if I decline to do it?'

'Then I must, so please tell me quickly what you intend.'

'How would you get away with it if you did it?'

'I would not, Mr Jardine. I might succeed but I would not long survive since suspicion would soon fall on me. The best I could hope for is a firing squad.'

'But you will take that risk?'

Veseli laughed. 'It is not a risk, it is certain I would die.'

'Who were you going to pass the papers to?' Cal asked.

That was a solution to one conundrum he had in his bath: the Czech did not insult him by denying there was someone, but there was no way he was going to reveal any more.

'If I depart this square, my absence will be noticed, for to do so when the Führer is speaking would be seen as a gross insult to him . . .'

There was no way of faulting that statement; Veseli stood literally head and shoulders above most of his fellow men. He couldn't move anywhere without it being spotted.

'. . . while you can leave without raising even a slight eyebrow, especially if you claim to have eaten something that disagrees with you and which forces you to return to the hotel.'

'The guards?'

'Tonight, they will be here in the square, as will every Nazi in the town. None will want to miss this.'

'The clerk at reception?'

Veseli pointed him out and also the Ice Maiden, standing next to Henlein, who was talking to Corrie, adding that the hotel would be practically deserted, given all the staff were rabid anti-Czechs if not quite National Socialists, while the guests had come specifically for this rally. It was not a residence for anyone not committed to the cause.

'The news of the movements of the Czech army may come before Hitler is finished speaking, but it is hoped not. Either way, Henlein will seek to flee and to do that he needs his car, which is parked in the same place as your own.'

'Though not without those documents.'

'But hopefully you will have them and when he sees that they are gone he will not hang around to find out who stole them.'

'Miss Littleton?'

'I will make sure she is escorted to safety. Both you and she, being foreigners, will be free to travel through the army lines when things quieten down and it has already been arranged they will not attack the Victoria but the headquarters of Frank's Nazis. Stay at the hotel and wait till order is restored.'

'It is still dangerous.'

'What can we do in these times without hazard, Herr Barrowman? Take those documents, give them to your government and let them know what that little Austrian bastard is really like.'

'And what will you be doing?'

Veseli laughed softly. 'Me, I will be starting a riot.'

Even with the babble of talk in the square the loudspeakers had been disseminating a sort of background growl, which was the audience at the Congress Hall in Nuremberg and that began to fade into silence.

Veseli managed one more point before the Cheb crowd followed suit. 'I will also tell you that inside that safe is a large sum of money, subventions from the German Foreign Office, which Henlein uses to fund the SdP. I would not object if you took that too and found a better use for it.'

'Noise?' seemed an apposite question and he was not talking about that which was abating now.

'Imagine what it will be like when the Führer is insulting my poor country.'

The hush fell and there was an expectant silence from both the assembled crowd and the loudspeakers, which emitted only a steady crackle now. Then the loud voice spoke out, like a guards drill sergeant.

'*Der Führer, Adolf Hitler! Sieg Heil! Sieg Heil!*'

The orchestra struck up with a patriotic march only to be overwhelmed as that '*Sieg Heil*' was answered by thirty thousand throats in a deafening roar of welcome for the godlike master, which drowned out its brass instruments, while those at the Cheb rally now had their arms outstretched too and were yelling just as lustily.

The hails went on for an age and so emotional were the folk around the square that they had their eyes closed and were near to ecstasy. It was a great trick to pull, that long walk up the avenue of adoring acolytes, a march with glittering escorts and tessellated banners that raised to a supreme pitch the soaring sense of anticipation, even if it was invisible.

By the time the baying had died away and he said his first quiet words, all over the Reich and in many places beyond, most listening were in the palm of his hand, ready to be manipulated into a frenzy.

'*Meine Kameraden.*'

It was his standard opening line and what followed was the usual guff, about when he had first decided that the Reich needed him and then responded, how in six years, with their help, he had raised Germany to the pinnacles on which it now stood. He would go on for certainly over an hour, sucking them in and making them believe these 'good comrades' were his inspiration instead of mere tools.

Slowly but surely the voice would rise as he recalled his own struggles, much magnified so they matched those of the nation: the glory and filth of army service, being gassed, the stab in the back that brought national humiliation and then the rebirth under his guiding hand, all the tropes by which Germans deluded themselves.

These were the kind of myths which turned rational human beings into clichéd trotting dolts. As he had reflected many times, as a Scot, his own nation was not immune, though they did not turn to murder to prove them, more inclined to fire themselves up with a dram.

Cal could not wait for the insults to start, as Hitler damned everything and everyone who did not succumb to his genius, and now that he had manoeuvred himself out of sight of Corrie he clutched his stomach, put the now empty napkin to his mouth, looked pained and made his way out of the square.

As he passed Jimmy Garvin the youngster made to move. The blast for him to stay still was furious and the language left no doubt about what he would do to him if he followed. Out of sight and in deserted streets – the Czechs who lived here were inside with the blinds drawn and the doors barred – he could pick up his pace.

The garage was at the back of the hotel and open. Inside were

Henlein's Mercedes, a few other smaller vehicles and Cal's Maybach. The box from the boot he wrapped in one of the blankets from the back seat, able to smile at the irony of their so-different purposes that day; the hunting knife he jammed in his trouser belt.

The back door led into a lobby and a set of uncarpeted wooden stairs that were used by the staff, which creaked alarmingly as he stepped on to them. On the grounds that being surreptitious was a bad idea he made his way up them and accepted the sound would be treated as normal to anyone who heard them.

He had to put the box down on the top step, where there was a bare light bulb, to look at the napkin and get his bearings – which was a bit of luck, since he heard a creaking himself; it was an old building cursed with loose boards. Someone was coming along from what he had identified as the main part of the building to the passage that led to the staff quarters.

There was no time for subterfuge. Cal headed for the first door and was relieved it opened to reveal a deep cupboard which, by the smell, he reckoned was full of linen. The door he closed behind him as soon as he laid the box on the floor, and he had the knife out and ready, prepared to kill and hoping that if someone came in it was not a maid.

That he would have to take a life he knew; this was too important to let anything like finer feelings intrude, and besides, he was in the frame of mind he had been in many times in his life: when it came to kill or be killed there was not much room for sentiment.

The creaking had become boots, which thudded as they reached the bare floorboards, rising then falling off as they passed the door, a slight shadow coming under where there was a gap that let in light. He waited for silence, then sheathed the knife and opened the door to peer out. Sure it was clear, he picked up the box and tiptoed off.

Going to his own room first was a risk but he wanted that Mauser in case he was disturbed. He would use the knife for preference but up against anyone armed only a bullet would save him. The weight of that in his jacket pocket dragged it down to one side in a way that would show anyone who saw him what he was carrying – that had to be accepted.

To see the lobby deserted was a surprise, but as Veseli had said, even the guests had gone to the event in the square, it seemed, and where he might have been seen by the guards had they looked round, he was safe from that for the same reason.

He was halfway across when the sound made him stop dead, that was until he realised it was snoring, and when he looked behind the desk there was the porter who had taken his luggage to his room, slumped in a chair fast asleep.

'You, old son, are in for a very rude awakening,' he said very quietly to himself as he walked away.

Where would Hitler be by now? He looked at his watch, mildly surprised at how little time he had used to get this far, a mere twenty minutes; the Führer would have hardly got going. Access to the office suite was by a heavy five-bar lock that, had he not had the key, would have needed some of Mr Nobel's finest to get it open.

How the hell Veseli had got such a key he did not know, but then he had no idea how long they had been planning this operation. He went through and locked it behind him. That napkin had told him where the emergency exit was, at the end of the corridor, and he checked that first.

The heavy wooden door to Henlein's own office was locked too, and that was a setback solved by the blade of his hunting knife, not without a tearing sound that had him still and listening for half a minute before he entered to find that the large windows gave him enough light from the street to see.

First stop was the radio, which he switched on to warm up, turning the volume dial right down low even before any sound emerged. Then he put the Mauser on top of the safe, butt out, where he could get at it easily. Next he took the bulb out of the overhead light and put it in his pocket, then put on the gloves, using his knife to cut into the explosive packaging, his nose wrinkling at the increased smell.

He had no option but to employ what professional safe-crackers would call a 'jam shot', something he had learnt from one of Snuffly Bower's mates, which came in very handy for blowing off the steel doors of bunkers or places where arms were stored. The Nobel 808 being malleable, he could press down the lock side of the safe in a continuous strip, jamming it into the very small gap.

It looked feeble but he knew the force even a small amount could produce: an almond-sized blob properly placed would blow any normal door to bits. The radio was warm now so he gave it a bit more volume and spun the tuner till he heard that rasping voice from *Deutsche Rundfunk*. Ear close to the speaker, he could hear that Hitler was getting a bit hoarse; by the end of his peroration he would be rasping.

What 808 he had left he packed as close to the lock as he could, which created a mass into which he could insert a detonator, that then connected to wires, they in turn being threaded into the terminals on the plunger. Carefully he took that and opened the door to the hallway, placing it outside where he would fire it, using the solid wall of the old building to protect him from the blast. Then he settled down to wait.

Peter just made his train by a hairy taxi ride from the Gare du Nord to l'Est and was able to settle down to sleep in a comfy couchette, this while Vince was fuming and still being denied access through the last checkpoint. It had taken all day for Noel McKevitt to find a hose that would fit the Humber but he was back on the road, barrelling north, using his diplomatic passport and plates to get through every checkpoint as a priority case.

Not that such progress was smooth: given the number of cars held up and the sheer quantity that had to move to facilitate his advance – not to mention the fulsome and loudly expressed curses he got for his temerity – each one took an age, so that when he arrived at the checkpoint where Vince was waiting it was dark, and fulminate as he might, it seemed the army had priority on the road ahead and not even a diplomat could make progress.

Sitting on the floor, gloves off, Cal was listening to Hitler as he started to heap insults on Czechoslovakia, which was a miserable little country which dared to call itself a democracy but was suppressing its inhabitants . . . in this state there were three and a half million Germans (his voice was really hoarse now) . . . the misery of the Sudetenlanders was terrible . . . Beneš was a liar and a cheat . . . on and on he went and each part of his increasingly deranged tirade was met with great repetitive cries of 'Sieg Heil!' from the audience.

It was the climax of the speech he was waiting for, that last point where Hitler would sweep his right hand like a sword across his chest, the sweat flying from his brow, his shirt soaked and his eyes aiming off to some point beyond those who were listening to him, to a Valhalla where even the gods of the *Nibelungen* were sat bolt upright in amazement at his brilliance.

Cal turned the radio up a fraction and moved out of the door to where the plunger lay, closed the door as much as he could without damaging the wires, slid down so his back was to the wall and listened, his pistol near his hand, to the berserk spectators creating a din that was now so loud Hitler could hardly be heard. He then took the lever in his hand. Faintly he could hear those in the square, loud enough to echo through the streets and penetrate solid walls.

'I'm sick of the sound of you, old cock,' he said, then twisted and pressed hard before immediately jamming his hands to his ears and opening his mouth.

To him it sounded as if the earth had caved in, but he had no idea how it sounded outside. Perhaps the folk at the rally thought thunder or maybe, since half of them subscribed to beliefs in mythical deities, that the gods had spoken; he had no time to wonder – he just picked up the Mauser and went in.

The room was a mess: Henlein's desk was mostly matchwood, the window panes blown out so compressively they seemed to have gone in one piece, only breaking when they hit the cobbles below. Out came the bulb to be screwed back in, and then the light could be switched on; it made no difference who saw that now.

The door of the safe was hanging open and there was the smell of burning, probably some of the contents. Hauling to get it right open he looked inside and started rifling through the mass of papers, pushing aside bundles of banknotes.

The one he wanted was easy to identify, a high-quality green folder with the gold device of an eagle with a swastika in its talons.

Taking it over to what was left of Henlein's desk, under the light, he opened it to see the top letter carried the address of the office of the Führer at the top and the Hitler signature at the bottom.

'*Hände hoch!*'

There was no time to see who it was or what they had; dropping the file he just spun quickly, dived sideways and as he did so put a bullet into the chest of the porter who had been asleep downstairs, which blasted him backwards. Rolling up on to one knee, the second bullet went into his head and he died for the fact that he was old, overweight and slow and had a key to the door of the office suite; that and because he was holding a gun.

Relocking the suite door, and this time leaving his own key twisted in the lock to stop anyone else gaining entry, Cal went back to the office and jammed the file down the back of his trousers. Then, using that blanket from the Maybach, he scooped in the bundles of banknotes, knotted it and headed for the emergency exit which took him out of the back of the hotel, through a door that, once closed, locked itself.

He was out in the alley and heading for the garage before he heard the first of the thudding boots coming to find out what had happened, which risked him being caught in possession of that bundle, so he resorted to an old trick burglars use to avoid getting caught with their swag just after a robbery. Carrying it at night, when they usually do their breaking and entering, they are bound to be stopped by a copper and questioned. The solution is to find a convenient bin, preferably with a lid, and dump the goods till daylight – the back of the hotel was lined with dozens of them.

Then, coming from where his car was parked, he heard the sounds of a big engine being fired up and doors slamming, followed by screeching tyres as Henlein's Mercedes swept out and past him, forcing him to press his body against the wall, able to see the alarmed face of the driver as it raced past and then a fleeting last glimpse of a worried-looking Henlein.

Entering the garage himself he ran to the Maybach and jammed the file of documents and the Mauser under the front seat, before locking it and heading back to the square to find Corrie.

CHAPTER TWENTY-FIVE

The sound of breaking glass was almost immediate and as Cal ran towards the square he could see, in the intervening streets, small knots of Brownshirts busy attacking what he supposed must be Czech homes and businesses, so occupied they ignored him. When he got to the old marketplace, the central square was still crowded but now with a mob baying for what they saw as justice for an oppressed minority.

Veseli stood out easily, his head and forage cap visible from a distance, and Cal made straight for him, barging through a crowd that had no desire to ease his passage, passing open yelling mouths chanting either indistinct Nazi slogans or curses aimed at their Czech neighbours and foreign devils, clearly still under the spell of the euphoria created by Hitler's speech.

They were facing some hothead who had got himself hoisted above the crowd and was waving a swastika, trying to make himself heard above the din. Cal knew by his contorted face and that flag he was not trying to calm them down but seeking to fire them up to commit some kind of anti-Czech pogrom.

He got to Veseli eventually, standing tall and looking fierce, to find Corrie close by in the company of Jimmy Garvin, the look of fearful greeting in both their eyes evidence of how uncomfortable they found it to be surrounded by a mob of excited ideologues slipping rapidly out of any sense of self-control.

It was hard to believe they could make more noise than previously but the truth was assailing his ears, making it hard to hear what was being shouted at him, and Veseli had to wait till he got closer and repeated himself to be understood.

'Herr Barrowman, you must get Miss Littleton back to the hotel and keep her there.'

'Can you give us an escort?'

'No, I cannot be seen to.'

That was followed by an exchange of looks that told the Czech agent that the safe had been successfully blown and it was testament to his ability to control his emotions that he did not smile.

There was no time to argue about protection, so Cal grabbed Corrie's arm and yelled to Jimmy to stay close, then began to elbow his way back in the direction from which he had come, finding himself more than once faced with some slavering and fist-shaking German, of both sexes, disinclined to allow them passage; it would have been impossible had he not spoken their language and even then it was not easy.

More than once he was tempted to let go of Corrie and give one of the men an uppercut but there were two constraints on that: first, he might lose her in such a packed crowd, and secondly, if he struck one of these maddened bastards he might find he had to fight them all; that was the way of mobs.

It began to thin towards the rear, they were all facing that flag-waving lunatic, but now there was a bit of clear space they found themselves being eyed suspiciously, which Cal countered by yelling '*Sieg Heil!*' and throwing out his arm, getting a like response every time.

Looking back, he saw Jimmy Garvin had been grabbed by a burly local dressed in lederhosen and was being shaken. The temptation to abandon the little sod was one that had to be buried; he knew too much, and added to that was an inability to stand by and watch anybody being bullied by anyone, anywhere.

Putting both hands on Corrie to keep her still, that accompanied by a hard look, he went back to help the cub reporter who, foolishly, was yelling in English, which was probably what had got him into bother in the first place.

Cal yelled in the man's ear to ask him to let the boy go, only to have him turn and spit in his face. The head butt might be known as a 'Glasgow kiss' but it was a fighting strategy close to every Scottish schoolboy's birthright. Cal's forehead hit the German nose right on the bridge and the blood was immediate, as was the way he dropped the struggling Jimmy.

Cal stepped back to give himself room and planted his foot hard in the assailant's leather shorts before grabbing a bewildered Jimmy and telling him to get moving, the one obvious danger being that the assault had not gone unnoticed. This being a situation that would not be solved by a Nazi salute, Cal hauled out his hunting knife to warn anyone against interfering.

'Corrie, get moving and run,' he shouted, backing away from a trio, who with knotted and furious faces had come to their comrade's aid. 'Get to the hotel and stay there.'

There were other shouts and they were coming from a group of men closing slowly in on him and he could not fight them all. Added to that, the blood-spattered fellow he had hit was groggily getting to his feet, swaying and in pain, revenge in his eyes.

He could outrun them and so probably could young Jimmy Garvin, the problem was Corrie and the shoes she was wearing, which had heels, not high, but were very much not the kind of footwear conducive to flight. He had, of course, not considered that she might come to the same conclusion.

The scream of 'Run, Cal!' came from behind, but what told him it was possible was first one of her shoes, then the other, flying past his ear, both aimed at German heads. They did nothing but impose a minor distraction but that was enough for him to turn and go, glad to see that she had not waited but set off and opened up a bit of a gap.

It might not have worked but for a burst of rapid gunfire which broke out. Cal thought it ahead of him, but in a built-up area with the sound able to reverberate there was no way of being sure, though looking back he saw the noise had imposed a check on the pursuit, either out of confusion or the notion of being shot had cooled their Nazi ardour.

Whatever, it created enough of an opening to give him confidence he could get to the garage and root out that Mauser, where if he did and they were still following he would not hesitate to shoot to kill. Looking back in the direction he was heading Cal saw that Jimmy was not being brave; he was well ahead of Corrie, his knees pounding, and the distance was opening, which if he carried on would take him to the station square.

'Corrie, down that alley on your right!' His free hand was in his pocket rooting out his keys. 'Go in the back door, it's quicker.'

The firing was sporadic but constant now, single shots that indicated maybe some of the Czechs were fighting back, but of more concern was that a couple of those in pursuit had not been fully deterred, and even over his own breathing he could hear their boots on the cobbles and worryingly they seemed to be getting closer.

About to dive into the garage, the sound of a revving engine echoing in the cavernous building slowed him enough to stop him being knocked over; a car shot out of the doorway, proving clearly Henlein was not the only one fleeing Cheb, but thankfully the car give him a breather because as it pulled out it went in the direction of his pursuers and they too had to slow to avoid a collision.

They had stopped in the doorway by the time he got the car door open, two well-built brutes and one of them had a club. In silhouette he could not see their faces but he guessed they would be smiling at the fact that he was probably trapped. Quickly he knelt, pulled out the Mauser and stood again, the weapon hidden behind the car door.

One of the pair was cursing him, his breath heaving from his exertions, but over that, also amplified by the nature of the building, was the sound of a club slamming into his palm. The words were chilling: not only were they going to beat him to a pulp but they intended to string him up to a lamp post, having cut off his balls and fed them to the dogs.

Callum Jardine was not by nature a cold-blooded killer; in the heat of the moment he would shoot a man to preserve his own life but rarely had he shot anyone out of hand. Had they not promised him the fate they promised they might have suffered less but their words marked them out as the kind of Nazi thugs he hated most, the kind that would beat an innocent person, a Jew or a dissenter, to death in full public view.

He lifted the Mauser, laid it on the top of the door to steady it, and said softly, '*Sieg Heil, meine Kameraden.*'

Then, at a range of a few feet, he put two bullets into each, filling the garage with echoing sound and sending their bodies hurtling back towards the door. As the echo faded the only sound left was of that club rolling along the concrete floor.

Going through to the front of the hotel, he thought at first it was deserted; certainly the lobby was, looking incongruously peaceful given the continuing sounds of sporadic gunfire from outside. It was almost with a sense of comedy that he palmed the bell on the reception desk, the one used to summon luggage-carrying minions.

'Can I get you a drink?' Corrie was standing in the doorway to the lounge, barefoot and holding a Martini glass that even had an olive on a stick. 'First decent Martini I've had since Prague. You want I should make you one, Doc?'

'I prefer Cal and a good whisky, but dare I say it is not safe to be standing here in the lobby right now? We'd be better off up in my room.'

'Why yours?'

'It overlooks the square, so we can see what's happening.'

'Why do I have the impression you know what's happening?' Cal shrugged and in doing so moved the pistol in his hand, which drew her eye. 'I looked for you in the market square while that speech I could not understand was driving me crazy, but you were nowhere to be seen.'

'I had a little business to do.'

'The rod being part of it?' she asked, looking at the weapon again.

'It wasn't supposed to be. Let's go upstairs and I'll explain.'

'Lead on.'

He went to take her hand and lead her up the stairs but that was withheld. 'I'll wait for the explanation.'

'You were in no danger, Corrie, I made sure of that.'

'Well I have to tell you,' she replied, her icy demeanour shattered and her eyes beginning to look tearful, 'it sure as hell did not feel that way.'

The front door of the hotel burst open and Cal dropped to one knee as a reflex, the pistol coming up in both hands. Jimmy Garvin, looking dishevelled and as if the hounds of hell were on his tail, stopped dead, emitted a small moan and began to mouth a plea for mercy.

'Thanks for looking after Corrie, Jimmy,' Cal said, standing. 'I won't forget to tell your friends how intrepid you are.'

At least he was decent enough to look abashed as Cal commanded them to get out of the well-lit lobby.

'No lights,' he said as they slipped through the door. 'Go over to the window and sit under the sill with your back to the wall.'

'Why?' asked the ingenuous young Jimmy.

'Safest place when there are bullets flying about.'

He himself went to look out and the first thing he saw was a line of what had to be Czech police being deployed, taking up their positions, fully armed and lined up outside the entrance to the station, which indicated to Cal the first batch of the army would probably be coming in by train.

'So?' Corrie asked. 'Do I get my explanation?'

'Later, when Big Ears is not listening; right now we sit it out till the Czech army gets here.'

'They're coming?' Jimmy asked, taking the silence as an affirmative. 'How do you know?'

'Do you ever stop asking questions?'

'It's what we do, Doc.'

'Why do you call him Doc?'

'Because, Jimmy,' she replied, her tone bitter, 'he's a cartoon character, not real.'

How do you tell someone, especially with a third person present, that your life works in different boxes? She was feeling used and probably abused, so he went over and knelt beside her, whispering, 'I know you're angry and I can guess why, but just hold it all in for a while and when we're alone I will tell you enough to reassure you that you were never in any danger.'

'Then who was I running from?'

'You throw your shoes at people, they get mad, Corrie.'

Her shoulders began to heave; it was funny and worthy of a laugh, but that soon turned to sobs as the pent-up fears surfaced and took over. He took her in his arms and held her close until they subsided and he got her onto the bed and told her to sleep, holding her hand until she went under.

'Can you hear a train?' Jimmy hissed, a few minutes later.

He was right, faint but unmistakable was the puffing of a steam engine, which grew louder until it was overtaken by the screeching of braking steel wheels. That was followed by the sound of shouting and both Cal and Jimmy watched as the troops emerged from the station to form up behind the screen of policemen.

'Are those machine guns?' Cal nodded. 'Is there going to be a battle?'

'There will be tankettes coming up the road from Liberec, artillery, and more troops as well. My guess is the Czech Government expected Hitler to declare war in his speech tonight and they intended to be on the move before he was. But the first thing they have to do is put down the locals in places like Cheb.'

'This I've got to see,' Jimmy insisted, as the troops began to march out of the square.

'Nazi HQ, Jimmy, is where the main action will be, and don't get yourself killed.'

As the youngster made for the door, Cal called him back. He had remembered his camera, which he now did not need, that or the film it contained.

'Take this with you – you never know, you might get something useful.'

With the coming dawn, progress through the roadblock was finally possible and his dip plates as well as his irate insistence got Noel McKevitt priority, albeit not without a warning that there could be fighting up ahead. Delivered in German, he understood it; given twenty minutes later to Vince Castellano in Czech, all he could do was look understanding and nod silently before heading on up the road to Cheb.

There was no way of getting up any speed for either man and it was not just because of the amount of traffic, brought about by the hold-up. The army might not be moving, but by their mere presence they created endless bottlenecks, as trucks, horse-drawn artillery pieces, petrol and water bowsers, tankettes and all the paraphernalia of an army on the march did their best to tell the world they did not care how much inconvenience they could cause.

Peter Lanchester was awoken to take his morning coffee a couple of hours after they had departed Berlin, and he naturally, being British, enquired if the train would be on time. He was then treated to a level of disdain he had rarely experienced from an irate conductor, a pompous little man in his over-elaborate uniform.

In a mixture of bad and minimal English, mixed with a stream of German he barely understood, he was told in no uncertain terms that on the railway lines of the Reich, every train ran to its exact schedule.

The Paris-Prague Express would reach Eger at 11.15 on the dot. What time it would get to stations further down the line and Prague was down to the less efficient Czechs and he could not guarantee a prompt arrival there.

How Corrie slept through the din of battle amazed Cal but she managed it; the Nazis in Karl Hermann Frank's headquarters were the most fanatical people in Cheb and would have put up stiff resistance anyway, but there was a chance they were reinforced by those SS troopers Veseli had told him about.

Machine gun fire went on for hours, into full daylight, as well as rifle shots which Cal presumed came both from within and without the heavily fortified building and which added to the clanging as bullets slammed into those steel shutters he had seen on his walk.

Slumber as she could, no one could stay that way when the artillery opened up: first the crump of the firing shell, soon followed by the blast as it smashed into concrete walls. Quietly, in between those noises and with a very necessary filter, Cal told her why he had come and how important it was that he did what he did, though he did not tell her what that was. It was really the way he had deserted her that was upsetting Corrie, especially after the intimacy they had shared the previous day in the woods and her room.

Cal knew enough about women to realise that they invested more heavily in a relationship than most men, which made them more vulnerable to the feeling that they might have made a mistake and allowed themselves to be seduced only for their bodies, not their being.

When they felt like that it was hard to find words that would provide enough reassurance, so Cal took the only way out he knew and to the sound of crumping artillery shells and pinging bullets they made love for the third time in less than a day.

'Full marks for stamina, Doc,' Corrie said as they lay quietly. 'Sorry . . . Cal.'

'Listen,' he said, knowing he had been partially forgiven.

'It's gone quiet,' she said. 'That means it's over.'

'A bit of it is, Corrie, but it's not over.'

'I'm hungry.'

'I doubt the cooking staff have shown up, but we can help ourselves.'

Jimmy Garvin was weary but ecstatic, having had a wonderful view of the assault on Frank's Nazi HQ, and he had used up Cal's film as soon as there was enough light to focus properly. Now he had to get to somewhere he could write the story and another spot from where he could send it to the news desk in London. The photographs were more of a problem; for that he needed a wire service and that was in Prague.

Still, if he could find a local camera shop he could get them developed. He headed back to the hotel, on his way passing a fair-haired, rather florid man asking a Czech army officer questions, forced to dodge out of the way as an old and oddly shaped car pulled up outside the hotel.

Cal and Corrie were in the dining room eating breakfast and he was invited to join them, but the scream Corrie gave as he made to sit down alarmed Jimmy, until she leapt up, ran to the door and threw her arms around the man standing there, who looked over her shoulder and said, 'Hello, guv, you been causing bother again?'

CHAPTER TWENTY-SIX

With the town restored to a sullen peace there was no bar to the Paris-Prague Express stopping at Cheb and it was bang on time, which got him a look from the watch-holding conductor who had stepped from the train to oversee the departure. Like Peter, that fellow was quite taken by the number of soldiers as well as the level of equipment on the platform: ammunition boxes, field rations and quartermaster's stores.

Stepping out of the station concourse he stopped to look round and was immediately confronted by the sight of the Victoria Hotel, which seemed to have had its windows blown out on one side of the canopy, and it was impossible to miss the sparkling glass that littered the pavement and road, which what little traffic was about, both wheeled and hoofed, was taking care to steer round.

The square was full of army trucks and horse-drawn wagons; knots of men in grey-green uniforms stood or squatted about, and the smell in the air of dust and cordite was one he recognised from his own years of army service – something was going on but he lacked the means to find out what.

No doubt Cal Jardine would enlighten him, though thinking on his man he wondered if he had had anything to do with what smelt like a battle in a place supposed to be at peace, the conclusion being as he stepped out that it was more likely than not, given his propensity to get involved in violence.

It was sheer bad luck that Noel McKevitt was taking a coffee in the now-reopened café, which was crowded with Czech officers who, even if he could not comprehend what they were saying, knew by the backslapping and loud jokes they were congratulating themselves, and since he had enquired of an officer outside earlier he knew why.

He was watching the Victoria Hotel from one of the windows, obliged, in order to see clearly, it being cold outside, to rub off the steam caused by the heat of massed humanity. McKevitt was too long in the tooth an SIS man to just barge in; he had no idea who this Barrowman was, or how dangerous he could be in contact – he could be anybody.

What he did know was that the means to find out if he was a resident in the Victoria was lacking; he had taken a slow walk by the guarded entrance and observed through the windows that lay either side of the double front doors that the lobby was deserted to the point of there being no staff. One of the staircases was guarded too but few people had gone in, bar a young fellow swinging a camera on its strap and the driver of a rather battered old Tatra.

The elegant gait of Peter Lanchester took his eye, but with his back to McKevitt no more than that. What made him stand out was his doubt about where the cars were coming from in a foreign country, something he had struggled with in France, only to realise it was similar to home. But in double-checking he turned his head and the sight of his unmistakable profile caused the Ulsterman to swear.

But there was a real plus; Lanchester made straight for the hotel entrance and went through the identification procedure, which told McKevitt two things: that this fellow travelling as Barrowman was connected to him and, as he had suspected, the bastard was messing around in his backyard. The next question was how to deal with that knowledge.

'What is this?' Peter exclaimed as he came through the entrance to the lounge and saw who was sitting there, now drinking coffee. 'A gathering of the clans?'

'What the hell are you doing here?'

'I came, Callum, dear boy, to tell you your cover has been blown.'

'He knows that, guv,' said Vince, grinning, 'I've just told him so.'

'You got the telegram I sent you?'

The 'No' was explained when Vince told him how long he'd been on the road.

'A quiet word, Cal, if you please.'

'Don't I get an introduction?' asked Corrie. 'Since you two seem such bosom buddies.'

'Not "bosom", but we have scrummaged together. Peter, this is Miss Corrine Little—'

'No surnames, Cal, the lady is a journalist.'

'How do you know that?'

All that got was a sharp jerk of the head and the two went into a huddle facing away from the table, to impart the news that McKevitt, whom he was obliged finally to name, was on the warpath, armed and looking for a Mr Barrowman, as well as how he had got onto their tail.

'I also have instructions from on high to tell you to abort.'

'No need, I have written proof that Hitler intends to invade, the date, and a list of targets the Sudeten Nazis are to sabotage to help him, signed by Schicklgruber himself.'

'And where is this wonderful bit of kit?'

'Later, when we are a bit less of a crowd.'

'Who else knows?'

'No one here.'

'Who's the young chap?'

'Jimmy Garvin, a journalist, works with Vernon Bartlett.'

'Cal, old boy, you're mixing in the wrong company.'

That's all you know, Peter, Cal thought; *that little bugger is going to write up the story and get it into his newspaper so that Chamberlain cannot sit on it, which he might just do given his record so far.* That had been the deal, though Jimmy had no idea what he was going to be allowed to see.

Typical of his breed he had only finally agreed when he was promised Corrie, still getting dolled up in the bathroom, was not privy to the same story; he might be young but he was a fast learner and Cal suspected that Vernon Bartlett would not get a sniff either.

'The only question is, Peter, how are we going to get it out? If I try to take it through the airport that risks a search and they are nervous right now.'

'Diplomatic bag would be best, with me to travel alongside, which I can clear through the Prague legation with a Top Secret tag so I can deliver it straight to Quex.'

'Mr Jardine?' Both turned to face Jimmy Garvin. 'Can I take your camera to get the film developed? I'd rather someone took the spool out who knows what they're doing.'

'I think there's a couple of mine on there, don't bother with those. But before you go, you might as well join us in a glass of champagne.'

'How jolly.'

'I don't see any staff, Cal.'

'Neither will you, apart from the odd chambermaid.'

He explained about this being Henlein's HQ, though he made no mention of the body Czech Intelligence had discovered when they began to search the offices. Right now they were starting to assess all the office files.

'They've already searched the accommodation and allowed us back into our rooms and given us the run of the rest, bar Henlein's bit. Everyone who worked here is either hiding in their cellar or has fled to Bavaria. So, we help ourselves, which means we will not stint on quality.'

In the end, because they were such patriotic Teutons in the Victoria, they had to settle for a couple of bottles of very good German *Sekt* and Jimmy, rather lightweight when it came to alcohol, after three glasses of sparkling wine was in a very jolly mood when he finally left to find a camera shop.

Noel McKevitt had gnawed on how to proceed since he saw Peter Lanchester disappear, because it had finally struck him how much he was out on a limb here on his own; he was beginning to curse himself for the way he had told Gibby Gibson that the station was shutting down.

Could he get some of the lads up here to help him? The only way to find out was to call the legation, and that meant abandoning his watch on the hotel. Given there was no alternative he dived into the station and found a phone, at first getting shirty with the Czech operator who pretended not to understand his German when he asked for the number.

'Gibby, it's Noel. I need your help up here. How many of the lads are still available?'

'None.'

'Wha'd'yer mean "none"?'

'Orders from Quex in person: stay still, do nothing.'

'The bastard.'

'Come in, Noel, come back to Prague.'

'You think I should?'

'I think you've got to, I'm afraid.'

He did not respond immediately, because he was wondering why the old sod had issued that order and there was only one explanation: it was to try and stop him finding out what he was up to. If there had ever been any doubt it was serious enough to threaten the man's career, that laid it to rest, and now it looked as though Quex was trying to turn the tables on him. If he went back to Prague he would be bundled back to London in disgrace.

'You're right, Gibby. I'll have a bit of a bite to eat and start heading back.'

Then he hung up, went back to the café and bought himself a Pilsner; he would have to do it alone. The problem was first to find out the identity of Barrowman, then connect him to Peter Lanchester. He had to be another SIS agent, one of those Quex had recently brought back in.

It did not take a genius to work out there was only one way to do it, so he drained his beer, left the café and headed for the centre of town.

* * *

369

Peter, standing by the Maybach and fingering the signature, was impressed. 'Cal, this is gold dust, do I get told how you got it?'

'That will be two dinners you owe me.'

Seeing the look on Peter's face he laughed, then he told him the story. The folder went back under the seat and the car was locked and they went out into the alley, not without a good look because, as Peter reminded him, McKevitt was on the loose somewhere and he might well be in Cheb.

'Is that secure, that car?'

'Yes, and don't ask why.'

Jimmy was struggling; he only had a little German, zero Czech, was slightly tipsy and the man in the camera shop had no English – he was also impatient because another customer was waiting.

'D'yer need any help, son?' Noel McKevitt asked. 'I have the German if it'll help. Most folks around here speak two languages.'

'Golly, what luck. I want the film developed, which he understands, but I don't want the shots at the beginning. I'm afraid my expenses don't run to paying for photos I don't need.'

'Expenses, is it?'

'Yes,' Jimmy replied, with no shortage of pride, 'I'm a journalist and I managed to photograph the Czech army attack and take the Nazi HQ.'

'Why, isn't that grand.' McKevitt reached past and picked up the Walz 35 mm camera. 'I'd've thought you would have had a bigger camera than this, you being a journalist, and all.'

'Oh, it's not mine,' Jimmy slurred, 'it's Mr Jardine's.'

'Jardine,' McKevitt said slowly. 'I'm sure I know a fella by that name.'

'Callum Jardine?'

It was like a set of toy bricks falling into place to make a whole: La Rochelle, Lanchester, those machine guns; if Callum Jardine was a man who operated in the shadows, those did not extend to an organisation like the SIS. There was no mystery now as to who Barrowman was. There were still gaps to fill, but they would come when Quex was put out to grass and he had his chair.

Too experienced to let any of that show, he rattled off in German what this young man wanted, then when the shop owner replied, smiled at him and said, 'They'll be ready next week.'

'Oh no,' Jimmy protested, 'I want them today.'

'Best dig deep then, son.' The face fell but not for long; he would get well rewarded for his story and anyway this stranger was talking. 'Did I not see you outside the Victoria Hotel this morning, son?'

'Yes, that's where Mr Jardine is staying.' He peered at McKevitt. 'And I'm sure I saw you as well.'

'Well, I'm not sure your Jardine is the same fella, but maybe I'll drop in and say hello.'

'Shall I tell him?' Jimmy asked, thinking it was the rather loud sports jacket that he remembered more than the face.

'No, I might be wrong and if I'm not, well it will be a fine surprise.'

'Right, Jimmy, the garage,' Cal barked, heading for the rear exit, leaving Corrie and Vince in the lounge to reminisce about Ethiopia. Peter had gone off to send a cryptic message to Quex to tell him not to fret. 'You get one look at this, make your notes and that's it.'

'What happens to the original?'

'None of your business, just get your stuff in the paper and make yourself a star reporter.'

Jimmy used the passenger seat and when he had finished his note-taking he was ushered out into the alley. The document was hidden and the car locked before Cal emerged to join him.

'You going back to Prague in that?' he asked. Cal nodded. 'Any chance of a lift?'

'There's four of us already,' Cal replied; then he had a thought. 'My friend Vince came up in an old Tatra, you can have that to drive back. I take it you can drive?'

'You have to in my job, nowadays, but who can afford a car?'

McKevitt had found the alley just by walking around the block, the back door guarded by one policeman who, when he made his second passage, looked at the man carrying the briefcase as he walked up to him, his hand going inside his checked jacket and coming out with a blue-and-gold-covered passport, addressing him in good if accented German.

'British legation, come to see some of my nationals.' Confidence is the key in a situation like this one; the Ulsterman actually put the passport in the man's hand so he could examine it. 'None of them hurt in the fighting as far as I know, but I need to make sure.'

He could have gone in the front door, which was also now guarded by only one policeman, the army having withdrawn, so there seemed no harm in letting him pass, given the only other people in the hotel were from Internal Security, rifling, he had heard, through a mountain of files.

The people who had passed him previously had done no more than go to the garage and back again, so, not anticipating any danger, he nodded and handed the passport back. McKevitt gave him a cheery wave and went through the door, while the policeman, a bit bored in truth, turned to watch him disappear through the door.

He only felt the tickle of the wire for a split second before it was pulled tight, then it was choking him, a knee going into his spine as he was pulled down, his hands tearing uselessly at his throat. Four men appeared, one in the same uniform as the man now dying and he took up station while the body was dragged into the garage by the others. Then they disappeared into the hotel, pulling out their weapons as soon as they were inside.

They saw McKevitt's back as he walked forward gingerly, the flap of the briefcase open, though they could not see the box camera around his neck. It mattered not as they disappeared up the wooden staff staircase, the noise they created making McKevitt turn to look; there was nothing to see.

Creeping through the lobby he could hear the sound of voices and some laughter, but a look into what had to be the lounge – it was full of settees – showed it empty except for a small suitcase and a canvas bag on the floor by an open doorway. The sound was beyond that and gingerly he moved forward, edging his nose round the door to the table-filled dining room.

They were all sitting at a circular board, eating and drinking without a care in the world, and it was obvious by the heightened sounds of conversation that they had been imbibing with gusto. McKevitt silently put his briefcase on the floor, flap open, and got his camera ready; all he needed was a shot, more than one if he could, of Jardine and Lanchester together and everything else would follow from that.

He would find out if, as he had suspected ever since that message had come from Brno, those machine guns had gone to the IRA, to be used to fight and kill his fellow Protestants in Ulster. And when the truth of that came out, this pair would go to jail, while the man who had failed to see that one of his new boys was playing him false would be out on his ear, and that was before it came out that they were risking a war with their carrying on.

'Smile!'

He said that loudly as he stepped into the middle of the door. Everyone looked, even those with their backs to him, and he clicked immediately before dropping the camera to advance the film, a broad smile on his face.

'Good day to you.'

'McKevitt,' Peter said, 'what the hell are you doing?'

'Finding out who your friends are, Lanchester, like the man sitting on the other side of that lady, who I suppose is Callum Jardine, or as you have chosen to call him, Mr Barrowman.'

'How the hell does he know that, Peter?' Cal said, his eyes on the doorway. 'I've never met him.'

'I don't know,' Peter replied as McKevitt took another photograph.

'Ask your little journo friend.' Cal looked at Corrie. 'Not her, the other one.'

A glance at Jimmy Garvin had him blushing, a question brought out the admission, the response to which was vituperative if also devoid of passion. 'You stupid little bastard!'

'When I show these to certain people, an awful lot of trouble for you two is going to come out in the wash.'

'We're here on SIS business, Noel.'

'You're here on Quex's business, which he has no business being engaged in, and he's another one for the chop, I can tell you.'

'You're out of your league, Noel,' Peter insisted, as Cal stood up and moved towards the doorway. 'I'll take the camera.'

McKevitt dropped to one knee and pulled the Webley revolver out of the briefcase he had bought at the same time as the camera. Cal, who moved at the same time, was just too slow to get to him, finding himself staring down the barrel.

The gunshot, even muted, made him leap sideways and he was still travelling when he realised the Irishman had not fired, just as he realised that more shots were following.

'What the bloody hell was that?' McKevitt shouted as a real fusillade came from the upper floors, as well as shouting and the screams of people obviously taking wounds. The Ulsterman was forced to turn just by the sheer mayhem he was hearing, and Cal rolled towards the door, his hand stretched out to grab his canvas bag and drag it inside.

'Everybody down!' he yelled, which made McKevitt spin back again and he guessed very quickly that the bag must have a gun. The shouting and screaming had moved to the staircase that led to Henlein's suite and the man was in two minds as he saw several men reversing down the stairs firing upwards, vaguely aware that two of them were not moving properly.

'Leave it,' he yelled at Cal, as he saw him rummaging in the bag, but he spun back to look through the lobby.

What the man on the stairs saw, when that shout made him turn round, was a man with a revolver coming in an arc to aim at him. He fired and his was a fully loaded automatic weapon, so McKevitt was hit by three bullets that threw him back against the frame of the doorway and half into the dining room.

Having no idea what was happening, Cal hauled out his Mauser then scurried forward on his knees to get the Webley out of McKevitt's dying hand, shouting to Vince to take care of Corrie, and to Peter to get closer. It was all a blur from them on; he saw a shape and knew it was deadly, so he fired off the last of his rounds and took the target out.

Peter was beside him and had got hold of the Webley, which he started to empty, but they were sitting ducks in the doorway and both took return bullets, Cal more than one, which had him seek to get behind the wall. He was vaguely aware of the shouting in German and he also heard the click of Peter's weapon – it was empty.

Looking up he saw two men, both carrying wounds themselves, with their weapons up and looking to administer the *coup de grâce* to both him and Peter. Suddenly their bodies began to jerk like rag dolls as, from behind them, the Czech police – or was it soldiers? – riddled them with dozens of bullets. The last thing Cal saw before he passed out was, at the same ground level as his own, the glazed eyes of Peter Lanchester.

He did not see Corrie or hear her scream for an ambulance, nor feel Jimmy help her to make him comfortable. The hand that slipped into his pocket and lifted his car keys was equally unknown to a numb and unconscious body. Vince was trying to help Peter, relieved to hear sirens in the distance, which he hoped were ambulances and not more police.

Whatever else Cheb had, the medical services were good; all three men were rushed to the emergency department of the local hospital but McKevitt was dead on arrival, while Cal and Peter were hanging on to life. The surgeons were Sudeten German but the Hippocratic oath knows no nationality and they worked hard to save their two remaining patients.

It was Vince who asked where Jimmy was; he was not in the hospital. Only when they could do no more and they returned to the hotel to sleep did they discover he was not there either. It was the next day before anyone looked in the garage and saw the Maybach was gone.

EPILOGUE

Side by side on deep mattresses and enclosed in crisp linen, Callum Jardine and Peter Lanchester were as comfortable as two men could be having suffered multiple bullet wounds and undergone several operations. The doctors who were treating them were of the opinion that news, good or bad, was inimical to a speedy recovery, but they knew from their visitors that things were dire. They had no idea how bad until Sir Hugh Sinclair turned up in person.

At first, during the official visiting time, everyone had been present: Corrie, Vince, Major Gibson and the aforementioned Quex. He had charmed Corrie with his old-world courtesy and was taken with Vince, as any once-active serviceman would be with another. But the time came when he asked for privacy so that he could talk to the two patients, one of whom was pressing in posing the obvious question.

'There is no doubt that having stolen your car, young Garvin searched it and found the Hitler document.'

'I tip him as future editor of a national daily,' Peter said, bitterly.

'So it never got to Chamberlain and the Cabinet?'

'Two different beasts, Mr Jardine, but let me explain. Young Garvin flew out of Prague with the goods and insisted on taking it not to the editor of his newspaper but to the proprietor, a fellow called Layton, and he spiked the story.'

'Did he spike the little shit with it?' demanded Cal.

Blinking at the vulgarity, Quex shook his head. 'No, he bribed him to forget it with a senior post, which, I am told, had Vernon Bartlett spitting blood.'

'If you spawn evil . . .' Peter intoned, leaving the rest to the imagination of the others.

'But Layton gave it to Sir Samuel Hoare, who in turn showed it to Chamberlain.'

'So he got it!' Quex nodded. 'Then why did he sign that rubbish bit of paper at Munich?'

'Don't you see, Mr Jardine, he was the saviour of the nation?'

'Destroyer, more like.'

'Never,' Sir Hugh said gravely, 'underestimate how far a politician will go for a bit of short-term popularity. The PM was cheered by thousands when he came back from Munich and it went to his head. He quite forgot he is the leader of a nation of millions who think him a dupe.'

'Who were these thousands?'

'Those who think they have something to lose by war other than their lives. Comfort, houses, businesses, and that is allied to a deep fear of Bolshevism and the working classes. Anyway, according to my good friend Duff Cooper, who resigned in disgust, Chamberlain saw it and dismissed it as propaganda, then embarked on his shuttling to and fro by air to suck Hitler's poison, with Mussolini as the convenient suppository.'

'With the result that he has the Sudetenland.'

'And will have all of Czecho soon.'

'Poland?'

'Will take the coalfields they have desired for so long only to lose them again. Once Hitler has Teschen, Danzig and the hundreds of miles of Silesian border they are doomed. Not that they think so – to hear them boast, a squadron of cavalry is a match for any tank.'

'Which,' Cal growled, 'was perfectly obvious a year ago to anyone who looked at a map.'

'Politicians are strange creatures. Chamberlain is now acting as if Munich was a deliberate policy to gain time to rearm, instead of what it really was, the worst piece of diplomacy our country has ever engaged in.'

'What did you do about McKevitt?'

'Treated him as a hero externally and a warning internally. No point in washing our dirty linen in public, but he has served to remind those who incline to ill discipline that the end result is unpleasant.'

'What drove him?'

'Ah, what else but that madness which afflicts Irishmen on occasions? He was sure those machine guns were going to the IRA and he set out to stop it by diverting them to the *Jeunesses Patriotes*.'

'Who would have used them on their own government.'

'A notion which did not bother McKevitt one bit!' Quex snapped. 'Then I became the target of his ambition, an affliction which progressively warped his judgement, I fear.'

'He's not unique in SIS?'

'Sadly no; but anyway, now to business, because you cannot stay here until you are fully recovered. The Germans will move into Eger within days.'

'I'm feeling pretty good,' Cal said.

'Your physician does not agree. What we are planning to do is employ an ambulance to get you both back home and your doctors will travel with you, all covered by diplomatic immunity.'

'That's a lot of money, sir.'

'On the contrary, Peter, the doctors have no desire to be here when the SS arrive, both being social democrats. They and their wives, who will be designated as nurses, will be much happier domiciled in England and for that their services are free. Their children we will get out by normal channels.'

There was a pause to allow him to be smug. 'And now we come to you, Mr Jardine.'

'The Tower, I expect.'

'An amusing and tempting idea, but not sound.' There was another pause, to gather his thoughts. 'You are the possessor of skills that are in short supply and, I might add, skills we are going to need very sorely in the coming years. It has occurred to me that having someone of your ability inside the tent might be better than having you running around outside.'

'Are you offering me employment?'

'Don't pay him,' Peter snapped, 'he doesn't need it.'

That got a thin smile. 'There is a war coming, Mr Jardine, and we can do nothing to avoid it. I am too old to be entering such a cataclysm. Peter will prosper both through his brains and his judgement.'

That got a raspberry from Cal.

'But you and your type are needed, Mr Jardine.'

'Type?'

'Killers. Or should I say imaginative eradicators of human vermin.'

'You should look after General Moravec, he's got some good people and he is, as I know to my cost, a wily old bugger.'

'Already arranged; he will come to England when the Germans take the rest of the Czech lands.'

'His agents?' Cal was thinking of Veseli.

'His to decide on.' Quex stood. 'Now I must go and seek to advise a government intent on adding to their foolishness.'

'Not possible.'

'Oh it is, Mr Jardine. They are talking about guaranteeing Poland's borders.'

'Vince, in my bag is a fortune in German marks. Could you do me a favour and take it to Prague and then fly home from there? Give it to Elsa Ephraim at the Jewish Emigration Centre and tell her it comes from the *Reichsbank*. She will be tickled to think she's using their money to get her people to freedom.'

The last person to talk to was Corrie and she was very mature. 'You're not free to marry and I'm not willing to give up my career.'

'So how do we stay in touch?'

She tapped her forehead. 'Up here, Cal, up here, where there are good memories. And – who knows? – we are flotsam who gravitate towards war zones. We both like trouble, so I guess we will meet more often than you think possible.'

'I hope you believe me when I say I want that.'

She bent forward and kissed him. 'Take care, Doc.'